AURORA RISING

LIFE ON PENNINGTON CREEK
BOOK 2

GLENDA CLEMENS

Edited by
JAN FORMISANO

Edited by
DAVID CLEMENS

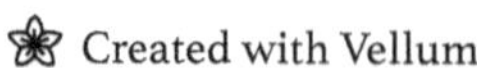 Created with Vellum

This book is dedicated to:
Lorraine Summers, RN.
She taught me the essentials
about women, their babies, and birthing.

BETA READERS AND EDITORS

Thanks to our Editors & Beta Readers
Without these folks, I would never finish a book!

Editors:
Jan Formisano
David Clemens

Beta Readers:
Cindy Brumley
John Brumley
Evelyn Harrison
Diana Yeatman

AUTHOR'S FORWARD

"There are few nudities
so objectionable
as the naked truth."
Agnes Repplier

This is the story of Aurora Harrison, Maggie's first friend, upon arriving in Tishomingo, Indian Territory, which is now the state of Oklahoma.

While most of the story is fiction, some of it is based on actual events. These events are foundational for Oklahoma and the story. They include The Trail of Tears, the formation of Indian Territory and Oklahoma Territory, and many broken treaties, including the Daws Rolls. Later, the territories, along with No Man's Land, joined and became the state of Oklahoma.

As a child growing up in Oklahoma, I believed every word spoken about our fair land and the people who lived in our state, Oklahoma. However, children's beliefs and thoughts give way to adult realities. I learned that life isn't always pretty, kind, or loving. As a friend of mine once said, "History is a bitch."

For example, while Pennington Creek is a real place that I love, and the story of how Pennington Creek got its name is real, I believe. Another example is that there are no log cabin homes in the areas on the map I've noted on the banks of Pennington Creek. Nevertheless, the characters in my story, Maggie, Aurora, Silas, and Clay, loved living in those homes and raising their children there.

Most of the characters are fictional. However, a few are not, such as William H. Murray (future governor of the state of Oklahoma), Mary Alice Hearrell (Mr. Murray's wife), the lawyers Treadwell and Lucas, Douglas Johnston, and other notable Chickasaw people, as well as a few white people mentioned, were real.

I've tried to ensure that any information, including criticisms and aspersions, about the real people of that time is as authentic as I could find within the annals of Oklahoma history.

It was a sad day for me when I learned some of what you will learn in this fictional story about William H. Murray. It turns out he wasn't a paragon of virtue or even a very good man, though, in my childhood, I thought he was terrific. Before I began writing this story, I was proud of him as a leader in Oklahoma. He was liked and even loved by many despite his flaws.

For these and many other reasons, I've included a list of my sources at the end of the book. It makes for good reading for history buffs, and if you are a history buff, you will find hours and hours of learning on those pages.

BEGINNING

Everything the power does
it does in a circle.
Lakota Proverb

Aurora's anxiety grew as she pulled her buggy to a halt in front of the new Chickasaw Nation Council House in Tishomingo, Indian Territory. It was her first time driving her buggy into town alone.

Six months earlier, Lester Blunt had tried to kill Aurora, her child Okchuli, and her husband, Clay. First, he planned to kill their neighbors, the Pennington family, so there would be no one to come to Aurora and her family's aid. However, he was thwarted and thrown in jail for his attempts to murder her and her family and friends. Now that he'd been released from prison a few days ago, after only six months of incarceration, Aurora was sure he was ready to cause mischief and make her life miserable.

She wanted to be fearless today, but the stakes were higher than ever for her. After all, she had a daughter who came to her in a basket on her front porch, a loving husband, and a cherished home. She knew that keeping Lester Blunt's evil intentions in mind was crucial. If he succeeded in ruining her life and that of her baby, Okchuli, she would have much to lose.

Aurora did not understand why he hated her so much and was determined to kill her and her baby. She felt his hatred was more than mere bigotry. At the same time, Aurora was determined to keep her child, herself, her husband, and her home safe from the evil intentions of Lester Blunt, a known bigot. She tucked her shawl around her baby, who slept wrapped against Aurora's breasts, then stepped down from her buggy, holding the baby close.

She was Chickasaw on her mother's side of the family and part Chickasaw and part black on her father's side. Her father was part Chickasaw from his mother, but his father had been a formerly enslaved person after the War Between the States. Her father was barely one year old at that time, but still, a lot of people held ill will against the enslaved people, and Lester Blunt loudly claimed them not to be human.

This morning, she had business with the Chickasaw Council. Her husband, Clay, worried he should go with her, but she wanted to go on her own, in part, to prove her bravery. For the first time in her life, she felt a little out of place being on her own this morning. She had never worried about being alone when she attended a birthing. As a midwife, she was often alone helping other women.

Still, this morning felt different. With Lester Blunt out of jail, she was nervous about seeing him or, worse yet, hearing his horrid deprecations of herself and her child. Her hope was that Lester Blunt would be nowhere around this morning. Working to be brave would never have entered her mind if it weren't for Lester Blunt.

As Aurora walked up the granite steps to the new Council building, she shuddered when she saw her nemesis standing next to the new brass-clad and glass door. She took a deep breath and let it release as she finished climbing the last few steps, trying to ignore the bully standing next to the building door.

He pulled the cigar he was smoking from his mouth, blew his

smoke at her, grinned, and said, "Well, now. If it isn't the half-breed woman and her toss-off baby."

She tried to ignore him, but he blocked the way into the building, pushing his foot against the door. Aurora said, "Excuse me, please, Mr. Blunt. I have family business to attend to at the Council Office."

He spat a wad of brown and green phlegm on the granite step by her foot. "There is no excuse for you, Aurora. When are you ever going to understand that?"

She pulled Okchuli closer inside her shawl and stood waiting, saying nothing while keeping her eyes on the building's door.

He snorted a bit of a laugh. "Cat got your tongue? Or do you only speak injun?"

She could take no more of his vile speech. She raised her head and looked up at him, looking directly into his eyes. "I speak English much better than you, Mr. Blunt, and you know that is true. I am a well-educated woman. I have graduated from Bloomfield Academy with honors. However, you are correct. I speak Chickasaw, English, Choctaw, and Kiowa. How many languages do you speak, Mr. Blunt?"

"Just good old plain English, and nobody had to educate me to be able to speak it. Now, little black injun, you should turn around and head back under whatever rock you've crawled from. Talkin' any injun words is vile and reprehensible."

Aurora ignored his taunts, reached for the new door's brass handle, and tugged at it. Of course, it didn't open because Lester Blunt kept it closed with his foot. On the other side of the door, another citizen—a white man—was trying to get out and pushed on the door hard enough to make Lester Blunt stumble. The man ignored Blunt and said, "Good morning, Mrs. Harrison. May I have the honor of holding the door open for you?"

"Thank you. That would be a kindness, Mr. Riddle."

"My pleasure and my blessings to you and your darling daughter."

"Thank you, sir." She walked into the building, let out a deep sigh, and walked down the hallway to Walter Thompson's office, where he was the Council Clerk. With Lester Blunt pushed aside and the door closing behind her, she could take a deep breath and let go of the fear Lester Blunt always brought to her life.

However, for today, she decided to try to block him from her mind—she had new concerns now.

She walked with her head held high, and as others saw her pass, no one noticed that she wasn't quite five feet tall. One woman thought, *now there goes a regal woman with her head held high, with her hair braided, crowning her head.* The woman smiled and thought of Queen Victoria of England, whom she'd admired all her life.

1

A danger foreseen
is half-avoided.
Cheyenne Proverb

After several minutes inside the office of the Council Clerk, Walter Thompson, Aurora knew her life had been irrevocably changed. She felt it was changing for good but also brought more risk and turmoil.

Her hands quivered with the papers she held, making a soft clicking sound as the pages rubbed together. To her ears, it sounded almost like crickets. Document against document rattled while she felt unsure about it all. She held back a smile that threatened to become a full-throated laugh. In doing so, she felt a chill prickle on her arms and neck as she shuddered, feeling danger was near.

She shook her head, looked up at the clerk, and asked, "What is this, Walter?" Her voice was a bit strident, and her baby daughter, Okchuli, tucked in her shawl, whimpered.

Before Walter could answer, she held up a hand and said, "Wait, Walter." She kissed her baby's forehead and hummed a soft tune.

Walter recognized the tune as one his wife had hummed to their son when he was sleepy but fussy. Now, Walter had a daughter as well as a son. His wife Mary hummed the same tune to their newest child.

He felt a frisson of love surrounding him as he listened to the soft, whispered tune filled with the harmony of mother and daughter. He couldn't help but think of Mother Mary holding the Christ child close. He smiled softly, knowing he thought of the Holy Mother whenever he saw a woman holding a baby. *I suppose every mother is holy, as are their innocent babes.*

When the baby settled, Aurora looked up and asked, "Please tell me why this is happening."

Walter sighed, then said, "Well, it's the Curtis Act."

"The white men broke another treaty?"

He nodded. "Yes, and we all knew to expect it but hoped it would not come. Now, what used to be our communal land of millions and millions of acres, we all shared—working the land together—is now to be apportioned out as individual allotments."

"Will every Chickasaw have an equal division of our land?"

"No, not exactly. There will be equality of a sort, though. Every man, woman, and child of the Chickasaw Nation will be allotted 160 acres of land. Each Chickasaw will receive the same amount of land."

"Is that the equal division of our millions of acres?"

"No. The Chickasaw Nation will no longer have communal land, and the land not allotted to our tribal members will be up for sale to anyone with money."

With a sharp, cold voice, Aurora gritted her teeth and said, "So, once again, the Great White President will steal our land from us."

"Yes, but we will all—every one of us, including our children— have our own land."

"But not the land we shared?"

"Correct. That land will be no more and, in fact, is no more."

Aurora looked at her sleeping baby, curled up in her shawl, and then back to Walter. She brushed away the tears on her cheeks and asked, "Does my mother know?"

"Yes. I talked with her yesterday."

Aurora pointed to a black walnut box hanging on the wall, with a black tube to talk into and another black tube to listen with. "My mother talked through that?"

"Yes."

"How can you be sure it was my mother talking?"

Walter grinned. "Your mother and I have been friends since our swaddling clothes. I would know her voice if she spoke from the highest mountain on the other side of the world."

"But she lives in Tulsa."

"Yes, she does, and I talked with her through the telephone." He pulled out his pocket watch and said, "I promised to call her back today and let you talk with her. It is time to call your mother."

Aurora nodded, licked her lips—she was a little nervous, and said, "I've never talked on such a contraption."

"It's called a telephone."

"I know what it is called, Walter. Still, it isn't natural. Does it hurt?"

"No, it does not. My ears felt your mother's truth, but I agree it also seems strange. Are you ready?"

"Is it safe for Okchuli to be close to the telephone?"

"I've been told it is safe."

They looked at each other for several seconds, and though Aurora wasn't sure it was safe, she nodded. "I would love to hear my mother's voice. It has been many months since we spoke."

"Good. Come. Stand by me, and we'll get your mother on the line. She is in the office of a lawyer friend of mine in Tulsa."

Aurora nodded as Walter picked up the telephone, put it next to his ear, talked into the tube with the local operator, and told her who he needed to speak to and the name of the lawyer's office. After a few minutes, Walter said, "Hello, Bradley. Is Mrs. Freeman there with you?"

"Yes, I'll give her the telephone if you're ready."

"We are." Walter waited, and when Aurora's mother was on the line, he said, "I hear your voice, Aponi. I'll hand the receiver to Aurora now. She is standing beside me."

He handed Aurora the phone, and she listened with the tube close to her ear. Walter tapped the tube attached to the wooden box on the wall and said, "Talk into this tube." Being not quite five feet tall, she had to tiptoe a bit.

Aurora asked, "Ishki?"

Aponi said, "Yes, Oshetik."

"Momma? Can you hear me?"

"Yes, dear, I can. Have you talked with Walter about the allotments?"

"Yes. I don't like it."

"Nor do I, but we have no choice. It is better to have a little land than no land."

"Why did you give your land to me?"

"Because I love my life in Tulsa. It is a city and vibrates in a way that makes me happy."

"I couldn't live in a city."

"No. It is not your nature, Oshetik. Your nature is to live close to the land and only with people who love you."

"That is my truth. I wish to see you, Momma."

"Your father and I will come to see you and Clay in your home. And most especially, we yearn to see your darling Okchuli. Your father and I will come there to see you, be a part of the dedication of the new council house, and Thanksgiving, too."

"It will be a blessing to see you both, Momma. I will prepare a space for you and Daddy."

"That would be nice. We want to spend as much time as possible with you. We will return home the day after Thanksgiving to avoid the winter weather."

"I'm eager to see you both and have you in our home. How will you get here?"

"We'll travel by train from here to Ardmore and then by coach to Tishomingo."

"What day are you arriving?"

"We have tickets to arrive on November 15th. Will that be a good day for you?"

"Oh, yes, Momma. I know you love Clay and will adore Okchuli."

"You are right, daughter. We love you and Clay and already adore Okchuli."

"Momma, are you sure about giving me your allotment?"

"Yes. You will use the land and use it well. Besides, if I ever need to live near you, I know you will honor me and make a place for me."

"Of course we will, Momma, for you and Daddy both."

"What about Lester Blunt? Is he still threatening you?"

"Yes, he is. I tried ignoring him, but he is hard to ignore. He still threatens to kill me and Okchuli, but he hasn't made any outright efforts to do so."

"Please take care. Maybe even be sure not to be alone."

"Most of the time, I'm with family or friends, Momma. He can't kill us all."

"Still be careful."

They talked for a few minutes more, then Walter tapped Aurora's shoulder and said, "Our time is up. Others want to use the tubes and wires."

Aurora nodded and spoke into the telephone tube, "I love you, Momma, and will burn sage to bless your gift to me and for your journey. In only ten days, you will be here. I love you!"

"I am eager, too. I love you, Oshetik."

Aurora handed the tube to Walter. He bid Aurora's mother good-bye, hung the tube on a large brass hook attached to the wooden box, and then turned to Aurora. "I've entered your allotments, your mothers, including her selling much of hers to Jacob Pennington, which now belongs to Silas Pennington, and Clay's allotment, too. It seems he has already paid his fifty dollars."

"Really?"

"Yes, really."

"Why does Clay have an allotment?"

"He married a Chickasaw woman and has a Chickasaw daughter. He is now Chickasaw."

She smiled. "Lucky Clay."

He grinned and nodded. "Indeed, he is lucky. Now, share this with your husband, Maggie and Silas. Keep these papers hidden in a very, very safe place. You don't need to worry too much, but things are unsettled around here. Having your papers will be your best protection."

"I thought you had everything entered here in the Council House?"

"I do, but never, ever trust the government—especially the white man's government. They will shake your hand, and when you look down, your hand will be gone. Our new building may be Chickasaw briefly, but I feel in my bones the white man will take it for themselves—as soon as they possibly can."

She smiled and nodded. "I agree."

"Good. Our records are your backup in case any idiot wants to, or tries to, take your land from you."

"I appreciate everything you've done for me, Okchuli, and Clay."

"It is my honor." He gently lifted the edge of the shawl, peeked at the baby, and smiled. "I think she's beginning to look a little Irish with her reddish-blonde curly hair."

"I think so too. Her daddy is proud to have his daughter look a bit like him."

"I have to say, though, I like her skin being more native. Are her eyes brown or blue?"

"They are brown and lightening a little, but her hair is red—like Clay's, her father."

He nodded and smiled, knowing—or at least he thought he was right in knowing—that the lucky baby was a cast-off of a young white woman. She and her parents moved to Ardmore a few days after Okchuli's birth. He crossed his fingers, hoping Lester Blunt did not know Okchuli was his niece's daughter by birth. For that matter, there was no reason for Auorora to know those facts.

Nonetheless, Okchuli was a beloved and beautiful child, and he honored her adoptive parents, Aurora and Clay Harrison. Although he was one of the few people who knew the baby's heritage, on the rolls, he had entered Okchuli as the birth child of Aurora and Clay. He knew the couple loved Okchuli beyond reason—just as every child should be loved.

"I'll walk you out to your buggy." He put the allotment papers in a heavy yellow envelope and returned them to Aurora. She folded the envelope and tucked it deep inside her shawl beside Okchuli.

Once settled in the buggy with Okchuli still sleeping, she asked, "Will you be part of the dedication of the new Council Building in two weeks?"

"Oh, yes. I'll have to keep everything moving while folks eat, dance, sing, and make more speeches than we wish to hear—especially those filled with lies."

Aurora chuckled. "Sounds about right."

"Will you be coming to the dedication?"

"Yes, we'll come with the Penningtons and now, with Momma and Daddy. However, we probably will not stay late."

"Lucky you."

She nodded. "Well, we have children who will become a rowdy nuisance as things get rolling, then grumpy after sundown. They are our convenient excuse for leaving early."

He smiled and patted her hand. "I look forward to seeing you, Clay, the Penningtons, and especially your parents. Let Mr. and Mrs. Pennington know I'm at their service should they have questions." He started to turn away but turned back to Aurora and touched her hand. "Listen. I don't trust Lester Blunt as far as I could throw him—which isn't far. He is a vile piece of flesh. Please heed your mother's warnings about him."

"I will. Thank you again, Walter, for looking out for me and our friends."

"It is my pleasure," he said, waving her on her way back to her cabin on Pennington Creek.

He sighed, shook his head, and muttered, "Someone needs to rid our town of Blunt, and the sooner, the better."

2

Aurora settled on the seat of her buggy and pulled a woolen blanket over her legs. She wrapped another shawl around herself and baby Okchuli. The baby was still soundly sleeping in the nest Aurora had made for her close to her chest.

She clicked to the horse, who obediently started walking down the red dirt road through the middle of the Town of Tishomingo, Indian Territory. As she neared the blacksmith's shop, she waved to Clay and gently stopped her buggy to speak with her husband. He walked over to the buggy and asked, "Did you get to talk with your momma?"

"I did."

"How did it feel?"

"Strange, but I loved hearing her voice. She and Daddy will be here the fifteenth—ten days from now—to stay until after Thanksgiving."

"I'm glad. We will feel even more like a family then. I put the extra canning jars you and Maggie needed in the back of your buggy."

"Thank you. I did notice." She sighed and said, "I have papers from Walter Thompson we'll want to discuss at home."

"Is everything all right?"

"Yes, but it is a bit overwhelming."

"Well, don't worry. Whatever it is, we can work it out."

She smiled and said, "Yes, we can, and I think it is all good news."

"Hooray for us!"

She chuckled and shook her head.

Clay said, "Hank is putting new shoes on Abner. He's a good horse but grumpy when he needs new shoes."

"Yes, he is."

"I'll head home as soon as he's finished, and we can have a good old-fashioned palaver."

"Exactly what I want."

"Good. Noah and I have some things to finish on the cellar later this afternoon. We'll have a few hours to talk about your chat with your mother and your visit with Walter."

"Thank you, Clay."

"You look a little worried."

"Not worried so much as befuddled. But I don't want to talk about it here. This is for our ears only—at least for now. I told Maggie I wouldn't be around until later this afternoon to help finish the canning. You come home as soon as you can, and we'll talk then."

He kissed her hand and then the baby's forehead. "You ladies take good care of each other."

Aurora smiled. "We will." She waved as she drove her small buggy home.

Clay waved back and turned to the blacksmith's shop and his friends Silas Pennington and Hank Smithson.

Neither Clay nor Aurora saw Lester Blunt—their nemesis—watching them as he hid behind a redbud tree losing its last leaves, but Walter saw him. He shook his head and muttered, "That man is wicked. He has been out of jail for a few days and is already back to his old tricks. I'll watch, and if he sneezes too loud, I'll let the sheriff know."

ON THE RIDE HOME, Aurora gradually relaxed. The air was clear and a little crisp, but not the deep, biting cold that winter would bring. The bone-deep cold was usually reserved for late December through mid-February or early March. For now, in the early November sunshine, she felt the beauty of everything around her. She loved watching the birds swooping—some flying south for the winter, some hunting for food. She loved the sounds and smells of the land where she'd lived her entire life.

She could see her log cabin home when she reached the curve of Pennington Creek, where she lived. Joy filled her heart, loving everything she saw before her. She smiled as she realized that with the papers Walter had given her, she could never be pushed off her land and out of her home unless some nefarious person decided to be wicked and steal her house and land. She and Clay now had legal standing, on paper at least, as members of the Chickasaw Nation. She hoped Clay would be happy with their legally owned land, including the land Silas and Maggie had given them.

The land was everything to the white people who grabbed every acre of land they could and paid little for their desires. Most did not understand that the land belonged only to the Earth and Sky. Now that she legally owned the land belonging to herself, Clay, and their daughter, including her mother's gift, every acre now belonged to her family.

Aurora clicked a bit to get her horse, Rosie, to go over the stagecoach bridge. She didn't blame the mare a bit. The bridge was made of wooden slats fastened together over a few rocks, with water running through it all and sometimes even over it. Once they were over the bridge and onto the red dirt path to her home, both Aurora and the horse settled down, glad to be home.

Once she had the buggy unhitched from the horse's tracings and Rosie was in her shed munching on hay, Okchuli began to fuss. Aurora laughed at her daughter, "Thank you for not fussing or crying until we arrived home."

The baby let out a loud, angry howl, pushing and tugging to get out of the shawl her mother had tied close to her chest.

"Ah, Okchuli. Hang on, sweetie. Let's get you a dry diaper, then we'll sit down, and you can drink your fill while I think through the day's events."

As she nursed Okchuli, she thought about her mother and father coming to visit and all the things she wanted to prepare for their time visiting. This would be the first time her parents would visit her home. She talked to her daughter and shared her thoughts, much as her mother had, she was sure. She'd always known that her mother's voice carried her thoughts, desires, and wisdom.

"Momma—your Granny, Chuli—used to talk with me all the time. Her house wasn't nearly as fine as this one, but she took great care that it was always clean and inviting. I'll want to dust and clean every nook and cranny, and then I want to have a few pretty things set about to welcome your grandparents."

Okchuli watched her mother's face as she talked. Now and again, she'd grin at her mother and let a few dribbles of milk leak out of her mouth. When she smiled, her mother smiled back at her.

Clay had been building a second story within their home. The framework was done, and the flooring was installed. His next construction would be a staircase. She thought, "I hope you can finish that bit before Momma and Daddy arrive, Clay. It would be nice not to have them sleeping on the floor by the fireplace."

She smiled and nodded, watching Okchuli as she nursed. She was sure that if she asked, Clay would finish the two upstairs bedrooms and staircase in the next ten days.

Okchuli grinned and said, "Mama!"

Aurora beamed at her brilliant daughter. She had said her first word, and Aurora was delighted. She answered her daughter, "Yes, I'm your mama!" She kissed the baby's cheek, lifted her to her shoulder to burp her, and felt tears of joy on her face as she rocked and burped the baby.

AT LEAST ONCE A DAY, Aurora would tell her daughter a story. Today was no different. She said, "I have a story to tell you, daughter," and she started:

Once upon a time, long ago, when our people lived close to the Big River, which the white people called Mississippi, a little girl loved playing in the mud. She made dolls—a baby, a boy, a girl, a Momma, and a Daddy. When her mother saw the dolls, she said, "We should put hair and clothes on your dolls."

The little girl said, "I don't have any tiny clothes for my dolls."

"Ah, daughter, it is time for you to learn to make clothes."

The little girl clapped her hands, delighted to learn how to make clothes.

Her mother gave her tiny bits of cloth and leather, a steel needle, and heavy thread. Mother guided the little girl's hands, and soon—within a few days—she had made clothes for all her dolls. When she showed her friends her dolls with the delicate dresses she'd made, they were amazed at the beauty of the clothes. However, one girl said, "I can make much prettier clothes. Your clothes are okay, but mine would be better."

"Have you made doll clothes before?"

"No, but everything I make is wonderful."

The little girl became angry and said, "You know nothing about making dolls or clothes!"

"*I know everything about everything,*" *the other girl answered.* "*Just you wait and see. Tomorrow, I'll bring out the dolls I make and their beautiful clothes.*"

The little girl asked, "*When?*"

"*I already said tomorrow, so you can wait until tomorrow and see.*"

The little girl raced back to her mother's home and told her mother what the other girl had said. Her mother said, "*Do not worry. Your dolls are fine; they love you and the clothes you made for them. Instead of worrying, hope the other girl loves her dolls and makes them fine clothes.*"

The little girl wasn't sure but decided to wait and see.

The next day, she sat outside, waiting for the other girl to show her dolls and their clothes. By the time the sun was going down in the west, the other girl still had not shown up, so the little girl went into her mother's house, ate dinner with her mother, and then went to bed with her dolls wearing their fine clothes.

When the sun rose, she woke up and went outside with her dolls in fine clothes. She waited, and she waited, and she waited, but the other girl did not come out to show her dolls and their dresses.

The little girl waited the next day, and the next, and the next, and many more. Finally, she asked her mother, "*What shall I do?*"

"*Leave your dolls in their fine clothes on your bed. Go to the other girl's house and ask her to come out and play. Do not ask about her dolls!*"

So, the little girl did as her mother asked, and the other girl said, "*I'd love to play, but I don't have any dolls with fine clothes. I thought I could do it, but I could not.*"

"*Don't worry. Let's play and have fun.*"

The little girl and the other girl ran, raced, climbed, and splashed the day away. When the sun was nearly down in the west, the little girl said, "*I liked playing with you. Would you like to make dolls tomorrow? I'll help you.*"

The other girl clapped her hands and said, "*Yes! I want to know how to make dolls and clothes for them.*"

And they played together the next day and many days after. The little girl taught her friend how to make dolls and fine clothes for them. Now, both girls could make dolls with dresses.

Aurora looked down and saw Okchuli had gone to sleep listening to the story. Aurora liked the story she'd made up and decided maybe writing a book of tales for children with illustrations might be a good idea—especially if it was for very young children. She thought of the story and how she and Maggie had become best friends who worked together for their best lives.

She smiled, nodded, and put Okchuli in her cradle to finish her nap.

3

————

When Hank Smithson finished shoeing Clay's horse, he turned to Silas and said, "I tell you, Silas, I think the honorable Mr. William Henry Murray is a bigoted buffoon and not to be trusted." He pulled a glowing, hot, iron horseshoe out of the coalbed with the long tongs he held in his left hand. He pointed it at Silas Pennington and continued, "He believes in himself more than any other being, including God, Moses, and Jesus, not to mention us mere mortals."

Clay chuckled but said nothing.

Silas grinned and scratched his head. "Well, then, why is it that the Chickasaw Governor Johnston has him as the legal counsel for the tribe? They must see something good in him to give him that position."

Hank picked up his hammer, ready to strike the hot iron he held in his grip, and pointed his giant hammer at Silas and said, "There's a whole lot in this weary old world I have no inklin' about, includin' why anyone would have such a man as Mr. Murray for the lawyer for our tribe."

He turned back to the horseshoe he was forming. His hammer struck time and again as he finished yet another horseshoe. He felt sure he could never have too many horseshoes at hand. First thing every morning, he formed at least a dozen horseshoes of various sizes that would be reworked for each specific horse hoof when needed, as he'd done now for Clay's horse.

While Hank worked, Clay Harrison chuckled and told Silas and the blacksmith, "My wife has the idea that with Mr. Murray's colloquial way of talkin', his inherent likeability, and his affable presence, might keep the white men from totally robbin' the tribe of its wealth —primarily the land."

"Being married to a Chickasaw woman myself, I wouldn't count on it," Hank said. Then, he put the newly formed horseshoe in the water barrel to keep its form by cooling it. Steam rose around the blacksmith, and he said, "Thieves never give up on the possibility of quick rewards no matter where they come from or to whom they belong in the first place."

"Do you think William Murray is a thief?" Clay asked.

"Oh, he's probably not an out-and-out thief but a little too slick to my way of thinkin'. However, I suspect he is an opportunist and a fairly shady one. He's the kind of fella that the less work he has to do to reap the benefits of any opportunity, the better he'll like things in his life."

Clay nodded. "I can see that."

Hank shook his head. "Still, I think you may be right, Clay. Although I don't have any use for bigotry, when I'm in the presence of Mr. Murray, I can't help but like him, if only for a moment. Then he says something mean about the Chickasaw or African people grinning the whole time, and I lose interest in him quickly. Lucky for him, he hasn't demeaned the Irish in my presence."

Both Silas and Clay laughed at their friend's comment about the Irish while they watched him pull the cooled horseshoe from the water and toss it in a pile he'd use someday on some horse.

Silas grinned and said, "I feel such a man, born in Toadsuck, Texas, no less, might want to be a bit more humble."

The other two men laughed while Silas continued. "However, I do not think humility is in his vocabulary or way of being. He came into *Okchuli Press* and asked that I make him a few thousand business cards. He asked how much the printed cards would cost him and what he would have to pay upfront."

"What did you say?"

"I said he'd have to pay half up front just like anyone else in town, and when the job was finished, he'd have to pay the remainder before taking the cards with him. He shook his head a bit as if that was too much to pay, so I suggested he go to the newspaper that's trying to get started and see what they'd do for him."

"So did he?"

"No. He said my costs were—and I'm quoting him exactly— "mud-slick road robbery compared to the highway robbery of the newspaper." Still, he tried to talk me down on the money, but I refused. I told him I had just opened my business and couldn't afford to give anything away."

"So, did you print the cards for him?"

"Of course. He had the money, though he didn't want to let go of it, and I had the press hot and ready to run. It was a match I couldn't forgo. I'm not an idiot just because I don't believe he is a bloomin' sage as some are callin' him. I'm fairly certain he might not even be a good man."

Hank chuckled as he began to work on a plow blade. "Good for you, Silas. I'm right there with you. Still, I'll shoe any man's horse if he has a few coins."

Clay smiled. "And on that note, I must get back home. I want lunch and a chat with my wife before Noah and I finish the cellar.

After lunch, Aurora and Maggie will be knee-deep in a sweaty and overwhelming canning day. I never thought we'd need more jars than we'd already bought. Turns out I was wrong. I put them in Aurora's buggy so they would have them if they needed them sooner."

Silas nodded. "Thanks, Clay. Those two women have a hankering to fill our dugout cellar with as many jars as they can cram in there."

Hank laughed. "My Mary is deep into canning, too. Speaking of which, thank Aurora for me, Clay."

"About what?"

"Mary asked Aurora why her blueberry scones tasted so much better than her own—finally!"

"Did Aurora tell her the secret?"

"Yes, but Mary wouldn't tell me what it was."

"Why not?"

"She said she would never risk her blueberry scones tasting this good by telling the secrets."

Clay laughed. "How do they taste now?"

"They're much better. They're still a little tough but edible and no longer too tart to swallow. It could be, though, that I'm just getting used to them."

Clay grinned as the other men laughed and said, "I'll tell Aurora thanks and thanks to you for shoeing Abner, Hank."

"Thanks for buying him off me! I have too many younger horses, and no one wants to pay for older ones like Abner."

"I like him fine. I've enjoyed his company. I don't need him to run a race or nothin' like that. Besides, having Abner allows Aurora to hitch up her horse, Rosie, to her buggy and tote things around. Abner's a good horse, but I know he needs a good shoeing when he gets cantankerous."

Hank nodded as he pounded the red-hot iron before him, working kinks out of the plowshare. "My pleasure. Just drop the money in the basket over there."

"Two dollars?"

"If you insist. Most folks only pay a dollar or less if I let them."

"No, sir! I'll not be cheating you even if you are a friend of mine."

"I'm relieved to hear it," Hank said, grinning. It'd be a shame for you to fall out of my good graces."

All three men laughed. Clay nodded. "Not only do I want to stay in your good graces, but I appreciate the care you take with your work, especially on my horse." He climbed onto his horse, waved farewell, and rode back to his home on Pennington Creek with the freshly shod Abner.

Clay liked coming into town now and again, especially to chat with folks like Hank Smithson, but he knew he could never live there. When he was less than a mile from the smithy's place, he felt himself relax and enjoy the peace of the land around him. It had rained the night before, and the red dirt didn't kick up as much dust as usual, though the road was muddy and sticky in spots. The air smelled clean, and the sky was a clear blue with a few cotton ball clouds, but not much of a breeze today.

A rabbit dashed across the road, but up in the sky, a red-tailed hawk was watching the rabbit closely. The rabbit zigged and zagged, trying but failing to avoid the hawk. The giant bird swooped down, and before Clay could whistle, the hawk had the rabbit in his clutches, flying away to a more amenable place to have his early morning lunch.

He grinned and said, "Well, Abner, one hawk's lunch is another critter's demise." The horse nodded in seeming agreement. Clay continued, "I suppose that's how the world goes round."

He watched the scissortail flycatchers, crows, and even another hawk flying around. As he continued riding up the road, he saw five turkey vultures cleaning up a small coyote at the side of the road. He slowed his horse a little to ride past and not disturb them too much, though he shuddered as he passed them. When he was a bit farther on down the road, he turned and grinned to see the vultures back at their roadkill, finishing whatever had caused the coyote to die.

He told his horse, "Abner when my time comes, I hope I'm in the ground before those dang vultures smell me. Their bald redheads and pink bills are just creepy." Abner nodded again, but this time, he neighed his apparent agreement.

Clay said, "I knew you'd understand. If you go before me, I'll do my best to see the vultures don't dine on you."

The horse nodded and neighed again and sped up a little too.

Clay chuckled, pleased with his life this fall morning. The further away from the vultures—those in town and those in the middle of the road—the easier his mind would be.

Thoughts of Aurora and Okchuli brightened his soul even further. He knew what Aurora was upset about. Walter had talked with him yesterday afternoon and told him what was happening. Until that conversation, Clay had no idea he could petition for an allotment simply because he married a Chickasaw woman. He wanted to take the opportunity but didn't have fifty dollars. Walter assured him his portion had already been paid.

Clay sighed and muttered. "I wish I knew who paid my allotment." It wasn't that he wasn't grateful, but more that he wanted to make his own way in life. Another thought slipped into his head. Perhaps it was Silas who paid the allotment. He decided he would ask him about it. "I know Silas is a good friend and has more money than I do, but still, I don't want to be beholden to him—or anyone else come to that."

He rode Abner across the stagecoach bridge when they got to Pennington Creek. It wasn't much of a bridge, and Clay muttered, "Someday, we'll all fall in that creek!"

Abner neighed and sped up a bit but stepped lightly. He didn't like the rickety bridge, but more importantly, he could smell home.

4

Aurora Harrison did not know whether to be happy or sad, laugh or cry, move forward, or give up. Giving up wasn't in her nature, and she knew crying wouldn't help, although she might feel better in the moment. She had a home, a lot of land—more than she knew until yesterday morning—a loving husband, a newborn daughter, and friends.

Still, she felt unsettled and wished not for the first time that she was still a little girl and didn't know about the complexities of being an adult woman.

She and Clay had discussed the land allotments, including who paid for his allotment. She had no idea, so she asked Maggie, who said neither she nor Silas had paid the price. They were trying to keep their money close because the printing press wasn't making enough money yet to spend such a sum.

Today, with a beautiful fall sun shining and glinting sparkles on Pennington Creek as it burbled around them and all their canning completed, Aurora sat with her first best friend, Maggie Pennington. Aurora knew she should be happy. And she was—mostly. She shook her head and thought *I'm a strong woman and should act like it.* But, somehow, today, she did not feel strong. She felt afraid and uncertain.

Maggie looked up from polishing the large silver platter she wanted to use for Thanksgiving dinner. It had been handed down from her mother and grandmother and many mothers before them brought from England originally. She watched her friend, wondering why she seemed so out of sorts today. She said, "Aurora, your people, the Chickasaw, have completed their monumental task—building the new Chickasaw Capital Building. Does it make you happy?"

Aurora nodded. "Yes, in its way, I suppose it does. It is a beautiful building that I'm sure will stand for generations. Yet, many of my people believe that white men will never steal from them again simply because of the building. They believe the building is evidence of their hopes and dreams as a people. For them, it represents some-thing solid for the future. I hope they are right, but I do not expect their hopes to come true."

"Why?"

"Do you remember me asking about the allotment payment yesterday?"

"Of course. Is that what is bothering you?"

"No, it is more that I am angry and worried about The Curtis Act."

"Is that the reason for all the allotments?"

"Yes, and about taking our people's millions of acres of communal land and doling out a few acres to each Chickasaw Native instead. Many more acres will be left over than all of the Chickasaw will receive."

"Really?"

"Yes."

Maggie saw the tears on her friend's face and the bundle of

papers under her hand. She pointed to the documents and asked, "Are those papers why you are distressed, Aurora?"

"I'm not distressed—exactly. I feel more adrift today than I've any reason to feel. I feel as if I were seeking a different shade of blue while looking at a sparkling, clear blue sky. It makes no sense. Perhaps it is simple unease bothering me, but I fear more is concealed underneath our blue sky."

Maggie set aside the platter and silver polish, wiped her hands, and then said, "The babies are napping; Clay is finishing the cellar with Noah, while Sarah is playing with Ben and Bea on the front porch—enjoying a warm, sunny day. Silas is putting the finishing touches on Adella's apartment above his publishing store in Tishomingo. We have a short bit of blessed time to be ourselves—just you and me, dear friend. We can have a cup of tea, a slice of your incredible fruit cake, and you can tell me what is really bothering you," she pointed to Aurora's hand, "and share with me what it is about those papers that make you sad."

Aurora smiled. "Sounds perfect. There's nothing terrible going on, but I feel a shadow of sorrow for some reason."

"Then come, dear friend, let's have a bit of tea, cake, and a chat."

The luxury of tea and chatting without children tugging at their skirts—or husbands, for that matter—felt delightful to both women. Maggie opened the cake tin and took out two slices, one for herself and another for Aurora. She placed the slices of fruit cake on small plates next to their tea cups and saucers. Once the tea was ready, the two friends sat back down at the table—this time side-by-side, watching the world around them through the big double windowed doors to the backyard. They could see the kitchen garden tucked quietly under mulch, waiting for winter and spring, and the paving stone sitting area for spending summer evenings.

Aurora pulled the papers close, unsure what to do—though she felt she must do something.

Maggie touched her friend's hand, which was covering the papers, and said, "Now, tell me what is causing you to worry."

"This will sound selfish, but I'm upset about the new council house and the hoorah all the white folks will make of the dedication in a couple of weeks."

"I can understand your feelings. Perhaps you are worried that the symbol of your people may become a celebration by white people, for white people."

Aurora nodded, "Certainly, that is hanging around the edges of my mind."

Maggie squeezed her friend's hand and said, "No matter how it turns out, I'll be with you."

Aurora smiled a bit. "I know, and I appreciate your friendship. My life has been a lot of lucky turns despite some of the hardships. I was lucky Clay found me and loved me. I was lucky when you and Silas became our friends and improved our lives. I was lucky when the stars gave me my dear daughter, Okchuli."

Maggie sighed. "We all have trials and tribulations, but occasionally, we get lucky. It's the best part of life."

"You're right. It is. Do you remember Walter Thompson, one of the Chickasaw clerks at the Capital Building who helped us?"

"Of course I do. I also remember him blushing over talking about women having babies. We didn't mean to embarrass him, but we wanted to be sure both our babies' births—Okchuli and Teddy— were legally recorded on the records."

Aurora nodded and smiled softly, remembering the joy of making sure her daughter, Okchuli, would be listed as her bodily-born child, but she felt sad at the same time. She would never regret the blessing of the foundling baby who appeared in a basket on the front porch of her log cabin late one evening nearly six months ago.

Still, she worried about many things and feared for the future of the Chickasaw people.

Maggie waited quietly, trying hard not to guess what was bothering Aurora or what the papers she kept touching had to do with her current emotional strain. Maggie thought *There were many perils in her life, and frankly, for all women, no matter the color of their skin or the money the families have.*

Finally, Aurora sighed and tapped the papers she had laid on the table. "I need to speak my piece, Maggie, but I do not want to hurt you and your family in any way. Walter gave me these papers yesterday. These papers are for you and Silas, but first, I want to share what I know. Walter wanted to be sure you and your family, as well as me and my family, would always have the land on which we live."

"Was there any doubt it was so?"

"Maybe. Maybe not. Neither Walter nor I are certain. With the Curtis Act looming, he wanted to be sure. This," she patted the envelope, "contains papers. These papers are a bit of a fail-safe for all of us."

"Let me guess. That nasty old Lester Blunt is raising a fuss about us—again."

"Yes, but his ire is primarily directed at me. His time in jail wasn't wasted, though. He has more concrete plans to have me and mine out of Tishomingo."

"I don't give a rat's skinny tail what plans he has. We are not leaving our home or land."

"Good," Aurora said and grinned at her friend's choice of unladylike words. "I want you to look at these papers Walter gave me, and then we can decide if we want to do anything. This set of papers is for you and Silas. I have the same papers for Clay and myself—hidden in a safe place. Perhaps we do not need to do anything, but I want us all to be ready for whatever comes next."

Aurora handed the papers to Maggie. Maggie looked at her friend for a moment, then picked up the sheaf of papers and read every page. When she finished, she looked at Aurora and asked, "What does this mean? I find this a little confusing."

"I did as well, but Walter explained it all to me. It means that Jacob Pennington bought my mother's land allotment and most of my allotment as well—I was a child then, and she had the right to do so. However, he did not buy Okchuli's allotment—because she wasn't born yet."

"Really? He could do that?"

"Yes. Really. It's more than Jacob deeded to you and Silas. More acres are west of Jacob's land and where Clay and I live. That is part of my allotment that Momma sold to Jacob. There are more acres all told than we knew, and it doesn't count Okchuli's or Clay's allotment."

"Are you certain?"

Aurora nodded, then shrugged. "Yes, most of my allotment, Jacob Pennington bought and then deeded to you and Silas upon his death. That remains yours and Silas's."

Maggie shook her head. "This makes my head swim."

"As it does mine. However, Walter has entered all of this at the council house, which is legally binding. I have similar papers, except you and Silas have your deeds."

"What about the five acres we deeded to you?"

"It is still ours unless you wish to have them back."

"Not a chance," Maggie said and chuckled. "I'm happy with my farm and my dear friend living nearby. I'll share all of this with Silas tonight after dinner. For now, I'll put these in his desk drawer. Let's finish our tea and cake. We can celebrate your great good fortune."

Aurora smiled, nodded, and hoped Maggie was right that it was good fortune. Still, nagging in her mind, she felt surely there would be a price to pay for such largess, and the price would be high.

5

Maggie touched her friend's hand and said, "You know I love you, not only as a friend but as my sister, shared in love. Please tell me what you are thinking."

Aurora nodded and smiled. "I feel the same way about you, Maggie. According to these papers, Jacob Pennington has purchased a significant portion of our allotments. However, my remaining 80 acres are still within the area of Clay's and Okchuli's allotments.

"Does your mother know all of this?"

Aurora nodded. "Yes. I spoke to my mother about it yesterday before Walter gave me these legal papers."

"What does your mother say? How and when did you talk with her about it all?"

"Walter allowed me to use the telephone in his office. Once we were connected, Walter left the room, closed the door, and I talked with my mother. Have you ever used a telephone?"

Maggie smiled. "Yes, Silas's parents had a telephone, and there was a telephone at the newspaper where Silas worked in Columbia, South Carolina, as well as one at the bank where his father was a part owner and manager."

"Well, I'd heard there were telephones in Tishomingo at a few businesses and the new council house, but I'd never talked on one."

"What did you think about hearing your mother's voice?"

"It was strange to hear her voice coming through the wires into my ears, but it also felt like magic. It sounded like her voice but also not her voice."

Maggie nodded. "I felt the same way the first time I heard Silas's voice coming from the newspaper to his parent's home on their telephone. However, I didn't take long to learn how to use it."

"Well, it was a new experience for me and felt a little like magic," Aurora said, tapping the papers again. "To the point of the papers and my mother's allotments, I can use that land however I wish, including selling it. All of our allotments, including what Jacob left you and Silas, are on the west side of Pennington Creek."

"I'm glad you have more than the five acres Silas and I gave you. It helps me feel closer to you."

"Why?"

"Now we are more equal in every regard, and I love that we are."

"Thank you. Momma is relieved it is all written out and legal at the Capital Building."

"I'm glad your mother is doing well and is happy, and I'm delighted she is coming in a few days. We'll have both our houses filled to the corners!"

Aurora laughed. "Yes, we will."

"I'm also glad you have legal papers of your holdings and our holdings. However," Maggie looked at the papers, "Why did this happen now?"

"Walter had heard that Lester Blunt was making noises about the

Pennington Creek property not being properly sold to Jacob Pennington."

Maggie said, "But these papers say differently, and they were dated long before Jacob died."

"Yes, they were, and the papers are also filed with the clerk's office at the new Chickasaw Council House."

"I thought they were calling it the Chickasaw Capitol Building?"

"Yes, that is true. Walter told me that some of our people, the Chickasaw, do not think they can hold onto the building if the Indian Territory joins Oklahoma Territory to create a new state for the United States. I fear he is right, and once again, we will not have our place to be. Still, they can't simply take away all of our land. Walter agrees and thinks that might be the only good thing in the Curtis Act."

Maggie nodded. "I hope you are right. Silas has heard some of the rumblings both from the native Chickasaw people and the white people who are already living here."

"Well, there are more and more white people coming here every day, and not all of them are good people. There are some who say the way the white people finally conquered our people was to build beautiful buildings, nice roads, stagecoach routes, telephones, telegraphs, and railroads on our land. Then all they had to do was keep white people coming here and buying up our allotments."

"Although most of our roads aren't really nice and we don't have telephones for most people, I agree, dear friend. The truth of the matter is that I feel guilty about having this land but do not wish to be elsewhere. I love my home, our land, and my friends."

"Don't feel guilty. My mother sold our allotments to Jacob Pennington, who deeded it to his nephew Silas and his wife, Margaret. Legally, this land belongs to you and Silas."

"I do understand, Aurora, and I love that you don't feel we've no right to this land. However, it's difficult to keep my feelings of guilt at bay. Please tell me why you are so distressed, though. It seems to me that legally, Lester Blunt can do nothing but be a cocklebur under our saddles."

"I'm afraid someone will take from me all I have worked for and dreamed of having—even the five acres you and Silas gave us."

"What makes you feel so strongly about this? You have a legal claim to everything."

"Many white people think we are savages—not quite human. I've heard Lester Blunt express those feelings about me directly. People like him feel they can plunder our lands, lives, and ways of being without remorse. It seems to me they are the savages."

"I agree, and it is part of why I sometimes feel guilty about it all."

"It is not your guilt, Maggie. The Chickasaw would welcome people with kindness and equality in their hearts. But that's not how it works for many white people."

"I agree."

Aurora said, "I remember a story of Desoto when he first came around the Chickasaw. The tribe welcomed him as an honored visitor and gave him food, shelter, and many blankets. The next day, he told Miko—the chief—he must give Desoto 100 of our people as slaves to carry all their goods. At dawn the next day, our brave soldiers decimated Desoto's camp, and many of them died. The few who lived, including Desoto, left quickly. In less than a year, he died of a fever on the banks of the big river you call the Mississippi."

"What a story! It's hard for me to know people from Europe did such vile deeds."

"I understand, but that was Desoto's guilt, not yours, Maggie. I told you the tale to remind you never to carry the guilt of another person's misdeeds. You have always been a blessing for Clay and myself."

"Thank you for your words, but love and kindness will not be enough. I think it would be best if you had a lawyer. The lawyer must be one the white men will listen to, and the Chickasaw will accept."

"That's exactly what Walter said."

"Did Walter give you an idea of who would be a fair and honest lawyer?"

Aurora smiled and nodded. "Sort of. Walter said there were more lawyers in Tishomingo than rooting hogs. He said, 'Most of them aren't worth a bucket of warm spit and could be just as destructive as rooting hogs.' However, he felt Mr. Murray might be a good place to start."

"Really? William Murray? Why him?"

"Because he wishes to marry a Chickasaw woman for her land, and she is smitten with him. Also, her uncle is the governor of the Chickasaw people. Her place in the tribe hierarchy is solid and above reproach."

"Does Mr. Murray wish to marry her only for her land?"

Aurora shrugged her shoulders. "Perhaps—I don't know. Maybe —if she is lucky—he wishes to marry her, at least partly for the vibrant and well-educated woman she is. But who knows? He will be glad to have her land and delighted to have a beautiful woman on his arm." Aurora grinned then and said, "Walter felt any man born in a town called Toadsuck, Texas, was perhaps more honest than not."

Maggie laughed loudly and asked, "He was born in Toadsuck?"

"Yes, indeed. Toadsuck, Texas. It's called Collinsville now, but Walter thinks that's only because the town's women, having more good sense than the men, couldn't stand the original name."

"What a world we live in."

"I agree. Mary Alice Hearrell is who Mr. Murray has set his hat for, but more importantly, she is the niece of the Chickasaw Governor, Douglas Johnston. So, Walter thinks if I ask Mr. Murray to be my lawyer, I will likely succeed in keeping all my allotments without question. No lawyer would dare to deny a Chickasaw woman her allotments, especially when he has planned to marry a Chickasaw woman precisely for that purpose—and perhaps even for love. One can only hope it is so."

"What happens to our home and land?"

"Walter has already made sure the deed for your land and Clay's land—the five acres—is a sealed deal between me, my mother, and the Chickasaw Nation. For Clay and myself, he has already paid his $50.00 for my allotment—at least, I think he is the one who has paid for the allotment."

"Really?"

"That's what the deed says."

"Ah, thank heavens for Walter Thompson! Now, all is right in our world."

"Maybe. Lester Blunt is out of jail now and trying to get a gang of white men to wipe me and mine off the face of the earth. He's also making noises about Okchuli being 'another half-breed.' I'll rip his heart out with my bare hands if he does anything to hurt her."

Maggie shook her head and blew out a big breath. "He is the worst of the worst! I'd call him a slug, but even slugs wouldn't crawl over his slime. What about the sheriff?"

"He's aware, but he pointed out that now that I have a legal claim to a lot of land, Lester Blunt will be more dangerous than ever."

Maggie nodded. "That's all the more reason to sign up Mr. Murray to be your lawyer quickly."

"I agree, but a lawyer's papers won't stop Mr. Blunt. It makes me sad to have all this turmoil and vitriol landing in my lap when my personal life is beautiful, and I have everything I'd ever dreamed of."

"I'm so sorry, Aurora. Let's wait and see what Mr. Murray says about it all."

"You're right. Thanks for listening to my woes."

"Anytime, dear friend."

Maggie stood up to clear the table when Sarah came racing into the house and asked, "Momma, can we go down to the creek?"

6

"Before you choose
a counselor, watch him
with his neighbor's children."
Sioux Proverb

Before Maggie could answer, Aurora stood up, tucked her shawl snugger around Okchuli, and said, "The water will be too cold to go swimming, but I'll go with the children to be sure that old black mother snake and her wiggly babies aren't around."

Sarah said, "I'll get the hoe, Aurora."

"Thank you, Sarah."

Maggie smiled. "While you and the children go to the creek, I'll finish with the silver."

Maggie watched Aurora with her baby Okchuli snuggled close in her wrap as her friend walked out with the children to the creek.

Maggie had quit carrying Teddy next to her all the time. He was now over six months old, growing like a weed, and too heavy to carry for hours and hours. She glanced at the cradle where her youngest of five slept. Now, she had five children with Sarah, whom she and Silas had adopted a few months ago.

She smiled, thinking of her family and all that had happened in their lives over the past eight months. First, adventure called them to move to Indian Territory. Indeed, it had been a tremendous undertaking, and so had each day since. Second, she and her husband Silas had been welcomed by Clay and Aurora, who had become dear friends with their family on Pennington Creek, Indian Territory, near the small town of Tishomingo.

She told herself, "I have much to be thankful for," and picked up the silver paste and cloth. She wanted to finish getting the platter ready for Thanksgiving dinner. She had a lot of work to do before Silas' parents from South Carolina arrived in less than two weeks for the dedication celebration of the Chickasaw Capital Building and Thanksgiving.

AURORA WATCHED as the children romped, tossing rocks and acorns into the creek. The fish, turtles, and frogs weren't interested in the stones, but the acorns were a different thing for all the creatures in the stream. Bea and Ben plunked acorns into the creek, where a giant catfish stayed close to the bank, eating the nuts. What he didn't eat, a snapping turtle did. As any snapping turtle would do, he snapped up any morsel that came his way. Further out, Sarah's acorns found the mouths of the perch and bass.

While the children played, Aurora sat on a warm rock in the sun, lowered her blouse, and let her daughter Okchuli nurse. Once the baby had her fill, Aurora held the baby across her shoulder, patting her back to loosen any gas bubbles in her stomach.

Sarah asked, "Does it hurt for you to let Okchuli suck on your breast?"

"No, it doesn't. I'm happy to be able to feed her at my breast."

Sarah nodded and said, "Momma says when I'm about 12 years old, my breasts will start growing."

"Yes, that sounds about right. Some girls' breasts start growing earlier and some later, but 12 years old seems about right."

"Why do we have to have bigger breasts than boys?"

"So you can feed your babies."

"Papa says it's kind of like cows and their milk."

Aurora bit her lip and held back laughter but smiled and said, "He's right."

Sarah nodded, picked up a flat rock, and let it skip across the creek. Immediately, both Bea and Ben tried to skip stones without success.

Aurora laughed softly, watching the children.

Sarah turned back to Aurora and asked, "What about bleeding?"

"Well, for girls, that happens around the time their breasts start getting bigger."

"Why?"

"So they can have babies."

"We bleed to make babies?"

Aurora touched her lower abdomen to show Sarah where the womb of a woman was and said, "We don't bleed to make babies, but your womb, which is down deep in your belly, has to bleed to be ready for a baby to be made."

"How does the baby get into the womb?"

Aurora started to tell her then, thought about how she'd feel if another woman described the ways of blossoming womanhood to Okchuli. She asked Sarah, "What has your mother told you?"

"Not much. Just the growing breasts and bleeding and wombs."

Aurora nodded. "Didn't your birth parents have hogs?"

"Yep, and every spring, there would be a whole passel of piglets sucking at her teats."

"Did you watch the piglets get born?"

"Yeah. It was messy, but the piglets seemed fine with it all. The sow grunted a lot and wasn't very nice for a bit. But I don't understand how the piglets got inside the sow and why they decided to come out."

"Well, did you see how the big pigs, like the sow, were together?"

"Oh! Yes, there was a big black boar. He was mean and kept crawling up on the sow's back until she kicked him and bit him, and he left her alone."

Aurora tried not to smile—unsuccessfully—and asked, "I wonder why he was on her back?"

"Daddy—my mean daddy—said he was poking her to have piglets."

"There. That's how it all works."

"You mean Momma's have to be poked by a big black boar to have babies?"

"Only if they are pigs. Pigs, or in this way of thinking, Sows have Boars, Cows have Bulls, Horses have Studs, and Hens have Roosters. Does that make sense?"

Sarah considered what Aurora had told her for several seconds, then nodded, blushed, and whispered to Aurora, "So, do women have men?"

"Yes. That's how human babies are made."

"UGH!!!!! No way will I want a man to poke me."

Aurora smiled and nodded. "Not yet, of course. You're still a child, although you are growing up. Someday—a long time from now—you might change your mind. But only when you are a fully grown-up woman—several years from now."

"Is that how Okchuli was born?"

"Yes," Aurora quietly answered and sat still, hoping Sarah had forgotten about the basket on her front porch.

Sarah saw how quiet Aurora had gotten, so she touched Aurora's hand. "I've forgotten all about the basket. I know for a fact Okchuli is your daughter."

Aurora squeezed Sarah's hand and said, "Thank you, Sarah. I appreciate that you have forgotten. It means a lot to Okchuli, Clay, and me. Your forgetting will help keep us safe."

Sarah swiped her hand across her forehead and asked, "Forgot what?"

Aurora chuckled. "Thanks, my dear young friend."

Sarah smiled at the endearment just as Bea squealed and shouted, "You hit me with that acorn, Ben!"

"Sorry," he said and grinned. "I thought you were a catfish."

Bea picked up an acorn and threw it at Ben. It hit him on the cheek. He shouted in pain—a tiny pain, mind you—a mere scratch—and started to fuss at his twin sister when Aurora stood up and said, "Let's go back up to the house, children. Before long, it will be sunset time, and I must get home and fix dinner for Clay and me. Besides, Okchuli has a wet diaper, and it's getting wetter."

"Okay," Ben said, "But she hit me with an acorn."

"I know. Perhaps next time you throw an acorn, you'll aim it anywhere except where your sister is."

"Yes, ma'am, but I don't like it."

"I'm sure truer words were never spoken."

Aurora worked hard not to smile as she ruffled his hair, and he quickly scraped his fingers through it to get it back to how he wanted it. He didn't understand why adults insisted on ruffling his hair. They wouldn't like it if he did that to them—not one bit!

Once they were back at the house, Bea raced inside to tell her mother about Ben throwing an acorn at her, and Ben told her how Bea hit him on the cheek with an acorn. "My goodness. Alert the press! The Great Acorn War!"

Aurora could no longer contain her laughter and laughed out loud. She shook her head and said, "Hopefully, they'll survive the day. For now, I need to head home and get dry clothes on Okchuli."

Sarah said, "Momma, I'll check on the hens and see if there are more eggs."

"Thanks, Sarah. I'll meet you at the well in a bit, and we'll carry water in for dinner."

Sarah nodded but was wanting time alone to think about poking and babies. It didn't make much sense, but she trusted Aurora wouldn't tell a lie about women and babies. Momma said she was the best midwife anywhere around here, and Sarah trusted her mother even more than Aurora. As she walked to the hen house, she remembered her birth mother and father and all the noise they made on their squeaky bed. Maybe that was poking.

She shrugged her shoulders and hoped somehow she could figure it out before her breasts grew and she started bleeding. She shook her head, wondering why she would ever need to bleed, where she would bleed, and where the blood would come from.

Knowing about things isn't always something I understand, she decided.

Now, there's an intelligent girl.

7

*"We will be
known forever by
the tracks we leave."*
Dakota Proverb

Clay was pleased with the nearly finished cellar. He tucked his hands in his pockets and looked down at nine-year-old Noah—Maggie and Silas's oldest child—as he, too, put his hands in his pockets, mimicking Clay's stance. Whenever he noticed Noah following his lead, it reminded him to be the best example he could be.

He grinned and asked the boy, "Well, what do you think now, buddy?"

Noah looked up and nodded. "I think it looks fine. I thought we were building too many shelves, but I guess I was wrong."

"I'm right there with you, buddy, but your momma insisted we have more shelves than we thought we needed."

"Yep. And she wanted a big bench, too. I like the benches in the middle."

"I agree. They'll be handy for sitting on or gathering food to bring into the house."

Noah grinned, "There's still a little more room, but not a lot."

Clay chuckled. "You're right. That's part of why we built two big cold wells inside the cellar today. Not only will they keep things like meats and dairy cold for several days—even longer during the winter —but they won't be taking up space on the shelves."

"Just like Momma said. I like the big bins for the potatoes, carrots, and yams, but still, it's a lot of jars."

Clay nodded. "You're right, Noah. I'm amazed how many jars Aurora and your momma could fill up with all the crops we grew this year."

"Momma counted the jars and said it would be enough so long as we take good care of things." Noah shook his head again and said, "Momma says we ate these same foods in South Carolina, but I don't remember that."

"Did you see the food being cooked?"

"No, sir, I didn't."

"Well, my guess is if your momma said so, it's the truth. What we fellas don't know about cooking could overflow these shelves and leave us knee-deep in our ignorance."

Noah laughed. "Yeah." He nodded and pointed to the cellar's roof. "Why did Momma and Aurora hang all those weeds on the ceiling rings?"

"Well, son, the first thing to understand is that one man's weed is a woman's herb or medicine. When they need one of the weeds to help us when we're ill, we'll be mighty glad we hung all of it up on the ceiling. Besides, it smells good with mint, lavender, sage, rosemary, basil, oregano, and what else I don't remember, but the wild critters don't like the smell. We want to keep critters out, and those weeds, as you call them, are part of keeping our food safe."

"I do like the smell, but not completely. Papa said Momma knows the right thing to do, mainly because she does it all for us, not just for herself.

"And there you have love, Noah."

Noah nodded. He liked how Clay talked about his mother, and it helped him feel his mother's presence in the cellar. He knew without a doubt his mother loved him, and that knowledge helped him every day.

He said, "I kinda like how the jars are different colors. I especially like the red sand plums and orange persimmons."

"That may be because they taste so darned good. Don't tell your Momma I cursed."

Noah grinned. He knew his Papa and Clay teased him with their curse words, but he also knew he wouldn't tell his Momma. He said, "No, sir. I won't. Still, all those jars lined up on the shelves are pretty —a rainbow of food."

Clay nodded, liking how the boy thought. "I agree. Let's get our tools stowed away and settle things for the evening." He patted his belly and said, "I'm lookin' forward to some fine vittles."

Noah patted his belly and said, "Me too," then he pitched in and helped Clay pick up the tools and put them back in their boxes. Noah asked, "Are we finished with the cellar?"

"Until Aurora or your Momma come up with more ideas."

"What will we do now?"

"I have two things on my list. The first one is to finish building the second floor of my house. I've talked with Silas about it all. Would you like to help me?"

"You betcha'! I want to learn all I can about building."

"Well, I'll check with your papa in the morning. I've got a lot of it framed and most of the flooring done. I'm fairly certain your papa will be okay with letting us finish out the house before we start anything else. I want it to be finished before Aurora's momma and daddy come to visit."

Noah nodded and scratched his head. Then he said, "Clay, I'm just a kid, but I keep worrying about something."

"What?"

"Why is Aurora afraid of Mr. Blunt?"

"Well, to my mind, it's a complex set of circumstances, Noah. Mr. Blunt doesn't like her because she is part Chickasaw and part black from her father's side of the family."

Noah shrugged and said, "That's silly. What difference does that make?"

"You're right as rain about that, buddy. The other thing I think is there's something about Okchuli that sets him off something fierce."

"Why? She's just a baby."

"Again, you are right, but maybe he knows which woman gave birth to Okchuli and left her on our porch."

"But, I thought Momma said she helped Aurora have a baby."

"Yes, she did, and we all know that Okchuli is Aurora's daughter."

"So why would anyone be mean about it?"

"Noah, I think you've got a fine way of lookin' at things, but Lester Blunt isn't a nice man to begin with. He doesn't like who and what Aurora is. Having Okchuli makes him even meaner. On top of that, he hates that your Momma and Daddy helped us and gave us the little cabin and five acres of land."

"Why would it matter to him at all?"

"I don't know, Noah. All I know for sure is he is out to get Aurora and maybe me too."

Noah shook his head. "I like Aurora a lot, and Okchuli is fine for a baby."

Clay chuckled, "You're right about them both. They are everything I love in my life."

Noah sighed and nodded as his brain returned to what he loved the most—building. "So what are we going to do after we finish your house?

"Other than my house, I think the next thing on our list of want-to-do is building a smokehouse."

"Cool." Noah scratched his head and asked something that had been bothering him about the smokehouse. "Do you think you and Papa will find a hog who will have babies?"

"Yes, I do. It's why we built the pig pen. We'll see if we can lure her in as soon as we find her."

"What's lure mean?"

"Well, it's when you—or something or someone—go after something you can't resist—like Aurora's fruit cake."

"I love her fruit cake."

"Me too, son."

Noah nodded. "When are we going to get a momma pig?"

"Soon as we find a wild one."

"What will she eat? Will she like us?"

"Oh, I've never met a sow yet who liked anyone, maybe even herself."

"What's a sow?"

"A momma pig."

"Oh. Why do animals have silly names? Why don't they have names like momma and poppa or boy and girl?"

"I have no idea, Noah. It's surely something to think about."

Noah scratched his head, and Clay smiled and continued. Now, as far as what she will eat when we find her, we'll probably use some of the leftovers from your Momma's and Aurora's canning. For example, the skins of peaches, plums, and persimmons, as well as the bits of corn cob, broccoli stalks, and bean hulls. Those things will taste mighty tasty to a momma pig. Your momma is saving back that sort of thing in a can by the compost heap. She's even added a little of the skimmings from butter making."

"That would not make me hungry!"

Clay chuckled and ruffled Noah's hair. "Me neither, son, but pigs like that sort of stuff, especially this time of year."

"Why?" Noah asked as he settled his hair back, how he liked it.

"'Cause the momma pigs—sows, you know—are thinking about breeding this time of year, and they get mighty hungry thinking about being a sow with piglets growing up inside her."

Noah asked, "Are there momma hogs and papa hogs?"

"Yep. It takes two to tango."

"What's a tango?"

"It's a sort of dance."

"Hogs dance?"

"Well, buddy, not exactly," Clay said, grinned, and shook his head, trying to figure out how to explain about hogs dancing. He was rescued when they heard a scratching on the door.

Noah looked up, startled, eyes wide open, and asked, "What was that?"

"I don't know. Someone—or something—is scratchin' on the door. Let's see who's comin' to visit."

Noah grabbed Clay's hand and said, "People do not scratch on the door. They knock."

"You're right, son."

Again, something scratched at the door, but this time, whatever was at the door also whined and then barked. Noah grinned and raced to open the door. "It's a puppy!"

Clay grabbed him just in time to keep Noah from opening the door. He said, "It could be a coyote, Noah, or other mean critter. Just because something sounds nice doesn't mean it is. Let me open the door first."

Before Clay could open the door, a loud voice boomed, "Quit being silly gits. Open the door! My hands are full."

Noah grinned. "It's Papa!" Before Clay could stop him, Noah opened the door, and the two puppies Silas was trying to wrangle jumped down from his arms and into the cellar. Noah wrestled with the puppies, rolling on the wooden floor of the cellar. He was giggling and squealing with glee while they licked his face. When one of the puppies started to squat, Clay grabbed him, gently tossed him on the ground outside, and said, "No peeing in the cellar."

Silas laughed. "Let's get them both outside to run around and piddle wherever they want." They watched the black, brown, and white puppies as they piddled and wrestled.

Noah asked, "Does Momma know about the puppies?"

"Not yet."

Clay shook his head. "I hope you know what you're doing, Silas."

"You and me too. As I rode out of town toward home, Hank

Smithson waved me to his smithy. His brother had a big box of puppies at the stables, and he was offering them free."

"And a sucker is born every minute. No puppy, nor kitten, nor child, for that matter, is ever free."

"I suppose you're right, but I always wanted a puppy, and my mother wouldn't hear of it. I figure they might come in handy with the children."

Clay scratched his head. "What kind of pups are they?"

"I don't know, and neither did Hank's brother, Simon. His wife said to get rid of the pups today, or she'd get rid of them her way."

"Well, Silas. Good luck. Our front porch is available if you need a place to sleep tonight."

Silas laughed. "I'm not worried. Maggie had a puppy as a child and talked fondly of her. I figure having a dog or two around might help distract the children a little and might also help keep snakes away from the yard."

"They can be good for that; certainly, your children will be happy having them around."

Noah asked, "Are they boys or girls?"

"Both are boys."

Clay laughed. "That will help ensure they are the only dogs—for now."

Noah asked, "Can I name them, Papa?"

"Well, son, I suppose you could, but how would you feel if I brought home a couple of pups and Sarah, Ben, or Bea named them before you could put your penny in the cup."

"I guess I wouldn't like that, but what if they want some silly, stupid name?"

"Well, that for sure is a risk. What's the worst thing that could happen?"

"I might not like the name."

"Would that be so bad?"

Noah sighed and rolled his eyes. "It would be annoying, Papa."

Silas grinned at his son's facial expressions and said, "I get that.

Truly, I do, but let's go home and see if we can figure out what to name the dogs together—as a whole family."

Noah sighed. "Okay, Papa, but if they come up with something I don't like, I will say so."

"I would expect nothing less, son."

Clay grinned. "I'll head on home. Aurora will be wondering about me if I'm not home by sundown, and we have a mere few minutes left of daylight."

"We'll head home too. Have a good evening, Clay. If you want a puppy, there's more where these two came from."

Clay laughed. "I'll think on it for a few years and let you know."

Silas laughed, picked up a puppy, and told Noah, "You carry the other one, and I'll carry this one."

Noah picked up the puppy and let him lick his face. He whispered to the puppy, "I hope we pick a good name for you. Either way, I'll love you."

Silas smiled and walked home with his son. When they were standing on the porch, Silas said, "Now, son, remember this is a family affair."

"I will, Papa, but I have some name ideas."

"I do, too, but we'll let Momma, Sarah, Bea, and Ben give their ideas, too."

Noah nodded but hoped they wouldn't come up with anything silly. Thankfully, Teddy was too young to put a penny in the cup!

8

———————

"All dreams spin
out from the same web."
Hopi Proverb

Maggie watched her children and the new puppies rolling around and playing on the sitting area floor but was having difficulty getting her thoughts of Auoroa out of her mind. Silas came over and kissed her, then asked, "A penny for your thoughts, darlin'."

She smiled. "I was just wondering about Aurora, hoping she is doing okay."

He nodded. "Well, Clay is home with her and Okchuli. I'm sure they'll come over if there is anything really wrong."

She smiled and nodded. "You're right, of course. I'm sure there's nothing more we can do—for now at least". She pointed to the children and puppies. "Where do you plan to have the puppies stay at night?"

"Well, darlin', I haven't thought that far ahead."

Maggie raised her eyebrows, grinned, shook her head, clapped her hands for silence, and said, "All the children, including the man in the house, listen closely to me. Let's be clear on a few things before anything else happens. I will not allow pee or poop on my floors anywhere in my house or the porches. I will *not* be the person cleaning up any pee or poop on my floors or the porches. The pups will sleep in boxes in the barn with the horses and the cow. Their job around here will be to watch after all the animals and alert us when something is wrong. I will not be the one to feed the pups, either. Are we clear on those details?"

All the children nodded, as did Silas, who said, "Yes, ma'am," and the children echoed his words.

She smiled at him and the children. "I get to veto any names I don't like. They need dog names, not baby names."

Noah groaned. "But Papa said we all had to work together to name them."

Ben said, "I don't know how to name puppies."

Bea, Ben's twin sister, rolled her eyes. "Anyone can name a puppy."

Maggie pointed across the room to the alcove and said, "Well, children, go to your blackboard and write some puppy names, and we'll see."

Bea said, "But I can't spell any names but mine and Ben and Noah and Sarah and Momma and Papa."

Sarah put her arm around Bea and said, "I'll help you, Bea."

"And me," Ben said.

Sarah smiled and said, "Let's get busy naming the puppies."

While the children were busy at the blackboard, Maggie turned to Silas and said, "I love dogs, but two?"

"Well, I figured the girls would want one to be theirs, and the boys would be the same."

She nodded, then shook her head, tried to scowl, but in the end smiled. "I must say, I'm pleased there's not a female mutt in our menagerie."

"I figured you'd prefer no extras coming along in a few months."

"Exactly so. You and the children are enough to care for." She kissed his cheek and said, "Now go wash up, husband of mine, and help me get dinner on the table."

Once dinner was on the table, Maggie said, "All right, children, come to the table and tell me the names you've come up with. But first, let's fill our plates and say grace. Then, while you eat, you can chatter away about the puppies."

And chatter away they did.

Ben said, "I like that they are both boys."

"I don't," Bea said and glowered.

"Well," Silas said, "I picked the two that wanted to come home with me. Remember, we didn't know Teddy would be a boy before he was born."

Ben shook his head. "No, Papa, I knew the day before he was born."

Silas nodded. "I'd forgotten about that. Still, most of the time, we have no idea whether a boy or girl will be born."

Bea asked, "Were there no girl puppies?"

"Yes, there were, but they weren't the ones that wanted to come home with me."

She squinted her eyes at her father but said nothing. She was pretty confident he wasn't being honest, but she wasn't sure. Silas licked his lips, thinking his daughter's glare might become more dangerous as she grew up. Maggie chuckled as her husband got a taste of how determined Bea could and would be.

Maggie said, "I'm sure your Papa brought home two wonderful pups. Now, who will tell me the names you came up with?"

Noah looked at Sarah, who nodded. He said, "Because the puppies are boys, we decided the girls would name the first puppy."

"That seems like a very judicious choice, Noah."

He nodded but didn't know what 'judicious' meant—still—since Momma was happy with him, he'd let it go. "So, the girls came up with the name 'Rover' because the puppies would be roving everywhere we went."

Maggie nodded. "I like it."

Noah shrugged. "It's okay."

Maggie grinned and asked, "Which puppy is Rover?"

Bea said, "The one with the white snout."

Silas said, "I like it too. Now, what is the puppy's name with the black snout?"

Ben said, "Ranger!"

"I like that name. What do you think, Noah?"

"Well, I wanted to be the one to name them, but you were right, Papa. We needed it to do it together."

"I'm pleased to hear you say so, Noah."

"Thanks, Papa. I wanted to name him Blackie, but when we decided on Rover for the first puppy, Ranger seemed like a better name for the second one."

"I think they are fine names." He looked around the table and asked, "Is everyone settled with the names?"

They all nodded, but Bea asked, "Are you sure there isn't a girl dog to bring home."

"I'm sure," Silas said. "We don't want to be greedy. Some other children and families need a puppy, and we got two."

"How many were there all together?"

"Eight."

Bea looked down at her hands and counted eight fingers, then tucked two away and counted her fingers again. She said, "That means there are six other puppies."

Silas nodded. "I'm proud you can subtract and figure that out, Bea. Education is a good thing."

She nodded but sighed and rolled her eyes. Sometimes, she thought her father wasn't very bright, but she loved him. She said, "Momma is teaching me, so I'm getting good at counting. She's smart, you know."

"Yes, I do know, and you are right. Your Momma is a smart woman."

Bea shook her head. "Still, there were six other puppies." She held up six fingers to prove her point.

"Yes, there were, and we took two that could have gone to other children's homes."

She looked at her father for several seconds and said, "I guess we have enough."

"I'm glad you see it that way, Bea. It shows you have a generous spirit."

She rolled her eyes again and got busy eating her dinner. She didn't feel generous, but she liked her father's words. She was eager to eat the wild red plum cake her mother had made for dessert. Momma said there would be cool, thick cream, too. But, still, she wished one of the puppies had been a girl puppy she could dress up like a baby girl.

UPSTAIRS, preparing for bed, the children chattered about the puppies. Sarah said, "Don't worry about them. They are with the hens, horses, and the cow. They'll be fine, and let us know if anyone comes sneaking around."

Ben shook his head. "But, I wanted to play with them. We barely had any time to play with them."

Silas said, "Don't worry, son. You'll have lots of time to play with them tomorrow."

"Promise?"

"Promise. Your momma knows all about puppies. She'll help you learn about caring for and loving them."

"And playing?"

Maggie chuckled. "Absolutely. Playing, too."

9

Once the children and puppies were all in bed, Maggie sat in front of the fireplace with her usual basket of darning on her lap. "Silas, I need to talk with you about something very important."

"I know, darlin'. I'm sorry I brought home the puppies without asking you. Truthfully, there were a lot of folks looking the pups over."

She chuckled. "That's not what we need to discuss, but I appreciate the apology. I love the pups, and they will be a big help with watching after the barnyard and the children."

"I'm going to pretend that's why I brought them home," Silas said, then blushed. "The truth is, as a boy, I never had a puppy and simply couldn't resist."

"Then, of course, you should have brought a puppy home. I'm assuming you brought two because you also wanted one for the children."

"That was my plan, and I'll tell everyone and anyone that asks—it was exactly my intention."

She smiled and asked, "What else happened in town today?"

"Well, before the pups showed up, I was talking with Hank. We wound up talking about Mr. William Murray."

She raised an eyebrow. "He's a bit of a popinjay, I think, Silas."

He chuckled. "Well, we agree on that for sure. I wasn't in town when he arrived in Tishomingo back in March or early April. However, there's a high-falutin tale I heard about his arrival. Apparently, when he ended up in Tishomingo, he stepped from a wagon wearing a Prince Albert frock coat and a derby hat. He was hard to miss, and most folk thought at the time he was a loud-mouthed dandy."

"So my feeling is correct that he is a bit of a popinjay?"

"Maybe. I suppose he has settled down a bit—bein' a lawyer and all with Mr. Treadwell and Mr. Lucas. I haven't seen him dress in such a foppish manner. Still, I wouldn't say I like judging a man based on his appearance. Now, how he talks is entirely different. He seems very sure of himself—my father would have called him cock-sure. I'm not ready to go that far, but I swear he could talk the skin off of a rattler. However, since Mr. Douglas Johnston, the Chickasaw Governor, likes him and has brought him on as counsel for the Chickasaw, I suppose he must be a fine man."

Maggie shook her head. "That doesn't prevent him from being a preening ass."

Silas laughed out loud. "Oh, Maggie, I love you dearly, but talking like that outside our cozy abode will get folks jabbering about your language."

"You're right, of course. Perhaps. Maybe if now and again women spoke their minds, things might be different. What concerns me most, though, is things are changing a lot for the Chickasaw people, and now it seems Mr. Murray is a part of it all. What do any of us really know about him? Is he a *fine* man or even a *good* man?"

"I catch your drift, darlin', and it's an important question. Still, I'm unsure what we can do about it all."

"I agree, but I'm worried."

"What worries you?"

"He's a white man for one thing and therefore can't possibly have the needs and lives of the Chickasaw people front and center in his mind."

"I think you're probably right. For now, he is a lawyer helping the Chickasaw people. He's busy litigating for the Chickasaw tribe and their people. When I hear him speak, though, I hear a politician."

"And my guess is he is pocketing a fair bit of change from the people."

"Exactly so. Hank says we could toss a cow pie, and we'd dirty the fancy coats of a dozen lawyers who would buy new coats rather than clean them."

Maggie chuckled. "It seems to me that the boon for lawyers may not be a boon for the Chickasaw or anyone else for that matter."

"Oh, it'll be a boon for some folks, but it will most certainly not be even-handed."

"I agree. I heard about the Curtis Act from Aurora. She's worried, too."

"I haven't read the act, but perhaps we could get a copy and see what it's all about."

"No need, I think. Aurora has a copy she shared with me and talked to me about. Rather than all the land of Indian Territory belonging to the tribes as communal property as had been laid down by previous treaties and their ancient ways of being, now the land is divided up to the individual members of the tribes as an allotment. Each man, woman, and child now has an allotment."

"What difference does that make, Maggie?"

"Your daughter explained to you earlier about her skills in math coming from my tutelage."

He blushed a bit, "I do remember, darlin'. However, I'll need more elucidation on this."

"Ah! You have the words, and I have the numbers or at least a few of them."

They both laughed, but Maggie continued. "Previous treaties set aside much more land for the tribe. Now, it is being allotted to each Chickasaw or Choctaw native *individually,* with a lot of land left over. So much more will be left over that the white people will soon—very soon—overwhelm the population of the Chickasaw and any other Native tribes."

"Really?"

"Oh, yes, Silas. Each native Chickasaw will get 160 acres. I'm not sure of the exact number of Chickasaw, but it boils down to millions of acres that will *not* belong to the Chickasaw but will be available to anyone to purchase. This is true of all the tribes in the Indian and Oklahoma Territories. What has always been communal lands for the Chickasaw will now be allotted as personal Chickasaw land to do with as they please. The white people will buy the rest."

"But that means that Indian Territory and Oklahoma Territory will no longer be tribal."

"Exactly. I believe that is the intention of the United States government. I also believe that statehood will follow the Curtis Act. We will be living in the State of Oklahoma in a few years."

Silas nodded. "I'd heard murmurings but had thought little of it until now." He shook his head and said, "This certainly isn't South Carolina."

"No, it isn't, but South Carolina and all the other states and other people across this land must understand that all the loss for the native tribes is because of us—white people. It's not just you and me but every interloper since the first ships landed on the northeastern shores of this continent."

"Ah, darlin', take care speaking such things out loud. I fear for your safety should your thoughts be heard outside our home."

She laid her darning in her lap and looked at her husband. She was so still and quiet that finally, Silas felt the hair on the back of his neck rise. He blew out a soft breath and whispered, "I hope you know I love you and agree with you."

She softly answered. "I know, Silas." She shook her head. "Still."

He nodded. "Yes. Still."

They both sat quietly for several minutes.

As the fire began to crackle on the last bits of fuel, Silas said, "We have much to account for. Yet, at the same time, I want to scream, 'it isn't my fault.'"

Maggie smiled at her husband and said, "That's exactly how I feel, too, dear heart. But it is the fault of every white person—it's not only our fault but everyone's fault who came to these shores and took land that was already in use and owned by the native people." Maggie sighed. "Still, Aurora feels strongly that this isn't our fault, but I feel sullied somehow."

Silas reached for her hand. "I'm relieved we are both understanding things together. I know for certain we will do whatever we can to help all our Chickasaw friends and neighbors. It will not be enough, and our way of life will inevitably become their way of life. Anything we can and will do won't be enough."

"No, it will not."

"Damn. I wish I'd let the puppies sleep inside. I could use a few puppy licks and cuddles."

Maggie squeezed his hand and smiled. "Well, you could go check on them and give them a bit of a snuggle."

Silas stood up, leaned over, kissed his wife, and let a small teardrop land on her cheek. "I'll be back soon, darlin'. I want to check on the pups."

"Good idea. I'll get ready for bed, and we'll talk some more."

He nodded, pulled on his hat, opened the door, and headed for the stable and puppies.

LESTER BLUNT STOOD in the woods and watched Silas Pennington walk into his barn. Blunt was eager to get rid of the Pennington family. He shook his head and muttered, "Just because their name is on the creek doesn't mean they have a right to be here or make friends with the injuns. It ain't right, and I aim to set it right, maybe even rename the creek to Blunt Creek."

He shook his head, knowing Blunt Creek would never sound as good as Pennington Creek. He pulled a fresh cigar out of his pocket, put it in his mouth, struck a match, and lifted the flame to the tobacco. Silas didn't see the flame or smell the cigar, but another man, a Chickasaw friend of the Pennington family, Conrad Davidson, stood nearby watching Lester Blunt.

He shook his head and thought *no matter what anyone says, some of the white folks are not worth spitting on.* That was how he felt about Lester Blunt. He sighed and muttered, *Of course, some of the Chickasaws aren't much better. Humans are a mixed lot.*

He was determined to see to it that Lester Blunt didn't live much longer. The time would come—when it was the right time—to remove that vile man from the soil around Pennington Creek.

The safety of Aurora and her child was his top priority. Keeping Okchuli safe had gone to the top of the list in his mind. He thought, *Now that I know I was her biological father, I'll move heaven and hell to keep her and Aurora safe. I'm not the right sort of man to raise a child, but I'll keep her and her parents safe.* He knew Clay loved Okchuli and would give his life to keep her safe. Between himself and Clay, they would be sure to keep their daughter safe.

He watched as Silas Pennington left the barn and headed to his home. When Lester Blunt finally left, Conrad turned and crept back into the deep woods and to his own home. It wasn't much, but he didn't need much. It was a small one-room affair that he'd built in a dry cave—more a deep depression in a big rock—near Devil's Den. He knew his home was blessed as it faced the east and the morning sun.

All he'd built was a framework within the cave and a wooden

front. In his home, he had shelves for storing his food, clothing, a few dishes, and cooking utensils. Another large shelf created an elevated place for him to sleep, sit, and read. He loved to read anything but especially stories. He'd read Mark Twain's *Tom Sawyer* and *The Adventures of Huckleberry Finn* so often he had to take care that pages didn't fall out. For him, his cavelike abode felt safe and secure.

Just as Aurora had done, Conrad had spoken to Walter Thompson and Mr. Murray. Conrad made sure that if he passed away, all of his property and land, including his home and allotment, would belong to Okchuli Harrison. Although Mr. Murray found it unusual to leave everything to an infant, Conrad made it clear that he would haunt Mr. Murray and anyone else for eternity if they tried to take away Okchuli's inheritance.

Friends who knew him thought he was crazy to live so close to a place where outlaws, robbers, and murderers used to live—maybe there were a few still around or, at the very least, their ghosts. When anyone showed up and got close to his home, he chased them off with his hair-raising screams and beating his little drum.

Seldom did he have to lift a hand to make interlopers leave. His bristling hair was tied with small rocks and bones, and his black-striped face paint was enough to send lookie-lous runny for civilization. He'd worn this visage for so long that he seldom had to add more black soot to the lines on his face anymore.

He walked past the big rocks that loomed over the whole area and looked up at the behemoth rock formations. He thought perhaps Lester Blunt was due for a fall from a high place. He grinned and whispered, "Thump!" and then giggled. He could see old Lester at the bottom of a giant boulder. He would be nothing more than a human bag of broken bones left to rot.

Many white folks came out to see the rocks and the creek, amazed at the giant stones. They'd swim when it was warm, have a picnic and a bit of a hike, and then, long before sundown, they would head back to the safety of their homes in Tishomingo.

No one wanted to be at Devil's Den when the sun went down. He chuckled at the silliness of the white folks. To his mind, there was more danger in town—even in broad daylight—than in Devil's Den. He stood at the edge of the woods leading to his house. He waited a few more minutes to be sure no one was around and then walked past another big boulder, ducked through a small crevice in the boulder, and entered his shelter.

10

When Silas returned from checking on the pups, Maggie kissed him and wrapped her arm through his. "Dear heart, we do need to talk about these papers. I have something you need to read, and then we can go to bed."

He nodded. "You're right. I just needed a bit of air to settle my thoughts and feelings."

Once they were settled in the sitting area, snuggled together, Maggie handed the sheaf of papers Aurora had given her as their copy of everything about their land and how they came to legally be bought from Aurora's and her mother's Chickasaw allotment. "Read these papers, and I'll tell you the rest of the story behind it all."

Silas sat back in his chair, lit his pipe, opened the papers, and began reading. He looked up at Maggie a time or two. He read the pages two times before sighing, shaking his head, and refolding the papers. "Does this mean we get to keep our land and home?"

"Yes, it does, but it also means Aurora has as much land as we have, and Okchuli will have her allotment in the future, too. For now, Aurora is the caretaker of Okchuli's land."

"Good. In a way, I feel better about it all knowing this. I still want Clay and Aurora to keep the five acres we deeded them."

"I agree and said as much to Aurora. The issue is that Lester Blunt is making noises about taking Aurora's land because she isn't full-blood Chickasaw."

"But her mother is full-blood Chickasaw, isn't she?"

"Yes, and her father is part-African but Chickasaw too. His father was a freedman after the war and married a Chickasaw woman. So, both her parents are considered Chickasaw."

Silas said, "I wonder why Lester Blunt hates Aurora so much."

"I'm not sure, but both Aurora and I wonder if it means that Okchuli was born to someone he knew or was even a part of his extended family."

"Really?"

"Yes. It turns out his brother, his wife, and their teenage daughter left Tishomingo just a few days after Okchuli appeared on Clay and Aurora's porch. There was gossip that their daughter—Lester's niece—was pregnant."

"Wow. Who was the father?"

"No one is sure, but what is certain it was a Chickasaw man."

"For a bigot like Blunt, that would be too much to bear."

"My thoughts exactly," Maggie said. "Regardless of that part of Clay and Aurora's lives, Walter Thompson suggested Aurora get a lawyer to help make sure her land and Okchuli's land cannot be taken by force. He also set things up so Clay could claim his allotment since he had married a Chickasaw woman. It appears Clay has already paid and claimed his allotment."

"I wonder how he could afford to pay for the allotment?"

"I have no idea, and neither does Aurora. Did you pay the allotment?"

"No, but if he'd asked, I would have, or at the very least, I'd loan him the money."

Maggie smiled. "Good. Aurora doesn't know, but she was worried that perhaps you'd paid the price. I wondered if the birth father of Okchuli paid the price."

"That could be, but I certainly didn't pay it. I am glad that it's settled on the books. No one needs to know where the money came from. My guess is someone paid it but swore Walter to silence. Walter knows more about everything happening in town than anyone else in town, except for Shirley at the dry goods store or maybe Hank at the livery."

"I agree. I think guessing about who paid the price and who the birth father of Okchuli was is something better left lying quiet."

"You're right, darlin'."

"Now, about lawyers," Maggie said. "Aurora doesn't know Mr. Murray, but Walter recommended him."

"Do you know why he recommended Mr. Murray?"

Maggie grinned and said, "Aurora and I think Mr. Thompson recommended him because Mr Murray has his hat set on marrying Mary Alice Hearell. She is the niece of the Chickasaw Nation's Governor, Douglas Johnston. The governor has appointed William Henry Murray, the lawyer in question, as legal advisor for the governor and the tribe."

"Ah. Now I get it. Walter wants to be sure Aurora has the best possible case for keeping all her land and Clay's allotment without questioning by folks like Lester Blunt."

"Yes, and though I don't know Mr. Murray, I suppose he is as capable as any other lawyer."

Silas shrugged and said, "Perhaps, but more importantly, having Mr. Murray on the side of the Chickasaw and the governor gives him a better chance of being sure Aurora's land remains in her possession."

"What about Lester Blunt?"

"I don't know. He isn't a good man, but he is a white man. Being a white man gives him some power, I think."

Maggie shook her head. "Today, Aurora told me something that makes me feel ashamed of being white."

"Really?"

"Yes, she said many of the Chickasaws believe that when the white people came along, they built pretty buildings and towns, dug wells, and made a few roads, and that was enough for some of the natives to hand over anything and everything to the white folks."

Silas nodded. "I can see her point of view. It brings no honor to white people, but she is right in the main. Regardless of skin color or speech patterns, humans will accept lovely things when they come their way even if it isn't in their best interests."

"That is exactly what Aurora felt, too. She has little regard for most white people. Her way of living is to wait and see how things go. But waiting might not be in her or our best interests."

"I'm glad we meet Aurora's standards," Silas said. "Even though I think she is right in the main, this isn't a time to wait and see. She needs to get Mr. Murray and the governor on her side. Mr. Blunt will do all he can to run her out of town and steal every stone, mud puddle, mouse, tick, and plant she owns."

"I agree." She smiled, thinking of her husband's picture of stones, mud puddles, mice, ticks, and plants. "Now. Enough of the politics swirling around us. How is your publishing business coming along."

Silas grinned. "It's great, and Adella is a godsend. She keeps the place looking spit and polished no matter what mess I make."

"Really?"

"Yep. She even fusses at me like Momma used to when I left a mess."

"Good for Adella! I hope you'll have learned enough and have things in order so you can start publishing regularly soon."

"It has been a slow slog with the building of Adella's apartment, getting all the parts we needed, including lots of sizes of letters and carving trays. Both Adella and I had to learn our way around the whole process. But I'm ready to print!"

"When is your first local letter coming out?"

"Monday morning—Adella suggested we call it *Weekly Beginnings* with Number 1."

"I like it."

"Me too. It turns out that Adella is a poet, too. She helps with typesetting, which helps a lot. I brought a sample of what we'll print on Saturday—tomorrow."

"May I see it?"

"Yes. I hope you'll like it." He handed her the paper with printing on the front and back.

She said, "I thought it would be smaller."

"We thought about it, but we will fold the big page into four sections, front and back. That was Adella's idea. This way, we would have room for pictures, and it would seem like a booklet more than just a flyer."

Maggie looked at the front page and opened to pages 2, 3, and 4. "I like it, Silas."

After she looked at those pages, she handed them back to Silas. He said, "Now, hold on, Maggie, darlin'. Ordinarily, the inside could be either 4 more missives or one large one. Open the paper to full size and see what's inside."

She opened the paper and gasped. On the left-hand side, top-to-bottom was a sketch of part of Pennington Creek, and on the right side was *How Pennington Creek Got Its Name, as told by Aurora Evangeline Harrison.*

"Oh, Silas! It is marvelous. Does Aurora know?"

"Not yet, and I want to keep it a secret until Monday."

"Where did you get the sketch?"

"From Aurora. I told her I wanted a large sketch of Pennington Creek that I could use for the paper. She made three sketches of different sizes."

"I'm amazed at her skill. Was it hard to carve out on the press block?"

"Sort of. It did take a little extra help from Adella. She added some smaller bits I couldn't copy very well."

Maggie nodded. "I can almost hear the water running. Can I read the whole thing?"

"Yes. That is why I brought it home. I need a proofreader who hasn't already read everything a dozen times. Adella and I have read it so often that we doubt we could find an error."

"Let's sit at the table, read it from the beginning, and mark anything that needs attention."

He stood up and reached into his pocket. He drew out a pencil and handed his wife the red-colored pencil. "Here is your implement for your part of our endeavors. You'll be our copy editor and proofreader."

She grinned. "I'm looking forward to making red marks on your paper, Silas."

He chuckled. "I feel like a boy in school. I was sure you'd be ready to mark away. It's the teacher in you."

She picked up the pencil and began to read. She marked a few places, but there were very few errors. When she finished, she said, "Once you get it published, I want a copy for us. I also want to frame the story Aurora told us."

"Great idea. I'll use a piece of our heavy cardstock to print the story. Maybe we could use some of Sarah's color pencils."

"Better yet, print two on cardstock, and we could get Sarah to do the coloring. Aurora is important to all of us, but without Aurora, Sarah might not have come home with us."

"Sounds great, darlin'. Now, how about we get to bed? With the fire down, it's pretty chilly in here."

She smiled. "I know exactly what you need to warm up, Si. Follow me."

And he did.

11

Work hard,
keep the ceremonies,
live peaceably and
unite your hearts.
Hopi Proverb

Saturday morning dawned bright and clear in Tishomingo, Indian Territory. Hank tugged on the bellows above his coal bed to heat the coals for another day of ironworking. When the coals were red hot, he began his morning ritual of making horseshoe blanks to start his day. He'd made two horseshoes when he looked up and saw Silas Pennington coming into his smithy shed. He nodded and said, "Mornin' Silas."

"Good morning, Hank. When I first arrived in town, I stopped at the post office to pick up the mail and then headed to your smithy. It's become a morning ritual."

"I welcome your company. Smithy work can be a lonely job."

"I'm sure," Silas said and lifted two jars. "I brought a couple of jars of red plums from Maggie. She said to tell you she loved the pups."

"I'm glad. I was a bit worried about you taking two pups home. Some women don't want them around at all."

"Oh, my Maggie loves dogs, although she relegated them to the barn with the cow and hens for the night. The hens were skeptical, but when I went out this morning, the pups were cuddled up with the hens."

"My guess is they're lonesome, not being snuggled in with their momma and the rest of the pups."

"I'm sure you're right. Maggie said she always let her pups sleep with the hens. Once they get to know each other, the pups are less likely to go after a hen."

"Sounds right to me."

Silas smiled and asked, "Where shall I put these preserves?"

"Oh, just set them over on that shelf," Hank pointed to a shelf where he kept more fragile things. He grinned and said, "My Mary loves plums and does a pretty fair job cooking them. I'm glad Maggie liked the pups. The rest were gone within an hour of your leaving."

"Good. I'd feel like a piker if any girl pups were left hanging around. Our Bea bedeviled me for quite some time about how surely I could have brought home a girl puppy among the six pups left."

Hank laughed. "Girls most assuredly make up their minds about things. No need to worry, though. Before long, some of those pups will be mommas, and there will be more dogs than you can shake a stick at."

Silas chuckled. "I'm certain you're right, though I see no need to have a litter of pups at my place."

Hank chuckled and shook his head. "It's the way of life around here, Silas. One day, you're a dog. The next day, you meet the bitch, then before you know it, pups are sure to follow."

"I hear ya," Silas said and grinned. "But really, two pups is enough. On another subject, Aurora needs a lawyer, and Walter Thompson—the clerk at the Chickasaw Council House—has suggested Mr. Murray because of his association with the grand high muckity mucks. I hate to talk poorly about any man, but I'm apprehensive about Mr. Murray."

Hank nodded as he hammered away on the iron horseshoe. "I agree. I guess, being a lawyer, he is making more than a few dollars. Later on, I'd bet he'll be a politician for years. Hell, he might even grow up to be a governor."

Silas shuddered a little. "It felt like a goose walked over my grave, Hank. Don't say such things. Fingers crossed, he will never be a governor. Sadly, though, I think you're right. He has a sweet tongue when speaking about our town, lands, and homes. Still, I don't like hearing him call the African folk coons and the Chickasaws injuns."

"Nor do I. On that score, he's no better than Lester Blunt. The war's been over for many years, and they have a right to be treated as the real human beings they are, and anyway, the good Lord put them on our Earth—a good enough credential for me."

"I agree, but I don't think Mr. Murray agrees with us or the Lord. I hear he's fit to be tied that the enslaved Africans the Chickasaws owned before the war were given land allotments and added to the Chickasaws' roles. According to the Chickasaws, they are Chickasaws if they are not enslaved anymore since they have nothing to begin their lives with. It seems to me the Chickasaws did the right thing."

"I agree, but I hope Aurora will not be upset with him and his antics. She is Chickasaw and African—but I suppose her father is considered Chickasaw. His family was given Chickasaw citizenship after the war. I agree that the Chickasaws did the right thing. The Africans couldn't be enslaved any longer, but after being with the Chickasaw for generations, they fit right into the ways of the Chickasaw."

"I might remind her of that. It might help her, and certainly, her father is Chickasaw—especially since he has Chickasaw and African blood—he has a right to his allotment."

"Good idea, Silas. My guess is she has forgotten or does not understand the possibilities. She is well-liked by many folks around here—other than the bigots, who are thankfully few—for now, at least."

Silas agreed. "She is important to all the women around here."

Hank nodded. "I know my Mary touts her birthing skills to any needy woman."

"I was talking about it with Shirley at her dry goods store. She's been working hard to sing Aurora's praises whenever possible."

"My Mary thinks Aurora hangs the moon and makes the stars twinkle, especially with her birthing chair."

"Good. I'm glad it helped her."

"It did. Our darlin' Sally is blooming. My Mary's birthin' was much easier this time, and I'm relieved. Our Ronald is soon to be three years old and is smitten with his baby sister. Thankfully, he's fully potty trained and feeds himself, which takes a big load off Mary."

"Good. I'll let Maggie know, and she can pass it on to Aurora."

Hank wiped his hands and asked, "How's Adella Rittenhouse doing?"

"She is doing great. I never have to worry about tidying the place, and she doesn't let anyone cheat me out of even a penny."

"I'm glad it's working out for her. Are the rooms above the store working well for both of you?"

"It's great for me. She says she loves it and doesn't mind climbing the steps to her home above the print shop. I did build her a commode chair for nighttime. I don't want her to fall down the stairs or have a lazy rattler bothering her at night."

"And they will do that, too! I followed your lead and made a commode chair for Mary and a little one for Adam. I'm ready for indoor plumbing, including a bathtub with running water. I hope we have plumbing for the whole town soon."

Silas nodded. "I've been thinking about how to have plumbing in our house. We'd have to have a septic tank, I suppose."

"Yes, you would. Even if we get plumbing here in town, those who live out of town will be on their own. Many folks in town already have them, and I should set up one, too. Oscar Cassidy is the honey bucket man around here and the best one to talk with you about the hows and wherefores."

"Where does he live?"

"On the northeast edge of town. I think it's about four streets, maybe five, from here."

"I'm surprised there aren't more street names yet."

"Someone will think of that soon—maybe even the vaunted Mr. William Henry Murray, Lawyer," Hank said and grinned. "Now, I've got more to do today than fashion more horseshoes and gab with you —fine as that is. Anyway, to get to Oscar's place, start behind the new Chickasaw building and follow that road till it ends. You'll recognize which house it is because of the honey bucket. He keeps it close to the road, but his house is quite a bit further down his lane and closer to the creek. He says it keeps the stench from invading the house."

"I bet it does. Thanks, Hank. I'd best be heading out to his place then."

"If the bucket isn't there, he's out hauling the foulness from other folks' tanks and outhouses."

Silas shook his head and laughed. "What an occupation!"

"I'm right there with you, buddy. I couldn't do it, but Oscar likes his work and is always busy. He says he's the king of all he surveys, whether hauling other folks' excrement or caring for his own home and land. When you see his house, you'll understand why."

"What do you mean?"

"Well, there's only one honey bucket fella in town, and he has a very nice place."

"Ah, from the outhouse to the bank then."

"Exactly so. Some folks work pounding iron, plowing the land, writing up legal hoorahs, printing stories, preaching, selling all and sundry things, and then there's Oscar. He takes the leavins and makes a fine living doin' so."

Silas laughed, waved goodbye to Hank, and rode his horse to his business venture, *Okchuli Press.*

He rode his horse, Whisky, to the back of the shop, where he had a small, lean-to shed for the horse. He filled his tray with hay and bucket with water and removed his saddle for the day.

When he opened the back door of the press shop, he smelled

smoke and ran racing into the central portion of the shop to find Lester Blunt smoking away on a big, fat cigar.

Mrs. Rittenhouse ignored Silas's entrance, leaned on her broom, and said, "I'll not ask you again, Mr. Blunt, to take your cigar outside. This is a press shop and very susceptible to catching fire."

"Oh, now. Don't go on so, Della," he said, tapping a glowing ember from the tip of his cigar to the wooden floor.

Mrs. Rittenhouse shook her head and said, "You have not been given leave to call me anything other than Mrs. Rittenhouse."

Lester grinned but said nothing.

She nodded and said, "You, Lester Blunt, won't be able to say I didn't warn you."

Before Silas could say or do anything, she turned her broom to hold it like a bat and swung it hard and fast on Lester's lower legs. He fell to the floor howling and dropped his cigar. She picked up the cigar, carried it out the front door, and threw it into a mud puddle in the middle of the road from last night's rain.

When she returned to the store, she saw Silas standing there smiling. She said, "Mr. Pennington, I suggest you remove the trash. I'll have to start sweeping my floor again with the mess he made."

As Silas went to Lester Blunt to help him up from the floor, Lester shouted, "I'll sue you blind, you hussy, and you too, Mr. Sassypants Pennington."

"Well," Silas said, "With that attitude, it seems you'll have to crawl out of here since I'm in no fair mood to help you."

Lester rolled over on his hands and knees and tried to stand up but could not. "I think that haridan has broken my legs!"

Silas sighed, shrugged, and asked, "Do you need my help?"

"I most assuredly do not!" Blunt shouted. He half crawled, and half stumbled to the door. He turned and said, "You haven't heard the last of this, Pennington. And you, Della, owe me a cigar!"

"I don't have a cigar, so you'll have to figure that out for yourself, Mr. Blunt."

Silas grinned, and once Lester had closed the door, he turned to Mrs. Rittenhouse.

She said, "Wipe that silly grin off your face and get busy. We have a booklet to print."

Silas tried—to no avail—to stop smiling. Instead, he said, "Yes, ma'am, we do, and I have a few minor corrections from Maggie."

"I figured you might. We've read the thing so much I can't remember my name, much less find mistakes."

"Well, there aren't many."

"Good. You get busy on that while I clean up the mess Mr. Blunt made."

"I think he has the perfect name," Silas said.

"I agree," she said. "He is certainly a blunt instrument whether in talking, working, or just standing around."

Silas laughed and went to the printing bed to reset the corrections for the first edition of *Weekly Beginnings.*

12

"The lazy ox
drinks dirty water."
Native American Proverb

After a day of working at the press with Mrs. Rittenhouse, they had printed two hundred of the booklets. When the papers were completely dry, Silas and Mrs. Rittenhouse folded the first *Weekly Beginnings #1*.

"I think we've printed enough, don't you, Mrs. Rittenhouse."

She nodded. "I'm worried about wasting paper printing more than we need."

"Well, come Monday morning, we'll know if we printed too few, too many, or just enough."

"Fingers crossed," she said, holding up a hand with her fingers crossed. Now, what will you do with the rest of your day?"

"First, I want to print one more thing—well, two of one thing."

"I didn't know we had an order."

"We don't. It's a special printing of Aurora's story. I want to print it on card stock, then I'll take it home for Sarah to color it."

"What a grand idea. I'm glad Sarah is doing well with your family."

"We've made it all legal and adopted her. She is our daughter, and we're all happy as pigs in slop she has joined us."

She shook her head at his antics but said, "I heard that, and I'm glad for all of you."

"She is sweet and kind and works hard with Maggie and Aurora. She also spends much time with the twins, which greatly helps Maggie."

"Does she like to draw?"

"Yes, and she is getting better each day. Aurora has been teaching her and the rest of the children drawing, but Sarah is the one who latched on to it the best. She has a few watercolors and loves them. She calls the watercolors and her colored pencils her treasures."

"I'm glad. She deserves much better than her biological parents gave her."

"Well, she's our daughter now and a blessing to our family. Let's print the cardstock so it will have time to dry before I head home."

They worked together on the printing, and when they finished, Adella said, "It is lovely. I'm sure Aurora will be pleased. When it is completely dry, I'll lay a tissue paper on top of it, wrap it with butcher paper, and put it in one of the big envelopes for you to take home."

"Thank you, Adella. That is a great idea. Now I have other fish to fry."

"Anything exciting?"

"You betcha," he chuckled. "I'm going to Oscar Cassidy's home to talk with him about sanitation ideas, including indoor plumbing. I think I'll talk with Clay and Aurora too and see if they want indoor plumbing, too."

"Very few folks have indoor plumbing around here. I'm not sure there will be many, either. Seems to me a luxury."

"Yes, it's true that having a well and an outhouse is convenient enough, but having indoor plumbing is also a safety factor for me. I don't want Maggie and the children to risk themselves from snakebites while washing at the well or going to the outhouse, especially when it's dark outside."

"I can understand that. Now that winter is approaching, the hours of light are shorter, too."

"Indeed they are. I don't suppose we can accomplish it very soon, but I want to find out how it could work."

She smiled and said, "Before long, you'll be a high lord sitting on your toilet perch in the house."

Silas laughed. "I hope you're right. I'll see you Monday morning, Mrs. Rittenhouse."

"Good day, Mr. Pennington. I'll leave your package for Aurora on your desk."

"Thank you, Mrs. Rittenhouse. Have a good Sunday tomorrow."

"I will." She smiled as she watched him walk through the building to the back door. She was happy to have a place where she felt safe and not beholden to anyone. She was also grateful to have work to do. Sitting around fiddling with needlework as her only occupation just wasn't her cup of tea. Although she enjoyed crocheting and knitting in the evenings and even occasional fine stichery work, she preferred more manual labor during the day.

She walked through the shop, ensuring everything was stored as it should be. She turned out the lights, walked to the back door, and saw Silas as he saddled his horse. She smiled, watching the horse, who loved his owner. She walked up the stairs to her home, where she planned a quiet evening of reading and rest. First, she took her shopping satchel and returned to Shirley's Dry Goods. She hoped there would be white crochet thread. She planned to create pretty little decorations for Christmas. She wanted to hang the white lace in the windows of her home, which faced the street below.

WHISKEY, Silas's deep red roan horse, was eager to be on the road. Silas rode his horse to Oscar Cassidy's home. When he arrived, he looked at the large, beautiful white house with a red door and black shutters. He said, "Well, Hank, you're right—that is some home. Looks nearly like a plantation estate." Since the honey bucket—though it smelled like anything other than honey—sat in the field close to the lane, he quickly rode on up to the house built on all the nasty residue of the town of Tishomingo, Indian Territory.

Silas tied his horse to the railing in front of the house and walked up on the wide veranda. The flooring of the veranda was painted a soft gray with fall foliage in large terra cotta pots. Flowers of all colors ran riot in the pots, while pumpkins were stacked on each side of the door, with branches of red cedar surrounding them. Alongside the house was a small creek running over rocks and flowing into the bigger Pennington Creek. He smiled and murmured, "It's a regular painted postcard."

He reached for the brass knocker on the deep red-painted door, but the door opened before he could use it. In front of him stood a man a few inches shorter than he, with red curly hair, bright blue eyes, and a face full of freckles. His grin was a delightful mix of welcome and question. He said, "Well, if it isn't the publisher of *Okchuli Press.*"

Silas smiled and nodded. "Yes, sir, I'm Silas Pennington." He held out his hand, and the man in the door took Silas's hand, grinning as he pumped it up and down a few times. Silas felt that even though he was taller than the man standing in front of him, he didn't have nearly the arm strength of the Irish man.

He said, "I'm Oscar Cassidy at your service, Mr. Pennington."

"What a relief. I need your help, but first, please call me Silas."

"Absolutely. Your Uncle Jacob was a friend of mine and a fine man to boot."

"Yes, he was."

"I'm assuming you need my honeypot for your outhouses."

"Well, I certainly do need that, but I was told you were also the man to talk to about getting a septic tank at my place and plumbing to my house."

"Well, Mr. Pennington, you were told the truth. Come on in, and we'll discuss the possibilities."

Silas grinned and followed Oscar inside. He followed him into his office and was surprised to see a neat office with files in order and a glistening roll-top desk. "Your office is terrific, and your desk is similar to my own at home."

Oscar nodded. "Your Uncle Jacob convinced me to buy this one. It cost a fair bit, but he was right. I can keep all my records close, which helps my financial endeavors."

"Well, it is a fine and impressive desk."

"Come, sit by my desk, and we'll work out what you need to modernize your home with running water, bathtubs, and flush toilets."

Silas sat by the desk as Oscar pulled out the writing board and said, "I'm not sure what I want or can afford."

"Well, don't fret over it all," Oscar said. "I had dreams of hot and cold running water, a bathroom with a tub for soaking, and flush toilets. I'd heard of some homes in Oklahoma City, Tulsa, and Guthrie with indoor toilets, tubs, and wash basins. I learned a lot about building such a room when I built our room for bathing and toilet needs. We even have running hot and cold water!"

"Well, that sounds mighty grand. My parents had a similar setup in their home in South Carolina, but I'm sure it's more than I can afford."

"Let's talk and sketch and see what we can come up with. You might be surprised. Your uncle and I chatted about this a few days before he died. He thought if he had running water and an indoor toilet, it might persuade you to hurry to Indian Territory."

"I wish I'd come sooner to see him before he died."

"I'm sure that is a burden for you, but you know, as I do, Jacob wouldn't want you to feel bad about not coming sooner."

"Thanks, Oscar. Wishes and horses and all of that!"

"You speak truly, Silas. Now, let's see what we can come up with."

The two men talked, and Oscar drew a sketch of Silas's home. Then he said, "My suggestion is that we clear out the space behind the fireplace. I've been to your home a few times when Jacob was around, and a few days before his death, I was there to see if we could turn the space into a bathing room with a toilet. Folks call it a bathroom. As I recall, he used that space for outdoor clothing, wood, and a few tools."

"Yes, and that is how it still is."

"Well, I'm certain you can find a way to relegate those things to other places in your home. We can even build a woodshed near the back of the house if needed."

"I agree. I think it's about six feet from the fireplace to the back wall."

"You are correct, sir, and it goes from the pantry wall to the front of the house."

Silas nodded and began to be hopeful of having a bathroom in the house.

Oscar sketched and pointed to the drawing. "We can heat your hot water by the fireplace. It won't be true running water but more a cistern. We can do the same for cold water, using rainwater as much as possible for the tub and toilet. We'll have to run pipes to a septic tank."

"Where would you put the septic tank?"

"I'd dig it right beside the outhouse. We know it won't contaminate the well water or creek that way. Besides, you'll probably use the outhouse when you're outside working until you get used to having an indoor bathroom."

"How much would the tub, toilet, pipes, and cistern cost?"

"All told, about fifty to sixty dollars, I think."

Silas nodded. "How much would you charge for helping Clay and me build the bathroom and get everything set up?"

"Well, since I wouldn't do it alone, how does ten dollars sound?"

"That sounds fine. Could we also put a sink in the pantry with running water?"

"Sure, and I won't charge you a penny more to do so—other than the sink itself and its pipes."

"That sounds grand. When would you want to get started?"

"Well, with winter coming on, it might be tough to get the digging done, so we'd best get that started right away. In the southern mountains and foothills where we live, hard frost doesn't happen until mid-December, but you can't count on it. I can have the furnishings here in a couple of weeks, but I have piping on hand from a few other jobs around here for others."

"Good. Now, I want to be sure we do the same thing for Clay and Aurora at their cabin. It seems to me it would be easier overall for the three of us men and my son Noah to help with the plumbing in both houses at the same time."

"You are certainly right there, Silas."

Silas nodded. "Now that we've settled the plan of events for our two houses, can you come to my place and measure it before we spend money?"

"Absolutely. How about tomorrow after church?"

"You work on a Sunday?"

"It's not exactly work. I think of it more as visiting a new friend and his family. What do you think?"

Silas grinned and nodded. "Sounds good to me."

Thus, Silas made another friend and was delighted at the possibility of an indoor bathroom for his family. He was eager to get home and talk with Clay, Aurora, and, of course, Maggie.

13

Silas rode Whiskey home with the sketches of the bathroom and the prints for Sarah to color. He smiled at the thought of Sarah coloring and painting the picture and story of how Pennington Creek got its name. Silas thought *I'm glad we have Sarah in the family, but more importantly, she let us into her heart. Her drawing and painting skills are getting better and better because Aurora was able to teach her the ins and outs of drawing and painting.* He hoped Aurora would like the picture.

He rode to the barn, unsaddled Whiskey, rubbed him down, brushed him, and fastened a blanket over his back to keep him warm in the chilly night. He filled his basket with hay and a few oats. He made sure the horse had plenty of water and was set for the night. He carried the package with Aurora's story and pictures into the house.

The children came running out to greet him, filled with questions about everything outside their Pennington Creek home. Sarah looked at Silas and asked, "Papa, what's in there?"

"Something special I want you to help me with, Sarah."

"Is it something for me?"

"No. It's better than that. It is something for someone else, and I need your artistic talents to help me with this gift."

Bea asked, "Is it for Momma?"

"Nope."

Noah smiled and said, "I don't think it's a dog. It looks too flat for that."

Silas chuckled. "You're right, son. I know better than to bring home puppies two days in a row. Let's get in the house, and as soon I can say hello to your mother, I'll show you what's in the package and why I need Sarah's help."

They all clamored around Silas as they walked.

Ben asked, "Why do you always talk with Momma first?"

"Because I love her, and she takes good care of us all."

Ben rolled his eyes. "That means you're going to kiss Momma."

"At least once," Silas said, grinned, and ruffled Ben's hair. Ben promptly used his fingers to put his hair back in place.

Bea grabbed Silas's hand and told him, "Teddy said 'Momma' today, Papa."

"Now that is something wonderful, isn't it?"

"I suppose. But Papa, Teddy didn't say 'Bea,' although I asked him to."

Noah laughed. "All he did was blow bubbles at Bea."

Silas laughed with the children, then looked at Sarah and asked, "You seem worried, daughter."

"Not worried exactly, but I can't figure out how I can help you with that package."

"Good. Mystery is something we can all enjoy from time to time."

"What's mystery?" Ben asked.

"It's something you want to know but don't know—yet."

Ben shook his head and muttered, "Mystery happens a lot around here."

Silas laughed as they stepped up on the porch. The door opened, and Maggie held Teddy perched on her hip. Silas smiled at his wife and son and said, "Hello, darlin'. I hear a lot of wonderful things have happened today."

She nodded and smiled.

Ben said, "Hurry up, Papa, and kiss her. I want to know the mystery."

"Me too," Sarah said.

Silas sighed and said, "Well, if I must."

Maggie laughed and said, "That's the price of entry into my home, fella."

He grinned, leaned forward, and kissed his wife and then Teddy. "I love you, Maggie."

"And I love you, Silas. Come on in and tell us whatever this mystery is."

"Let's go to the table. I have a project for Sarah that I think will be a grand surprise for Aurora."

Maggie smiled, knowing what was in the package. She let Silas make a production of unwrapping the picture and story of how Pennington Creek got its name.

The children gathered around the table—each vying to be the closest to their father. Silas opened the package, pulled back the tissue paper, and turned to Sarah. Bea slipped under the table, through Silas's legs, and then on his lap. He grinned and asked, "Are we all settled."

Everyone nodded but Ben was a little grumpy because Bea cheated to get on Papa's lap. Silas rubbed Ben's head—who quickly put his hair in the right order—and then Silas said, "Sarah, your Momma and I talked about this last night. We think it would be nice if you could use your watercolors and colored pencils to highlight this picture. We want to frame it and give it to Aurora as a gift. She has worked hard to help us in our new home. Now that she has a baby and her own home, too, she works to keep us all well and happy. I printed two so we can have your coloring of the picture, too."

Sarah moved closer to stand beside her father. She smiled and said, "Oh, Papa. It's beautiful. Will the water ruin the ink?"

"I hadn't thought of that, Sarah."

Maggie said, "We can test on the page you brought home, Si."

"Good idea, darlin'. The ink is a combination of oil and water, so it might be a problem for the watercolors."

Sarah touched the paper and said, "I can put a little blue on the edge of the creek and highlight the banks with a brown pencil. I'd have to be careful not to touch the letters."

Maggie said, "I'm impressed with your idea, Sarah. What other ideas do you have?"

"Along the side, I can use pencils with some watercolor. There is one other thing I'd like to try."

Silas asked, "What would you like to try?"

"I want to sketch Aurora's face in the upper right-hand corner with her long, waving black hair dropping close but not on the letters."

"Have you tried sketching people's faces?"

"Yes, Papa. Aurora has taught me how to sketch just about anything. Leaves are the hardest, but I'm getting better. I think my sketches of the family and Aurora, too, are pretty good. Aurora says I'm getting better every day. Let me go get my sketchbook, and I'll show you."

Sarah was racing up the stairs before Silas or Maggie could say anything.

Silas smiled, kissed Bea's cheek, and said, "Bea, I need you to get off my lap for a bit."

She slid off his lap and watched as her father said to her mother, "Let me hold Teddy for a bit, darlin', while Sarah gets her book."

Maggie handed the baby to him and said, "Here you go, Papa!"

Silas kissed the baby's cheek and said, "Papa loves you, Teddy," who promptly drooled a bit and tried kissing his father but with his mouth open. Silas laughed, and Teddy giggled, too.

Then Teddy said, "Papa!"

Silas beamed. "Yep, I'm your Papa."

Bea scowled and tugged on Silas's pants leg. She looked up at the baby and said, "I'm Bea!"

Teddy laughed and clapped his hands, then blew a few bubbles at Bea, who shook her head and rolled her eyes.

Before anyone could say anything more, Sarah returned downstairs, set down her sketchbook on the table, and said, "Papa, let me hold Teddy, and you and Momma look at my sketches. Aurora has been teaching me a lot about drawing."

Silas opened the booklet, and as he turned each page, he felt the love Sarah had given each sketch. She had drawn Bea with a scowl and her hands on her hips. On the following page, Bea clapped her hands and laughed. Ben, Noah, Maggie, and himself were also in the booklet. Silas said, "Sarah, I had no idea you could draw this well."

"Thanks, Papa. I couldn't have done this on my own. Aurora taught me about faces and how to add shading to make them seem alive." She reached into her pocket and pulled out another book. "This is my sketches of the flowers, fruit, vegetables, and animals, including the pups, hens, cows, and horses. Most importantly, at the end of this booklet are sketches of Clay, Aurora, and Okchuli."

Silas took the booklet and smiled at each sketch until he got to the ones of Aurora and Okchuli. There were even a few sketches of Clay, grinning, with his cowboy hat pushed back in one drawing, and then in another sketch, he pulled down his hat over his forehead while he dangled a piece of straw in his mouth. He leaned against the barn with his right leg cocked up to balance himself.

Silas sat at the table and motioned for Sarah to sit beside him. He said, "Your sketches are terrific, Sarah. How would you like to come work at the press shop after school a few days each week?"

She beamed. "I'd like that, Papa." She pointed to her favorite sketch of Aurora and said, "I was thinking this sort of sketch on the upper right-hand corner of the story."

"I think it's perfect." He looked at Maggie and asked, "Did you know Sarah could do this?"

"Not really. I've seen Sarah sketch the pups, hens, food, and flowers, but not of all of us. She is much better at sketching than I am."

Sarah beamed. "Thank you, Momma. I love doing it. The first faces I drew weren't good, so I burned them. It was when Aurora taught me about perspective and emotions that I got better at drawing faces. I didn't want you to know I was sketching you so I could figure out how your faces change when you're doing work, talking, or taking care of Teddy."

"I'm so glad you did, Sarah." Maggie hugged her and said, "You go put your sketchbooks up in your room. Papa will put the big picture you'll work on in his desk so it doesn't get harmed for now."

"Okay, Momma. I'll be right back to help with dinner." Sarah raced back up the stairs and into her room. She tucked the booklets into her trunk under her window. She whispered, "Fingers crossed, I can do more painting and sketching. Beats doing laundry and scrubbing the floors any old day." She chuckled and said, "I'll still want to help Momma though." Then, as she walked out of her room and onto the staircase landing, she thought, *I like helping Momma and playing with Bea, Ben, and Noah.*

She walked down the stairs and heard her father say, "She is a good girl, but I don't want her to think she must always work. She's still a child, like Noah. Although they are both nine years old and think they're just about grown up, they need time to be children."

"Me, too," Bea said. "I don't like working."

"Well," Maggie said, "Whether you like it or not, we all work together. But there will always be time for playing."

Sarah smiled as she entered the living and dining areas. "I'll help you with dinner, Momma."

"Thank you, Sarah. I've got dinner ready and would appreciate your help preparing it for the table. Noah, you get the plates while Ben gets the napkins and Bea gets the silverware."

Bea sighed. "Yes, ma'am."

Maggie chuckled. "And remember, children, working with a cheerful heart brings blessings to everyone around you."

Bea sighed again and said, "Yes, ma'am. I'll try. I promise."

The rest of the children smiled and nodded.

Maggie kissed Bea's cheek. "Thank you, sweetie. I love you."

"Do you love me more than Sarah or Noah or Ben or Teddy?"

"No. I love you all the same with all my heart."

"How can you do that? Don't you run out of heart?"

"Not a chance of that happening. Momma's never run out of heart or love."

"Promise?"

"Absolutely."

Bea smiled and nodded. "I'll get the silverware, Momma."

"Thank you, Bea. I knew I could count on you."

Bea smiled, but she wasn't sure about hearts, love, and children. Regardless, she was hungry. She believed her mother loved her at least as much as everyone else.

She crossed her fingers, hoping it was true.

14

The younger Pennington children cleared away the dinner table while Silas helped with washing the dishes. Sarah put away the leftovers for tomorrow's breakfast and lunch—out of the reach of mice and bugs.

Noah went to the barn, made sure the animals were all snug in their places and fed the dogs, Ranger and Rover, some of the leftovers from the family dinner. He checked to be sure the chicken hutch was closed. Both Ranger and Rover liked to sleep with the chickens, which made a lot of sense to Noah. The dogs could watch over things through the fencing and make sure the chickens were safe.

The chickens found they liked having the two puppies in their hutch. The dogs added extra warmth, and they watched out for the foxes, coyotes, and snakes.

Maggie worked on the pantry table, making another loaf of sourdough bread for the next day as she did every evening after dinner.

Once Sarah had put away the leftovers, she carefully watched her mother add the sourdough starter, flour, and a few chopped dried fruits. Once the dough was mixed, Maggie scattered a bit of flour on the table and kneaded the bread until it was very elastic. She then put the dough into a greased cast iron pan and covered it with the lid.

Sarah asked, "When can I start making the bread, Momma?"

"Well, I suppose as soon as you would like."

"Can I make tomorrow's bread?"

Maggie nodded. "I think that's a fine idea, Sarah. Why don't you get one of your empty journals and start making your own cookbook?"

"Well, I don't have any recipes yet."

Maggie raised her eyebrows and said, "Well, it's my opinion every young woman should have her own recipe book. If you feel you are ready to start making the daily bread, you'll need a recipe."

Sarah's mouth dropped open, and she nodded. "You're right, Momma. I'll get one of my journals and use it as my recipe book. "Can I start writing some of your recipes tomorrow?"

"Absolutely. Now, for this evening, do you remember which stone I put the pan on with the bread?"

"Yes, Momma."

"Good. Then, if you go put the bread to rest and rise, I'll clear up the mess I've made."

Sarah nodded, took the castiron casserole dish with its lid covered snuggly, and smiled. Tomorrow, she would start learning to cook, and somehow, she felt a little more grown up. She was excited to be making her own recipe book.

She'd seen her mother's recipe book with ribbons separating the types of cooking. As she thought about the recipe book she thought about drawing the steps in every recipe. Her next thought was perhaps Papa would print our recipe book.

Once all the chores were done, everything was clean and where it should be for the night, Maggie said, "Now, children, it is Saturday night, which means tomorrow morning we'll go to church. I have your shoes polished and your Sunday clothes cleaned and pressed, hanging on your walls, so don't mess them up tonight."

"We won't, Momma," Noah said. "What about when Granny and Pops get here? Where are they going to sleep?"

Silas said, "I was thinking we could use the empty stall in the barn for them."

Maggie slapped his arm more than gently and said, "Silas! You know better than that. Do not tease the children."

Noah grinned and said, "It's okay, Momma. I can sleep with Ben."

Before Maggie could say anything, Sarah said, "I can sleep with Bea, Momma."

Maggie smiled. "Well, if you children think it won't bother you too much, I think it is a fine idea. My thought was Papa and I could give them our bed, and then Papa and I would sleep on the floor."

Silas gasped and shook his head. "Really, Maggie? Was that really what you were planning?"

"Absolutely. But the children's idea is a good one. We can move Sarah's bed into Noah's room so Granny and Pops can sleep together."

Sarah nodded. "When we move the beds in Noah's room, in my room, we can bring up a box as a table and two chairs so they can have some space for quiet time."

"That's a grand idea, Sarah," Maggie answered. "I think you children have come up with a marvelous solution. For now, it's time to go to bed so you can be up and dressed for church in the morning."

"Oh, Momma, do we have to go to sleep right now?" Noah asked.

"Well, I can't make you sleep, but I want you to go to your room, be quiet, and prepare yourself for sleep."

"Can I read the new book Granny sent me? I want to know what adventures Alice has next. Besides, I worked hard all day long helping Clay build his upstairs rooms."

"I know you work hard, and I'm proud of how you helped with

Clay. You may read for a while, but I expect everyone to have their lights out before long."

Noah nodded. "I wish we could read in bed, but the lantern would burn the bed."

"And that," Maggie said, "Is exactly why I don't want you moving your lanterns. The lanterns are to stay on the table by your bed and not be moved."

"Yes, ma'am," Noah answered. "I won't move the lantern." But, he thought perhaps he could sit on the side of the bed and read. He'd give that a try and see how it worked. Instead, he asked, "Papa, do we get a story tonight?"

"Sure, son. I want us always to have story time before bed."

Sarah grinned. "I love story time. It's one of the best things we do together."

"I'm glad to hear you say so, Sarah."

"Me too!" Bea said. "I love stories about me."

Silas said, "Well, tonight is not a story about little girls. It's a bit different. Are you all ready?"

Noah nodded. "As soon as you fill your pipe, Papa."

Silas grinned, picked up his pipe, and filled the bowl with his favorite tobacco. He struck a match and puffed a bit on the pipe, then said,

In another time, another place, and another house, there lived a boy who loved to read stories. He loved them so much that he would read for hours and hours. This was usually fine, but as he got older, he had to work hard all day to help his father and mother.

He'd shovel and rake the barn clean, then gather the eggs from the hens, milk the cow, brush the horses, carry the eggs and milk to his mother and help her strain the milk, wipe the eggs, put the milk in the cold cellar, and finally put the eggs in the egg bowl and cover them with the egg cloth.

Although he was getting tired by this time, he knew he had work to do with his father. So, off to the fields, he went to help his father plow the ground, plant the seeds, and water them so they would grow.

When that work was finished, the boy and his father built a new build-

ing. He wasn't sure what the building would be, and when he asked his father, the answer was always, "You'll see."

So they hammered and sawed for the rest of the day. Whatever they were building wasn't finished yet, but his father said, "You did a fine job today, son."

"Thanks, Papa," the boy said, "but I'm tired now."

"Me too. While I gather the tools and put them away, you carry some water for Momma. She will need it to cook our dinner."

So the boy went to the well and pumped the water into the two big house buckets. While pumping the water, he said, "We need more children! I'm the only one doing anything around here."

His father heard him and said, "Your sisters and brother are working too, just as you and I and Momma are doing. More sisters and brothers would mean more work."

"But I'm tired! I do all the work!"

"Now, hang on there, son. I saw your sister helping you gather the eggs this morning."

"Oh, yes. I forgot sister helped me."

"Then your brother swept out all the stalls while you carried the fouled dirt and straw to the compost heap."

"Oh, yes. I forgot brother helped me."

"And I saw your Momma, brother, and sister carrying two buckets of water this morning while we worked in the field."

"You're right, Papa. Now, I remember seeing them working."

"So," father asked, "Who exactly does the most work?"

The boy nodded and said, "I understand, Papa. It's up to all of us." The boy yawned and said, "I'm eager for dinner to be finished so I can read before I go to bed."

Papa yawned and said, "Me too, son!"

Maggie clapped her hands, as did Sarah, but Bea, Ben, and Noah just sat looking at their father. They hoped there would be another line or two of the story to make them happy. But it was not to be.

Silas tamped down his tobacco in his pipe, relit the tobacco, puffed a few puffs, and sat waiting quietly.

Bea rolled her eyes, yawned, and said, "I'm going to bed."

"Me too," Ben answered.

The twins kissed their parents and started up the stairs, as Sarah chuckled and said, "Goodnight, Momma and Papa. I loved the story."

Silas nodded. "Thank you, Sarah. Have a good night's rest, daughter."

Noah sat looking at his mother and father, who said nothing.

After a few short minutes, Teddy whimpered, and Maggie said, "Well, there's my call for the last diaper change and nursing before bedtime." She stood up, went to the cradle in the corner of the room, picked up the baby, took him to her bedroom, and changed his clothes. Afterward, she returned to the great room, sat in her rocking chair near the fireplace, opened her blouse, and began to nurse the baby.

Noah watched her, then turned back to his father and sighed. "You're right, Papa. We all work hard all day, but I still want to read before bed and sleep."

"I do, too, son. However, you might consider reading just a chapter or two a night and then going on to sleep to be ready for another day."

"I will try, Papa," Noah said. He stood up from the table, kissed his father's cheek, and said, "I love you, Papa."

"And I love you, Noah. You're a fine son, and I'm proud of you."

Noah smiled and nodded but said nothing for fear he would cry.

He walked over to his mother, touched the baby's head, and then kissed his mother's cheek. "I love you, Momma."

"I love you, Noah, and I'm delighted you are my son."

Noah blushed a little but smiled. "Thank you, Momma." He went up the stairs and to his room, glad he had a few minutes to read before turning down the lantern in his room.

So it was at the Pennington house that the children were in their rooms, with Bea and Ben tucked into their beds, yawning, while Noah and Sarah each read for a bit in their rooms. Teddy was tucked into the cradle, and Maggie hoped he'd sleep the night through.

She turned to Silas and asked, "What do you have in your mind, dear heart? I see the gears turning in your head."

Silas chuckled. "I could never hide anything from you, darlin'." He patted the table and said, "Come let me show you my next big idea."

She smiled, sat beside him, and said, "I've only one question, Silas."

"What's your question, darlin'?"

"How much?"

He grinned. "I can never put anything past you."

"I sincerely hope not, Si. Now, tell me how much this is going to cost."

"Sixty dollars."

"My word, Silas! That's a lot of money."

"Yes, it is, but I feel it will pay off in the end, and things will be easier for you. Let me show you what Oscar Cassidy can help me with."

"You mean the honey bucket man?"

Silas chuckled. "That's him all right."

"But we pay him two dollars each time he comes and cleans out the outhouse. Is he raising his rates?"

"No, but he will be helping me put in a septic tank."

"Why would we need a septic tank?"

"For the flush toilet, pantry and bathroom sinks, and a bathtub. We'll have running water and even hot water, too."

Maggie's eyes widened, then she smiled and hugged Silas. She kissed his cheek and said, "It will be worth every penny, my love."

"I thought you might like it."

"Like it? I love it. I can't imagine not carrying water into the house in full buckets. Can we do this?"

"Yep. We've enough room behind the fireplace for the toilet, bathtub, and sink. I think I saw some old mirrors upstairs, so we won't have to buy one for over the sink."

"Oh, Silas! It sounds lovely. Indoor plumbing is the best surprise you've ever given me."

"It pleases me to see you happy, but mostly, I wanted to do this to keep you and the children safe in the evenings when going to the outhouse. Besides, lugging water from the well is heavy work that could be made easier with plumbing."

"The commode chairs have worked fairly well, Silas."

"I know and we might still use them in the middle of the night, but the more I thought about how much work you and the children do simply carrying water, the more I wanted to make your lives easier. We can use some of Uncle Jacob's extra money to create a bathroom behind the fireplace and a sink in the pantry for washing dishes and cleaning vegetables. Oscar told me that Uncle Jacob was planning to do exactly what I want to do."

"He was a forward-looking man. I can't wait for how much easier my life will be with cooking, cleaning, and much more. Have I told you what a marvelous husband you are?"

"I think I remember a few times."

She grinned. "Come to bed and celebrate with me, Silas."

"I am but your humble servant."

"Oh, I don't know about humble."

"Servant?"

"If you must."

15

Good and evil
cannot dwell together
in the same heart,
so a good man ought
not go into evil company.
Delaware Proverb

At the Harrison home, Aurora sat beside Clay in front of the fireplace as she nursed Okchuli. They loved their log cabin home nearly as much as they loved each other.

Despite the mess in the house for now, Aurora was happier than she'd ever been. Clay and Noah had spent the day working on getting the two upstairs bedrooms closer to being ready for company. There would be a guest bedroom and a nursery.

Aurora smiled as she thought of the nursery. She'd never expected to have a child, and knowing her daughter would have a lovely room made Aurora happier than she'd ever thought she would be.

She lifted the baby to her shoulder to burp her and said, "Okchuli is getting bigger and bigger."

Clay chuckled. "Well, darlin', that's how babies become adults."

She rolled her eyes and shook her head, smiling. "I know. It's just that this will be my only baby, and every moment with her flies by far too fast."

Clay wrapped his arm around his wife and daughter. "I know you don't believe it, but I know deep in my heart we will have more children."

"Well, there are occasionally children around who need a place to be with a family, like Sarah was."

"And that's terrific," Clay said. "But in my dreams, I dream of more babies we will have. I even dreamed I would need to make our house bigger to accommodate our children."

She chuckled. "Your dreams are something else, my love. I know you've said before that we would have more babies." She sighed. "I know I can't bear babies since that awful night when I was raped and beaten by several men."

Clay nodded. "Do you ever dream about them?"

"NO! That wouldn't be a dream. It would be a nightmare."

"Well, I dream about your babies—the ones who will be born from my seed and your womb. I adore Okchuli, and I'm so happy she is our child, but I know deep in my heart you will bear at least two more children."

Aurora brushed away a few tears and nodded. "I don't see how that can be, but I believe in your dreams. I'll hold out hope that your dreams will come true and I will have more babies in my life."

Clay didn't argue about where those babies would come from, nor did he know the why and how of it all, but he knew in his dreams the children would be born of Aurora. He did say, "I hope your doubts about bearing children aren't because of how Lester Blunt is being mean and threatens you."

"I don't think I am doing that, but every time he is mean to me or threatens me, all I can see is the men beating me and raping me over and over. I never see their faces, just their fists and penises."

Clay shuddered a bit. "If I thought for one moment Lester Blunt was one of those men, I'd kill him with my bare hands."

"Please don't think of doing so, my love. I need you too much in my life to risk meting out the throttling he richly deserves."

"I won't, but just to be clear, the only reason I haven't killed him already is because I want to be with you and Okchuli rather than swinging on the end of a rope."

Aurora shuddered. "I love you but never even consider doing such a thing."

"I won't."

"Please, promise me, Clay."

"I promise I will not do any harm to Blunt, at least harm that might kill him."

She smiled. "A good thumping might present itself, but be sure you don't lose control and go too far."

"I won't. I promise."

WHEN AURORA and Clay lay side-by-side in bed, he said, "I'm worried about your safety, sweetheart."

"Oh, you shouldn't be. I am seldom alone, and I'm not the least bit afraid of Lester Blunt and his ilk."

"Well, there are a lot of folks pouring into Tishomingo. The Curtis Act is beckoning many folks to our corner of the World, and many who are mean-spirited like Lester Blunt. I don't understand why he hates you unless he has done something to be ashamed of."

"I know, and I agree. I would think it is simple bigotry, except for Okchuli. He's become increasingly mean since she came into our lives."

"Makes me wonder if he's the birth father."

"I thought of that, but he has black hair, and his wife is Chickasaw. With Okchuli's curly red hair, I think the father must be someone else. Besides, she's never had a pregnancy, so if he is the birth father, it isn't his wife who bore Okchuli."

Clay shook his head. "I can hardly imagine any woman willing to let him in their bed."

Aurora nodded. "I agree, and I promise I will watch out for him. I have an appointment with Mr. William Murray on Monday morning."

"Good. I'll be going in with you."

"I don't think that's necessary, Clay."

"I do. Going into town with Maggie or simply to the council house is one thing. But going into town to meet with a man you've never been introduced to is another thing. Additionally, I find his arrogance quite off-putting. I certainly do not like the way he speaks of native people like you or the African people."

"I agree, Clay, but I want the white man's law behind us just in case. I want no one to question our legal claim for our land. Paying a few dollars to a lawyer might help keep us from being kicked out of our homes and land. I will not give up the best home, life, and friends I've ever had."

"I understand, darlin', but still, I'm worried about you going to meet with Mr. Murray alone for the first time."

"I suppose you're right. Every time I go into town, it seems a hundred more people are roaming around. It feels a bit overwhelming."

Clay pulled Aurora close in his arms. "I know you are a brave, kind, and generous woman. Some folks, especially Lester Blunt and William Murray, might well want to take advantage of your kind and giving nature. With your husband beside you, they might think twice before doing anything nefarious. I trust you completely, but I am still old-fashioned enough to want to protect you and our daughter."

She smiled and kissed his cheek. "I'd be delighted if you came with me to meet Mr. Murray."

"Good. Now that Okchuli is snug in her bed, I'd like your undivided attention."

"Undivided?"

"Yes, ma'am."

"Well, a woman's gotta do what a woman's gotta do."

He chuckled, loving her more each day.

LATER THAT NIGHT, as Clay snored beside her, Aurora felt more anxious about Lester Blunt and the allotments than she was willing to tell Clay. It wasn't that she didn't trust Clay. It was two things.

First, she felt if she talked about her fears and anxiety, she might be inviting evil into her life.

Second, she didn't want to risk losing their home and land. It was the second thing that made her feel an urgent need for a lawyer to stand up for herself and her family.

She smiled and thought, *I have a real family, including a lovely, sweet daughter. I have a home that is more than I ever expected I would have. I have so much that losing it all, I think I couldn't go forward.*

She looked out the bedroom window and watched as the full moon began to rise. She prayed to the moon, "Please keep my daughter, my husband, and my home safe. I'll keep working hard and doing good wherever I can so long as my family and I are safe."

She knew a full moon could not banish all the risks facing her, but in the light of day, she felt confident she'd be able to stand up to the vile people who wished her harm. Then she thought *it might not be enough, but I am a strong woman, maybe stronger now than ever before. Indeed, with the sun's rising, my token, I will feel its power.*

LESTER BLUNT HAD FOUND a new set of cronies to hang with. None of them knew Clay and Aurora yet, so things heated up quickly when he started telling his version of their relationship.

One scruffy fella, new to Tishomingo, said, "How can a white man even want to touch a leftover slave, much less an injun one?"

"I feel the same way," Lester said. "It might be because he's Irish. I've heard that the Irish will settle for about anything so long as good whisky is around."

A different man shook his head and said, "Hey, now. Let's not knock good whiskey or the Irish. My lovely wife is Irish, and I thank God she is in my life every day. Still, I don't think injuns and folks with different colors of skin should be allowed to drink whiskey. I am Scottish, so good whisky is right up there with mother's milk in my mind."

All the men laughed, and Blunt said, "It's not the whisky I'm knocking. Dammit all! I'd have to be drunk as a wobbly skunk to touch a woman like her."

One fella shook his head and said, "You have no real problem to my mind. You don't have to touch her."

A lot of muttering followed, and a few men—including the one who spoke up—excused themselves with various reasons such as 'the wife will tan my hide if I'm not home for dinner,' 'I've got cows to milk at home,' and 'I'm too dang tired to talk about all this', which might even have been true.

Once they left, Blunt said, "It takes strong men to keep the women in line. My wife never threatens me about when, where, or what I'm doing. Besides, milking the cows is a woman's work. No self-respecting man would milk a cow when he has a wife to do such piddling work."

A few more men left without excuses but quietly exited while others talked. By the time there were only five men left to keep their vile nattering, Lester knew these men were of his frame of mind, at least for the time being.

Lester said, "I don't believe for a minute that Aurora Harrison birthed that baby."

"How can you know that?"

"I'll tell you how. My wife heard from a close friend of Aurora's mother that Aurora couldn't bear babes. She said a bunch of men raped her so violently that her womb died and closed shut."

"That's disgusting. Did no one do anything about the men?"

"Why would they? She's part slave and part Chickasaw."

The man stood up, shaking his head. "No matter who or the color of their skin, raping a woman is evil. I'm outta here!"

With only four men left, Lester was furious. "Of all the lily-livered crap I've ever heard, that's the worst of it. Any woman who is injun and slave leftovers is fair game in my book."

The four men looked around, and none of them said a word. Finally, Lester said, "Ya'll just git up and git on outta here. Ya'll aren't worth the turds that come out of your bunghole."

As the men left, Lester kept muttering about how awful his lot in life was. "My god, what lily-livered men to think a woman like Aurora was even human. Hell, she's barely even a beast and isn't worth the spit I wasted on her a few days ago. The only reason I have a Chickasaw wife is for the land, and she damn well knows better than to stand up to me or for someone like Aurora. Besides, when we raped Aurora, we were doing righteous work. Putting a half-breed woman in her place was something we had a right and obligation to do!"

Sadly, none of the men heard his muttered indignation.

ONCE THE MEN were out of earshot, one said, "He's a dangerous man. The less I see of him, the better off I'll be."

Another nodded. "I don't love slaves or injuns, but that there man is plumb crazy. Live and let live, I say."

The third one said, "I don't know about crazy, but I do know he is dangerous. The less I'm around him, the happier and safer me and my family will be."

The fourth man said nothing but nodded. He would go to the sheriff's office in the morning. He knew what had happened before with Lester Blunt trying to burn out and murder the Penningtons and their children, as well as Clay and Aurora and their newborn baby. He thought highly of Sheriff Harvey and how he sent Lester packing and locked him up in jail for several months.

From tomorrow morning on, he planned not to think of Lester Blunt. For sure and certain, he wouldn't be around the man.

16

As the night deepened, Aurora dreamed of her home, life, husband, and daughter. She saw black splotches in the sky, but there seemed to be a bubble of light surrounding her and her family. When she dreamed of Tishomingo, she saw some blackness but more light. The light helped keep her spirits filled with joy and love despite the tribulations of life.

Her dreams shifted to the next week when her mother and father would arrive. She was relieved Clay, with Noah's help, was able to finish the upstairs rooms and staircase. Only paint and linseed oil were needed to finish out the second floor of their house. In her dreams, the rooms were lovely and inviting, just as her mother's home had always been.

Her dreams softened her anxiety. She knew her mother and father would have a safe, comfortable place to sleep while they were here. She felt her heart soar and knew when her mother held Okchuli in her arms that she would love her granddaughter nearly as much as she loved her gift of a child.

Suddenly, her dreams changed. As her dreams deepened, she began to hear a voice in them. She didn't know the voice but felt it was a loving and honest voice. She knew when she woke, she would need to write the dream in her journal.

A chill raced up her back, and a voice in her dream said, "Watch out. Lester Blunt won't give up until you and Okchuli are dead."

"Why would he kill Okchuli?"

"He knows who fathered the child."

"Do you know who fathered the babe?"

"Yes. His brother's daughter was in love with Conrad, and they lay together a few times. The woman's father was incensed that she was pregnant by a Chickasaw man. She refused to tell her father who the man was, so neither her father nor her uncle, Lester, knew Conrad was the birth father."

"Thank you for telling me. Why does Lester hate me so?

"He hates you because of who you are and that you are mothering his brother's granddaughter. He feels shame over the birth of the baby."

"He should feel honored that a baby is loved."

"Yes, but that is not his nature. Just before they moved, the brothers fought. The brother denied his daughter had ever been pregnant. He gave Lester a black eye and split lip for his trouble."

"I heard they moved."

"But Lester did not, and he isn't one to let any perceived evil—no matter how big or small—go untended. Of course, there is nothing evil about you, Okchuli, or her birth mother and father, for that matter."

"Okchuli and I are both good women. Okchuli especially is without evil."

"Yes, but that doesn't fit into Mr. Blunt's way of thinking, and his way of thinking is very limited."

Aurora shuddered and whined a bit. Clay wrapped his arms around her and whispered, "You're safe, my love. We're all safe."

Once she was quieter and sleeping deeply, Clay carefully left their bed to check on Okchuli. He carried his pillow and pulled an extra blanket from the shelf. He had no idea what had disturbed his wife's sleep but felt danger approaching.

He crept to his daughter's cradle and watched her breathing softly with her eyes closed and thumb in her mouth. He smiled, kissed her forehead lightly, then lay on the floor beside her and slept there for the rest of the night.

Evil was afoot—he could feel it in his gut and bones. He was determined he would not let anyone harm his daughter or his wife. They were the moon and sun to him.

Aurora's dreams deepened as the night continued its rest. She dreamed of Clay protecting her and Okchuli while he helped everyone around him. She dreamed of her womb and felt her womb become ripe. There was an ache with the ripening but also a new joy.

Her mother whispered in her dreams, "All will be well. You are blessed and loved. All your children will honor you."

The moon watched over the cabin near Pennington Creek. As the night deepened, the moon's path began to go below the land, others in the firmament watched over the family. The child was special in many ways to many beings, including many humans.

Aurora woke early as usual and was surprised that Clay wasn't in bed beside her. She grabbed her shawl, wrapped it around her shoulders, and walked from the bedroom to the living area to find Clay sleeping on the floor beside Okchuli's cradle. She smiled and turned back to the bedroom. She dressed and washed her face, then unbraided her long hair. As she finished undoing the two braids, Clay stepped up behind her, wrapped his arms around her, and said, "I love the sunlight on your hair. As the sun rises, I'm always glad my Aurora is with me. You light up my life."

She smiled, turned, and kissed him. Looking up into his face, she asked, "Were you worried about Okchuli?"

He nodded. "A little. I just felt I needed to be beside her for the night."

In the living area, Okchuli rolled over and cried from her cradle.

Aurora smiled. "Let's see what we can do to help our daughter this morning."

Clay agreed with his wife and followed her. He was concerned about her anxiety, but even more so, he was concerned about how he had felt the previous night. He had a strong feeling that something evil was near and wanted to harm his daughter while she was sleeping. Despite the fact that he knew logically that she was safe, he still worried about both Okchuli and Aurora.

Aurora picked up the baby and said, "My goodness, dear one, you need to have dry clothes." She turned to Clay and asked, "Will you bring dry clothes and a dry diaper for Okchuli?"

"Of course," he answered, glad to do anything to help his wife and protect his daughter. While he went to the chest where Aurora kept the baby's things, Aurora removed the wet diaper and clothes. Then she wrapped her shawl around Okchuli and opened her blouse to nurse her baby.

The baby latched on and sighed with relief to be in her mother's arms, suckling, for not only was she hungry, but she'd also felt darkness in the night. Clay walked back into the main room and saw the sunlight streaming through the windows on his wife and daughter. He stood quietly watching the Madonna and Child in his very own home. A few tears came, and then Aurora said, "Come sit with us, Clay."

He wiped his face and sat beside his wife and daughter. He said, "It is a beautiful sight to see you in the beam of the sun's light with our daughter in your arms."

"Thank you, Clay. I love having her in my arms and the sunlight. Now that she's not ravenously hungry let's put dry clothes on her so she doesn't soil everything in sight."

He chuckled, handed Aurora the diaper and clothes, and took the baby from her arms. He kissed the baby's cheek, and Okchuli laughed at him. He said, "Ah, daughter, your Daddy loves you."

She clapped her hands, laughed, and said, "Dada," and then she let loose her bladder onto his clean, dry pants.

"Ugh, Okchuli. Is that any way to treat your Daddy?"

Aurora laughed, and Okchuli giggled and clapped her hands. Aurora reached for the baby and said, "Go on and get clean, dry pants, Clay. I'll get her dressed and finish nursing her. It's Sunday, and I have a special breakfast for today."

He kissed his wife's cheek and said, "You're the best." He touched the baby's cheek, grinned, and said, "You, on the other hand, are on my shortlist!"

The baby kicked her feet, grinned, and said, "Dada!"

"Okay, girly," Clay said, "I'll let you off the hook."

Aurora laughed. "You're a softy. Go on and get cleaned up so you can milk the cow and bring in the eggs. I'll have breakfast ready by the time you finish."

17

"One has to face fear or
forever run from it."
Crow Proverb

While getting dressed for church, Aurora felt cramping low in her belly and decided to go to the outhouse rather than use the commode chair. The chair was fine for urine, but she relegated anything else to the outhouse.

She walked out to the backyard and the outhouse. The sun was brilliant, and the wind was soft, although the chill of an early November morning hurried her along. She sat on the seat and waited for her bowels to move, but they didn't. She wiped herself only to find blood on the scrap of old muslin. She shook her head and muttered, "I can't have babies. I have not had bleeding since the rape years ago."

She folded and fashioned another cloth to protect her clothing and walked back to the house, trying to think about the matter. She had not been using any herbs since she started nursing Okchuli. Prior to Okchuli's arrival, she had been taking herbs daily since she was raped. *I wonder if that is why I'm bleeding.* She shook her head and decided since there wasn't much blood, she would wait and see what happened. She muttered, "Momma might have some ideas. She'll be here in a few days. She, too, was a midwife, so I hope she'll know what to do."

She tried not to think of her dreams. She decided not to take too much stock in dreams. At the same time, she knew when she had such a profound dream, she should pay attention. She picked up her journal and re-read what she'd written about her dream. She wrote another sentence in the journal: *if it is possible for me to bear a child of my own womb, I would feel honored. I don't want to get too excited, though. This could be something terrible.*

She closed her journal and finished dressing for church.

CLAY AND AURORA went to church with Maggie, Silas, and their children, but Aurora couldn't stop worrying, and the cramping didn't ease up. By the time church was finished, Aurora knew she needed relief from the cramping.

When they were home, she brewed some willow bark tea for their Sunday dinner. At least that would help the cramping.

Clay helped her set the table, and just as they were about to sit down, he saw a dark stain on Aurora's skirt. "Darlin', are you okay?"

"Yes. Why do you ask?"

"There's a stain on your skirt. It looks like blood."

Aurora turned, lifted her skirt, and saw the blood had seeped through. She sat down and began to cry.

Clay quickly sat beside her and asked, "Are you ill, Aurora?"

"I don't know, but I'm terrified, Clay."

"Why? What is going on?"

"You know my uterus was scarred when I was raped. I never had another time of bleeding after the rape. The doctor said I would never bear a child. This morning, I started bleeding. I'm sure it is vaginal blood. I'm having a lot of cramping, too."

Clay nodded. "I have an idea."

She shook her head at her husband, thinking he wouldn't know anything about a woman's body other than making love and babies. She asked, "Really?"

He smiled at her, took her hand, and said, "Yes. I'm not a midwife, but I know about animals and how they birth."

"It's not the same, Clay. At least not entirely."

"I know, but let me tell you a story. We had an old cow that never had a calf, but she'd give milk almost on demand. Years passed, and then one morning, when we went to milk her, she stomped on any foot that got close to her. Daddy wanted to kill her, but Momma said no to Daddy's idea in a hurry—good milk cows are hard to come by, and Momma thought maybe the cow simply needed a break. So, instead of butchering the cow, Daddy turned her out to pasture where there was an old, cantankerous bull in the pasture. It was like two tetchy cows getting to know each other. When he mounted her at his first opportunity—several times—we had a clue about what the cow wanted. He kept mounting until she'd had enough and sent him packing. Several months later, she laid down in the barn and delivered her only calf."

Aurora laughed. "I've never heard of such a tale, Clay."

"Are you doubting the veracity of my story, darlin'?"

"Well, it is a tall tale, Clay."

"No, ma'am, it is not. If Momma and Daddy were still living, they'd back up my story."

"So, even if I believe your story—which I will take just as you told me—what does that have to do with me?"

"Well, we are coming up on our first wedding anniversary. From the beginning, I strongly felt you would have children, and I believe Okchuli is our first child. She is close to six months old now, and you've been nursing her all that time. Could it be that nursing her allowed your uterus to heal?"

"I can't see how, but I suppose it could. Still, the doctor sewed up some of the tears in my cervix and vagina and said he couldn't be sure, but he didn't think I'd ever be able to be pregnant."

"You've been nursing Okchuli a bit less over the past few weeks as she learns to eat other foods."

Aurora nodded. "Maybe things are changing for her and me both, but I don't see how this could be anything else but a bad omen."

"Hang on, now. How long do most women bleed each month? I know sort of how it works but not the details."

She chuckled. "Most women bleed three to five days and a few longer. It happens every 28 to 34 days. For a lot of women, they have bleeding in the new moon or full moon."

"Good then. We have the New Moon in a few days, right?"

"That's right, Clay."

"I'm glad we agree on that, at least."

She laughed, and he took her hands and said, "You go clean up while I finish setting dinner on the table. We'll worry if your bleeding gets heavy or it's still going on by next Sunday. Your momma will be here shortly after that. She might have some fine ideas."

"You're right. I love you, Clay."

"I love you too. You are the light in my life. I'd give up my life at a moment's notice to be with you."

"That doesn't make any sense, Clay."

He grinned. "And for that reason alone, you must be with me for the rest of my life. Someone in my life must reason well."

She kissed him, stood up, went to the bedroom, and found a few old rags she could use. Once she was cleaned up and had washed the blood out of her skirt, she sat beside Clay at their table and drank her willow bark tea.

Clay asked, "Do I have to drink that tea? It tastes like it came off a dung heap."

"Well, having never tasted dung heap tea, I'd have to leave it to you as to what it tastes like. But no, you don't have to drink the tea. You can drink water or even coffee. Coffee's staying warm on the hearth."

He laughed and said, "Thank heavens."

She smiled at her husband's antics but soon was thinking about the bleeding. It wasn't much—just a few spots and cramping—but she still wasn't sure it wasn't something terrible. Yet, she allowed a bit of light, a little frisson of hope, to bloom in her heart. *Maybe Clay is right.*

AFTER LUNCH, they worked together in the upstairs rooms, painting the walls and sanding the floors. They planned to wax the floors in another day or two. Aurora couldn't help but think how it would be to have children in these rooms.

Clay was thinking the same thing but also about expanding their home. He thought, *"If Aurora can bear children, we'll need more than two extra rooms. I'd be happy to build as many rooms as needed."* He wanted to be calm about the possibilities, but he simply couldn't help but hope for children in the future.

Aurora still felt trepidation about the bleeding, although she was trying to accept a miracle instead. She knew the bleeding could mean several things. *Maybe something in my womb has broken loose. Perhaps it's something even worse—something that could kill me. But my dream was so real and I'm sure the Universe wouldn't send me such a dream without the possibility of it being true.*

She shook her head and forced herself to think positively—to wait and see if the bleeding stopped in a few days. She prayed it would be that her womb had finally healed. Maybe having Okchuli in my arms and drinking the milk I have in my breasts gave the rest of my body the ability to be a complete woman.

She decided to smoke sage in their home and put fresh cornmeal in all the corners. *When the Sun rises tomorrow, I'll give thanks for my life. Maybe the Sun will bless me for my name, if nothing more.*

MONDAY MORNING DAWNED bright and clear. It was a cool, crisp morning with a little breeze. Aurora and Clay, with Okchuli wrapped close to Aurora's breast, drove their buggy into Tishomingo to speak with Mr. Murray, the lawyer. She was nervous but trusted that Walter Thompson had given her excellent advice.

Neither Clay nor Aurora spoke of the bleeding, though. Both felt talking about it might jinx things. Of course, they both also knew that talking about something like this couldn't change the outcome. Their mere thoughts or words didn't have that sort of power.

Clay wasn't worried but had difficulty not being excited that they could have more children. He was certain that without Okchuli in their lives, the possibility of more children would never have occurred to either of them. He smiled, remembering the meaning of his daughter's name: 'awake.' He thought, *maybe our daughter brought life to her momma and me, too.*

Aurora watched her husband's face and asked, "What caused you to smile, Clay?"

"I was just thinking about Okchuli, how much I love her, and how happy I am that she came into our lives."

"Yes, she is a miracle."

"More than that, her name means *awake,* darlin'. I've been thinkin', maybe she brought you healing and awakened your body as a woman."

She nodded. "Maybe. It's only been a short time. Today is day two, and the bleeding is a little heavier, but the cramping is better. Let's not worry or fret about it unless it gets worse."

"I'm with you, darlin', but I have a gut feelin' it will get better and better. I'm happy as a pig in slop."

She laughed. "There he is—my happy pig farmer."

"Yep. Now, we're here at the law office of Mr. William H. Murray, Lawyer."

"Let's get this part over with. Then I want to go to Shirley's store. We need sugar, flour, and coffee. I also need more muslin."

"That all sounds more fun than talking with a lawyer."

Aurora chuckled. "Let's go meet our legal bigot and see if he's willing to help us."

18

"If the white
Man wants to live in peace,
Treat all men alike.
Give them all the same law."
White Elk

They sat in straight-back chairs in front of Mr. Murray's desk.

The lawyer said, "Mr. Walter Thompson has outlined the situation very nicely. He is a meticulous man, and Mr. Johnston feels he is one of the best and most honest of men."

"That's a relief to me," Aurora said. "Our family has always thought Mr. Johnston to be a good judge of character. I'm counting on his judgment for your honesty with us, Mr. Murray."

Without even a bit of pink blushing, Mr. Murray nodded and said, "Of course, of course. As regards Mr. Johnston, truer words have never been spoken, Dear Lady. I intend to be certain you have no legal problems from this day forward."

"That would be a relief, Mr. Murray."

Murray nodded again and turned to Clay. "Now, Mr. Harrison. It says here that you paid your required allotment cost. Is that true?"

"Yes, it is."

"Good. I'm glad to hear it. Some folks have tried to steal rather than honestly pay for their land."

"I'm dead set against stealing, Mr. Murray. Besides that, because I've married a Chickasaw woman, therefore I am considered Chickasaw. So I feel I'm covered in both directions."

"Yes, sir, you are, and I appreciate the quickness of your mind." Mr. Murray shuffled the papers around, and after a few minutes, he pulled out a sheet of paper and wrote a note that said he'd read all of the documents and was confident the land of the Aurora and Clay Harrison as well as their daughter Okchuli, was adequately and honestly recorded at the Chickasaw Council House and therefore could not be taken from them. He clipped the letter to the papers and slid them back into the heavy envelope Walter Thompson had given Aurora.

He handed the papers back to Aurora and asked, "Might I see your baby?"

"Of course. She is the delight of our hearts," Aurora answered. She stood up and unwrapped the shawl she'd wrapped Okchuli in. Clay stood with her, observing the lawyer. She uncovered the baby and smiled at the sleeping baby.

Mr. Murray stood and came to her side. He smiled and said, "To my mind, there's nothing more beautiful than a baby. And, Mr. Harrison, that curly red hair proves your parentage, and you, Mrs. Harrison, I see the Chickasaw beauty she will become."

"Thank you, Mr. Murray," Clay said. "I'm delighted with both my wife and my daughter."

"What a blessing you've been given."

"Yes, sir. I am a blessed man. Just out of curiosity, though, why did you ask to see our baby?"

"Ah. I'd heard some vile accusations that the child was a foundling and not of Mrs. Harrison's womb."

Clay was very quiet and stared at the man. In a few seconds that felt like hours, Aurora took care with her words and said, "There was a time we thought I could not bear a child, but I've been blessed with Okchuli."

"Well, I'd heard you were barren because of a terrible encounter with ruffians."

"You mean my being brutally raped and beaten by several men in this town?"

He did blush—a bit. "Yes, that's what I'd heard. I'm so sorry you had to suffer such a vicious encounter and worried that you might never be a mother. I wonder why anyone would think you could not bear a child?"

"For a few years since the rape, I had no womanly discharge. A doctor helped stop the bleeding from the rape and said he doubted I'd ever bear a child."

"But that's no longer the case?"

"Exactly. Is there any reason why I would show anyone my bloody clothes to prove my fitness as a woman and mother? I'm very willing to do so."

Clay sucked in a breath and held it tight. He was worried Aurora had been too bold, but Mr. Murray sputtered a bit, blushed, and said, "Dear Lady, and I mean dear lady in the best possible way, of course, you do not have to show evidence of fertility. The babe in your arms is testament enough for me."

"Good. Then we need never to speak of it again."

He nodded, but Clay released his breath and said, "Of course, if you hear anyone suggesting my wife isn't a complete woman, you know how to set folks straight."

"I'm not sure..." Mr. Murray spluttered, but Clay held up a hand, interrupted the lawyer, and said, "That is what I would expect of any good, honorable man or woman, including you, to do, especially about an honest and much-needed woman in the community."

"Of course! Of course! I've heard you're the best midwife in the area. Only a cruel, mean-spirited person would throw aspersions on you, Mrs. Harrison."

Aurora smiled and held out her hand. "Thank you so much for all your help today, Mr. Murray."

He smiled, took her hand, and kissed the back of her hand. "It was an honor to meet you, Mrs. Harrison. I enjoyed getting to know your husband and see your beautiful baby."

"Thank you, Mr. Murray. Will you attend the Celebration of our new Council House on the 17th?"

"Absolutely. I've even been asked to give a speech."

"How nice for us all," Clay said, smiling to conceal his anger. "I'm sure as time goes on, people will remember you and every word you've said, and every speech you've given and every word you've written. I expect your words will appear in newspapers and maybe even a few biographies."

William Murray preened a bit in what he thought was a grand compliment. "I live only to serve the Chickasaw and the town of Tishomingo. However, I do appreciate your confidence."

William Murray, lawyer for the Chickasaw, entirely missed the meaning of Clay's words.

ONCE CLAY and Aurora were back in their buggy and heading to the Dry Goods Store owned by her friend, a Chickasaw woman, Shirley Duncan, Aurora asked, "Did you mean what you said to him as a compliment?"

"Not in the way he thinks. He is a preening ass but may be useful to us for the time being. Sadly, I think Hank was right that Mr. Murray may become a politician."

"Really?"

"Oh, yes. He even said he might become a governor someday."

Aurora laughed and said, "God help us all!" Okchuli wiggled in the shawl. Aurora said, "I think our daughter's closeness to me all day may end. Not only is she getting heavier to carry, but she is awake more often and wanting to be unconfined."

"I was wondering about that too."

Okchuli said, "Mama," and reached up a hand to her mother.

Aurora beamed and kissed the baby's hand.

"There you have it, darlin'. She's talking and not just to me."

Aurora laughed and turned the baby to see the town as they went to Shirley's store. It took a few minutes longer than usual as people walked through the street willy-nilly, and horses were coming and going and crossing without looking out for oncoming buggies and wagons.

Clay said, "I have a request for you, Aurora, for our first wedding anniversary."

She tucked her hand around his arm. "I have a request too."

He said, "You go first."

"Thanks, Clay. Friday, the eleventh of November, is our anniversary."

"I did remember, darlin'."

"Good. Here's my request: I want to invite Shirley, the Penningtons, and Hank and Mary with their children to our home to celebrate."

"Sounds like a great idea."

"Good. What did you want from me and Okchuli?"

"There's a new fella in town who takes photographs. I want a photograph of our family to have in our home."

"Is it costly?"

"Three dollars, including a pretty frame."

"I think we can spare that, can't we?"

"I think so. We don't spend much on frills in our lives, but I want to have a photograph of our family, year by year."

"It's a lovely idea, Clay. When will we do it?"

"I have an appointment for Wednesday morning. Will that work for you?"

"Yes. It allows me to be sure Okchuli and I are in our best dresses."

"What about me?"

"I'll brush your suit coat and your good trousers. Because this is for us and everyone in the family for future generations, I'll even iron the creases sharp."

Aurora said, "Shirley, Friday is our first anniversary, and we'd like to invite you and a few other friends for a potluck party."

"Oh, that sounds like great fun. Who else are you inviting?"

"I thought Mary and Hank and their children, plus Maggie and Silas and their children, too."

"How exciting. Will this be your first party at your home on Pennington Creek?"

"Yes, it will."

"Great. You make your fruit cake, and I'll take care of talking with Maggie and Mary. We'll plan a perfect party to celebrate your marriage."

Aurora turned to Clay and said, "I saw some baby dolls over there, Clay. Maybe we could take one home for Okchuli."

"Please," Shirley said, "Let her pick which one she wants, and it will be my gift to Okchuli."

Clay grinned, took Okchuli from his wife's arms, and went to the shelf with dolls.

Aurora said, "Thank you. Now, I need some more muslin. Doesn't have to be fine linen."

"Sure. Are you making towels or using the fabric for rags."

Aurora leaned forward and whispered, "For women's bleeding."

Shirley's mouth opened, and she quietly asked, "For you?"

Aurora nodded.

Shirley beamed. "Good for you, my dear friend."

"Fingers crossed it's not something terrible. For now, I'm going to pretend it is simply my womb healing and waking up."

"I'll cross my fingers and send a prayer to the Universe for your best outcome. Now. I have some small pieces of cloth that are washable for just this purpose. Let me show you. A lot of women are using them and like them."

"What a relief. I wasn't sure what to do."

"Of course not. You birth babies but don't have to deal with the routines of womanhood."

"Until now."

"I'm certain it will be for now and the future."

"From your mouth to God's ears."

"That's my plan."

19

When leaving Shirley's Dry Goods store, neither Clay nor Aurora saw Lester Blunt approaching them. Clay was carrying Okchuli—holding her new rag doll—while Aurora had the bag of food and cotton pads.

Lester shouted, "Hang on a minute, Clay."

Clay looked up at Lester but told Aurora, "Let's get you and Okchuli settled in the buggy."

"Good idea."

She put the food in the back of the buggy, climbed up on the seat, and took Okchuli into her arms as Clay handed the baby to her. She wrapped her daughter and the baby's doll close to her.

Lester was close and shouted again, "I said I wanted to talk with you, Clay."

Clay answered, "I have nothing to say to you."

"What I have to say is in your best interests. Trust me on that, boy."

"I'm not your boy, and besides, you are the last man in Tishomingo I would trust."

"That's as may be, but listen to my proposition."

Clay stood blocking the buggy, his wife, and his child as Lester walked closer. Lester puffed on his cigar as he stood a few inches away from Clay and said, "I'm going to make you a one-time offer, Clay."

Clay shook his head. "You will never have anything to offer me that I would want."

"Even money?"

"How many millions of gold coins do you have?"

"That, of course, is none of your business, but I'm offering you one hundred dollars for that dinky ass place where you live."

"Sorry, I can't help you, Lester, since I don't have a dinky ass place. And if I did, I would not sell it to you."

"Why? Just because you've made the mistake of your life by marrying an injun-nigger and call the cast off leavings of another injun your daughter."

Clay had no intention of saying or doing anything else, but his fists reacted before his thoughts reached them. Before Aurora could stop her husband, he'd slugged Lester and left him lying on the road with blood gushing from his now crooked nose.

Clay said, "No thanks for your vile offer, Lester. Never speak about my wife and my child in such odious terms if you plan to continue to walk above the sod." He climbed into the buggy beside his wife and child and headed home.

Lester screamed and spluttered. "You broke my nose, and I'm going to kill you and kill your squaw after I finish with her! I'll stomp that baby into the mud where she belongs!"

Shirley was standing outside of her store. She'd seen and heard the whole encounter. She said, "You are no longer welcome in my store, Mr. Blunt."

"I go where I wanna go!"

"Except here in my store."

Hank was striding across the street with one of his hammers in hand. He asked, "Are you all right, Shirley?"

"Yes, I am. I appreciate your concern, Hank."

Lester struggled to get up from the mud puddle where he'd landed. No one bothered to help him. Once he was standing, he pulled out his handkerchief and said, "I'll see all of you folks in the ground for harboring that vile woman and her supposed husband, Clay Harrison."

Hank swung the hammer in his hand back and forth and said, "I'd hate like hell to get your nasty blood on my favorite hammer, Lester."

"You wouldn't dare!"

Hank kept swinging the hammer in bigger and bigger arcs. "I just might dare for you, Lester."

Lester shook his head and stomped away while trying to stop the bleeding from his nose. Hank sighed and said, "Something has to be done about that man."

Shirley nodded. "I'll talk to the sheriff when he comes by today."

"He's been coming by a lot," Hank pointed out.

"I've asked him to check on things on the main street here a little more frequently to protect the businesses and the people who work here. We have more and more people moving in, and I felt we needed to be alert. I also asked him to ride herd on Lester."

"That's a great idea. I'll talk with the sheriff too. I don't want anything to happen to Aurora, Clay, or their baby."

"I agree with you, Hank. Now, how about something more pleasant?"

"Yes, please!"

She told him about the plans for Clay and Aurora's first wedding anniversary celebration. He said, "Sounds good. Besides, all of us celebrating with them might help keep Lester from stirring up any more trouble."

"I wouldn't count on it."

"No, but it might help, even if just a little, and even if just for our friends."

AN HOUR LATER, the sheriff entered Shirley's store and said, "Just here to check on things."

"I'm glad, Sam. Lester's been being a right old pain in the keister again."

He shook his head. "That man doesn't have the sense to shut his mouth and just go on and live his life. I don't know how Lenora puts up with him."

"You and me both, Sam. What's going on now is he doesn't seem to be able to stop harping on Aurora and Clay Harrison." She related the story of the morning events, and he shook his head and said, "Once an idiot, always an idiot with that man."

The little brass bell over the door dinged, heralding another customer. The sheriff said, "I'll let you get on with your customers, Shirley. I'll talk with Mr. Blunt and try to settle him down." He turned to the man who'd just entered the store and said, "Conrad, it's good to see you. How are things out at the den?"

"Once the picnickers, hikers, and swimmers head back to town, it's a perfect, quiet place."

"Good to hear. I need to keep moving." He waved his goodbyes to both Conrad and Shirley.

Conrad asked Shirley, "What's that sorry excuse for a human being, Lester Blunt, up to now?"

"Same old, same old. He's bound and determined to either run Clay and Aurora out of the area or, better yet, kill them and their darling Okchuli."

Conrad shook his head, and a few of his braids and rocks and bones whispered their sounds. He said, "It would be a blessing for us all if he simply vanished."

Shirley touched Conrad's hand. "You aren't planning anything, are you?"

"Not particularly."

"You are wearing your warrior braids and face paint."

He nodded. "I'm Chickasaw, same as you. Killin' ain't something I'd do unless there were no other options."

"Are you talking about Lester Blunt?" Shirley asked.

"I'm talking about my responsibility to Okchuli and her mother. I think maybe putting a little fear into Blunt might help him find a better way of being."

"Is that likely?"

He shrugged his shoulders. "I like most of the white folks just fine, but Mr. Blunt is the worst kind of human—although it's hard to see him as a human. His wife is Chickasaw, too. It's a wonder she can't get him to settle down."

"I think she has tried, but it is dangerous for her to try."

"He's hurt her?"

"She tries to hide the bruises, and I have heard her excuses about being clumsy."

Conrad gritted his teeth. "I like Lenora a lot. I'll sing for her. Too bad her husband isn't clumsy enough to do himself great harm."

Shirley chuckled. "Now, that would be a blessing for us all."

"Yes, it would. For now, I need some coffee, flour, and sugar. Milk, if you have it, would be a treat."

"So happens I have milk and all the rest you need."

He nodded and thought about Lester Blunt. *A mighty fall at the Devil's hand might suit that idiot just fine.* He continued to think on the subject, unsure exactly how it might happen, but it certainly needed to happen.

SHIRLEY CLOSED the store early and rode out to Maggie and Silas Pennington's home on Pennington Creek. She wanted to talk with them about the party for Clay and Aurora, and she also wanted to stop in and be sure Aurora was doing okay. It would be a great blessing if she were able to bear children. It would also be a great horror should the bleeding be from some dangerous malady.

Maggie and Aurora were sitting on the front porch watching the children play when she arrived at the Pennington home. She tied her buggy and horse to the railing in front of the fence, approached the two women, and said, "The wind is getting a bit brisk."

Maggie smiled and nodded. "Aurora says we'll have a light frost tonight."

"That's what my almanac and bothersome knee say, too."

Maggie chuckled. "Come sit with us for a few minutes. The children never seem to run out of the need to play."

"Where's Noah?"

Aurora said, "He's helping Clay build a bed for my parents."

"That's nice. I heard through the grapevine that Clay built two rooms where there should have been an attic."

"Yes, and he's done a fine job. He's a good builder and carpenter."

"He's done work for me, and you are right. He is very good with hammers, nails, and wood. Have you told Maggie about Friday?"

Maggie smiled, "Yes, she has, and I'm excited. She's also told me about her bleeding."

Shirley nodded. "I'm going to keep faith that it is nothing serious and hopefully means you might be able to have more babies if you want them."

"I do want them. I'm trying to do what Clay asked me to do."

"What does he want you to do?"

"Not worry about it and think that perhaps my womb is healed and functioning as it should be. He thinks it is because I quit drinking most of the teas I used to drink. I took them to keep my womb safe, which might also have been making it difficult for me to conceive."

"Why did you quit using the herbal teas?"

"When I started nursing Okchuli. I wanted my milk to be wholesome for my baby. Lately, however, she has been nursing less and eating more regular soft food. She loves eggs and mashed potatoes."

"Does she have teeth yet?"

"No, but she is drooling and even a little fussy rubbing her gums." She pointed down where Okchuli was with Teddy. "They are working on trying to crawl, and occasionally they make progress—mostly they're flopping about like two fish out of water. They both reach for toys, but Okchuli cries when Teddy grabs her doll. She loves the doll, and I thank you for the gift, Shirley."

A sudden screech from Okchuli as Teddy grabbed her doll made Shirley laugh. She said, "I'll bring Teddy a soft doll when I come out on Friday."

"That would be great," Maggie said. "Let's talk about the party. This will be our first party since we moved here."

Shirley said, "It's been too long for me too. Now, Aurora, you'll make your excellent fruit cake?"

"Yes, and I'll make sweet whipped cream to go with it."

"Perfect. Now, Maggie, Mary, and I will do the rest of the cooking."

Maggie laughed. "Exactly what will Mary be making?"

"I don't know, but we want to keep her in the loop—so something easy and tasty."

Maggie nodded. "Something she can't mess up."

The women laughed, chatted, and planned a great party for Friday evening. Before long, Okchuli and Teddy had had enough of playing on the porch and were ready for their mommas to give them some milk to drink and dry pants to wear.

Aurora said, "It's getting cooler. I'll head on home with Okchuli and get dinner started."

Shirley asked, "May I walk with you and see what your husband has created?"

"Yes, please."

Maggie called her children into the house, including the crying Teddy, who was ready to suckle.

20

"Be first at the feast,
And last at the fight."
Native American Proverb

In small towns, gossip is the best way to learn who is doing what, how, why, when, or even to whom. Tishomingo, Indian Territory, was no different. It was becoming a bustling town on the frontier. Most of the folks were kind and generous, but some were downright worthless regardless of the coins in their pockets.

A fine example of such a creature would be Lester Blunt. Word quickly spread of Lester Blunt being bested by Clay Harrison—right in the middle of the street. Why? Because Mr. Blunt continued to spout vile aspersions on Mr. Harrison's wife—this time loudly in public.

At the same time, Hank Smithson backed up Mr. Harrison with one of his mighty hammers just in case Mr. Harrison needed his help.

He didn't.

Most folks thought it was high time someone gave Mr. Blunt a right good thumping. As the story traveled through the town, it became a full-on beating Mr. Blunt received rather than the one well-placed punch on his nose. Some heard Mr. Blunt had nearly bled to death from just that one mighty clobber of Mr. Harrison's fist.

No such luck for the town.

However, no one said much about Mrs. Rittenhouse taking out the mean bully—the very same Lester Blunt—with one swipe of her broom across his legs a few days previously. With no blood involved and no public reckoning, her perfect aim with her broom remained unknown to most. The few who knew about it thought it an elegant dispatch for the malicious man.

Not a single citizen of Tishomingo ever gossiped about Lester Blunt's wife's numerous bruises and scratches. Not only did they fear her husband, but they all felt sorry for her. She was a kind and friendly woman, who cooked better than anyone in town. To dine at her table was a real treat. Everyone wanted to help her. Still, no one knew what they could do to help her without embarrassing her.

Of course, Mrs. Blunt didn't know what to do either, so she quietly waited, hoping there would be some way out of the mess she was in. Divorce was unthinkable for Lenora Octavia Blunt, Lester Blunt's wife. To her mind, her only saving grace was the herbal teas she drank daily. She was determined never to have a child from Lester Blunt's dribblings.

Now, in the town and environs, it was Friday evening, and folks had planned for the evening to be one of friendship and fellowship. Some went to the barn dance just outside of town. Others visited their neighbors, and some—primarily young folks—walked outdoor paths holding hands and wondering when, or even if, they would go further in their sparking. Many people hoped for love on this beautiful, moonless, and unseasonably warm evening in November.

Not everyone thought of love. Another man, a quiet man, contemplated how Lester Blunt might meet his permanent demise all on his own—or mostly on his own. When will that happen? Who knows.

Regardless, the man felt the time had come when putting up with Lester Blunt's meanness was too much for a quiet man to tolerate.

His plan was elegant in its simplicity. He wouldn't need Mrs. Rittenhouse's broom, Hank Smithson's hammer, or Clay's fist. All he would need to do was to appeal to the greed of Lester Blunt, who—with any luck—would step a little too close to an edge.

The quiet man nodded and could almost hear the splatting of broken bones and bruised skin. He didn't like what needed to happen, but he was tired of letting evil run rampant, harming innocent people who were simply getting on with their lives.

The quiet man thought Lester Blunt's soul had shriveled up and died long ago. All that was left for the hate-filled man in this plane of existence was for his body to join his soul.

ON THIS LOVELY NIGHT, at Aurora and Clay Harrison's home, their closest friends brought food and gifts to celebrate their first wedding anniversary.

Above the fireplace was a large photograph of the young Harrison family in a lovely frame. Clay stood behind his wife, Aurora, with his hand on her shoulder while she sat in a dark red velvet chair with their daughter, Okchuli, on her mother's lap. Though the photograph was black and white, Clay could see the colors in his mind every time he looked at the photograph. Both Clay and Aurora smiled, but Okchuli stole the show with her clapped hands and a big, laughing grin. Yes, the baby's hands blurred slightly, but the joy was evident. Everyone thought the photograph was perfect.

Silas Pennington said, "I love that picture." He turned to his wife and said, "Darlin', we need to get a portrait of our family."

Clay chuckled and said, "I'm not sure the photographer has a big enough camera for your brood, Silas."

Silas laughed. "I'll be sure he does."

The adults crammed around the table to eat dinner while the children sat on the floor, which Okchuli and Teddy thought was a perfect compromise. Their mothers watched carefully to be sure the babies weren't given anything that they wouldn't be able to gum into submission before swallowing.

After dinner, they all went upstairs to admire the attic Clay and Noah had built. Silas said, "I'm proud of you both."

"Thanks, Daddy. It may have taken longer than necessary, but Clay worked hard, so it didn't bother me much."

Everyone, especially Clay and Silas, laughed at the boy, who was turning the usual joke on his father and Clay.

Clay clapped his hand on Noah's shoulder and said, "In all serious-ness, Noah is becoming a fine carpenter. He thought of making two beds and pushing them together for adults who wanted to be in one bed. Otherwise, each bed will be fine for children or single adults."

"That's a great idea, son," Silas said.

"Thanks, Papa. I got the idea because it's what we're doing for Granny and Pops next week."

"Yes, and as I recall, you and Sarah kept me from having to sleep on the floor."

Maggie chuckled, "Or worse yet, for us to sleep in the barn, which was Silas's idea."

The men laughed, and the women shook their heads and thought —'men!'

Once back downstairs, the men went to the porch and smoked their pipes. The younger children were getting tired, so they sat with Noah and Sarah, who were telling them stories they'd read.

When the table was cleared and all the dishes dried and put away, Maggie said, "Sarah, will you tell your father it's time for Aurora's present?"

"Yes, Momma." She jumped up and went to the porch to tell her Papa it was time for the gift for Aurora.

Aurora said, "I don't need a present."

"Yes, you do," Shirley said.

Mary said, "Never say no to a present. Accept it and say thank you or whatever lovely thing you can say."

"Thank you, Mary. I will."

Everyone smiled and nodded at Aurora's acceptance of giving thanks when something lovely and kind was coming her way.

Sarah came back in, stood beside Aurora, and put her hand in the woman's hand. Maggie smiled and nodded at Sarah as her father brought Aurora's present.

Silas said, "I'll hold it for you while you unveil it, Aurora, but remember that you are part of the creation before you do. With all your teaching of art you've given her, Sarah made this present much more special."

Aurora nodded, reached for the cloth, and pulled it off. In front of her was the story she'd told them about how Pennington Creek got its name. She asked, "Who did this?"

Silas said, "Mrs. Rittenhouse used your sketches of the creek when she carved the blocks for the printing press. Sarah highlighted the creek with her colored pencils and watercolors."

Aurora touched Sarah's drawing of her looking down on the creek. She hugged Sarah close and said, "Thank you. This is a terrific present."

"Well, first, Mrs. Rittenhouse and Daddy made it for the *Weekly Beginnings*. But it was Daddy who thought we could print and frame it, and Momma suggested I could do a bit of watercolor and colored pencil to make it special."

Aurora asked, "Sarah, this is very special. Who suggested the drawing of me?"

Maggie smiled and said, "That was all Sarah's idea, and she drew it all by herself."

Aurora nodded. "I'm not surprised. She is getting better every day.

I loved the first *Weekly Beginnings* and was pleased to have the story on the inside. I told Clay I wanted to keep it."

Clay smiled. "The story is great, and the way it was laid out is perfect."

Shirley said, "I've heard nothing but good things, Silas. People have talked about the *Weekly Beginnings* all week long. I'm keeping my fingers crossed that you can keep it up."

"Well," he said, "With all the talent around me, there's no reason we can do this for years and years."

Mary said, "I love this, Sarah," and then she turned to Silas. "Do you know I write poetry and short stories?"

Hank nodded. "I think they're excellent."

"Great. Bring some by, and we'll get Sarah to illustrate your poems and stories and add them to our *Weekly Beginnings*."

Mary turned to Sarah and said, "I like your father's ideas of doing other drawings for the poems and stories."

"Daddy says I can help a few times every week after school."

"That will be grand," Mary said. "Before long, Sarah, you will have folks wanting your drawings and paintings."

Sarah blushed, shrugged her shoulders, and said, "Maybe," but deep in her heart, she was pleased and hoped she'd become a good enough artist to someday be well-known for her work.

Aurora said, "I have faith in you, Sarah. You are already an artist. Now. I don't know where to hang this beautiful painting of my story."

"I do," Clay said. "I think it will be perfect hanging at the end of the dining table so we can see it daily."

Aurora smiled. "I like it."

AFTER EVERYONE HAD GONE HOME and Aurora had nursed Okchuli for the last time before bed, she sat in her rocking chair admiring their photo above the fireplace. She said, "Thank you, Clay, for the photograph. I love looking at our family."

He nodded and said, "Me too, darlin'. My heart tells me another baby will bless our home and love in a year or two."

She smiled. "My bleeding has stopped for whatever reason. I'm hoping you are right. I'll feel more hopeful after I've talked with Momma next week."

He puffed on his pipe and nodded. After a few moments, he said, "I don't care how many children we have in our home or how they come to us. I care about loving you and any child who comes to us. A child we create would be lovely, but I would not love that child more than Okchuli."

"I'm pleased to hear you say so, Clay. I feel the same way. I know our daughter came to us to seal our family with love and belonging."

"I can't say it better than that."

"Good. Are you finished with your pipe?"

"Yes. I am."

"Good. Let's go play under this moonless night."

He smiled, stood up, and took her hand in his. "I am but your humble servant."

She chuckled at him saying so, just as he did every time she suggested going to their bed. She said, "I love a humble man."

"Only for you, darlin'."

She laughed, and they went to their room.

OUTSIDE, the quiet man carefully walked through the rocks along the creek. He climbed to his abode through the cracks and crevices at Devil's Den. Inside his home, he said, "Soon, the people I love the most, especially Okchuli, will be safe from Lester Blunt."

21

─────────

*"Always assume your
guest is tired, cold, and hungry,
and act accordingly."*
Navaho Proverb

"Momma, I'm ready!" Bea said.

Maggie said, "Good job, Bea. Now, let me take a look at you."

Bea smiled and twirled around, then said, "See, I'm all dressed and ready to go get Granny and Pops."

"What about shoes?"

Bea looked down at her bare feet, back up at her mother, smiled, and said, "I forgot."

"Well, go get your shoes and socks. Be sure you use clean socks."

"I will, Momma," Bea shouted over her shoulder as she ran to the stairs and her bedroom.

Silas laughed. "She's a pistol."

"Truer words were never spoken," Maggie said. "I'll go upstairs and make sure the children have tidied their rooms and have their clothes on."

"I'll come with you, darlin'. I'm just about as eager to get into town as Bea."

CLAY ASKED AURORA, "Are you ready to go into town?"

"Yes, but the coach isn't due for a couple more hours."

"I just don't want your Momma and Daddy standing around waiting for us to bring them home."

Aurora laughed. "Well, you could go upstairs and be sure everything is tidy up there for them. But don't wake Okchuli. She'll be up longer than usual today."

"What if she's already awake?"

"She won't be."

He nodded but knew Okchuli was as excited as he was to have Aurora's parents here. Oh, he knew that she didn't understand it all, but he was sure she knew today would be special—or at least that's what he told himself when he went upstairs to sit by her new crib —a bed he and Noah had made. Of course, after he sat there watching her sleep for several minutes, she woke up, and Clay whispered, "Shhhh. Don't tell Momma you're awake, or she'll fuss at me."

Okchuli smiled at her father, said, "Papa!" and yawned, waving her hands.

Neither Okchuli nor her father saw Aurora watching from the doorway.

Clay said, "Okay. Just for a minute now. But we have to be quiet." He stood and picked his daughter up from her bed. He kissed her cheek, and she reciprocated with her open mouth and gave him a slobbery kiss on his cheek. He couldn't help laughing out loud, and neither could Aurora.

She shook her head, "You two are quite a pair."

"Yes, darlin', we are boon companions."

She walked over to her husband and daughter. "Let's get her dressed for now. I hope we don't have wet clothes halfway into town."

"I'll leave you two to work out the details, and I'll check out the other bedroom again."

Aurora smiled as she watched her husband go to the bedroom he'd built for her parents. She knew he was as excited as she was for her parents to arrive. He'd met them a few times but had said, "I'm feeling happiness overwhelm me now and again."

"I'm glad, Clay. I love our home and all the work you put into building a second floor with two bedrooms."

"Don't forget the storage room."

She nodded, "Which is empty except for Okchuli's cradle."

"Still, we'll find more things to put in there as time goes on."

She nodded, pleased he'd remembered. When he said, "We'll want to hang on to the cradle because I'm certain we'll use the cradle and Okchuli's baby bed another time or two or ten."

She laughed and remembered how much she loved his faith in her and everything around them. It helped to keep her grounded and not worrying too much. *Talking to Momma will ease my worries, I'm sure.*

CLAY AND AURORA sat on the buggy bench with Okchuli tied close to her mother with Aurora's shawl, but now she faced forward. Okchuli clapped her hands, giggled, and looked at everything around her—her first look at the trip from their home into Tishomingo.

Aurora said, "I like your idea of the extra benches on the sides of the buggy, Clay."

"I saw some similar pictures in a book at Shirley's store. They were advertisements, but I realized I could make it so two more adults could ride with us. Then Silas added two long benches on the sides of his wagon."

"My goodness. He could haul all of us with his wagon."

"Yes, he could, but we decided we'd each take our own, so if there were any problems, some could stay in town, and the others could head home."

"Well, since my parents and the Penningtons of South Carolina will be on the same stagecoach, I don't think there will be problems."

"You're right, darlin', but I want everyone home, safe and sound, so you and your Momma can palaver over your womb and see what you come up with."

Aurora laughed and tucked her arm around his. "What a man you are, Clay. Lucky for you, I'm head-over-heels in love with you."

"I'm delighted with you and our daughter. I'm the luckiest man in Indian Territory."

"You are lucky, indeed. I hope Momma and Daddy will be happy and love Okchuli too. We will have many hours for Momma and me to talk, but I'm no longer worried about it all."

"Why?"

"Because the bleeding was short and the cramping was only the first few days. If it were something awful, the bleeding and cramping would not have stopped. I trust my body now more than ever before."

He nodded. "I'm relieved, darlin'. Still, I hope you'll talk with your mother about it all."

"I will. I promise."

CLAY PULLED their buggy close beside the Pennington Family's buckboard. Silas, Maggie, and all their children were already in town. Bea rushed over to Aurora and Okchuli. She said, "I dressed all by myself today!"

"Good for you, Bea. It looks like you did a fine job, too."

"Yep. I almost forgot my socks and shoes, but Momma reminded me."

Clay laughed. "I have the same sort of problem sometimes."

Bea nodded. "When you want to get going, it's easy to forget shoes. I was 'cited to see Granny and Pops. Where are they?"

Everyone laughed except Ben, who said, "I hate not having my shoes on, especially outside."

Clay ruffled his hair and said, "I'm sorry, Ben. I love wiggling my toes in the grass."

Ben shook his head and quickly ran his fingers through his hair back the way he liked it.

Watching his brother, Noah smiled and said, "Hey, Ben, let's look in Shirley's window."

Ben quickly followed his older brother. Once they were standing side-by-side, looking in Shirley's window, Ben asked, "Why do grown-ups always ruffle our hair?"

"I don't know, but I wish I did."

"Well, I don't like it."

"Me neither."

Shirley tapped the window and motioned the boys to come into her store. They quickly went through the door and into her store. She said, "You boys were having a serious conversation out there. Is there a problem?"

Noah shrugged his shoulders, but Ben said, "Yes! Why do grownups always ruffle mine and Noah's hair?"

"Does it bother you?"

He nodded.

"I'm not sure, but I have two possible ideas. Would you like to hear my ideas?"

Both boys nodded.

She smiled and said, "Maybe they love you so much they want to touch you. Could that be it?"

Noah said, "I guess so, but I don't think they'd like it if we did it to their hair."

"Well, I'm certain you are right, but there is a more important and secret reason why."

"Why is it a secret?" Ben asked.

"Because adults know it but usually don't remember it. They ruffle boys' heads anyway without thinking."

"That doesn't make any sense without knowing why," Noah said.

"I agree, and the older we get, the more we do many things without thinking about it or knowing why we do what we do. Let me tell you the secret." She bent over and whispered to them, "Boys are magic, and adults want to have a little magic in their lives."

Ben grinned and nodded. Noah's eyes were wide. "Are you sure?"

"Yes, sir."

"When does the magic go away?"

"I'm not sure that it ever does, but I think when you become an adult, people don't remember boys have magic."

Noah nodded. "I guess that's right."

Shirley smiled and ruffled both boys' heads.

Both boys laughed, and Silas poked his head in the door and said, "Come on, boys! The coach is nearly here." He waved to Shirley, "Good to see you, Shirley," and shuffled the boys back outside to greet their grandparents. Of course, Silas ruffled both boys' heads, but the boys ran their fingers through their hair to put it back in place without worrying about the adults messing with their hair.

Shirley chuckled and went back to dusting the shelves in her store. However, she thought she was right about boys and their magic.

THE CHILDREN CLAPPED and jumped up and down as the coach approached—even Teddy and Okchuli clapped their hands.

Aurora squeezed Clay's hand and asked, "Am I too old to clap my hands and jump up and down?"

He laughed. "Of course not. I'll clap and jump with you and the children."

Both Aurora and Clay clapped their hands, and when the coach was in sight, Aurora couldn't help herself. She jumped up and down. Clay loved watching her joy and wished not for the first time that he could sketch fast and furiously to keep the joy and delight on his wife's face. There were many times he'd seen her happiness, but today's was because her mother and father were coming to visit and see their child.

Sarah was busy sketching Aurora and Okchuli while she stood beside Clay. He looked down and said, "When you have that finished, will you make one for me?"

She grinned. "Yes, I'd love to. Aurora taught me how to draw, and I love her nearly as much as I do Momma."

He hugged her a little and said, "I think it's impossible not to love Aurora or Okchuli or Maggie for that matter."

Sarah grinned and pointed as the stagecoach stopped the team of six horses in a cloud of red dust. Once the coach was standing still, one of the men driving the coach jumped down to open the doors and help the people inside come out.

Silas's and Aurora's mothers were the first two out of the coach. Then came their fathers. Ben and Bea raced to hug their grandmother. Bea said, "Granny, I dressed myself today!"

"That's grand, darling." She hugged Bea, turned to Ben, and asked, "How are you doing, Ben?"

"Good. I'm glad you're here."

"Me too," she answered and ruffled his hair. This time, Ben smiled but still rearranged his hair like always.

Noah saw and was proud of his little brother. When he was closer to his grandmother, he said, "I'm glad you're here, Granny. Where's Pops?'

She hugged him and said, "Right behind me."

Before Noah could go to his grandfather, Granny said, "You've grown a lot, Noah."

He answered, "Yep," and didn't fuss or grimace when his grandmother ruffled his hair.

Shirley smiled, watching the children and their grandmothers and grandfathers. The boys' hair was ruffled a lot, but there was no fuss about it. They just smiled and rearranged their hair. All the grandparents oohed and awed over Okchuli and Teddy.

Shirley loved seeing them all happy and together. She came

outside to greet Aurora's mother, Aponi Jane Freeman, a dear friend. Her friend preferred to be called Jane, though. When she'd hugged her daughter and had her granddaughter in her arms, she turned to Shirley and said, "Isn't she just the cutest baby ever, Shirley?"

"Yes, she is. I'm so glad you've come to visit Jane. I've missed you and Johnathan so much."

"I missed you too, but I love living in Tulsa. How's everything here."

"Good mostly, but turning into a circus."

Jane looked around and said, "Seems like there's as many white people as Chickasaw folk roaming around in town."

"You're right. I expect in a few months there will be more white people than Chickasaw throughout all of Indian Territory."

Jane nodded. "That's how it is in Tulsa. Of course, there aren't a lot of Chickasaw up there. Still, I love living there."

"I'm glad. Will you be at the dedication of the new building?"

"Yes, and I'm looking forward to it. It is beautiful and seems more elegant and useful than the old log cabin Council House or even the old brick building."

"I agree. There isn't another building in town as magnificent as the new Council House."

"And that's as it should be. I should join the family, but we'll return to town for the dedication in a few days. Hopefully, we can have a time or two to spend more time together."

"Let's plan on it."

They hugged, and Jane returned to her family.

Shirley looked up to see Lester Blunt glaring at the families. He didn't see her, however, which relieved her. He seemed very angry, and he jerked his cigar out of his mouth, broke it in two, and stomped off in the other direction.

The sheriff saw and followed Blunt to be sure he went home and nowhere else.

The quiet man, Conrad, a friend of Shirley's, Aurora, and the Pennington family, nodded to Shirley and followed the sheriff.

Shirley felt a little chill on the back of her neck. She thought *things are coming to a head with Lester Blunt. I hope nothing terrible happens to my friends.*

She felt a mighty reckoning was coming for Lester Blunt.

She was right.

22

Once Aurora's parents' cases were loaded in the buggy, Aurora said, "I want to sit in the back so I can talk with Momma."

"That'll be fine, darlin'. Once we get the ladies and Okchuli settled, Johnathan, why don't you join me upfront so we can get to know each other better."

"I'd like that, Clay. We moved a few weeks after you two married, and we've not had time to talk man-to-man."

"Hopefully, you'll approve of how things have gone. We are happier now than a whole hive of honey bees with the best queen in the world."

Johnathan grinned and nodded. "That's exactly how I want my

daughter's life to be." He'd known from the start that Clay was a good man and that although he wasn't Chickasaw, he loved his daughter. As far as he was concerned, Aurora and her mother were the best women in the world. That demanded their husbands be good men, too. He was pleased with Clay.

The men helped the women climb up into the back of the buggy. Clay was glad he'd thought to have a stepping stool at hand. Climbing into a buggy isn't always easy.

Clay and Johnathan sat on the buggy's seat up front and talked while in the back, Aurora said, "I've missed you so much, Momma."

"And I've missed you, daughter. I'd thought—maybe even hoped —you might give in and join us in Tulsa."

Aurora touched her mother's hand and said, "I considered it, Momma, but both Clay and I love our lives down here. Besides, there are very few midwives around here, especially with you gone and a few others who moved away. Besides, I love being a midwife."

"I'm sure it keeps you busy."

"Yes, I am. I deliver three or four babies every month and visit all the women and children in the area who need my skills."

"Have you thought about finding another young woman who wants to become a midwife?"

"Yes, I have. Shirley told me she knows a young woman who might be interested. She's going to talk with her and let me know. She's a little young, but Shirley says she is determined to be a midwife."

"That will be wonderful."

Aurora said and smiled. "I couldn't do all I do without your teaching me. Every baby I deliver is a blessing for me that you made possible, Momma."

"I know you are an excellent midwife. Do you get paid enough for your work?"

Aurora nodded, then shrugged. "I don't get paid much money. Mostly, I'm paid in trade for things like eggs, sausages, bacon, and canned goods. All of that saves me money, so I count it as money. A few folks give me five to ten pennies when they have it. I never turn anyone away who needs me, even if they pay me nothing."

"I'm sure you're a blessing to everyone around Tishomingo. I'm proud of you, daughter. But, please don't sell yourself short."

"I won't, but I would never turn my back on a woman and baby in need."

"Of course you wouldn't."

Aurora smiled, "I love what I'm doing and feel I'm helping people. I can't imagine doing what I do only for money."

"I understand, sweetie, but remember you are worthy of being paid for your services. I'm pleased that you understand the purpose of midwifery—helping women and babies be healthy. You are a good woman."

Aurora beamed. She loved that her mother thought of her as a grown woman and no longer treated her as a child. She said, "I'm excited for you to see the birthing chair Clay bought me. It's a marvel and makes birthing easier for me and the mothers."

"I'd heard about those, but I don't do any midwife work anymore."

"Why not?"

Her mother shrugged. "At first, I was just working on settling in at our home in Tulsa, but now, I'm writing stories."

Aurora smiled. "Tell me about your stories, Momma."

"Well, it turns out folks like to have weekly stories to read in their newspapers, and I like writing stories. The best part is I get paid a penny for every five hundred words. Of course, the editors choose which words stay in and which are taken out. Still, I make a bit more money—more than I made being a midwife—without having to be up all night, several nights a month."

"I'm glad Momma. I love being a midwife. I'm too much fascinated with midwifery to let go of it yet."

"And that's as it should be."

"However, I'm also writing, Momma. Silas Pennington is helping me to write and publish a book on midwifery and caring for children and women. He hopes to publish it in two or three months."

"Is he a publisher?"

"Yes, he is. When we return to town for the celebration, I'll show you where his publishing business is. He named his business *Okchuli Press.*"

Okchuli clapped her hands and said, "Chuli!" and then laughed at the sound of her name.

Jane smiled at her granddaughter and said, "Now, isn't that something? May I hold my granddaughter for a bit?"

"Of course!"

Aurora handed Okchuli to her mother and said, "Let's give Gram some time with you while Momma talks."

Okchuli kicked with delight, and once she was in Jane's arms, the baby gave her one of her open-mouth, slobbery kisses and said, "Gam!"

Jane laughed. "Yes, sweetie, I'm your Gam."

Aurora beamed at the two most important women in her life— her mother and her daughter.

Her mother said, "Now you were telling me about the publishing business of Silas's."

"Yes. When he asked if he could use Okchuli's name, I said yes but wondered why. He said, 'The whole point of publishing is to let folks know what's going on and hopefully keep them awake in their hearts, minds, and souls. Okchuli is the perfect name for the business.'"

"So, he knew the meaning of Okchuli's name?"

"Yes, he did. I shared the meaning of her name with their whole family. They are good people and our best friends—they feel like family." She chuckled and said, "Bea, their youngest daughter, said about Okchuli, 'She's always sleeping and hardly ever awake.' I told her to wait in a few months, and she'll be awake all the time.'"

Jane smiled and said, "They seem like a good and honorable family."

"They are, Momma."

Okchuli clapped her hands and said, "Momma!" Then she smacked her lips.

Aurora smiled and said, "That's her sign that she wants to nurse."

Her mother returned the baby to Aurora, who opened her blouse and let the baby suckle as they rode along the red dirt road to their home. She sighed and looked around the lush land they were driving through.

Her mother saw her daughter's face and asked, "What is bothering you, daughter."

"Something I need to talk about with you."

"Luckily, I'm sitting right here watching you nurse your baby. Tell me what is worrying you, daughter."

"My body. I want—no, I need—to talk with you about the rape."

Jane shook her head and asked, "Why do you want to dredge all that up, Aurora? I'd think tamping it down would be easier on you."

"I'd learned to live with it, Momma, and wasn't bothered much by it until about a week and a half ago."

"What happened?"

Aurora looked at Clay and her father's backs and saw them chattering away. She motioned to her mother and leaned closer to her. "I bled last week, and it seemed normal."

Her mother sat back and smiled. "You quit taking the herbs to keep your uterus calm, didn't you?"

Aurora nodded. "I did so because I wanted to be sure it was safe for Okchuli to nurse from my breasts."

Her mother touched Aurora's hand and said, "The doctor suggested we keep your uterus calm so it could heal."

Aurora nodded. "I remember, but I also remember he said I'd never have babies."

Her mother shook her head. "No. That isn't precisely what he said. He told us he thought you wouldn't be able to bear a child, not that you for sure and certain would never be able to have a baby."

"So, I might be able to bear a child from my womb?"

"I think you might. It's been over three years, and without you taking the herbs, your body might have chosen its path forward."

Aurora nodded but couldn't stop the tears from falling. Her mother handed her a soft cotton handkerchief she'd tucked in her sleeve and said, "Things happen as they should, daughter."

Aurora took the handkerchief, wiped her tears, and nodded. "I know, Momma." Okchuli grinned, dribbled a bit of milk, and said, "Momma."

Aurora smiled, wiped the milk from around the baby's mouth, and said, "Yes, I'm your Momma."

The baby started to nurse again, and Aurora looked at her mother. "I'd decided having Okchuli would be enough for me. The night on the porch of our home, when we found Okchuli, changed everything for Clay and me. She is a miracle in my life. I stopped drinking the herbs in my tea to be sure she was safe while I was nursing her. I wanted what she was drinking from my breasts to be safe and help her to be strong and healthy."

"You did the right thing," her mother said. She patted Aurora's hand. "Wait and see what happens, sweetie. It may mean something but may mean nothing at all. If you get sick or have heavy bleeding, you'll have to see a doctor, but otherwise, if you start having regular bleeding each month, without lots of pain, I think you are fine and may well have children from your womb."

Aurora smiled. "Clay has said all along I would have children. He was happy our first child was Okchuli, but he dreamed about me having babies from my body."

"If you do have a baby from your womb, how will he feel about Okchuli?"

"That she is his first and beloved daughter."

Jane smiled and nodded.

Aurora continued, "I hope to have more children. It would be a gift from the stars if they were born from my body."

"I think the possibility is strong, my dear daughter. Now, enough about worry and what might be. Tell me all about Okchuli and Clay and your house."

"Ah, my home is a castle to me. It's about as big as your house was, but there's something about it that is special. And even more, Clay built a second floor with two bedrooms and a storage room. He's planning how to make the whole house bigger."

"And the land?"

"My heart loves the land where we live."

"What about Devil's Den?"

"It's close, but none of Devil's Den is on our property—Walter Thompson ensured our boundaries were outside the den."

"He's a good man. He's always been a good friend to me. I'm eager to see your home and your land."

"And I'm eager for you to see our home, Momma. It is more than I'd ever thought to have."

"That's as may be, but it and every gift the Universe gives you is exactly what you deserve."

"Thank you, Momma."

Both women watched the birds flitting by, even in the cold of November. As the buggy took them on the red dirt road to Pennington Creek, Aurora sighed and watched a puffy cloud float across the blue sky. In the north, she could see a darkening and hoped there would be no snow yet. Rain would be a blessing, but snow would be a hindrance.

She saw four vultures sitting at the edge of the road and wondered if they were hungry or just waiting for something dead to show up. She shuddered a bit, thinking of vultures and Devil's Den. She shook her head and pointed to the bridge. "It's a rickety old thing, but somehow it gets across every time we need to cross."

Jane nodded and smiled. "I remember the bridge. Walking across is treacherous unless you're walking across the water."

"It still is," Aurora answered.

Jane watched her daughter and wondered what was casting a shadow over her life.

23

*"A man must
make his own arrows."*
Winnebago

While the women chatted about Clay and Aurora's home, the men were doing the same on the front buggy bench.

Johnathan said, "You're married to my daughter, and this is only the second time we've met. We haven't had time to talk and share. Tell me more about yourself, Clay."

Clay nodded and told his father-in-law, "I've worked mostly as a farmer for most of my life, and I learned the carpenter trade along the way. Our house didn't have an attic, but the ceiling was high enough to put in a second floor—so I did exactly that."

"I'm impressed, Clay. Building a second floor from the inside must have been a monumental endeavor."

Clay chuckled. "Well, sometimes it felt like a task beyond my skills. For example, I was worried about how to frame the whole thing for it to be safe."

"I can't imagine even trying to do such a thing. How did you work it out?"

"A friend in town is a great builder. I've worked with him building houses, barns, sheds, and the like in the area. When I asked about making a second floor without destroying the roof of our house, he drew me a sketch of how to tie it into the braces already there. It was a bit fiddly and not as easy as I thought. After I tied in the bracings for the frame, he came out and took a look. He gave me a few more suggestions, and then all I had to do was frame and finish out the rooms."

Johnathan laughed and shook his head. "You make it sound like it was easy peasy."

Clay chuckled and shook his head. "No, sir! It was hard work— some of the hardest work I've ever done. Noah—Silas's boy—helped me most of the time, and Silas occasionally had time to lend a hand."

"You mean that small lad of Silas's helped with the building of your upstairs?"

"Yes, sir. He seems to have a knack for it. I swear he was born with a hammer in one hand and a nail in the other. He's not good with the saw yet, but I think that's because the saw is nearly as long as he is tall. With a hammer, My Lord, that boy has the knack. It takes him two or three whacks, and that nail is set and set properly. I figure by the time he's bigger with stronger muscles, he'll be a one-whack wonder!"

Johnathan laughed. "An amazing young man."

"Indeed he is, and he is a good and thoughtful boy. Every step of the way, I was careful, though. These rooms will be where my children spend much of their time."

"Children?"

"Yep. I have faith in my dreams, Johnathan, and my dreams tell me Aurora will bear babies of her own. I dream about them almost every night."

Johnathan nodded but was quiet for a bit. His daughter had been through a terrible ordeal when she was beaten and raped, and he had doubts about whether her body could bear a child. Still, what a blessing that would be for her and the whole family.

He sighed and said, "Now, about this second floor you built: What was the most difficult part?"

"Tying the beams into the walls of the downstairs beams and studs. Luckily, Silas's uncle, who built and owned the cabin before us, left bare beams visible inside the house, so we didn't have to tear things up very much."

"Sounds like an enormous undertaking."

"It was. It's the most challenging building I've ever done." He grinned and nodded, "I keep trying not to be too proud of myself, but I can't seem to help crowing about it all."

Johnathan chuckled. "Hells bells, lad. I'd be shouting to everyone around about my amazing building skills."

"Thanks for that, Johnathan. I'm pleased with the outcome, and Aurora is happy with the results."

"Good. Keeping your wife happy is your number one job in life."

Clay cocked his head and looked at his father-in-law. "I'm glad to hear that, Johnathan. I can't imagine anything she would want that I wouldn't get for her. Aurora is the queen of my life."

"Then you must be the king. You are the one who takes care of her in every way you can so she can take care of your children and her home."

Clay nodded. "I agree. My momma and daddy died soon after I met Aurora. It may sound daft or mean-spirited, but in some ways, their dying makes my life easier."

"How so, son?"

"It's not that I don't miss them. I do, and I love them. It is simply that they didn't understand my love of Aurora—not being a white woman—or why I'd marry a woman who thought the house and home were hers no matter what else happened."

"Did they live around here?"

"Close by, but not in Tishomingo. They lived up close to Reagan. They sold their house and moved back to Mississippi. I stayed here."

"But they died?"

"Yes, they did. A few months after they left Tishomingo, I got a telegram telling me my father had gotten in a fight with some fella and his friends—I have no idea what the fight was about. Anyway, late one night, they robbed and killed my parents, then burned down their house."

"What happened to the men?"

"I never heard anything more. My best guess is their lives were cut short by the end of a rope around their necks. Still, even though I loved my parents, I had to move on with my life, and my heart was with Aurora. They didn't understand but didn't say anything terrible about Aurora, which helped my soul—just a bit, though."

Johnathan nodded and said, "I'm glad, son."

"Thanks, Johnathan. Aurora lights up my life. We married soon after my parents left and started working to make our way in the world."

Johnathan nodded. "We moved to Tulsa shortly after you wed. We talked about waiting to move, but Jane wanted to move to a bigger town. Aurora was wed and happy, leaving us to follow our plans. I know she had help from Shirley, Jane's best friend, but I wasn't sure how everything worked out until she sent us a letter telling us you two were working and living with folks as they needed. Later, in one letter, she even mentioned Jacob Pennington offered you the small cabin."

"I remember when she wrote that letter."

"We didn't have any details of where she was living. She didn't want her mother's house, so we sold it."

Clay nodded. "Yes, she told me, but I wondered why she didn't want her mother's house."

"She said as soon as she could that she wanted to live in the surrounding countryside of Tishomingo. She didn't want to live in town. Where did you two live?"

"We lived here and there, but nothing to write home about. Sometimes, we had a place to be for a few weeks while working for someone. We had to sleep in our buggy for a few nights, which was very uncomfortable. Then, the fellow who owned the feed and seed place gave us a room out back to live in exchange for working with him. Aurora made a bit of money as a midwife along the way, and we saved every penny to have land and a home to call our own."

"Is that how you got the place you live in now?"

"No, sir, and that's another miracle in my life. Silas's Uncle Jacob offered us the cabin that is now our home. We lived there while I helped him finish building the big house where Silas and his family now live. When we finished that, we went back to the feed and seed store to work and live."

"Why didn't you stay in the cabin Jacob Pennington offered you?"

"It felt too much like charity and a handout to Aurora and me. Neither one of us could feel honorable living there."

Johnathan was quiet for a few minutes. Finally, he said, "I understand, son. However, now you live in that cabin you turned away from out of pride."

Clay blushed and nodded. "They say pride goes before a fall, and we fell pretty low. When Jacob died and left his place to Silas and his family, Silas asked us to move into the little cabin to watch over things. They were still in South Carolina and wanted the property taken care of. It was a blessing that we still couldn't reckon our good fortune the day the telegram asked us to live there and watch over things until they arrived in Tishomingo. That very same day was when the feed and seed store owner fired us."

"Why?"

"Oh, not because we weren't doing good work, but he was losing business because of Aurora and me working and living there."

"Really?"

Clay nodded his head, sighed, and said, "Some of the bigots around here say horrible things about her because she is part African and part Chickasaw. And, the same people don't think very highly of me being Irish."

Johnathan shook his head and sighed. "Some humans don't seem very human at all. I'm sorry, son, about all that happened."

"Thanks, Johnathan, but I'm not. All that happened taught us a lot, and now that Silas and Maggie are here, our lives are a miracle."

"How so?"

"They deeded us five acres and the cabin."

"That's an amazing gift."

"I agree, but we became fast friends. It wasn't exactly a gift but a lifelong promise to do all the extra work around the property so Silas could have time to write and run his publishing company. They wanted to be sure we stayed on long term."

"He sounds like a kind and generous man as well as a prudent one."

"He is, and his wife is too. We love them as if they were family."

As they approached Pennington Creek, the horse balked at the bridge across the creek. Clay clicked his tongue at the horse to get her to cross the rickety bridge. No horse he knew liked that bridge, and no horse could understand humans taking the risk. The horse quickly picked up the pace to get to the other side without falling into the creek.

Once they were over the bridge, Clay said, "We're nearly home, Johnathan, and I'm delighted you and Jane are here. I think you'll like our place. I know we love our house and our land. Aurora has a lot to tell you about the land."

"Her mother told me a bit about it." He smiled as he saw the cabin with a white picket fence around the yard and some flowers still hanging on until the first hard freeze happened. A field of pumpkins and winter squash was a beautiful backdrop for the whole place. He nodded and said, "It looks much better than when Jacob lived here."

"Yes, it does. Aurora works every day in the yard and gardens. She is amazing. I truly think—as the adage goes—if you gave her a sow's ear, she'd make a lovely silk purse out of it."

Johnathan chuckled. "I'm glad you feel so loving and proud about my daughter. I think she is tremendous, but maybe that's because I'm her father."

Johnathan was quiet as he helped his wife, granddaughter, and daughter from the back of the buggy. He was furious about how some had treated his daughter and her husband in Tishomingo. Both Aurora and her mother were quiet but determined women. He knew they could handle anything they needed to. Still, he wanted to horse-whip all those who'd cast aspersions on his daughter. He thought, *I wish I had known about it all.*

It wouldn't have changed anything, of course. Regardless, a father should feel precisely like Johnathan does about his daughter.

JOHNATHAN AND JANE carried their luggage into their daughter's home while Clay took the horse, Rosie, and buggy into the small barn. He unfastened the traces from the horse, rubbed her down, and gave her some oats in her trough with a water bucket next to her feed.

No one saw the quiet man watching through the brush and trees as Lester Blunt crept through the woods. The quiet man, Conrad, would protect Aurora, her husband, her home and land, and especially her children. Conrad knew he was Okchuli's birth father and carried the blessing of Aurora and Clay, as her parents, close to his heart. He felt it was his responsibility to protect Aurora and his child not only because he was Okchuli's birth father but because his honor as a warrior demanded it.

24

"We will be known forever
by the tracks we leave."
Dakota Proverb

While Jane and Johnathan settled their luggage in the guest bedroom, Aurora changed Okchuli's clothes and tucked her into bed. Jane quietly joined Aurora, looking around the room. "Clay did a marvelous job constructing this floor of your home. I'm sure Okchuli will love this room for many years to come."

Aurora nodded and hugged her mother. "I love every nook and cranny of my home, but this room is special. Clay fiddled and fussed to have everything for Okchuli's room just right, and he did the same for the rest of the house."

"I didn't know he'd done anything other than adding the upstairs rooms."

"Oh, he has done several things for our home. The pantry has a sink now. We don't have running water inside yet, but Clay ran a drain pipe from our house outside close to the outhouse. I still have to carry water in, but I love being able to wash the dishes and vegetables in the sink. He and Silas have plans for indoor plumbing, including bathtubs and indoor toilets in both our houses."

"That's marvelous."

"I think it is a miracle. Oscar Casey, the honey-bucket man, has all the plans laid out for both houses, and the men are working on getting it all ready before we have a hard frost. For now, the sink makes my life much easier."

"I'm sure it does. We have indoor plumbing in Tulsa. It makes me feel like a queen."

Aurora chuckled. "I'm beginning to feel the same way in our home. I love our home." They left the baby sleeping and walked to the guest room. Aurora asked, "How's the room we've set up for you and Daddy."

"It's a lovely room. I'm impressed with Clay's building and carpentry skills. He built a chest under the window and a closet for clothes."

Clay poked his head in and grinned. "I planned to create an environment no one would want to leave."

Johnathan stood behind him and chuckled. "Well, son, you've done a fine job. I agree with Jane. It is a lovely room. Most of all, I like the double windows facing southeast. We'll have a lovely sunrise and nice breezes, too." He walked to the windows and looked across the creek into the woods. Only Jane noticed his jaw tighten and his chin lift a little. He said, "Clay, I'd like to walk around the place if you don't mind."

"Sure. You want company?"

"That would be terrific. I haven't been here in a long, long time."

Jane watched her husband and son-in-law leave the room and crossed her fingers. Aurora was so eager to show her home to her mother that she didn't notice the anxiety on her parents' faces.

Downstairs, Aurora and her mother began the preparations for dinner while the men walked around the nearby property.

Jane stood before the fireplace and said, "This is a lovely photograph of your family, Aurora."

"Thanks, Momma. It was a present to ourselves for our anniversary. Clay wants to have a photograph of our family every year to celebrate our marriage."

"What a lovely idea. He seems to be a kind and generous man."

"Yes, he is, and I love our lives together. Come see the other piece of art in the dining area."

Jane followed her daughter, and when she saw the story of Alonzo Pennington and the beautiful sketches, she said, "This makes me so happy. You told the story perfectly. Did you do the sketches?"

"No, Sarah Pennington created the drawing of me, and Adella Rittenhouse drew the part of the creek they couldn't stamp on the printing press."

Jane nodded. "I knew Adella could draw, and she did a fine job. The drawing of you is marvelous. Sarah doesn't look to be more than ten years old."

"She's only nine years old, Momma."

"Are you certain?"

"Yes. I taught her the basics, and she took to drawing as if it were the most natural thing in the world. She even did surreptitious drawings of her family, Clay, and me. She did such a fine job that Silas has her coming into town to work with him and Adella on the weekly newsletter he prints."

"Do you have a copy of the newsletter?"

"Yes, I even bought one extra for you and Daddy of this one so you'd have the story to keep."

"After dinner, I'll want to read the whole newsletter. Now show me what I can do to help you with dinner."

Clay was surprised when Johnathan started walking into the forest on this side of the creek. He asked, "Did you see something?"

"Someone."

Clay was surprised at the terse response and felt the hairs on the back of his neck stand to attention. "Who did you see, Johnathan?"

"Two men. One was Lester Blunt and the other was a friend of mine.

"Is your friend a friend of Lester Blunt?"

Johnathan shook his head. "No, I'm certain he is not. He loathes and despises Blunt nearly as much as I do. It looked like he was following Lester, but I don't know why."

"Lester Blunt is a revolting man." Clay swallowed irritation and asked, "Do you think your friend is intentionally following Blunt."

"Absolutely." He squatted and gently scooped a few leaves away. He looked up at Clay and said, "See here. There are shoe prints of a heavy man."

"How can you know those are prints of a man and a heavy man?"

"Well, this impression is of a white man's shoe, and the impression goes pretty deep. So it belongs to a heavy man who is probably white." He pointed a few feet away and said, "You see that feather on that branch over there?"

Clay nodded. "Looks like a crow feather, but it's tied onto the limb with leather."

"Yes, it is. I think my friend is letting you know that Crow is looking out for you and your family and watching the evil man who threatens you."

Clay nodded. "I am an easygoing man, but if Lester Blunt comes close to my wife or daughter, it will be the last thing he does on this earth."

"You and your family are blessed to have crow looking out for you."

"What about your friend? Is he looking out for us, too?"

Johnathan nodded. "I'm confident he is. He is a good and kind man but very quiet. He lives alone, deep in the woods, in a cave near the creek. He isn't a social person, but a good person."

Clay nodded and looked around the area. From this spot in the woods, he could see his home and most of his property. He shuddered a bit. "I don't like the idea of anyone snooping on my property."

"I don't either. I know my friend will do you no harm, but Lester Blunt is a malicious piece of humanity and is willing to abuse and torture anyone he doesn't like."

"How has he kept out of prison so far?"

"Well, the law around here is merely a loose approximation of the law. I did hear he was jailed for six months for trying to burn down Silas and Maggie's home."

"Yes, and we were next on his list."

"Keep your eyes open, son, and at night, be sure everything is locked up."

Clay smiled, noticing Johnathan had referred to him as 'son' all day. He said, "I will. Are you sure your friend is a good man?"

"Yes, I am. He is simply a very quiet man who loves living in solitude. He occasionally works as a guide for folks moving into Indian Territory, but he doesn't spend much time around people if he can help it."

They walked further along the creek, and Clay said, "I'm seeing a lot of crow feathers tied to the trees around here."

"I did notice them as well. My friend is trying to protect you and your family."

"Well, I'll welcome any help he offers, including crows and their feathers."

Johnathan nodded. "I'm glad you are willing to accept our ways."

Clay nodded and asked, "But you're African, right?"

"By blood, but also Chickasaw. My mother was Chickasaw, and since the war, all my family are Chickasaw. I grew up in the Chickasaw ways of being, seeing, and feeling. I'm Chickasaw, through and through, though my skin is brown mixed with black."

Clay smiled. "I'm glad to be married to Aurora and pleased she is Chickasaw."

"Why?"

"I didn't set out to marry a Chickasaw woman, but I hated what our government in Washington had done to all the native tribes. None of the treaties seem fair or kind. Folks may spout a lot of Christianity, but it doesn't show up in our treaties."

"You are right about that, Clay. However, all we can do is do the best we can. That means we are kind, good, loving in everything we do with the hope that at the end of our lives, we have done the best we could with the time we were allowed."

"Sounds right to me. Can I ask you something?"

"Of course, son. You can ask me anything."

Clay grinned. "Well, you've been calling me son all day, and I appreciate it. What would you like me to call you?"

"I'd feel blessed if you called me Dad."

"Well, Dad, that feels right to me. Thanks for visiting us and helping me look out for our family."

"You're welcome, son, and I love the light in my daughter's eyes when she is around you."

Clay swallowed back sudden tears. He tried to speak but found himself unable to for a bit. When he could talk, he said, "She is my light, and I appreciate your words, Dad."

The two men kept walking, with Johnathan pointing out crow feathers along the way. As the sun lowered, Clay said, "We should head back to the house. I don't want Aurora to worry."

"Good idea," Johnathan agreed.

The men both knew that families come together in all manner of ways. What is essential is the love of family and the care we give to each other. This concept is foreign to fellas like Lester Blunt.

AURORA AND HER MOTHER, Jane, chatted and worked together, preparing dinner. Jane said, "I think this is the first dinner you prepared that I've had since you married, Aurora."

"Yes, it is. Thanksgiving is next week, but I prepared a special dinner for us tonight."

"Good. We can have a special dinner again next week on Thanksgiving Day. Dinner smells terrific."

"I've baked a deer roast with pumpkin and turnips. We'll have corn and squash to go with it. For dessert, I have a wild plum cake and whipped cream."

"That sounds terrific, sweetie."

Aurora smiled at her mother's endearment. "I'm eager to see if I have bleeding again at the next new moon."

"I'll keep my fingers crossed for you."

Aurora felt excited and said, "I can hardly wait to be pregnant with a child from Clay."

"Will that change how you feel about Okchuli?"

"No. She is the daughter of my heart. I know who her birth mother is but not the birth father."

"Does her birth mother live around here?"

"No. They moved to Ardmore."

"Have you ever talked with her about the baby?"

"No, I didn't have the chance. They moved about a week after Okchuli appeared on my front porch."

"Ah. So her parents feel shame."

"Yes, I suppose they do, and that is a sadness, I think, for them all."

"You are right. Are you sure you don't know who the birth father is?"

"So far, yes. However, I've had dreams about him, and he protects his daughter."

"Who would do you or your daughter harm?"

"Lester Blunt."

Her mother shook her head. "What a repulsive man."

"Yes, he is. Right after we moved in here and the Pennington family moved into Jacob's big house, he and some of his gang came to kill us and burn us out of our homes. Noah, Maggie's oldest boy, scared them away with a shotgun."

"Why didn't you tell me?"

"There was no point, Momma, and you couldn't change anything. It was over quickly, although it was frightening."

"I could wring his fat neck and slice open his bloated belly!"

Aurora chuckled. "I'm sure you could. Instead, the Sheriff put him in jail for six months."

"My guess is Lenora blossomed during those six months."

"I don't know for sure, but I saw her in Shirley's store one day. She looked at Okchuli and said, 'What a marvelous daughter you have, Aurora. She is the spitting image of you and your dear husband Clay. I'm certain Jane will be delighted to see her granddaughter.'"

Jane laughed out loud. "Now, that is the woman I remember going to school with. If she likes you, she'll ensure everyone around you likes you too."

"What if she didn't like me?"

"She'd be polite, but that would end things for her."

"Did she like you?"

"Yes, she did. We were great friends until she started dating Lester Blunt. Things cooled off quickly then."

"Is she Chickasaw?"

"Oh, yes, but Lester Blunt is white through and through and in all the horrible ways of some white men."

"I'll say a prayer for her."

Jane smiled and hugged her daughter. All she could think about was how sweet and kind her daughter was and how brutal and mean Lester Blunt was. She knew Lester Blunt considered Aurora's graceful way of being a weakness. Someday, he might understand that his vile way of being was mere cowardice and that Aurora is a stronger person than he gives her credit for. However, she doubted he'd ever change.

25

"It takes a
whole village to
raise a child."
Omaha Proverb

Bea clapped her hands. "Momma said we don't have to study today."

"That's right," Sarah agreed, "but we do have a lot of things to do before we go into town for the celebration and dedication of the new Chickasaw building."

"Why?"

"Well, Momma said we'll go and see all the falderol, but we won't stay for dinner because it will be too dark."

"What about Granny and Pops? Are they going to stay for dinner?"

"They and Aurora's parents will stay for the fancy dinner and dance. We'll be coming home before dark."

"But I want to dance too!"

Sarah laughed, picked up Bea under her arms, and twirled her around the room a few times, with Bea giggling in delight. "Now that we've danced, are you ready to go downstairs for breakfast?"

"Is breakfast ready?"

"Oh, yes. Everyone else is already up and downstairs with Momma and Papa."

"I hope they didn't eat all the biscuits. I'm hungry."

"Let me finish this last braid, and we'll go downstairs." Sarah finished braiding her little sister's hair and reassured Bea there would be a biscuit for her. "I'm sure Momma made enough for everyone."

Ben stuck his head into the girls' room. "Momma said to hurry if you want a biscuit. They're going fast!"

Noah followed his brother and laughed. "There's plenty, but breakfast is ready, and Momma is making us all wait for you girls."

Sarah said, "I'm hungry. What about you, Bea?"

"I'm starving. Are Pops and Granny already downstairs?"

"Yes, they are. Daddy and I had already milked the cow, and Granny and Pops gathered the eggs while Momma fed Teddy. Come on! We're all hungry and waiting on you."

"I'm ready," Bea said and dashed through the door.

Sarah laughed at her little sister. "Ya'll go on. I'll be down in a few seconds."

Noah smiled and nodded, "Don't take too long."

"I won't."

Once they were all gone, Sarah picked up her journal and wrote:

I'm nervous about today, and I'm not sure why. I love Granny and Pops, and they didn't ask any questions about how I became their grand-daughter. They just hugged me and accepted me. For some reason, their hugs seemed to seal the deal for me as a member of the Pennington family. I love that Granny and Pops liked my painting and sketching of the Alonzo Pennington story. Momma wants us all dressed up because the man who shoots pictures on paper will be set up in town. Momma wants us all in a family picture—even me. Granny and Pops want a picture of all of us, including them. I'm happier every day than the day before because I am the daughter of Maggie and Silas Pennington. I love Daddy's mother and father, too. Yippee! I have grandparents who love me!

Sarah sketched Granny and Pops on this page, closed her journal, and tucked it into her pillowcase. She didn't write anything wrong or mean about anyone, but she felt the words she wrote and the sketches she drew were her secret storytelling to herself.

AFTER BREAKFAST, Sarah helped her mother clean up the dishes and store away the food. She asked, "Do you think Granny and Pops would like a sketch of themselves?"

"Oh, Sarah, what a lovely idea. Would you do black pencils or colored pencils?"

"I'd start with regular black pencil but then add some color. Maybe with watercolors, then highlighted and outlined with colored pencils."

"I think they'd like it a lot. Would you be willing to give it to them in the next few days?"

"No. I want to send it to them as a Christmas present."

"Great idea, honey. They will love it."

Sarah kissed Maggie's cheek and said, "Thanks, Momma," and ran out of the room and upstairs.

Maggie smiled, thinking of how much she loved Sarah and truly felt she was her daughter. Then she sighed, thinking of the hard times Sarah had gone through in her life and how resilient she seemed. "She's amazing, and I know good things are ahead for her."

Maggie dried her hands on a towel, checked that everything was put away, and took off her apron. She hung it on a hook by the pantry door and glanced over at the back wall and the penciled-in rectangle where a sink would be installed in a few weeks. She grinned and said, "I'm ready and a little jealous Aurora already has a sink installed at her house."

UPSTAIRS AT AURORA'S HOME, Jane was talking to her granddaughter as she changed the baby's wet diaper. When she finished, she picked up Okchuli from her crib. The baby giggled and gave her grandmother one of her open-mouth slobbery kisses. Jane laughed, "Gam needs to work on you having less slobber with your kisses, girly."

Okchuli laughed and said, "Gam!"

Johnathan poked his head in the nursery door and asked, "So, you're Gam now?"

"Yes, I am. What is your name, Granddaddy?"

Okchuli clapped her hands, said, "Dah!" and reached for Johnathan.

He smiled, took the baby in his arms, and said, "Dah will do just fine."

Jane chuckled and said, "Okchuli, you should kiss Dah."

Okchuli grabbed Tom's face and gave him one of her slobbery, open-mouth kisses. He laughed and kissed the baby's cheek. "Thanks, Okchuli."

She nodded and said, "Chuli!"

"Chuli it is."

Aurora stood in the doorway, watching her parents with her daughter. When her parents turned around, she laughed. "She has told me 'Chuli' is her name a few times."

"Go with the flow, darlin'," her father said. "Children know what they want, and letting them have things their way as often as possible gives them power or at least lets them test their power a bit."

"Thanks, Daddy. I appreciate the advice. I wonder when I'll quit needing your advice?"

"Long after, both your mother and I are in another dimension."

She hugged her father and mother and said, "Many years from now."

Aurora yawned and said, "Forgive me if I yawn a bit today. I was up from about midnight to four this morning delivering Jessica Riddle's baby boy."

Johnathan asked, "Did you go alone?"

"Yes, just like always."

"With all the hoorah from Lester Blunt, I don't like you going anywhere alone, especially at night."

"Well, if I don't go alone, I must wake Clay and Okchuli too. We've talked about it a lot. Most of the time, it's either broad daylight or deep night. I think Lester Blunt is too lazy to get up in the middle of the night and harm me."

"I wonder if there's someone else to help?"

"I can't imagine who, Daddy. I can't just leave women alone in their time of need because I'm afraid."

"Are you afraid?" he asked.

"No, I'm not, but I do take care. I bring the shotgun with me and carry a lantern, too. Usually, when I go out at night, the husband or older child comes to get me."

"Do they take you back home?"

"Sometimes, especially if it is still dark."

Johnathan sighed. "I guess that's better than nothing."

Okchuli clapped her hands, said, "Momma," and smacked her lips.

Jane and Johnathan laughed, and Jane said, "I take it she's hungry."

"Yes, she is."

Johnathan said, "I'll leave you ladies to care for each other, and I'll go find Clay."

"He's outside getting things ready for us to go into town for the celebration."

"Then I need to be out there helping him." As he walked out of the house and to the barn, he muttered, "Maybe Conrad can help until something is done about Lester Blunt."

Jane watched her daughter sit in the rocking chair, snuggle her baby, and let her nurse. She said, "I love seeing you nursing Chuli."

"I love doing it, Momma."

ONCE BOTH FAMILIES loaded up children, grandparents, and picnic baskets for a late lunch, Silas told his father and mother, "I'm glad my parents are here to see our home and town."

His father, Tom, said, "Well, I came out to visit Jacob one time about ten years ago. He lived in the small cabin where Aurora and Clay now live."

"We'll have to go visit them before you leave," Maggie said, "It's not the same log cabin you remember."

Noah said, "I helped Clay build an upstairs inside the house for extra bedrooms."

"Really?"

"Yes, sir. He's teaching me about building."

"Do you like building?"

"I do. I like it a lot. I want to be a builder or maybe even learn how to draw up buildings for others to build."

Marietta, Silas's mother, said, "You know, we have a University close to where we live in South Carolina where they teach young men and women exactly what you're talking about. You could learn to be an architect."

"Does that mean drawing buildings to build?"

"Yes, it does."

Noah nodded. "So if I went to that school, could I return home when finished?"

"Certainly you could."

Maggie smiled. "You'll have to learn many things I teach you, Noah before they let you go to their university."

"I'll study extra hard, Momma."

"Especially math and geometry."

He was quiet for several seconds and said, "I'll work hard on math. I kind of like math. I don't know what geometry is, but I'll learn it."

Silas nodded and smiled. "I like how you think, Noah."

Noah grinned. "Thanks, Daddy."

Maggie said, "Geometry is the beginning of learning and understanding how to build things. It's all about the angles and how they work."

"Then I want to learn a lot of geometry, Momma."

"I'll teach you the rudiments, but I'll have to study up on anything more than simple geometry."

Tom said, "I'll send you some geometry books and see if I can find a fundamental architecture book."

Noah said, "Thanks, Pops! With those books, I'm sure Momma can teach me about them."

Maggie grinned. "Maybe. I'll have to learn and study, too."

Her mother said, "Won't hurt a thing. Perhaps even Silas could learn a thing or two."

Silas shook his head. "Now we're headed for trouble. Let's get loaded up and go to Tishomingo before I learn anything else."

Everyone laughed. Noah knew his father was teasing him, but he also knew his father had no intention of learning how to do anything other than writing, reading, or publishing. That was fine in Noah's mind. He loved to read but had no desire to write or publish anything. He was eager to learn more about building.

26

> *"I was born*
> *on the prairies where*
> *the wind blew free, and there*
> *was nothing to break the light of the sun.*
> *I was born where there were no enclosures."*
> Geronimo

When the two families in their wagons arrived in Tishomingo, Clay said, "My Lord, but this doesn't look like our sleepy little town."

Noah said, "Wow! There are hundreds and hundreds of people here, Papa."

"You're right, son. Folks are ready to celebrate."

Although the official celebration was scheduled for the evening, all the business folks in town had set out their wares in front of their buildings, ready to sell whatever they could on this special day. It wasn't every day there was the possibility of making a profit, even if only a few pennies.

People were everywhere, and there were few places where anyone could safely leave their buggies, buckboards, and horses. Silas motioned to Clay to follow him behind *Okchuli Press,* where they would park their wagons and horses. Once their wagons and horses were settled, Silas said, "Now, children, I want you to stick close to Momma or me. There are a lot of folks in town I don't know."

Noah said, "I'll help Momma and Papa."

"Good. We're counting on you, son."

Noah beamed a bit happy his mother and father trusted him to help with the younger children.

Sarah said, "I'm happy to help too, Noah."

"Good," he said, "Keeping Bea and Ben out of harm's way is a big chore."

She laughed and said, "Bea and I will be close together while you and Ben do the same."

Bea asked, "What about Teddy?"

"I think Momma can handle him all by herself."

The adults laughed but were glad the older children took pride in helping their younger siblings. Sarah was delighted to be a part of the family and no longer worried about what anyone in Tishomingo thought about her. She was beginning to know people differently because of helping her father at *Okchuli Press.*

She knew part of her no longer feeling out of place was thanks to Mrs. Rittenhouse. As folks came into the press shop to buy the *Weekly Beginnings*, they saw a different Sarah than the ragged, rough-spoken child of her birth parents. Folks saw a young lady who was loved and cherished by the Pennington family.

Silas said, "Let's go in through the press shop. I want to show our business to Granny, Pops, and Aurora's parents."

Silas's father said, "I'm looking forward to seeing how my investment is used."

"I think you'll be pleased," Silas told his father.

He showed everyone the press. His father had invested the money for the machine. Bea cocked her head back and forth and said, "It looks like a big black grasshopper, Papa."

Silas grinned, "You're right, Bea. Lots of folks call this particular press *The Grasshopper* just for that reason."

Both Thomas and Marietta walked around the big machine. When his mother started to touch it, he pulled her hand away from the machine. "Momma, you'll get ink all over your white gloves and dress if you aren't careful. Mrs. Rittenhouse, Sarah and I always wear leather gloves when working on the press."

His mother looked at her fingers and nodded. "I do have a little ink on my fingers." When she started to use her lace handkerchief to wipe off the ink, Sarah quickly handed her a shop rag and said, "Granny, you'll ruin your pretty hanky. Use this old rag."

Marietta smiled. "Thank you, Sarah, for looking out for me and my clothes."

"You're welcome, Granny."

Silas pointed to the front window and said, "I see Mrs. Rittenhouse outside with the table she and Sarah decided we should have.

Sarah nodded. "Daddy wasn't sure about having a table, but Mrs. Rittenhouse was sure, and I agreed with her. Of course, we should have a table and sell today's special newsletter."

Thomas patted Sarah on the shoulder and said, "I'm glad one of my grandchildren has the sense to know what her father needs to make a profit."

She blushed but felt pride welling up inside. She said, "Thanks, Pops. I like working with Daddy and helping him."

Silas nodded. "And she works hard and does a fine job."

Sarah beamed, then said, "I want to go see Mrs. Rittenhouse. She's set up the table outside. Come on, Bea. Let's go."

MRS. RITTENHOUSE SMILED as Sarah and Bea came out to the sidewalk. She'd taken Sarah under her wings and was working on being not only a good worker but a good young lady. She said, "Good morning, girls."

"Good morning, Mrs. Rittenhouse," Sarah said while holding Bea's hand.

Mrs. Rittenhouse beamed at Sarah's proper greeting. She said, "Good morning, Miss Sarah. I'm eager for the day."

She nodded and said, "Me too. I see you already have set up a table in front of *Okchuli Press.*"

"Yes, dear, I set out the past newsletters and the special one for this day."

Sarah nodded and pointed to a poster standing on the table. "I like the poster we made."

"I do, too. You did a fine job of doing the lettering and the bits of birds, flowers, and other nature, Sarah."

Sarah glowed and felt a little taller. "Thank you, Mrs. Rittenhouse.

The poster said: *Old newsletters are free for the taking. Today's special newsletter will cost you three pennies.*

Silas and the rest of the family joined Sarah and Bea. He said, "I don't remember talking about the special newsletter being three pennies instead of the usual one penny, Mrs. Rittenhouse."

"It's a special day, and people will talk about it for years, Mr. Pennington. They'll keep this newsletter as a keepsake, so they should cost more. However, for your parents, I suppose one penny will suffice."

Before Silas could say anything more, his father said, "Not on your life, Mrs. Rittenhouse. Three pennies is a bargain, regardless of whether it's a special day or an ordinary one. I want ten of them, if you please, Mrs. Rittenhouse. My friends in South Carolina will enjoy reading what you and my son have published."

She nodded, then counted out ten newsletters, handed them to Thomas Pennington, and held out her hand for thirty cents. "Remember, Mr. Pennington, this isn't the work of only your son and myself but also your granddaughter, Sarah. Her sketches are lovely and make our newsletter even more inviting."

He smiled, handed her exactly thirty cents, and said, "Thank you, Mrs. Rittenhouse. You're right about my granddaughter's skills. She creates lovely pictures to add to the newsletter. And you, dear lady, have done a fine job today, as I'm sure you do daily."

Sarah beamed, and Silas chuckled. He shook his head. "I'll leave the table with you, Mrs. Rittenhouse. It is obvious you have the right of things for today." He walked around the table and saw another poster. He grinned as he read the poster and said, "I can see you've outdone yourself, Mrs. Rittenhouse." He looked at Sarah and asked, "Did you have a hand in this?"

"Yes, I did, Daddy, but it was Mrs. Rittenhouse's idea. I agreed it was a perfect thing to do."

Maggie went to stand by her husband and laughed. "Mrs. Rittenhouse and Sarah, this is a grand idea."

The poster informed every passerby that they could have a colorized heavy card poster of the story of how Pennington Creek got its name for ten cents.

Sarah said, "Mrs. Rittenhouse and I printed off fifty posters. Then, I colored them with my pencils and watercolors. We figured selling only one would pay for the ink, cardstock, and printing."

Silas nodded and looked at his daughter. "I think it's a fine idea, ladies."

Sarah beamed at her father's approval and that he called her a lady. Moment by moment Sarah was feeling more like a Pennington and certainly more than nine years old. She even felt a little taller as she held her head high.

Silas asked Mrs. Rittenhouse, "Have you sold any posters?"

"Yes, sir. I've already sold four of them, so we've made our profit for the day."

He laughed and said, "Thank you, ladies, for your industrious and terrific ideas. Now, family, let's see the new building and the gardens surrounding the place."

Mrs. Rittenhouse said, "Mr. Pennington, the elder, allow me to keep your newsletters dry and wrinkle-free inside the store. You can pick them up on your way back to the younger Mr. Pennington's home."

"Thank you, dear lady. I also want one of those posters to take home."

Silas said, "This time, no charge if you please, Mrs. Rittenhouse."

"Of course, Mr. Pennington." She beamed as she watched the Harrison and Pennington families walk away to see the sights in town today.

Sarah turned around and waved to Mrs. Rittenhouse, who returned the wave. Mrs. Rittenhouse felt happier than she had in a long time. She muttered, "My goodness, I miss my dear departed husband, but I love my life now. Sarah is turning into a jewel of a woman." She turned back to the table to sell more newsletters and posters.

Thomas Pennington felt great pride in his son and his family's accomplishments. The sense of pride filled his heart more than even the possibility of making a profit on the press. It was more a matter of his son finding his feet in the world and creating a new life for himself and his family. In simple terms, he was delighted with his son and his son's family.

Johnathan Freeman felt relief that his daughter, Aurora, had found a man who loved and honored her and that she had chosen well the friends she'd made. Now, if the vile Lester Blunt would leave them alone, he felt strongly all would be right in their world. He crossed his fingers, hoping for them and the future.

All agreed that family and friends were the most crucial things in their lives.

THE DAY WAS A BIT CLOUDY, but the sun broke through between the clouds, making the day feel less like late autumn and more like spring. There was a gentle breeze now and again, yet considering today was November 17th, it was a perfect, warm day. Everyone wore light jackets, sweaters, or shawls, and the noise of people talking and laughing ebbed and flowed.

The new Chickasaw Capital Building gleamed with rosy warmth

as the sun graced the building on the highest hill in Tishomingo. It was the center of the small Indian Territory town.

The gardens surrounding the structure included several crepe myrtles that would bloom in the spring, a rose garden, and a holly hedge with red berries. Scattered around were various pine and cedar trees that, over the years, would grow tall and shelter the building. A large oak tree that the builders took care not to harm during the construction of the building took an honored place near the new and graceful structure. There was a park next to the new building where folks could sit at a table or spread their blankets on the lawn.

After touring the new building and seeing everything it had to offer, the Harrison and Pennington families found a space near the rose garden to sit on quilts and have their late lunch together.

Bea and Ben were chasing and racing while Noah and Sarah watched the young twins to be sure they were safe. None of the children noticed a quiet man standing nearby. When Aurora looked up and saw him, she smiled and waved for him to join them.

He nodded and came to stand by the group, and Jane stood and said, "Conrad, it's nice to see you."

Johnathan stood beside his wife and shook Conrad's hand. "I hope you are doing well, Conrad."

"I am doing very well and content with my life."

"That's more than many people ever have." Johnathan turned to Thomas and motioned him to join them. "Thomas, this is a dear friend of our family."

Thomas shook Conrad's hand and said, "It is a pleasure to meet you. Do you live around here?"

"Yes, a bit further north and west of your son's family home."

"I'm Jacob's older brother."

Conrad smiled. "I'm pleased to meet you. Jacob spoke of you and your family often. I'm glad your son has taken over the property Jacob built."

"I'm pleased he has done so and has started a fine publishing house."

Conrad said, "I bought one of the posters today about Pennington Creek. My guess is Jacob would have loved to have that poster."

"I'm sure you're right."

Johnathan said, "My daughter, Aurora, told the story just as it is on the poster."

"I remember her mother telling the story the same way when we were children. I hope Aurora and her family are doing well."

"They are, with the help of the Pennington family and others who watch out for her well-being."

"That's what friends are for, Johnathan."

"Indeed. Come and greet Aurora and her husband. Her baby is a sweet and beautiful girl."

Conrad smiled and followed Johnathan. He hadn't had the opportunity to greet his daughter, Okchuli, but would never ask to see her either. To do so might cause her and Aurora harm. Clay stood up as the men neared, and when introduced to Conrad, Clay said, "Silas told me how you helped him and his family make their way from the Mississippi River."

"Yes, and it was a blessing to get to know them."

"I heard that you and Aurora knew each other as children."

"Yes, we did. She has always been a good friend to me."

Clay nodded, "Come and see our daughter, Okchuli."

Conrad followed, nodded to the rest of the family, then squatted beside Aurora and said, "I've not met your daughter, my friend."

Aurora smiled and saw he was wearing his warrior face. She nodded and raised the baby to him, and said, "Tushka, this is Okchuli."

Okchuli grinned and kicked her feet. "Thank you for understanding, Aurora," Conrad said, taking the baby in his hands, "You are nearly as lovely as your mother, Okchuli."

She said, "Chuli!"

He laughed, and the baby reached for his face. He allowed her to kiss his cheek in her slobbery, open mouth way. He swallowed back tears and said, "Thank you, Chuli. I am glad you are awake. You are a baby any mother and father would be delighted to have."

Okchuli tugged on his braids, and he laughed, so she followed suit and laughed, too.

He kissed Okchuli's cheek, returned the baby to Aurora, and said, "You chose the perfect name for your baby. She is alive and well and awake, for which I am delighted. I wish you, your husband, and your baby many blessings."

"Thank you, Conrad. Your blessing is welcome. I appreciate everything you do to protect us."

He smiled and sighed. He held back tears and said, "It's the very least I can do, dear friend."

Clay watched the interchange and immediately saw something of Okchuli in Conrad, even though he had painted black stripes on his face. He would wait until later when Aurora could explain the paint to him. Of course, he could not be sure that Conrad was the baby's birth father; regardless, he would welcome him to their home.

A quick thought of knowing came to Clay's mind, and he knew what he must do for his daughter and wife and perhaps even for himself. He said, "Conrad, you will always be welcome in our home. Please visit any time you wish or need. We would honor your presence as a member of our family."

"Thank you, Clay. I appreciate your words and might sometime come to visit."

"Good." Again, Clay said, "We will always welcome you as family."

Conrad nodded, understanding Clay's intention. He smiled and said, "I must go about my way today. I hope you all have the blessings of the day and all the days of your lives."

Aurora nodded and said, "Blessings for your life, Conrad. Be safe."

"I will as the spirits wish," he said.

As he walked away, Sarah watched him and said, "I like Conrad. He's always been good to me."

Johnathan nodded. "He is a good man with demons inside his head occasionally."

Noah said, "I like him."
Clay nodded, "Me too."

27

"*Trouble follows sin
as surely as
fever follows chill.*"
Hopi Proverb

The following day, Aurora sat with her mother, Jane, Maggie, and Maggie's mother-in-law, Marietta, around Maggie's large table. She shrugged her shoulders and sighed. "Yesterday's celebrations at the opening and dedication of the Chickasaw Capital Building brought me joy but also left me feeling anxious and uncertain about life itself."

"What makes you uncertain, daughter?"

"Most of the previous afternoon and early evening were spectacular and happy events. I loved being with our two families. We all joined in celebrating the opening and dedication of The Chickasaw Capitol building. It is easily the most beautiful building in Tishomingo, Indian Territory, and may well be for years to come.

Still, I think it is mostly in vain for the Chickasaw. I have a feeling the white man will take over everything in our lives as soon as possible."

"I agree, daughter. You're right about the building. It is the center of the town. I know your thoughts are probably true. It will stand for the Chickasaw as long as our people live here, but I'm certain the white men will take it as their own."

Aurora nodded. "I believe you are right, Momma. However, it was a beautiful and joyful time yesterday. I'm so happy you, Daddy, and Silas's parents were here to rejoice and celebrate with us." She shrugged and said, "But now, the day after celebrating our people's great accomplishments, I feel lost and unsure for the first time in many months."

"I'm sorry, sweetie."

"Perhaps it is the culmination of events that seemed to pile up. I know this should be a time of rejoicing with all the Chickasaw."

Maggie nodded and held her friend's hand. "Maybe you're simply tired from all your work yesterday. Not only did you get your family rounded up to go into town for the celebration, but you also helped bring another baby into the world. I'm exhausted just thinking about all you've done in the past day or so."

Aurora pulled her handkerchief from the long sleeve of her dress and wiped a few tears from her eyes. "I'm certain it all is simply becoming a bit much."

Maggie chuckled. "You are right. It is all becoming a bit much. I'm exhausted from yesterday, too, and I didn't have to get up in the middle of the night to help bring a new life into the world."

"Hear, hear," Maggie's mother-in-law, Marietta, said. "I'm amazed at all you and Maggie do with your children and the farms. It makes me tired even to consider all you two do."

"I agree, Marietta," Aurora's mother, Jane, said. "I know I did all the things these two young women do at their age, but there is no way I could do it all now. I was exhausted by the time we left. I was glad we didn't stay for the fancy dinner and dancing."

Maggie nodded. "Me too! I was relieved when Teddy set up such a roaring fuss—at high pitch—to be fed we were given the grace to leave honorably."

Jane chuckled. "I think all the children were restless and overwhelmed with the endless falderol. I know I was."

Aurora nodded. "And I, too, was fed up with it. All the glittering paper lanterns, nearly royal promenades, and speeches—most of them given by white men who married or wanted to marry Chickasaw women—all of it went on far too long. And we didn't even get to the fancy food or dancing!"

Marietta said, "I did notice the men and wondered why so many white men chose to marry Chickasaw women."

Jane nodded. "According to our laws, a white man becomes Chickasaw with marriage and is given his fair allotment of land."

"That explains a lot," Marietta said. "Even the sainted William Henry Murray had a lot of nice things to say about the Chickasaw."

Aroura snorted, "He was nothing more than an impoverished Texas lawyer and school teacher until he showed up here in Tishomingo—a mere few months ago. He was so poor he couldn't pay the coach driver for his ride from Ardmore."

Maggie nodded. "Yes, he was stone-cold broke when he arrived here in Tishomingo. However, we should not be surprised that he is climbing the biggest ladder in the area. Governor Johnston, uncle to Mary Alice Hearrell, depends heavily on Mr. Murray and his skills in politics, writing, and making speeches. I heard William Murray will ask Mary Alice Hearrell to be his wife soon. Climbing that ladder might well help solidify his fortunes."

Jane nodded. "Yes, I'd heard that too. She is a full-blood Chickasaw with her allotment of land—land white men want. I'm sure she'll marry him, even though other white men are keeping an eye on her should she demur."

Marietta nodded. "And well, they should! She is lovely and well educated."

Aurora said, "Yes, she is, but Mr. Murray is a man who knows how to speachify at a moment's notice and could make a hen shake off her tail feathers if he'd ask her to."

Maggie laughed at her friend's vision, but Aurora continued in high dudgeon. "I could see Mary Alice's glittering eyes watching him across the room. His words seemed to be magic for her. It didn't hurt that he glanced at her primarily throughout the speech. And that soft, sweet smile he afforded her made my eyes roll. Yet, he can bring tears of joy or sorrow from his lips quicker than a bee can sting."

Maggie smiled and asked, "Do you think he is a good man?"

"It's too soon to tell, but I'm certain he isn't the worst. Some of the worst are full-blood Chickasaw." She sighed and shook her head. "Sometimes it all feels hopeless."

"What feels hopeless?" Jane asked.

"Humanity, I suppose."

Maggie smiled. "Ah, the way you talk, Aurora. Your command of the English language is remarkable, and not because you are a native. I'm certain it is because you are brilliant."

"I wish it were true, but thank you, Maggie. I was at Bloomfield Academy when Mary Alice Hearrell was there. We were classmates, although not close friends. Even among the Chickasaw, there is a hierarchy. She is far more brilliant than people give her credit for, and I wish I had her brain. Socially though, I am a half-breed to most folks minds—I'm far outside the scope of her society."

Jane sighed and shook her head. "I worry about her and other white men. Some of them are honorable, and some are scoundrels."

The women were quiet for a bit until Aurora sighed. She looked down at her hands and then at Okchuli sleeping nearby on a quilt next to Teddy. Their hands were touching.

Jane smiled and said, "The babies seem to be close friends already."

"Yes, they are," Maggie said. "I count it a great gift. They seem to be bonded in some way."

Aurora lifted her head, turned to her mother, and said, "Can I ask you a serious question, Momma?"

"Of course you can. What is bothering you?"

"Well, it isn't about yesterday's new building or big party. It's deeply personal. It's about Conrad."

Jane swallowed. She thought she knew what her daughter was going to ask. "What do you need to know about Conrad?"

"When he held Okchuli yesterday, I had a distinct feeling, maybe even a knowing, that he is her biological father."

Jane nodded. "I had the same feeling too. Okchuli's eyes are exactly like Conrad's except for their color, and so are her ears."

Maggie furrowed her brow and asked, "Her ears?"

"Yes," Jane touched her left ear and said, "She has a little crease on her left earlobe, just as Conrad has, and a bit of a point at the top of each ear, just as Conrad has."

Marietta said, "I'm not sure what you are talking about. I thought Okchuli was the product of yours and Clay's marriage bed."

"That is exactly what I want everyone to believe," Aurora said. "The reality is she was left on our porch, in a lidded basket, with her cord and placenta still attached and not tied off. Nor was the blood of her mother washed off. She was blue and barely breathing. I had to tie off her cord to avoid blood loss. Then, I massaged her and warmed her up to get her to breathe correctly. It's why we named her Okchuli, which means awake."

"Oh, my dear. I don't know what to say other than I think she is your child and was meant to be with you."

Aurora smiled at Maggie's mother-in-law. "I thank you for your kindness, Marietta. We know how blessed we are. Until recently, I thought I could not bear a child of my own. Now I have a beautiful, lovely daughter, and the possibility of being fertile may be in my future."

"Then you are doubly blessed. The awakening may have been Okchuli, but perhaps it was also your womb. Without Okchuli, you might never have any other possibility."

Aurora reached out and touched Marietta's hand. "Thank you for the blessing you've given me. I agree."

"You are welcome, my dear. Don't fret over Conrad. I did not feel he wished anything but blessings for you, your daughter, and your husband. He sees you as a bonded family and perhaps even part of your family."

Aurora nodded, and Maggie said, "Now that we've settled what a fine couple Aurora and Clay are with their darling baby Okchuli, let's not worry about Conrad. He seems to be a fine man who can care for himself." She waggled her eyebrows, grinned, and said, "Mary Alice may be a different story."

Jane laughed, and the other women followed suit. Jane said, "I hope Mary Alice's future is at least half as bright as yours, Aurora. If she marries Mr. Murray, as I'm sure she will, I'm certain she can stand up to him when she wishes to. The wishing, you see, is the courage and power of the Chickasaw women. We make a wish, work hard toward that wish, and our wishes come true."

Maggie nodded. "I think that is true of all women, but why, oh why, would a beautiful, accomplished woman like Mary Alice Harrell want to hand her wishes to a banty rooster like Willam H. Murray of Toadsuck, Texas no less?"

The women howled with laughter enough that both Teddy and Okchuli woke and cried for their mothers to soothe them with their breasts.

Jane sat back and watched the two young women nursing their babies. When she turned to Marietta and tilted her head, Marietta smiled and nodded. She said, "I'd like to go for a walk with Jane while you ladies tend your babies."

"That's fine," Maggie said. "Hopefully, the men will be back to milk the cow and bring in the eggs."

Her mother-in-law laughed. "Hope springs eternal, dear girl."

Maggie smiled and turned back to the baby in her arms.

28

Marietta and Jane walked side-by-side on the calm, sunny day along Pennington Creek. The children playing on the porch wanted to go with them, but Marietta said, "Jane and I are just becoming friends and want a little time with just the two of us."

Bea nodded. "Sometimes Momma and Aurora want to be just the two of them."

Marietta smiled and said, "Then you understand."

"Yep."

Sarah said, "Why don't you take the hoe—just in case? On a sunny day like this, the snakes might be out."

Marietta didn't know what to say, but Jane said, "Thank you for thinking of us, Sarah."

Sarah handed her the hoe that always stood by the door and said, "Remember, don't think about killing the snake. Just whack his head off. The dying will take care of itself."

Jane chuckled. "It's been a while, but I do remember. Thanks for the reminder."

Sarah nodded and turned back to her sister and brothers. They were playing tic-tac-toe with their chalk and slates. Sometimes, she let Bea win, but it was tough getting Bea to think about what her next mark should be.

As the two women walked away from the house and down to the creek, Marietta said, "I've been living in a city so long that I don't think about nature. I assume my rose garden is a benevolent place."

"Maybe for the roses, but the worms think the robins are violent creatures, and the bee thinks the rose is only there for its succulent liquid, while the rose cares nothing about the bee other than spreading its pollen."

Marietta laughed. "To everything under the sun, there is a time, a place, and a way of being."

"Exactly so. Now that I live in Tulsa, a big city, I find myself less and less able to handle the rawness of nature. Watching Aurora and Maggie reminds me of Our Mother."

Marietta shook her head. "Our Mother? I thought you were Aurora's mother."

Jane laughed. "I am, but I am also a daughter of the mother of us all—Mother Earth."

"Ah. Now I understand your words. I grew up the child of a rich father and mother surrounded by servants. I can hardly cook a meal anymore and was never very good at it when I tried. I watch Maggie and Aurora quietly get on with things and make marvelous meals with only a fireplace."

Jane nodded. "I have a big, fancy wood stove, hot and cold running water, a bathroom, and a kitchen. Yet, in my neighborhood, my life is nearly ancient compared to the folks with gas stoves and ovens, gas lights, and iceboxes with ice delivered daily."

Marietta said, "I no longer even try to cook. I have servants who do all of that, but we, too, have iceboxes with daily ice delivery. I think our stoves are gas, but if not, they are wood—and large. Some say that soon, there will be electric stoves, ovens, and refrigerators instead of ice boxes. Soon, cooking on an open fireplace will be for a time long gone. We have gas lights in the main rooms and a telephone in the house."

Jane nodded. "I don't have a telephone in the house, but they are running lines to have them in all the homes in Tulsa. We can always go to the post office and use the telephone for a penny per call. They are talking about building payphone boxes, but the call will cost a nickel. I suppose someone will make a profit off the call boxes."

"Certainly they will. We have those in Columbia, South Carolina. I've never used one since we have a personal phone. I've no idea how much it costs to use the call box phone, though, or even our household phone." Marietta shook her head. "I suppose I seem silly to you. I don't even know how much money I spend weekly on groceries. My husband has an accountant who does all of that."

Jane tucked her hand through Marietta's arm. "I don't think you are silly. You are a kind and generous woman. I know your husband can give you luxury, which is fine, but the most important thing about you is that you are a good and kind woman and a good mother. Silas is a good man. Your tutelage of him shines through."

Marietta patted Jane's hand. "Thank you, Jane. Watching our daughters make something out of nearly nothing is a blessing. I'm proud of both Aurora and Maggie and what fine mothers and women they are."

Jane stopped, pulled Marietta closer, and whispered, "Be still." She raised the hoe and whacked off the head of a rattlesnake poised to strike.

Marietta stood with her mouth open, then smiled and said, "Impressive. Sarah was right to hand you that hoe."

"You could have done the same."

"Not without practice. I'd probably hack off my foot if I were given a hoe. What do we do with the snake?"

"This," Jane said, and using the hoe, she tossed the snake's head and body into the waters of Pennington Creek. Then, she said, "The turtles and fish will have a high old time for lunch today."

Marietta laughed. "It's a turtle-eat-snake world around here."

"Yes, and sometimes the other way around, but usually only if a baby turtle or turtle egg is there to be eaten by a snake."

"You're kidding? What about their shells?"

"Snakes around here cannot eat adult turtles, but they can and will eat newly hatched turtles or turtle eggs. Snakes prefer softer things like salamanders, fish, frogs, insects, birds, and their eggs, rabbits, or squirrels."

"So only smaller animals—not humans."

Jane laughed. "They can kill humans with their bite but can't eat them because we are too big. Whatever they can swallow, they can and will eat."

Marietta chuckled. "Sounds like some men I know."

Jane laughed, and they continued walking and talking about their lives and children. On the way back to Silas and Maggie Pennington's home, Marietta asked, "Is Conrad a good man? He looked like a warrior yesterday."

Jane said, "Yes, he did, and he is a warrior in many ways. However, he is a good man. He is a shy man but, at times, needs to be alone. He prefers being alone and rarely wants to be with others. He is a distant relation to our family and both he and Aurora have been friends for their whole lives. He has preferred being alone since late childhood. He will help anyone who needs help but is not a social creature."

"What about Okchuli?"

"I am certain Conrad is the birth father of Okchuli. I am also certain he doesn't wish to interfere with my daughter's family. Clay is my granddaughter's father. It is rather like Sarah being a Pennington and is daughter to Silas and Maggie."

"That's a relief for you, I'm sure. Clay and Aurora seem totally in love with their daughter. Now, tell me about this man, Lester Blunt."

"Never has there been a worse example of the creator's hand. He is vile, and when he gets an idea about anyone, he never lets it go. I am worried about my daughter and her family."

"Is there nothing that can be done about him?"

"He was in jail for six months after he tried to burn down Silas and Maggie's home. He's been out of jail for a few weeks."

"Why didn't I know about that?"

"I've no idea, Marietta, but my best guess is that Silas didn't wish to worry you. However, Noah was the hero that night."

"Noah? How so?"

"He got his father's shotgun, put one shell in the chamber, and when Blunt was ready to shoot Silas, Noah blew a hole in the ground right in front of Lester Blunt's foot. Apparently, Noah said, "Oops, Mr. Blunt. I'm sorry. I meant to hit your head. I'll give it another try." The boy cocked the shotgun, and Blunt quickly took off."

Marietta laughed loud and long. When she could stop laughing, she said, "I shouldn't laugh, but that is a fine tale. I adore my grandchildren, but Noah is special to me."

"I can understand your feelings. He is smart, kind, and ready to do what needs to be done at a moment's notice. He has a strong affinity to protect those he loves."

"I agree. Thanks, Jane, for the story. But why is Mr. Blunt so dead set against Aurora?"

"I'm not sure, but I believe it is because he was one of the men who raped and beat Aurora."

Marietta asked, "Does Aurora know who did it?"

"No, they followed her home one night after she'd gone to deliver a baby. I was already at another woman's home doing the same, so she had to go. When she was close to home, several men grabbed her, blindfolded her, stuck a rag in her mouth, and began to rape and beat her."

"Does she have no idea who did this to her?"

"Only that she was certain it was older men, and they smelled of whiskey and tobacco. Because of the blindfold, she couldn't be sure whether or not they were white men, Chickasaw men, or of other color."

Marietta shook her head. "It could have been anyone. They could have killed her."

"Yes, they could. I worry it is because I fell in love with Johnathan many years earlier and wouldn't go out with Lester. From the time I started going out with Johnathan, Lester raved about John not being a real human because he is part African and part Chickasaw. When Aurora was born, Lester called her a half-breed and nigger injun kid."

"That's awful, Jane."

"Yes, it is, but Aurora said at one point one of the men said, 'Let's kill this nigger injun,' but another man said, 'Leave her be. She'll die on her own soon enough.'"

"How did she get home to you?"

"She crawled and almost made it home before she passed out. When I came home, the sun was beginning to rise, and I saw my daughter bleeding and unconscious on the ground in front of our home. I screamed, waking Johnathan, who came racing out in his underwear. We gathered up our daughter and brought her into the house. I did everything I could think of to heal her while Johnathan raced into town to get the doctor."

"But she lived."

"Barely," Jane said. "The doctor sewed up lacerations in her vagina and cervix and recommended I give her herbs to keep her from having monthly bleeding so her uterus could heal. It was two days later when she finally woke and immediately started weeping."

"How awful for you all. So you think Blunt was one of the men?"

"Yes, I do. If I could figure out how to kill him and not get hung, I'd do it in a heartbeat."

Marietta looked across the creek and asked, "Why are crow feathers tied in the branches?"

"I think it is Conrad's doing to help protect Aurora and her family."

"I hope that helps."

"Hope is slim when evil is afoot," Jane said.

Marietta shuddered and nodded. "Let's go home. I need to be with my grandchildren."

"Me too."

29

*"Deeds speak louder
than words."*
Assiniboine Proverb

Adella Rittenhouse was busy cleaning the printing press with Silas while Silas's father watched the two people work. He smiled and said, "Thank you, son, for letting me watch you work on your printing machine. I'm impressed with what you've done."

"I'm glad you were here to see it in action, Dad. After all, this printing press was your idea, and you've funded the endeavor."

"Yes, and I'm glad I thought of it. At this rate, you'll have your portion of the press paid off by next year."

Silas wiped his hands and said, "I'm hoping even sooner." He turned to Adella and said, "I think we're finished cleaning the press, Mrs. Rittenhouse."

She nodded. "We printed a hundred more than usual for this

week since all the newsletters we printed were sold out yesterday for the celebration."

"Fingers crossed we sell them all."

Mrs. Rittenhouse said, "Don't be a worry wart, Mr. Pennington. I'm confident we will sell out the *Weekly Beginning* and maybe have some sales of the posters, too. We sold all the colored posters with the story of how Pennington Creek got its name and have requests for more than fifty more."

"I know, and we'll get those printed tomorrow. I'll see if Sarah will come in tomorrow and do the color work."

"I'm sure she will. She is a fine artist. You and Mrs. Pennington should be proud of her."

"We are, indeed. She is a fine artist and a kind and loving daughter and sister."

Thomas Pennington nodded. "I'm very pleased with your family, son. Your children are delightful, and Sarah seems to have fit right in and very quickly."

"Yes, she did, Dad. I think she'd never been given love in any form, so she worked hard to acclimate to a loving family and home. We love her as if she'd always been our child."

"I'd glad, son."

Adella said, "I firmly believe that any child, given enough love and tutoring about life, can grow up to become a fine adult."

The little brass bell over the door tinkled, alerting them to a possible customer. When Silas saw it was Lester Blunt, he sighed heavily and shook his head. He wiped the ink off his hands and went to the front of the store. He said, "Lester, I'm surprised to see you in my establishment."

Lester puffed on his cigar and blew a big cloud of smoke directly in Silas's face, who didn't acknowledge Blunt's attempt at being rude. Thomas Pennington stood beside his son and said, "Son, I'm surprised you let anyone smoke in this building. Between the ink, alcohol, and paper, plus being a wooden structure, it is ripe for burning the place down."

"Aww, don't go on so, old man," Lester said. "I won't be but a few minutes." He turned to Silas, held out his hand, and said, "What say we let bygones be bygones."

Silas ignored Lester's hand and said, "Certainly, Lester. As soon as you're gone, I'll be happy to say goodbye—begone—to your sorry ass."

Thomas jerked his head to look at his son. He was about to speak when Adella walked to them and stood beside Silas with her broom. She said, "Mr. Blunt, please take your cigar outside. You know the rules here in our establishment. You can see the *No Smoking* signs on every wall, the window, and the door. Of course, I'm assuming you can read. If that isn't the case, I'll happily read the signs to you."

Lester scowled but took the cigar out of his mouth, dropped it on the floor, and put out the smoking cigar with his foot, grinding it into the oak floor.

Adella came toward him with her broom, and he stepped aside quickly. She glared at him, then swept the still-smoking cigar to the door, out on the boardwalk, and then onto the dirt road. She stood with the door open and her broom in her hand. "I'll stand here until the stench is completely out of our establishment, Mr. Pennington."

Silas nodded, and the elder, Mr. Pennington, smiled. Lester reddened, turned back to Silas, and said, "As you know, I own the two buildings on either side of your establishment."

"Yes, I do, and I wondered why they were sitting empty."

"Well, that's what I wanted to talk with you about. I'm thinking of selling them and relocating my endeavors closer to the new injun building."

"How much?"

"Probably more than you can afford, being the loser you are."

Silas ignored the taunt and turned to Adella. "Mrs. Rittenhouse, will you please see if Mr. Murray has a few moments to spare?"

"Yes, sir. I'll be right back."

She quickly left, and Lester grinned as soon as the door closed. "I guess you don't have enough money to buy your next suit of clothes, but I'm willing to sell it to you and carry the note—as a loan, you understand."

"I understand about loans, Lester. I'm not a big fan of loans. How much for both buildings? They are sitting empty with no sign of becoming used soon."

Lester grinned and scratched his head. "Well, now, I'm not sure. Your Uncle Jacob was a friend of mine..."

Before he could finish the statement, Silas said, "My Uncle Jacob was an honorable man. I can't see him spending a moment with you unless he was forced to."

Lester chuckled and shook his head. "If I didn't want the cash to start at a more amenable place, I'd be happy to wipe the floor with you, Silas Pennington."

Silas felt his father stiffen at the crude behavior and talk of Lester Blunt. He touched his father's arm to remain still, but before he could say anything, Mrs. Rittenhouse entered through the back door with Mr. William H. Murray, Lawyer in tow. Both she and Mr. Murray heard the threat made against Silas.

"Good day, gentlemen," Mr. Murray said.

Both Silas and his father turned to Mr. Murray. Silas smiled and motioned for Mr. Murray to come forward. Mr. Murray nodded, stepped from behind the printing press, and said, "Mr. Silas Pennington, I'm at your service, sir."

"Thank you, Mr. Murray. I was wondering if you could draw up a bill of sale for me."

"Certainly. Who is selling what to whom?"

"Mr. Blunt, our eloquent guest here, wants to sell the two buildings on either side of my own. He hasn't named a price yet, but when he does, I want to buy his buildings."

Mr. Murray brushed his long, wooly mustache with his fingers, walked to Mr. Blunt, and asked, "What's your asking price, sir?"

"I haven't decided."

"Do you know it is against the law to talk about selling something without giving a price, Mr. Blunt?"

"I did not know that."

"So, Mr. Blunt, before we go further, do you intend to sell the buildings as mentioned earlier?"

"Yes, sir, I do."

"What is your selling price for both buildings."

"Two hundred dollars—each."

Mr. Murray snorted and shook his head. "That is more than two times what the buildings are worth, sir." He turned to Silas and asked, "Do you have cash to buy these buildings?"

Silas nodded and said, "It depends on whether we can agree on a rational amount of money for the sale. I don't want to cheat anyone, nor do I intend to be cheated."

Mr. Murray nodded. "I agree, Mr. Pennington." He turned to Mr. Blunt and said, "Unless you're willing to offer these buildings for sale at a rational price, we've nothing else to discuss."

Lester reached out and touched William Murray's arm. Murray scowled at Lester, who quickly removed his hand. He said, "Now hold on, Mr. Murray. I haven't said I won't come down in price."

"I'm a busy man, Mr. Blunt. Give us a rational price for the buildings, one more time and one more time only. Otherwise, I suggest you leave this establishment."

Thomas Pennington enjoyed the confrontation but took care not to show his glee. He was certain Mr. Blunt had met his match with his son Silas and Mr. Murray and was eager to see how it all played out. He worked hard not to grin with glee.

Blunt swallowed and said, "I misspoke before. I am asking for two hundred dollars for both buildings, meaning one hundred dollars each." Mr. Murray started to speak, but Lester Blunt held up a hand and continued. "I know that is a high amount, but I think all these buildings will be worth more within a few years."

"Then why are you thinking of selling the buildings?"

"I have plans to build another, nicer building for myself, closer to the new Chickasaw Capital Building."

Mr. Murray nodded and said, "Mr. Pennington, if you have a piece of paper I can write on, I'll fill out the bill of sale of these two buildings. We'll have to go to the Capital Building to get the deeds. You must have the money in hand at that time."

"I can have the money in an hour or less."

"That will be fine. Regardless, once I write the paperwork and you and Mr. Blunt sign it, this bill of sale will be legal and binding on all parties."

"I understand," Silas said.

"And you, Mr. Blunt, do you understand?"

"Yes, I do. Please proceed."

Adella said, "Mr. Murray, we have fine writing paper in Mr. Pennington's office."

"Thank you, Mrs. Rittenhouse. Gentlemen, let's go to Mr. Pennington's office."

Adella noticed Blunt was sweating and kept running his finger around the neck of his shirt collar. She smiled and thought *It's high time you felt the heat, Mr. Blunt.*

Once Mr. Murray, Silas, and Lester Blunt were in Silas's office, Thomas Pennington, in a quiet voice, asked, "Do you know where the money is, Mrs. Rittenhouse?"

She nodded. "If you'll follow me, we can get it right now."

She locked the shop's front door and motioned for him to follow her. She poked her head in the office door and said, "I'll be back soon, Mr. Pennington. Your father is escorting me to the dry goods store for some needed items."

Silas nodded. "Thank you, Mrs. Rittenhouse. We'll be here waiting for you."

Once Adella and Thomas were outside, she said, "Follow me, Mr. Pennington. Your son wanted to have money close on hand for needed purchases. Ink and paper can be costly. We buy both in bulk to keep the costs down, so we keep a few hundred dollars on hand for that need. Of course, we'd never leave much money in the store or my home upstairs. There's no need to make things easy for a thief."

Thomas chuckled. "I knew you two had something in mind."

"Yes, and I, for one, am glad. Mr. Pennington and I have discussed the two empty buildings, and your son would have offered to buy them soon. We have discussed some ideas about the possibilities for those buildings."

"Such as?"

"A nice place to sit and eat breakfast and lunch for one. For the other, my heart desires a library and bookstore in our town."

"I love both ideas and would like to help in those endeavors."

"That will be something you'll want to discuss with your son. Now, follow me."

They walked over to the horse shed behind *Okchuli Press*. She walked into the shed, petted both horses and gave each a scoop of oats in their troughs. She pulled a rug from the edge of the trough and placed it on the ground between the horses. She lifted a piece of wood between the two troughs, lifted the pile of hay out of the way, and pulled out a leather bag filled with money. She stood up and said, "This, Mr. Pennington, is the cash on hand for the business."

"You just leave it out here with the horses?"

"Yes, sir. Most folks don't bother to look where the animals spend their time. I believe you might find money under some of the hens at your son's home, and the outhouse is a good place, too. I always preferred using the compost bed."

He laughed and said, "I'll keep this story quiet, but I'm impressed with my son and you too."

"Oh, it wasn't his idea. Since I no longer have a standing home but live above the print shop, I'd forgotten about the compost bed and outhouse. That was Maggie's idea. She says not only do men underestimate women, but they underestimate the places and sources of work women have. My mother kept her extra money under the slate slab in her cold well—even my father had no idea."

"I knew my son married well, but I didn't understand how well."

"Indeed he did. I think Mrs. Pennington is a brilliant and kind woman. It's an honor to know her. Let me put the hay and lid back on and the rug, too, then we'll walk back into the office."

They walked back into the printing office just as the men had finished writing the bill of sale. Mr. Murray pulled out his pocket watch and said, "If we go to the Capital building right now, we can have this sale done and dusted before the close of the day."

Mrs. Rittenhouse handed the bag of money to Mr. Pennington

and said, "Don't spend it all in one place, young man. We have a business to run, you know."

Silas grinned and nodded. "Yes, ma'am."

"I'll finish tidying up around here and be available should you need me later."

"Thank you, Mrs. Rittenhouse. We'll not be long."

"Good."

Lester Blunt said, "I sure as shootin' wouldn't let anyone talk to me that way, especially a woman."

Thomas said, "Mr. Blunt, the fault is in you, not Mrs. Rittenhouse."

Blunt shook his head. "Like son, like father."

"And with good reason," Mr. Murray said. "Come fellows, let's finish this sale. Mr. Blunt, I'll take the keys to both buildings now if you please."

"Why?"

"Because I want no fuss at the Capital building, and I don't trust you further than I can spit."

"My guess is you can't spit far with that silly-assed mustache."

Mr. Murray grinned and said, "Exactly, Mr. Blunt."

30

"The one who
tells the stories, rules
the world."
Hopi Proverb

Once the sale of the two buildings was completed and Mr. Murray paid for his legal services, Mrs. Rittenhouse said, "I want to open your new buildings, Mr. Pennington."

"As do I. Which one first?"

"I think they are both about the same size and building inside. The one on the west side doesn't have much by way of shelving."

"Then let's open the one on the west side first." Mrs. Rittenhouse, along with Silas and his father, went to the building, pulled out the key, and Silas opened the door. They walked in and looked around.

Adella said, "Well, it's exactly how I remember it."

"Were you thinking of using this building as the library?"

"No, the other building already has lots of shelves. I thought you could get Mr. Harrison to wall off an area in the back of this space for cooking and cleaning dishes."

"I think I heard my name!"

Adella and Silas turned to see Clay Harrison standing at the open door.

Silas smiled. "You arrived just in time for our purposes."

"And what might that be?"

"Well, I've bought this building and the one on the other side of *Okchuli Press*."

Clay nodded. "What are you going to do with this one?"

Silas said, "Mrs. Rittenhouse has some ideas for both spaces. Go ahead with your ideas, Adella."

Thomas watched all the interchanges, and for the first time in his life, he felt his son was at least a bit smarter than himself. The idea of listening to a woman's thoughts about empty spaces would never have occurred to him. But, then again, neither would it have occurred to him to hide money in feed boxes by the horses or in the compost heap. He was eager to hear more about his son and Mrs. Rittenhouses's ideas.

She turned to Clay and said, "Well, this used to be a bar of sorts, and I use the term loosely. You can see a few tables with chairs that are in pretty poor shape. The bar and mirror on the west side seem to be in good shape but dirty."

Clay asked, "Were you planning to open a saloon, Mrs. Rittenhouse?"

She slapped his arm. "I most certainly not! I thought of blocking off the back half, setting up a bakery and cooking area, and offering breakfast and lunch for a reasonable price."

"What would you do with the bar and mirror?"

"I'd have baked items, such as pies, breads, cookies, and such, available for sale for folks to take home to their tables. Rather than alcohol splashed on the bar, we'd have food people could use on the bar."

Clay nodded and counted the number of tables and chairs. "You have ten tables and thirty-five chairs plus eight stools at the counter.

If I could make a suggestion?"

"I'm all ears, Mr. Harrison."

He grinned. "If you put the baked goods on the counter behind the bar and kept the stools and bar as they are, you'd have room for eight more single customers. Many men, especially single men, are used to eating alone and will be more comfortable eating a fine home-cooked breakfast or lunch at the bar. You'd still have baked goods for folks to take home, too."

Adella smiled and nodded. "I like the way you think, Mr. Harrison."

"Thank you, Mrs. Rittenhouse."

"Please call me Adella, Mr. Harrison."

"Only if you call me Clay."

She nodded, and then Clay looked at Silas and said, "You will want to have running water, sinks, and shelves for the cutlery and dishes, pots, and pans."

"I agree. Let's get Oscar Cassidy to do all the plumbing, including a water closet with a flush toilet. When can you get started?"

"Noah and I have finished the smokehouse, so I'm available whenever—at least until a sow with a full belly of piglets comes along just waiting to have her babies."

"Good. Do you think Noah is ready to ride into town alone?"

"As long as he feels ready, I think he is ready. But, I'm happy to bring him in after lunch."

Adella said, "It's none of my business, but if Clay rode with Noah for a few days or weeks and maybe worked together here so he was comfortable in town, he could certainly ride the few miles from your home to here."

"I think you're right, Adella," Silas said, "In fact, I need to do the same thing with Sarah coming into town to work in the print shop."

Silas's father said, "You know I used to ride all over the place when I was Noah and Sarah's age. I'd be worried about them now that we live in a city."

Clay nodded. "I understand, Thomas, but I guess folks that like living in cities will want to be up in Oklahoma City, Tulsa, or Guthrie."

"I'm sure you're right, Clay. Now, son, why don't you and Adella show us the other building and what you have in mind."

Adella smiled. "If we can make a library in the other building, I'd be in hog heaven."

The three men laughed, and Silas said, "Then let's get at it."

IN THE SECOND BUILDING, Thomas saw exactly what Adella wanted to do with the revamping of the second building. There were many shelves in the building, and he could see in his mind books lined up, ready for someone to borrow and read. There were three small tables and a few wooden chairs.

Adella said, "I think it would be nice to have a few more comfortable chairs and low tables for those folks who want to sit and read at the library." She turned to Silas and said, "I also thought, Mr. Pennington, that since we're getting requests for printing books, we could sell them right from our store."

Silas nodded, and Clay said, "I think that's a fine idea, Adella. We could also have a doorway between the printing area and the library. I'd have a half door you could latch from the printing side to keep folks from getting too nosey."

Thomas nodded. "I like the way you and Adella think, Clay. Imagine buying a book from *Okchuli Press* and reading it in your library next door."

"Exactly, Mr. Pennington."

He looked at his son, "You'll have to hire more help, especially for the cafe you're talking about building."

"Yes, and there are a lot of good cooks around here."

Adella nodded. "I have many friends who are widows or women whose men have just up and left for greener pastures who would appreciate the possibilities of making a little money for themselves."

Clay said, "I think the library part of the endeavor can be ready in a week or so. Noah would love to be a part of it all."

Silas chuckled, "Yes, he would, but let's not bring in a big batch of books before we're ready to open the doors. I swear if he's not hammering, he's reading."

Thomas laughed. "And that, son, is grand."

"Yes, it is, Pops."

CLAY WALKED INTO HIS HOUSE, where his mother-in-law was finishing cooking and setting the table for dinner. "I saw Aurora and her father riding off toward town. Is everything all right?"

Jane nodded. "Yes. Aurora was called to a birthing, and Johnathan felt he should ride with her. It'll be dark when the baby is born in a few hours."

Clay nodded. "I've been thinking and worrying about her riding off on her own like that."

"You're right to be concerned. While working as a midwife, I always insisted that whoever came to me for help must ride with me from my home to theirs and back to my home."

"I wondered about that and even asked Aurora about it. She said she felt safe going on her own and wouldn't listen to my thoughts on the subject."

Jane shook her head. "She's always been headstrong and thought she was invincible."

"Even after being accosted?"

"Even then, or perhaps more so to prove herself. After she was brutalized, I worried that perhaps she had a death wish or didn't care if she died. But now, things are different. She has her child to care for."

"I agree."

Jane chuckled. "So does her father. Today, John told her, 'If you don't care enough about your well-being to be safe, you can't possibly be a good mother and wife.'"

Clay shook his head and whistled. "Those are strong words, Mom."

"Yes, but they are true. She must take care of herself first before taking care of anyone else."

"You're right, of course, and I should have put my foot down about it long ago."

"Yes, you should have, but now you have a golden opportunity to do so. Might I suggest something?"

"Please do!"

"The first time I went to see a woman who was pregnant, I told her I required a husband or older child to ride to our house to get me and ride with me to their home when she was ready to give birth. Then they would also ride back with me to my home once the baby was safely birthed."

"Sounds like a good idea."

"I also told them my fee for each visit was three cents, and the delivery cost was ten cents."

"Did they pay?"

"Mostly. Those who couldn't pay my charge almost always gave me eggs, butter, milk, or bacon. Some even gave me preserves and canned goods. Those things equal money I didn't have to spend, so it worked out fine."

Clay nodded. "Thanks for sharing all of that, Mom. I haven't pushed very hard on these things because Aurora has always seemed strong and sure of herself."

"Of course she is, and she'll always be so. Still, she has a greater responsibility to her children than any other mother's children now. I hope she remembers her primary duty as a mother."

A cry from upstairs stopped their chatter. He said, "I'll go upstairs, change Okchuli, and bring her down. Did Aurora leave some milk?"

"She did. John made a little wooden cup for Okchuli. We'll see if she can drink a little milk with the cup.

AFTER CLAY CHANGED the baby's clothes, he carried her downstairs, telling her about everything he'd done that day and how there would be a fine library and bookstore in Tishomingo where people could come and read and even borrow books. He said, "And your Uncle Silas is also going to print books, even for little girls."

Jane smiled. "Is that true, Clay?"

"Oh, yes. Sarah has the idea to break up the story of how Pennington Creek got its name into a children's book."

"Even with the hanging at the end?"

"Yep. I think she's planning to have Alonzo Pennington climb back up in the wagon and start singing and fiddling, and gradually, he will fade away except for the fiddling and singing."

"Oh, my! What a terrific story that will be."

"I agree. I have to say, meeting up with the Pennington family has been a real boon to my life. Everything in my life feels like a miracle, but we all have had to work hard."

"And that's the secret to getting miracles. Work hard and take good care of each other. Miracles abound."

Clay nodded. "Yes, ma'am. Now let's see how our baby does with drinking from a cup."

Okchuli grabbed for the cup and sipped and dribbled but got most of the milk in her tummy and not on it. When she finished, she held up the cup and said, "More."

Clay and Jane laughed, and Jane said, "Coming right up, my lady."

LESTER BLUNT WAS none too happy to see Clay, Silas, Mrs. Rittenhouse, and Silas's father poking around in what just a few hours ago were his buildings. He went to the local saloon, drank a few shots of Tennessee Whisky, and started bemoaning his sad life.

He told one fella, "That lawyer man tricked me."

"Well, it sounds like you still got a good deal. I wouldn't pay more than fifty dollars for both buildings."

"That's not the point. The point is that uppety Pennington clan has outdone me again."

Another man shook his head. "You should never have offered those buildings up for sale."

"I'll burn the whole damn town down before I'll let those folks get away with stealing from me."

Conrad heard what was being said and went to the sheriff's house. Within half an hour and a few more shots of whisky, Lester was in jail again on drunk and disorderly charges.

Conrad was a quiet man who seldom participated in the town of Tishomingo's life, but Lester Blunt was a problem—not only for the town but for him and his family. It didn't seem to Conrad that Blunt would ever learn any lessons that most folks took for granted. Something had to be done. Besides, his poor wife, Lenora, deserves a better life.

WELL, as we all know, things are coming to a boil, and something has to be done for the best of everyone. But who and how? For this night, things are fine, with Blunt snoring on the jailhouse floor, drooling out of the side of his mouth, and vomiting occasionally. He was happy enough with his dreams. He dreamed of gold and silver coins just out of his reach. Will his dreams come true?

31

Johnathan Freeman rode side-by-side with his daughter, Aurora. She smiled as the sun rose and began singing her birth song. Her father listened, and when she finished, he sang his birth song. As the sky brightened, Aurora asked her father, "Why do some Chickasaw have a birth song and others do not?"

"I do not know, daughter. I know many of us around here like having a birth song, sung only by themselves but given to us by our mothers."

"I like having a birth song. Momma named me Aurora because I was born as the sun was rising. She had read about a Roman goddess of that name and loved the name and the goddess. My birth song is one of gratitude to the Sun and Mother Earth."

"Your mother still reads the stories of different people's gods and goddesses. She is an amazing woman."

Aurora smiled. "I agree. What about your birth song, Papa?"

"My birth song is one of freedom and large rocks."

"Why?"

"I was born a freeman, and my mother loved the large rocks around here. My grandparents took the name Freeman after the war between the states. My grandfather fought with the Chickasaw at the Battle of Devil's Den. He died a few years after the war. My father married a Chickasaw woman, and he sang my birth song, the same song his father sang to him, with me every morning about how the rocks shelter the creek and protect those who lived nearby."

She nodded. "I wish I had known him, but knowing your mother was a blessing too."

"I miss her. I feel her presence here, surrounded by nature, strange boulders, and rocks. I hear her voice in the flowing water."

"I'm glad Papa. Do you like living in Tulsa?"

"Yes, I do, and your mother is happy there, which makes me happy."

"I am happy here."

"And for that, I am happy, too, daughter. There is a lot of happiness in all our lives."

They rode quietly for a few minutes, enjoying the beauty of the early morning. Mists hung in a few places close to the creeks and ponds. As the sun rose a bit higher birds were busy swooping and catching morning breakfast on the wing. A rabbit poked its head out of the ground and quickly ducked back in as Aurora and her father rode by. The chattering of squirrels in the trees let everyone know it was time to start the day.

John sighed and said, "I wish to ask a favor of you, Aurora."

"If it is in my power, I will do as you ask."

"I'm certain it is in your power, but your will is sometimes strong and hides your power."

She laughed. "You and Momma did not raise a kitten, Papa."

"Nor did we raise a silly woman, daughter."

"Papa! I am most certainly not a silly woman."

"Well, sometimes, your strong will overwhelms your good thinking. I am asking you not to leave your home alone after dark."

"But babies are born when they decide, not when the sun decides."

"I agree, but your mother never went out alone to birthing, especially at night. She required her patient's family to come for her and stay with her until she was back safely at home."

Aurora nodded. "I know, and I'll try to do better."

"Trying is inadequate now that you are a mother, Aurora. Since it seems you may bear more children, you must take care of yourself so you can take care of Okchuli and your other children as they come. Your children are the most important thing in your life. They depend on you for everything. Do you imagine Mother Earth and Father Sky would hear your song if you ignored danger?"

Aurora brushed away tears and said, "You are right, Papa. When I first started midwifing, I never went out alone."

"What changed, daughter?"

"When Clay asked me that, I said I didn't know."

"What is your answer now?"

"I hate the answer."

"Do you have an answer you love?"

"I would love to have all babies born in the daylight."

Her father chuckled.

She nodded and continued, "I understand nature does not work that way. Babies are born when it is their time—regardless of the sun, moon, or stars. I come when called to birth the baby and leave when it is settled at its mother's breast."

"That's as it should be, daughter. But why do you risk your life, the life your daughter needs, going out alone at night."

She stopped her horse, leaned over the horn of her saddle, and wept. Her father stayed on his horse and waited for her sorrow to be released. When she could calm herself, she said, "Before Okchuli, my life was no longer important."

"Not even for Clay?"

She shook her head. "I've betrayed him, Papa."

"How so?"

"By not caring enough for my life even though he loves me and would die for me."

"But you might have died on any night, daughter, alone. I believe you've put your life on the altar of *not worthy*. You've made yourself a sacrifice. Why would Clay or any man love such a woman?"

"I don't know. He is a better man than I am worth."

"That is not for you to decide. You are worth every star in the sky to him. He's asked you to let him go with you at night to birth babies. You've said no because you don't believe in your worthiness and the worthiness of your life. You sing your death song when you go out at night alone."

Aurora jerked her head up and shouted, "Papa! No!"

In a quiet voice, he answered, "Yes, daughter, you do, even if you do not use your voice. I love you. Your mother loves you. Clay loves you. Okchuli loves you, and all your friends love you. Please honor their love, my love, daughter, and do not ride out in the night alone singing your death song. Will you do that?"

She brushed away tears and nodded. She sat quietly in her saddle for several minutes, and her father quietly waited. When she could speak without tears, anger, or fear, she said, "Yes, Papa. I promise I will not go out again alone in the dark."

"Good. I'm hungry, and sure, your mother has cooked us something marvelous."

Aurora smiled and started riding, and her father followed, pleased with his daughter. In less than a minute, Clay came galloping toward them. She felt fear and anxiety, and when he was close to her, she asked, "What's wrong?"

He smiled. "Nothing now. I needed to see you in the morning sun."

"The sun is up, and I promise never to go out in the night alone again."

"That's good because I'd decided that if you did, I'd simply follow you no matter where you were headed."

"What about Okchuli?"

"I'll figure out how to bind her to me as you do. But, not understanding the ways of women and babies, I'd probably make a mess of it."

Aurora laughed. "Probably. I'll teach you the binding methods. For now, I'm hungry."

"Good. That's the other reason I came to find you. Your mother wouldn't let me eat until you were home. I'm getting fair famished."

Aurora laughed, as did her father, and they rode home together with the morning sun shining on their hearts.

LESTER BLUNT GROANED as he realized he'd missed another chance to destroy Aurora. He was beginning to wake up in the puddle of his vomit and drool in the Tishomingo jail. His head pounded, and when he tried to sit up, he vomited again. When he could sit up without vomiting, he muttered, "I'll kill that nigger injun if it's the last thing I do on Earth."

The jail deputy unlocked the cell door in a few minutes and handed Lester Blunt a bucket of water, old rags, and a scrub brush. "When you've got your puke cleaned up, let me know. If it's at least as clean as it was when you were tossed in here, you can go home."

"This is woman's work!"

"Not around here, it ain't. Around here, he who spews does the cleanin'. If I were you, I'd get started. We don't serve breakfast or lunch around here. If you're here at dinner time, we've got some gruel you might keep down."

Lester choked and heaved but didn't vomit this time.

The deputy chuckled and said, "Or maybe you'd prefer to simply clean up your mess and go home if your wife will have you."

"She'll do what I say."

"Well, that's right handy for you. You can leave as soon as you do what I say." The deputy turned and returned to the jail's front office, waiting for Lester Blunt to clean up his mess.

JANE HELPED Aurora clear the table, and Clay said, "If you're up for it, John, I'm going into town and getting started on Silas's next endeavor."

"What's his next endeavor?" Aurora asked.

"He's bought the buildings on each side of *Okchuli Press.*"

"That's a surprise."

"Yep. He'd talked about it a time or two, but it seems he made enough money with the folks in town buying his newsletters and posters to pay for the purchase. He and Adella have been discussing what they'd do if they had those buildings. Now they have them, and there's building to be done."

"I'm surprised Lester Blunt didn't try to hoodwink him."

"Oh, he did, but Mr. Murray made it clear the price of the buildings must be rational—at least, that's what Silas said."

"Good," Aurora said. "You and Papa go while I talk with Momma. We must prepare things for the weekend and start planning what we want to cook for Thanksgiving."

AS JOHN and Clay rode into town, Clay said, "I hope I was clear but not too rough about my feelings with Aurora riding out alone at night."

"No, son. You were right and willing to let yourself seem incompetent."

"Oh, I wasn't joshing about trying to figure out how to tie on that shawl the way Aurora does. I've watched and watched, and I get lost about the third tuck and wrap she does."

John laughed. "Well, lucky for you, you don't have to worry about that anymore."

"I'm especially relieved I don't have to worry about Aurora riding out alone at night. I think Lester Blunt is serious about doing her harm."

John shook his head. "I have never understood Lester Blunt. It seems he is getting more and more pigheaded and determined to cause harm."

"I agree. I don't wish him ill will, but I wish he'd leave my family alone. He's the only fly in the ointment of my life."

"Well, for today, let's let him be and hope for the best. Tell me about the plans for these two buildings."

"It is Mrs. Rittenhouse's idea. We will turn the building just west of the press into a cafe and bakery. There will be breakfast and lunch plus prepared foods like bread, pies, cakes, cookies, and such to buy and take home."

"That's a great idea. With so many folks moving in and many of them single men, they will probably make a short-run profit."

"I agree. The building on the east will be a bookshop and lending library."

John laughed. "I'm fairly sure that won't make much profit."

"I agree, but you never know. Besides, Silas and Mrs. Rittenhouse's newsletter, *Weekly Beginnings*, is a big hit. They sell almost every pamphlet they print. Folks like to have stories to read."

"I do, too. It helps to make the mundane and tedious bits of life seem much easier to bear."

"That's it exactly," Clay said, pointing down the street. Lester Blunt was smoking a cigar on the opposite side of the road and staring at the *Okchuli Press* building. "Now, speak of the devil—there he is."

John shuddered and said, "Let's ignore him and get on about working on Silas's and Mrs. Rittenhouse's dreams."

"Good idea."

32

———

*"When the fox
walks lame, the old
rabbit jumps."*
Oklahoma Proverb

Conrad left the telegraph office and tucked the paper in his pocket. He was pleased to have another job leading a family from the Mississippi River to Broken Bow in southeast Indian Territory. He would use the money for provisions for winter in the home he'd built in his deep cave. He liked to be as much like a bear as possible in the winter. He'd stay snuggled and warm in his cave, eat a little, read a lot, do the necessary things of life, and sleep for ten to twelve hours a night.

His life of solitude never felt lonely, but he enjoyed meeting new people and helping them find their way in Indian Territory. This would be his last journey in 1898. By late February or early March 1899, he'd be ready to guide another family west. His life was good, and he felt no need to be anywhere other than on his horse's back, guiding folks, or spending time in his cave.

He looked up to see Lester Blunt staring at the three buildings of Silas Pennington. Blunt's scowl was more profound than usual and a cause of worry for Conrad—a lot of worry and even a little fear. He couldn't in good conscience leave on this next journey to the Mississippi with Blunt still causing problems for the people he loved. Conrad walked across the street and went to stand beside Lester Blunt.

Blunt turned to him and said, "What do you want injun?"

"I wondered why you sold those two buildings if you didn't want Silas Pennington to buy them."

"I wanted his money and had nothing I wanted to do with those rickety old buildings. He's serious about making something out of them."

"Sounds like a good thing to me."

"That's all you know."

"I suppose so. I hear one of the buildings will be a lending library and bookstore."

"That's what I heard, too. Why would anyone want to sit around reading, never mind spending money on a book?"

"I rather like reading books, Lester."

"Yeah. You're just another crazy, lazy injun, too."

"I've got to head to Shirley's place and put in my order for my next trip."

Lester nodded. "Beats the dickens outta sittin' around readin' a book."

"Good day, Lester."

Lester pulled on Conrad's sleeve. "Why do you spend all your time on those dad-blamed rocks piled all around Pennington Creek?"

"Well, I guess one man's rock is another man's treasure. Good day, Lester."

Lester snorted. "Not yet, it ain't."

Conrad walked across the street to Shirley's store. As he turned to go inside, he saw Lester stomp out his cigar, turn, and walk away back home, muttering and shaking his head. "I hope Lenora is all right," Conrad muttered, then walked into the store.

Shirley had walked closer to the door and heard what Conrad had said. She told him, "I think Lenora is on the edge of leaving him."

"A fine idea," Conrad said. "I suspect he beats her, but she denies it."

"I think so, too, but what can we do? I've offered to help her, and she always smiles and says, 'In time, it will all work out.' I suppose it will."

Conrad nodded. "One way or another. I'm heading out for the Mississippi River in a few days, so I need some provisions."

"Another family coming to Tishomingo?"

"No. This one wants to go to Broken Bow."

"Another fine place to live."

"Yes, it is, but I'm rather partial to around here."

Shirley smiled. "Me too. Let me see your list to be sure I can prepare it for you."

"Thanks. It's nothing much and certainly not fancy." He handed her the paper and his leather traveling pouch. "I've got the smaller pouches inside too. You always pack it right, so I'll leave all that to you."

She read the list and nodded. "I can have this ready for you the day after tomorrow. Do you want to put it on credit for when you get back?"

"No need. I've enough money to pay for it now. How much?"

She smiled and said, "Let me put pen to paper and see." She walked to the counter, laid the paper on the counter, put numbers by each item on Conrad's list, and said, "That'll be 3 dollars and 18 cents."

"About what I figured," Conrad said, pulling his money pouch from his pocket and giving her the coins. He said, "I'll see you Monday before noon."

"Sounds perfect, Conrad. Are you okay? You seem a little down or fretful."

"Not particularly, but I'm fine. Just wish Lester Blunt would grow up and be a better person."

"I think it's too late for that."

"I do, too. I hate that Lenora is stuck with him."

Shirley nodded. "It's hard to get a divorce unless another woman is involved, and even then, it's a hard thing to do when a white man is involved. Beating your wife is considered necessary for some around here."

"Not for me and not for most Chickasaws. It's the white men who think beating a woman is necessary. Lester takes it all out on her but doesn't go too far. After all, he's only Chickasaw by marriage. He can't afford to lose his allotment."

"I know, but I don't have to like it."

"Me neither," Conrad said, turned, waved goodbye, and left the store. On the ride back to his home, he stopped a few places, thinking of how a person could find themselves on the wrong side of the rocks. He returned to his cave, got out his drum, and talked with the elders in the sky.

LENORA TRIED NOT TO CRY, but the pain was immense. When Lester was too weary to beat her anymore, he said, "I should divorce you. I've poked you time and again, and after all these years, not one single baby has popped out of you."

She wiped the blood from her nose and said, "I would love to have a baby, Lester. I can't imagine how it would be for us to be a real, loving family."

He snorted. "Love has nothin' to do with you bein' barren. I know that for a fact."

"Ah, so you have a child, not of my womb?"

"That's none of your business. I'm hungry."

"I'll get dinner started," Lenora said, turning away from her vile husband. She'd thought of a hundred different ways to kill him, but none of them would leave her safe from the law of the white man. *If I were married to a Chickasaw man who beat me, I would have recourse at the council. I simply have to put up with it until he finally does something stupid enough or wanton enough to kill himself.*

Shirley had offered help, but Lenora was worried that Shirley would put herself in danger if she tried to help. The last thing she wanted was for another woman to be in harm's way because of Lester Blunt. She couldn't think of another woman who would allow him near her and didn't think he'd fathered a child. She knew no women who had a child and weren't married.

Of course, it could be a married woman, but still, who would want to be with him? If my father hadn't forced the marriage, I wouldn't be with him. My father died a few years ago. Hopefully, Lester will die soon, too. Jane's in town. Maybe she has some ideas.

When dinner was served and on the table, Lester sat down and ate until every bite was eaten. There were never leftovers at their home. Even when Lenora tried to cook enough to have leftovers, Lester gobbled the food down in a frenzy of gluttony. *Maybe Jane could help me figure out a way to poison him without poisoning myself. He eats without tasting a bite of food. He would never even notice.*

33

"Beware of the
man who does not talk and
the dog that does not bark."
Cheyenne Proverb

Monday morning was a clear but cold, crispy day. Lester didn't care a fig about the weather as he rode his horse close to Pennington Creek.

He muttered, "I have bigger fish to fry, and by God, I'm killin' that nigger injun today if it's the last thing I do!"

He climbed out of his saddle and tied his horse to a small cottonwood tree behind a large boulder where the horse was difficult to see. He quietly walked through the woods along Pennington Creek, watching for rattlesnakes and water mocassins. Getting bitten today wasn't on his agenda. He had no intention of dying out here in the wilderness.

While Clay and Silas were in town with the grandfathers of the family, hammerin' away on his old building, Lester's agenda for today was to mete out his vengeance on the women and their brats. He grinned when he realized he wanted to kill every damned woman and their brats too. His main goal for the day, though, was to kill that half-breed injun nigger, and her toss-off baby. "If'n I get to kill that snotty Pennington woman and her brood, all the better. It will be like the cherry on top of the cake."

The stagecoach bridge was a rickety mess, but he was sure he could safely cross without being seen. All the cottonwoods were moving in the breeze, even though he didn't feel the chill.

It was true the bridge was a rickety mess, but he was wrong about not being seen. Conrad Davidson had watched him tie up his horse and head for the creek. Conrad left the horse alone for now, but later, he'd be sure to untie the poor animal and send him back into town without that heavy brute he usually had to haul on his back.

Conrad was confident his plan would work, and there would be no need for Lenora to poison her husband or anyone else to murder him. Besides, Conrad decided it wasn't murder if someone was stupid enough to reach for a treasure that didn't exist.

Aurora was working outside in her garden, gathering the last of the fall squashes. She heard a voice that sounded like Lester Blunt and looked up. She stood quiet and still with Okchuli snuggled close in her shawl, watching the trees across the creek.

Lester brushed crow feather's out of his face and muttered, "Fucking injuns thinking feathers could do a damned thing." Once the words were out of his mouth, he felt a chill creep up his neck and wrap around his head. He turned around and looked right at Conrad but didn't see him. Aurora could see them both. Lester shook his head and crept across the creek onto Silas and Maggie Pennington's property.

Conrad tapped Blunt on the shoulder from behind when he was closer to the house proper. Blunt started to scream, and Conrad clapped his hand over the white man's mouth.

Aurora put down the pumpkin she held and began following the two men. She thought, *I don't know what is happening, but I've had more than enough of Lester Blunt. With any luck, today will be his last day on Earth.*

"Quiet!" Conrad hissed in Blunt's ear, and Blunt nodded. Conrad looked over Blunt's shoulder and saw Aurora quietly following them. He told Lester, "I found Jacob's hoard. Would you like to go with me and carry it out? I can't carry it all by myself."

Blunt nodded, and Conrad said, "If I move my hand off your mouth, will you be quiet?"

Blunt nodded again.

"Not a word, Blunt. You got that? Not a single word out of your mouth until I say you can speak. You speak, you die. Understand?"

Blunt nodded again.

Conrad nodded at Blunt and then raised his hand slightly to motion Aurora to come with him. He said to Lester, "Follow me. If you even whisper or ask a single question, I'll slit your throat and let you bleed out where you stand, choking on your blood. Understand?"

Blunt paled and nodded again.

Conrad removed his hand from Blunt's mouth and crept along the trail at the edge of the rocks behind Clay and Aurora's homestead and onto the larger rocks. Aurora followed quietly, hoping Okchuli didn't wake. At the next curve of the creek, Conrad motioned to Blunt to keep quiet and cross the shallow pool across the stream.

Once out of the stream, Conrad led Blunt up on the boulders of Devil's Den, but not near his home in his deep cave. Aurora crossed the stream when Conrad and Blut were out of the creek. She knew he never allowed anyone near his home. She ignored the cold water creeping into her shoes. When Conrad and Blunt could see all the land around them, and there were only a few more boulders to climb, Conrad let out a coyote howl.

Aurora smiled, knowing the coyote would help them if needed.

She watched from behind a small shrub as Blunt grabbed Conrad's arm. Conrad shook his head and motioned for quiet. Soon, a coyote was at Conrad's side. He patted the coyote's head and kept climbing, knowing Aurora was following him. The coyote looked over his shoulder at her and nodded. When they were on the highest peak of the pile of boulders and rocks, Conrad held up his hand to signal they were close and to be very quiet. He motioned for the coyote to sit and stay. The animal did so but remained alert, waiting for Aurora to come this way.

Conrad motioned to Blunt to follow him down a short gravel trail and sidled through in a crack between two gray boulders. Blunt followed but struggled to get through the close boulders. His belly was almost too big to get through. Finally, one of the buttons on his shirt popped loose. When through the gap, he bent, picked up the button, and put it in his pocket. He stood next to Conrad, who motioned for quiet, placing a finger to his lips.

Aurora quickly followed through the narrow opening, glad Okchuli stayed sleeping.

Conrad walked to the edge of the boulder and beckoned Blunt closer. He whispered in Blunt's ear, "If you look down, you will see a chest. It looks like an old sailor's chest. It is filled with money, including silver and gold coins and a few jewels too."

Blunt took a step toward the edge of the boulder and looked down. At first, he saw nothing but sand, rocks of all sizes, including some big enough to be small boulders, and a trickle of water from the creek—simply a tiny stream not even ankle deep. He shook his head, and Conrad whispered, "Look a little more to your right, Lester, and you'll see it in the shadow of a willow tree."

Aurora came closer, within arms reach of Lester Blunt. Conrad held up a finger for her to wait.

Lester did as he was told and nodded. He grinned and looked at Conrad, who motioned for him to say nothing. Lester turned back to the creek to look down. Lester saw an old sailor's chest on the sandy bank beside the small trickle of water at the creek, with a small willow tree shadowing the area. He nodded and kept looking down. "I see it!"

Softly, nearly quieter than the breezes surrounding them, Aurora began to sing Blunt's death song. Blunt shuddered but said, "Wow. It's real."

"Yes, it is," Conrad whispered. He joined Aurora, singing Blunt's death song.

Blunt kept looking at the treasure hoard and asked, "How can you sing at a time like this?"

"This is the perfect time and song for you today, Lester. Do you want to see what's inside?" He softly snapped his thumb and fingers.

Blunt nodded but didn't hear the finger snap. Coyote heard. Blunt took another half-step toward the edge of the giant boulder, but the coyote was behind him and nipped at Blunt's heel before he could take another half-step. Blunt turned around quickly to kick the dog, saw Aurora standing there singing, and felt a coldness flood deep in his belly. Before he could say anything, Aurora raised her arms, sang louder, then clapped her hands. Suddenly, Blunt was in the air, on his back, looking up at the clear blue sky.

Following him was his button.

Lester wanted to shout but couldn't open his mouth. Before he could think another thought, he landed on his back on the rocks and sand below, where, a few moments ago, a large chest filled with gold and silver had never rested.

The button plopped on his chest.

Now, the only thing lying by the trickle of water was Lester Blunt, with blood pouring out of the back of his head and onto the sandy verge of the creek. The chest, filled with gold and silver, and even the willow tree were gone—not even a will-o-the-wisp whisper was there.

Conrad patted the coyote's head, wrapped his arms around Aurora and Okchuli, and said, "I should have invited you."

"You did, and I thank you for it."

He nodded, kissed her cheek, and said, "Go on home. I'll finish the rest."

She nodded and kissed his cheek, then walked away.

Conrad and the coyote turned and walked back the way they'd come while Aurora took a shorter, more direct trail home, singing her birth song as she went.

Conrad gave the coyote a rabbit he'd killed earlier, and the coyote raced away to his den to eat his easily won dinner. Conrad walked down the boulders and to the grassy verge at the base of the pile of rocks. He patted a stone and said, "Thank you for your help." He went through the dark woods toward Pennington Creek.

Again, Conrad crossed the rickety bridge, which was more stable than most folks or horses thought. He went to the cottonwood tree beside a smaller boulder where Blunt's horse was tied. He gave the horse water and then untied the beast from the tree. He told the horse to go on home, and the horse gladly obliged. He checked the ground to be sure that only Lester Blunt's shoe prints and those of the horse were visible.

When he was confident that only Lester Blunt and his horse could be assumed to have stopped at this place, Conrad walked the few miles into Tishomingo. His plan was to stop in Tishomingo, get his horse and supplies for his journey, then head east to the Mississippi River. From there, he would help a family find their way to Broken Bow, Indian Territory, near the Mountain Fork River.

Conrad watched the red-headed turkey vultures flying above Pennington Creek, nodded, and said, "Your feast awaits, my friends."

Perhaps, he thought, *I should take my own life. But Blunt had a choice all along the way. His greed beckoned him and took him to his maker's hands. What the maker does with him is up to the maker. I'll await my death for another time.*

He nodded and began to sing his birth song—just to be sure his soul, heart, and mind were in their proper way of being. He let the blessing of the sunny day and his music wash over him. He prayed to the great god that when Lester Blunt returned to the lands of humans again, he would be a better man.

Once in town, he went to Shirley's store to pick up the necessary provisions for this journey. Shirley smiled and said, "Isn't it a wonderful day, Conrad?"

"Yes, it is. I feel like all creation is blessing us this day. It feels bright and new."

"I agree. I gathered your usual things for your trip, Conrad." She handed him a leather pouch filled with food, flour, sugar, flint, coffee, chocolate, and tobacco.

"I thank you, Shirley, for all you've done for me."

"We are friends, and helping each other blesses us both. I suppose you won't be back for Thanksgiving."

"No. Besides, that is a white man's celebration. I'll wait for the solstice and then rejoice."

"Good man. Take care and come back home in one piece, dear friend."

He smiled and nodded, then turned to leave until Shirley called him back. He looked over his shoulder to Shirley, and she said, "I saw Lester Blunt on his horse riding toward the Pennington's place. Did you see him there?"

"No, I did not, for which I am grateful."

She shook her head. "I wish he would leave them alone, especially Aurora."

"Have wishes ever worked for you, Shirley?"

"Now that you mention it, occasionally they have."

"Then may your wishes come true, dear friend."

He smiled and waved, and she returned his wave with a smile.

Once he left the store, Shirley said, "I hope you are safe, Conrad. I'd hate to have you out of my life."

Conrad tied the leather pouch to the back of his saddle, double-checked his saddle bindings, patted his horse, Soba, and stepped up into the saddle. Once settled in his saddle, he turned the horse to the east and started the long ride to the Mississippi River.

The further he was out of town, the more he felt the burden of the day lift. He smiled and said to the sky, "Thank you for the blessing of this day." As each mile passed, his soul felt easier. He was sure his friend Aurora and his daughter Okchuli were safer, with Lester Blunt gone from the world of men. He'd not intended for Aurora to witness Blunt's death, but as he began this next journey, he realized her presence was needed for her healing. He hoped that Lenora would be blessed as well.

All day, he rode. Off and on, he would sing his birth song, knowing it was the best way to clear his soul of the shame of Lester

Blunt's death. His birth song, a song of life among the rocks and trees, was lifting him closer to a calming of his soul.

Most folks did not notice the vultures gathering at the lonely spot in the Devil's Den by Pennington Creek. Those who did see the Turkey Vultures, with their blood-red heads, gathering for a feast quickly turned away, glad they were not on the menu.

34

"Don't be afraid to cry.
It will free your mind of
sorrowful thoughts."
Hopi Proverb

Early Monday afternoon, Lenora Blunt looked outside her window to see Lester's horse standing in her roses—again. The horse often stood in the rose garden along the front of Lenora Blunt's house when Lester was drunk and couldn't ride the horse. Lenora would usually ride the horse into town and drag her husband home—sometimes literally dragging him behind the horse.

She shook her head at the sight before her and said, "If that vile man is drunk again, I might just conk him on his head and be done with it."

She shook her head, walked out to the porch, and saw the horse standing there as if it didn't know what to do with herself. Lenora walked down the steps and caressed the horse on her nose. She said,

"What's up with that bully that rides you all over every acre around Tishomingo? Oh, my sweet Dolly, did he leave you on your own again? I'm sure that would be better than lugging him about day after day."

The horse laid her head on Lenora's shoulder and sighed.

Lenora smiled, hugged the horse, took the reigns, and said, "Come on, darlin', and let's get you some water."

Dolly obediently followed Lenora to the water trough outside the barn and began to drink. She liked her name and was relieved Lenora called her Dolly. The man never called her by her name but sometimes called her 'Nag,' an expression of meanness.

Lenora called out, "Lester, you good-for-nothing piece of shit. Come on out here and take care of your horse. Dolly deserves better than you give her."

All was quiet, and Lenora tied the reigns to the post by the trough and said, "Hang on Dolly, and I'll go find that waste of flesh I married. You drink up, darlin'."

She went into the barn and found no one. Even the milk cow was out in the meadow, munching away. She went to the hen house to see everything as usual, with the hens pecking away and the rooster annoying them repeatedly. She walked around the house and barn and found nothing unusual—except that her husband seemed nowhere around the place.

She sighed and returned to the horse, standing as if waiting for Lenora to do something. She gathered the reins and said, "Well, Dolly, let's go into town and see if his sorry ass is there. Often enough, maybe too much, he's just left you standing outside the bar, drunk on his ass though not usually this early in the day."

It was less than a mile to ride from the Blunt home at the edge of Tishomingo to the local bar, where she usually found Lester, too drunk to remember what he was doing and where he spent a lot of time barking about all the supposed miseries of his life.

Once inside the bar, the bartender, Barney, said, "I ain't seen him all day, Mrs. Blunt. I did see him ride out toward the west of town, but that was early this morning before I even opened up."

"Thanks, Barney. I'll check with Hank and Shirley. They probably know where he is."

Lenora checked with Hank, who said, "I haven't seen him, Lenora. It's been quite a while since I told him not to come back around my place." He blushed and said, "Of course, that does not apply to you, Lenora."

She smiled. "I know Hank. He isn't much of a man, and what there is isn't worth a penny's worth of chaw. Still, as his wife, I feel obligated to find and help him if needed."

Hank saw the bruises on Lenora's face and said, "Maybe it's time to let him take care of himself."

Lenora smiled and touched her face. "I decided this time I wasn't going to cover for him. I'm not going to do him harm, but I'm not going to help him. He doesn't know yet that from now on, I cook for one—me."

"Good on you, Lenora. I can't say I blame you a bit. I'll let you know if I see him, though. For now, leave Dolly here and let me check on her feet. It's been a fair bit since she was properly cleaned and shod."

"Thanks, Hank. I'll go see if Shirley has seen him."

Hank nodded, took Dolly inside the barn, and got his pick out to clean her hooves. She indeed needed new shoes. He muttered, "I tell you, Dolly, you and Lenora are worth a fair sight more than her useless, hateful husband."

Dolly blew out her lips in agreement and nodded.

Hank smiled. "Let's get your feet in better condition."

The horse nodded and relaxed into the good hands of Hank Smithson.

Shirley said at her store, "I saw him riding west, out of town, on Dolly. That was quite a while ago, too."

Lenora pointed at Hank's blacksmith shop. "Hank's working on Dolly right now. She came home, but Lester did not. I can't imagine where he could be. He'd never walk anywhere he could ride, so I don't expect he sent Dolly home without him."

Shirley chuckled. "I'm sure you're right. Can I say something that isn't any of my business?"

"Sure you can. I might not like it, but unlike my husband, I won't throttle you if you tell me something I don't like."

Shirley smiled and nodded. "Good. Why in the hell do you not send that creep you married out of your life? Gather up his crap and leave it outside your door, Lenora. You know you have every right to do so, and no one in the tribe would fuss at you if you did."

Lenora laughed and then moaned as she wrapped her arms around her abdomen.

Shirley asked, "Are you okay?"

"Mostly, it's just bruising, but this time was too much. He doesn't know it yet, but I'm done with him."

"What a relief. Listen. You kick his ass out of your house and then come to town and talk with Adella."

"Why?"

"Because she is taking the building Silas bought on the west side of *Okchuli Press* and turning it into a cafe. She needs a cook, and you'd be perfect for the job. I already told her she should get you, and she was willing to wait to put up a *Help Wanted* sign so long as Lester wasn't around."

"Really? How much money?"

"I heard $45.00 per month to begin with."

Lenora grinned. The store door opened, ringing the little bell, just as she said, "I'll talk to her now before anyone else has a chance at the job. Then I'll go chase down the sheriff."

Laughter sounded behind Lenora, and the sheriff said, "I'd guess it won't take much chasing, Lenora. What's up?" He held up a hand and looked at her face. "He's been beating on you again."

"Yes, but it isn't going to happen again. Lester left the house early this morning, grumbling about me not making him pancakes, got on his horse, and left."

"I thought I saw Dolly at Hank's place."

"Yes, you did, and I'm glad your eyes are working right, Sheriff. A man in your position needs good eyes." He smiled and waited for her to continue. She said, "About an hour ago, Dolly came home without Lester. I've been trying to find him but haven't had any luck."

He looked up at Shirley, who said, "I saw him heading west out of town a few hours ago."

He nodded. "My guess is he fell off his horse and hurt himself. I'll go find his sorry ass and bring him home."

"Not to my house. He's done living with me. I don't care a tinker's damn where he goes so long as it isn't my house."

He smiled. "I'll find someplace to park him and let you know what I find."

"Thanks, Sheriff. I'm heading down to talk with Adella about her need for a cook."

"Good. I love your pecan pies, plus your biscuits are the best around."

She laughed. "Thank you, Sheriff. You have good eyesight and good taste, too."

He grinned, tipped his hat, and said, "Ladies, I'll talk with you later."

Aurora walked into her house and saw her mother sitting in the rocking chair, reading a book. Jane looked up, smiled at her daughter, and saw she was a little pale. "I thought you were in the garden, but then I saw you walk away along the trail behind the Pennington's home. I assumed you needed a little quiet time."

"Yes, but it wasn't quiet time. I had something I needed to do," she told her mother, and then asked, "Will you help me with something important?"

"Of course. What do you need?"

"I need a cleansing of myself, Okchuli, and our home."

"Shall I sing for you?"

"Yes."

"Anything in particular?"

"Putting evil out of my life, Momma."

Jane felt a slight tremor in her chest and asked, "Did you do someone harm?"

"I sang his death song, Momma."

Jane nodded. "Good. He's been in need of his death song for a long time. Do you have dried sage?"

"I do, and there is an eagle feather above the hearth."

Her mother nodded and said, "You and Okchuli should bathe while I prepare myself, the sage and the feather."

"Thank you, Momma."

"I count it a blessing, daughter."

THE DAY WAS MOVING QUICKLY at *Okchuli Press.* Mrs. Rittenhouse and Silas Pennington had finished printing the week's *Weekly Beginnings* and had the pages hanging up to dry to be folded later. Then he went next door to what would become the new cafe to help his father, Noah, Clay, and his father-in-law with the construction and remodeling of the building.

Clay said, "The building itself is stable and sturdy, but there needs to be some shoring up in a few places, and then we can finish the interior framing."

"It's looking good, Clay. How long do you think it will take?"

"Well, I think we'll have the rest of the interior finished and ready for use in a week or two. In the meantime, Hank knows a man with a wood stove with two large double ovens, six-pot positions, and a large built-in grill and griddle. He's asking a hundred dollars for it."

"What's the new price?"

"Around three hundred, but it hasn't been used in over a year and was just sitting in his barn, providing a home for the mice. He's been trying to sell it the whole time."

"Is he willing to come down some on the price?"

Silas's father laughed. "It turns out he was willing to lower the price. When I offered him $50.00 cash today, he asked, 'including hauling it out of my barn today?' I said yes, and so there you have it, son."

Silas laughed, "So we'll go get it out of his barn and haul it over here."

Johnathan said, "Already done and dusted. You want to see it?"

"I do!"

ADELLA RITTENHOUSE WAS busy writing a poster for reasonably priced, clean, used chairs and tables. When she finished that poster and another one for a well-educated woman to run the library and bookstore, she put them both up in the window of *Okchuli Press.*

Lenora walked in just as Adella finished putting the posters in the front window. Adella smiled and said, "You a sight for sore eyes, Lenora."

"Yes, I am. I have sore eyes, a bruised belly, and a few other achy places."

Adella wrapped her arms around her friend and said, "Please tell me you kicked him out."

"I did or will when I see him again. He took off this morning and hasn't come back. Dolly came home alone and stood in my rose bushes until I came out and found her."

"Poor horse. He was never kind to her. What happened?"

Lenora sighed, shook her head, and said, "I've no idea. The sheriff has gone to find him."

"Good. Let him deal with that sorry ass man."

Lenora laughed and said, "I agree. When I get home, I'll gather all his things and set them outside the fence of my home. According to tribal law, I have every right to do so. I'm done."

"Good. Are you ready to go see your cafe?"

"What? I heard you were starting a cafe, but I'm certain it isn't mine."

"Well, it was a figure of speech. Come on, and let's see what's going on next door. Of course, without question, you are hired. $45.00 a month, to begin with, starting today."

"Perfect." Lenora sighed and said, "I need to cry but also to jump for joy."

Adella said, "Go for the joy, my friend." She led Lenora out of the press shop, locked the door, and walked hand-in-hand with Lenora to the cafe next door. When they walked in, Lenora said, "I can see it already. Where's the cooking area going to be."

Silas waved from the back of the room and said, "Back here, Lenora. My dad already bought you a big old stove to cook on."

She smiled, walked to the stove, and said, "This is a marvel." She turned to Silas and said, "Do you have cleaning materials and rags?"

"We do."

"Good. I'm of a mind and urge to get busy making this place my place to cook and share with friends and family."

"We can certainly put you to work." He looked at Adella and asked, "You hired her, right?"

"Yes, and she starts today."

35

———————

"If we wonder
often, the gift of knowledge
will come."
Arapaho Proverb

Once Aurora bathed herself and Okchuli, who howled with the indignity of being bathed, she dried herself and the baby and put clean clothes on them both. She entered the living area, sat in the rocking chair, and nursed Okchuli.

Her mother walked in and said, "I've smudged the outside and inside of the house except for your bedroom. I'll do that next. Where would you like to have your cleansing?"

"I think in our bedroom."

"Good. You finish with Okchuli and come into your bedroom when you're ready.

ADELLA WENT BACK to *Okchuli Press* and started folding the *Weekly Beginnings*. They usually would have done so on Saturday, but with the whirlwind of life, including guests, the new building dedication, and all the family coming and going, they ran out of time. She sighed and said, "Who ever thought I'd be this busy at this point in my life."

The little bell over the door dinged, and she looked up to see a tall, young Chickasaw woman with her long, shining black hair sweeping nearly to her hips. Adella smiled and stood up. "Welcome to *Okchuli Press.* My name is Adella Rittenhouse. You seem familiar to me, but I'm not sure."

The young woman smiled. "I'm Emma Crawford."

"Of course you are! It's been a long time since I've seen you. You're no longer a little girl. You've grown into a beautiful woman, Emma."

"Thank you, Adella. I finished my training at Bloomfield and taught there for a few years until I decided I was ready to come home. I want to create a life for myself in my own way."

"Good for you, Emma. How are your parents?"

"They're doing very well but are eager for me to marry."

"And you're not as eager as they would wish."

"Exactly so. They yearn for grandchildren, but I plan never to marry a man and become chattel."

"Only time can tell what each of us has in store for our lives.

"You are right, of course. Emma turned and pointed to the window. "I want to have the librarian job you've advertised."

Adella nodded and smiled. "I'm glad you came along. I've worried a bit about having a sign in the window that I'd be stuck with someone I don't like or who isn't suitable."

Emma turned, took the poster from the window, and handed it to Adella. "I'm tempted to rip up this poster, but how about you and I talk while I help you fold the newsletters? If you like me and I like you, you can decide whether or not we need this poster."

"You are right. Pull up a chair, Emma, and we can talk while we fold."

Emma sat down, picked up a newsletter to fold, and started the chat. "I loved teaching, but I was teaching the same things, day after day and year after year. I'd much rather be of help, and reading is a great way for anyone to learn more about everything in our world."

"I agree. So let me tell you my vision."

The chatting continued with Adella sharing her desire to have a lending library and a place for books Silas Pennington would print to be sold. Folks could borrow books or sit in the library's quiet and read. Books would be sold, loaned, and shared.

When they had nearly finished the folding chore, Adella said, "Emma, I think you'll be perfect for the library and bookstore. Your pay will be $45.00 per month to start. As time goes on and markets change, we'll adjust. You'll have a lot of work to do every day."

"When do I start?"

"You already have. Helping here in the press is part of your job. We'll go next door as soon as we finish the folding, and I'll show you our plans. There's a lot of dusting and cleaning that needs to happen right away. We'll have to gather books to share as well."

The little bell over the front door of *Okchuli Press* tinkled, and both women turned and looked up.

Adella smiled, stood, and went to greet the young woman with three children walking behind her. Adella said, "Good day, Rose. How are you and the children doing?"

"We're doing fairly well, all things considered."

"I was sorry to hear that your father died so soon after your step-mother died."

Rose sighed and smiled, "Yes, and here I am, a mother by default."

"I'm sure it is a tough thing for you."

"Yes, ma'am, but not all bad. The children work hard with me. I love them and know they are a joy in my life."

The littlest boy, Joseph, said, "Rose is our Momma now. I like how she cooks."

Adella laughed. "I'm sure she is a fine cook. Now, I've forgotten all your names."

He said, "I'm Joseph, but I like being called Joe. My twin sister is Jolene."

Adella looked at the little girl. "Do you like your name, Jolene?"

"Yes, I do. It's what my Momma wanted me to be, and I love her. I love my Momma Rose, too."

"I'm sure you do." Adella looked at the older boy and said, "If I remember correctly, you're Adam."

He nodded. "Yes, ma'am. I like my name fine, too."

"Thank you for letting me know. How old are you, Adam?"

"I'm ten. Jo and Jolene are five years old."

"Well, I'm sure you are a good big brother. I have some peppermint candies if you, your sister, and your brother want one."

Adam smiled. "I'll never pass up candy."

"Me either," Jolene said, and Joe said, "Me too!"

She handed each of them a peppermint candy and then turned back to Rose, looking over her shoulder at Emmaline.

Adella smiled and said, "I don't know if you two young ladies have met each other."

Emmaline stood up and nodded. "I did meet Rose at Bloomfield, but she left school before I did."

Rose said, "My second mother became ill after the twins were born, so I left school and came home to help."

Adam said, "Rose has been our mother for a long time. Daddy died a year after Momma, so Rose has been caring for us and the farm."

Emma said, "Rose sounds like a fine woman."

"Yes, she is the best Momma around."

Rose blushed, turned to Emma, and said, "They are a handful sometimes, but Adam is a great help to me."

"I'm ten years old," Adam said, trying to stand taller. "I'm nearly old enough to help with the plowing."

Emma turned to Rose and asked, "Do you do the plowing, too?"

"No. I hire that out. We must have alfalfa, grasses, and hay to feed the cattle. I care for all the close-in farm animals and the kitchen farm. Now that Adam is older, though, he is a big help."

Adella handed Rose a *Weekly Beginnings* newsletter, and Rose gave her a penny. "Thanks Adella. I love reading the newsletter. I can't afford to buy books to read, but I read every newsletter a few times every week."

"I know you love to read. I have a few leftover newsletters of the special edition for last week's celebration. They are free if you'd like to have one."

"Yes, please. I didn't have enough money to buy it."

Adella turned away, and Emma closed the gap and said, "Rose, I'd like to visit your home. I'm sure we could become good friends."

"That would be very nice. I don't have the leisure of having friends but would love to have you visit. Monday is the only day I come to town. We're headed to Shirley's store to get some needed items. You'd be welcome to come for dinner this evening if you'd like."

"I would so long as you let me bring dessert."

"That would be very nice. Do you know where we live?"

"No, but my mother will know."

"I'm sure she will. Come whenever you're ready."

Emma nodded. "I will after I finish talking with Adella."

"Good. I look forward to the visit."

After Rose left, Adella said, "She is a remarkable young woman. She loves to read, which brings me back to our plans for a library. Let's set these newsletters out on the table on the boardwalk."

"Don't some folks steal them?"

"No. I put out the leftovers from previous newsletters for free. For the new newsletters, we charge a penny, and every week, we have exactly as many pennies as we put out newsletters. So far, stealing hasn't been a problem."

Emmaline smiled and said, "I like how you think Mrs. Rittenhouse."

"Please, call me Adella so I can feel free to call you Emma."

"I'd like that a lot."

"Come, and let's set up the table, and then we'll go next door to the library and bookstore."

Aurora went into her bedroom, holding Okchuli in her arms. The baby was sleeping, and Aurora was sure it was because of the hike they'd had to the boulders of Devil's Den.

Jane said, "Just so you know, Aurora, I'm very proud of you and how brave you've been."

"Thanks, Momma. I didn't touch him, but I did sing his death song and gave a loud clap. He stumbled, fell backward off the boulder, and landed in a bit of a stream, crashing his head on a large rock."

Her mother nodded. "How do you feel about it all?"

"I thought I'd feel anxiety or fear or even shame, but I do not. All I feel is relief."

"Good. That is what I think you should feel. Let's smudge Okchuli first, and then you can lay her on your bed while I smudge you."

Aurora nodded and held out her darling daughter to be cleansed from the day's events. Then she lay the baby on her bed and stood while her mother smudged every part of her body, wafting the smoke with the eagle feather and the dried sage she was burning.

Emma stood amazed when she and Adella entered the store next door. She smiled and said, "My goodness, we have many shelves here already that will work nicely for books."

"I had the same thought," Adella said. "Come back to the east side corner and see the desk. You might like it for your workspace."

Emma followed Adella, and when she saw a large oak professor's desk, she smiled and said, "It is perfect. The drawers on either side will make it easy to keep things tidy. However, I think it should be more in the middle of the library so I can see everyone and be accessible to the patrons if they need me."

"I agree. There might be a few books like dictionaries and encyclopedias that we wouldn't want to lend out. Perhaps a couple of tables towards the back where folks could sit and make notes would be useful for those larger books."

"Yes," Emma said, smiling. I'm beginning to understand the layout."

"Good. Come over here. I want to show you my other idea. You may not have met Clay Harrison yet, but he is a builder and friend of the Pennington family. He will make us a Dutch door between the library, bookstore, and printing shop."

"I can see that being very helpful."

"We can leave the top of the door open most of the time, but when the press is running, it's fairly loud and might disturb readers."

"Yes, it would. Having the door top open most of the time will also remind everyone that we are a publishing endeavor, a bookstore, and a lending library."

Emma walked around the room and began to map out what could be done in her mind. Adella watched her and smiled, knowing she had an excellent librarian for the business. Emma said, "Well, I'll wear work clothes tomorrow. I'll want to dust and clean every inch of the store."

"Good. I've advertised to buy comfortable chairs and low tables. Even if someone doesn't wish to buy or borrow a book, I hope they will spend some time reading and enjoying our establishment."

"I like that idea, Adella. What's the name of the library going to be?"

"I have no idea, but I'm sure Mr. and Mrs. Pennington will come up with something."

Emma asked, "Do you already have some books?"

"Very few, but Mr. Pennington's father will send some crates of books. Most will be for lending, and a few will be for references. We have also discussed having the free newsletters scattered on tables so folks can sit and read them and then take them home or leave them for someone else to read."

"I like your ideas a lot, Adella. I heard there's a newspaper coming to town."

"I'd heard that too. We'll connect with them and see if they'll give editions of the newpapers to the library. We will also ask for donations of books. I'm sure some folks would gladly give their books to our purpose while reading and borrowing books they haven't read yet."

Emma walked around the room again, then back to Adella, and said, "Thank you, Adella. Today, you might have given me a life I can live with and enjoy."

"Even living with your parents?"

"In time, I'm sure I'll live where I belong. For now, I'm happy to start this endeavor with you. It feels like exactly what I should be doing with my life."

"Good. Now, let me sketch the way to Rose's house. I've heard that Shirley has some lovely Gingersnap cookies for sale. She also usually has raisins, prunes, and dried apricots."

Emma beamed. "It sounds perfect, Adella. My day keeps getting better and better."

WHEN AURORA'S mother finished the smudging, the two women went outside and sang their birth songs to the heavens, and the heavens welcomed their voices.

36

*"Ask questions from
your heart, and you will
be answered from the heart."*
Omaha Proverb

Emma returned home to her parent's house and told her mother, "I'm going out for dinner this evening."

Her mother asked with hope in her eyes, "A new beau?"

"No, Momma. Not a beau, but maybe a girl."

Her mother nodded. "I remember a friend—a man, mind you—who loved a man. He said, 'We are two spirits that recognize our love for each other.' I thought they should be allowed to be joined together in marriage. But still, at the time, I worried for them, and I was right. Both men were beaten to death and left laying, bloody in the middle of the road with their genitals cut off and stuffed in their mouths."

Emma swallowed back her grief and horror and shook her head.

"We are two girls who knew each other at Bloomfield Academy. I like her a lot, but I don't know if we will feel a bonding of spirits."

"What's her name?"

"Rose Grace Grantham."

Her mother nodded. "She is lovely and works very hard caring for her stepmother's children."

"Yes, I met the children today when she came into town for her weekly shopping. We were at Bloomfield together for a short time. She is lovely, generous, and caring. The children love her and refer to her as Momma Rose."

"She is a good woman but has a lot of burdens on her back. Take care, daughter. Be certain of your soul before you let your heart take over."

"Yes, Momma, I will."

Her mother reached out and held Emma's hand. "Your father has told me he thinks your spirit seeks a woman, not a man."

"Will you be disappointed if I am?"

"No. Never that. However, I do worry. Take care and keep any endearments close to home. In the public eye, many wicked thoughts and actions can destroy even the strongest love."

"I don't believe that, Momma. I can't. If love is true and strong, it will outlast cruelty."

"I hope you are right, but please take care."

"I will. May I tell you my other wonderful news?"

"Certainly."

"I have a job working for Mr. Silas Pennington with Adella Rittenhouse."

"At his publishing house?"

"No. Next door."

"Doesn't that empty building belong to Lester Blunt?

"Not anymore. Mr. Pennington bought the building and will turn it into a lending and reading library with a bookstore, too."

Her mother's grin broke out like sunshine after a rain and blessed Emma's soul. "You'll be the librarian?"

"I will. I started today by helping Mrs. Rittenhouse fold the

Weekly Beginnings *newsletter*. Then, we went through our plans for the library and bookstore together. Tomorrow, I'll start cleaning and arranging the bookstore and library."

Her mother smiled, pleased with her daughter, and said, "I'm proud of you, Emmaline. You'll be the perfect person for the new endeavors. I bought one of the weekly newsletters when I was in town. It gets better each week."

"I think so too. Now. I need to be on the road to Rose's home. I promise not to be late."

"Have a good visit, daughter. I like Rose a lot, and if she is the woman for you, I'll welcome her to my heart."

"Thanks, Momma. It's too soon to tell. This is simply an evening of getting to know each other better and hopefully becoming friends. That may be all there is, too. Give Daddy a kiss for me when he gets home."

"I will, daughter."

Emmaline's mother, Rebecca Crawford, watched her daughter climb on her horse. Her usual men's pants showed under the skirt of her dress. She bundled her hair in a loose bun at the nape of her neck and pulled her hat on her head—an old leather hat of her father's. She waved goodbye to her mother with a bright smile on her face.

Rebecca looked toward the sun setting in a few hours and said, "May all the gods bless you, daughter." She returned to her house to wait for her husband, Harold, to tell him all that had happened. She knew it would be hard on him, but he was a kind and gentle man. She hoped kindness would be enough.

WHEN SILAS, Thomas, Johnathan, Clay, Noah, and Mrs. Rittenhouse closed and locked all the establishment doors, Silas said, "What a day we've had. I want to get home before the sun sets."

"Indeed," said Adella. "I know you didn't meet Emma, but she is perfect. You can meet her tomorrow."

Clay said, "I agree, Mrs. Rittenhouse. She is the perfect woman to run the library and bookstore. She is kind and loving but takes no guff from anyone. Add to that, she's smart as a whip. She's been a little at loose ends, but this will suit her down to the ground."

Before anyone could say anything else, the sheriff, Sam Harvey, rode up on his horse, stopped before the group, getting ready to leave, and said, "I need a couple of fellas with a buckboard. Silas, would you be willing?"

"Sure. What's going on?"

The sheriff looked at Noah and sighed. "Perhaps we could talk a bit in a more quiet spot."

"Sure," Silas said.

Thomas interrupted and said, "I'll ride home with Noah, son. This old man is ready to put his feet up."

The sheriff smiled and nodded with relief. He waited until the elder Mr. Pennington had left with his grandson Noah, then said, "I'm relieved your father took your son home, Silas. There's a dead man on the north edge of your property."

Silas felt befuddled and asked, "What?"

"Yeah. I'm sorry, Silas, to have to tell you this. Lenora asked me to go looking for Lester. I found him."

"He's dead?"

"Yes."

"How?"

"It looks like he fell or was pushed off a high boulder at the edge of Devil's Den. I am fairly certain he fell. I found his prints around on the ground but no other prints. Well, that is if we count his horse's prints on this side of the creek and a few coyote prints near the base of the boulder he fell from."

"Of course, I'll help you. Will you need more than me?"

"A couple of you would be nice. If you could load his body up and bring him back into town before he's eaten up completely by the vultures, that would be a great help. You can get a tarp from the jailhouse. The deputy will go with you out to Devil's Den. But, fair warning: The vultures have been at him already. There must have been nearly a dozen having their dinner. You'll find him where they are feasting. I need to go see Lenora and talk with her about his death."

"Of course, Sam," Silas said. "Where shall we take him?"

"The deputy will show you. We'll keep him in the shed behind the jailhouse. We use it for this sort of purpose and other grisly needs. We'll deal with him in the morning. Unless I find a reason to suspect foul play, we'll go ahead and bury him tomorrow."

Silas nodded. "He wasn't a good man, but I never wanted him dead, just out of my life."

Clay nodded. "That's how I feel, too. He was so mean and vile to Aurora that I'm finding no forgiveness in my heart despite his death."

"Well, no need to worry about it now," the sheriff said. "He's gone, and that's that. I suspect he was up to no good and fell, landed on his back, and hit his head on a big old rock. We'd all best get onto our labors before the sun sets and darkness settles in."

They all nodded and went their separate ways to finish the sad and messy end of the day.

Clay, Johnathan, Silas, and the deputy were tired and discouraged hours later. It had been a horrible business getting Lester Blunt wrapped in a canvas tarp, carried out of the creek, up the boulders, and into the buckboard wagon. Nearly a dozen vultures had been at him. His tongue was gone, as were his eyes and cheeks. His belly had been gashed open, but his button lay on the sand beside him. His jeans were torn to shreds, and the muscles of his thighs and lower legs were ripped off the bones. Silas tossed the button onto what was left of Lester Blunt's body.

The stench was awful—at least so the men thought. The vultures were none too happy to see any of the men—except Lester Blunt, of course.

Once the men picked up as much of Lester Blunt as possible, they wrapped the canvas around him and put him in the buckboard for his last ride to Tishomingo, Indian Territory. Lester had no more worries about 'nigger injun women' or any of the other myriad things that had annoyed him in life. He certainly would have upset the vultures if he'd had any way of knowing what was going on around and on him—but even that last bit of meanness wasn't given to him.

The deputy said, "He probably thought he'd found some treasure or another and walked too close to the edge and wound up killing his silly self."

Silas asked, "Why would he be hunting treasure out there?"

"It happens all the time, Mr. Pennington. We hear all kinds of differing stories of various outlaws, including Belle Starr, Jesse James, and his gang. We've been told for ages they'd hauled a lot of silver, gold, and jewels in various trunks and cases and hid them in caves in Devil's Den—yet none has ever been found."

"Really?"

"Oh, yeah. It was even rumored that your uncle, Jacob Pennington, had a hoard of money hidden near his place."

Silas shook his head and grinned. He knew his wife had already found that 'hoard.' It was a lot of money—but not the millions everyone thought might be around Devil's Den. And Maggie didn't find it in a cave but in a large tin box on the pantry's top shelf. It was now scattered in various places on their land—mostly under hen boxes, a hole covered by rocks beside the outhouse, under the compost bin in a tin can—places like that—women's places, you know.

Silas said, "If I find a hoard, I'll tell you, fellas." Then he grinned. "Maybe."

They all laughed as they returned to their buckboard with Lester Blunt's remains. At the jailhouse shed, they unloaded their gruesome bundle and laid Lester Blunt's remains inside the shed.

Silas said, "We'll all want to come and help with the burial of Lester Blunt."

"To be sure he died?" the deputy asked.

"No. We want to be much kinder than he ever was and honor his wife. It's the very least we can do for her."

The deputy blushed and nodded. "I'll let Sheriff Harvey know. I'm sure he'd appreciate your help, and Lenora will be grateful."

"Good. We'll come into town as soon as possible."

The deputy watched the men ride away in their buckboard. He felt embarrassed not to have been a better man than Lester Blunt had been. He muttered, "I need to remember if I want to be a good man, I need to act like it. I'll try harder."

Good idea.

37

Hopi Proverb

Silas, Clay, and Johnathan rode together in Silas's buckboard back home to their families. Johnathan said, "I've known Lester Blunt for years and years. He has always been a mean-spirited man, but I can't say I wanted him to die. I wanted him to be a kinder man. However, if any man needed to leave our Earth and come back another time, it was Lester Blunt. Still, my heart aches for him."

Clay looked at his father-in-law and asked, "Really?"

"Yeah. He was a wounded soul, I'm sure. He did not seem to know how to be a good man. My heart aches for him because the vultures got to him."

Clay nodded. "Well, although I'm not sad he is dead, I'm glad it's not me being gnawed on for an afternoon dinner."

"Me too, son. I will want to go to his wife and help her with her husband's burial. She is Chickasaw, and we should show her honor by helping her bury her husband."

Silas nodded. "You're right, John. I never had a moment's use for Lester Blunt, but Lenora deserves our honor."

Clay nodded. "I hear he was cruel to her."

"He was," John said. "Lenora tried to love him when they first married, but she was only fourteen. He beat her often and mercilessly. When he would beat her, she would try to learn what she could do to make him stop. I remember once when she said, 'I can't tell if I'm a dullard because I married him or because I don't know how to please him.' Your mother-in-law said, 'I think if Lester could please himself, he wouldn't need to harm you.' I think Jane was right."

Clay nodded. Finally, he said, "I'll try not to hate him. I certainly won't rejoice in anyone's death, but honoring him will be hard. Right now, I'm relieved he can no longer threaten harm to Aurora."

Silas agreed. "I'll happily bury him, help his wife any way I can, and even pray for his soul—but that last bit will be hard."

John said, "It is for us to pray for our souls that we learn the lesson of Lester Blunt and never allow our greed, anger, folly, or brutality to destroy our being."

Clay took his father-in-law's hand and said, "Thank you, Dad. Your words help."

Silas said nothing but thought of the love in his life. His parents, wife, and children were all blessings of love and hope. He found himself surprised to feel sorry for Lester and hopeful for Lenora.

LENORA SAT at her kitchen table with the sheriff and cried. He held her hand and waited until she could gather her thoughts and release her tears. Finally, Lenora said, "I'll want to bury him behind the barn."

"Why there?"

"It was the only place I ever saw him sit still and contemplate life. Occasionally, I'd find him there, and he'd say, 'Lenora, sit with me a spell. I love the feel of your hand in mine.' So, I would sit with him. He would tell me stories of his family and stories of others. They were always kind and loving stories. However, once he tired of storytelling, he'd say, 'Get up off your ass and cook me some dinner—I'm hungry.' I would get up and fix dinner. Sometimes, we'd have even a few days of love and honor, and I wondered if I could quit the herbs and have a baby. But soon, he'd be drunk again and come home to beat me and rape me."

"I'm sorry, Lenora. He did not give you the honor a husband should give a wife."

"I'm sorry, too. I used to think the fault was mine, but I no longer believe that."

"Neither do I."

"Still, I want him to rest in peace behind the barn. It's the only place I know where he was ever at peace. I'll lay the remaining whiskey bottles in the house with him."

The sheriff chuckled. "That's a fine thing to do, Lenora, and the best way to send him to his next beyond."

She nodded, reached for the sheriff's hand, and sat quietly at her table, glad to have a friend who would hold her hand and not raise his hand to her body.

The sheriff watched her and thought, *I wish Lenora had found a loving man rather than a devil. My wife died nearly ten years ago, and I haven't felt the touch of a woman's hand since. I know Lenora is reaching out to me for comfort, but her hand in mine gives me comfort, too. It's been too long since I allowed myself to look anywhere for comfort. Lenora deserves a better life, and perhaps I do too.*

They sat quietly for nearly an hour, and then Lenora said, "Let me know when you're ready, and I'll get some folks to help me dig the grave."

"No need. I know there are lots of folks around here who want to honor you. We'll want to dig Lester's grave for you."

"Are you sure?"

"Absolutely. I'll let you know when we get started."

Lenora smiled and said, "Thank you, Sam."

"It's my honor, Lenora."

SILAS DROPPED Clay and his father, Johnathan, at Clay's home, then headed to his home and family. He struggled with the stench and horrifying sight of the vultures eating away at Lester. He cried the rest of the way home and stopped the wagon by the well. He could see no stain of Lester's body on the wagon but decided to wash it down anyway. He pulled up a bucket of water, sloshed it over the bed of the buckboard, pulled off his shirt, and used it to wipe down the wagon. When he finished, he wrung out his shirt, set it on the buckboard, climbed up on the seat, and drove the buckboard and horses to the barn.

While unhitching the horses from the wagon in the barn, his father came out to help him. They quietly worked together, and when they finished, his father said, "Maggie is fixing you a hot bath in your bedroom. When you're ready, she has dinner for you too."

"Thanks, Papa."

"Was it awful?"

"Worse than I could ever imagine."

"I worried it would be when I saw the vultures," Silas said, but nothing more as they walked toward the house. When they were at the steps to the porch, Silas said, "I'm going to make it my life's work not to hoard and long for money or possessions. I'll take good care of my home, family, and our money, but I never want greed to overtake my soul."

His father wrapped his arms around him and whispered, "You are the best son a father could ask for." After a few moments, he added, "But you're wet and cold and getting me wet and cold. Let's get inside."

Silas nodded and chuckled. "Thanks, Papa."

He walked into his house, and Maggie smiled, "You're going to catch a chill running around with no shirt and damp clothes hanging on you."

"Aw, darlin', I was hoping just this one time, you'd let me come to the dinner table without a shirt or washing up."

"Dream on, cowboy. I have a hot bath waiting for you in our bedroom and dry, clean clothes on the bed."

"If you insist."

"I do."

ONCE HE WAS BATHED and warm and dressed in clean, dry clothes, Silas went to the dining area and sat down with the family for dinner. He said, "Thank you so much for waiting for dinner for me. It is a true blessing."

Bea said, "Teddy couldn't wait, but he was drinking milk from a wooden cup."

"Now, isn't that something grand and wonderful? Is he already asleep?"

Ben nodded. "Yep. I'm ready for him to talk more and play with us."

Silas grinned. "It'll all happen in time, son."

Marietta beamed at her son, proud of him and his love for his family. She said, "Noah's been telling us all about the construction in town."

"Well, Clay is right. Noah's a fine builder. We'll have to keep him out of the library, though."

Noah grinned and shook his head. "The library is still just a dream. Sawing, hammering, and all that goes into the building are already happening at Lenora's cafe."

Maggie asked, "Is that going to be the cafe's name?"

"I hadn't thought about it, but I think it's a grand idea."

Thomas said, "Now it's my turn. You won't believe the big wood stove I bought today."

Maggie looked at him and asked, "Not for our house, is it?"

"Nope. It's a fine stove but way too big for your house."

She smiled and kept the chatter going as long as they were all around the table. Later, Silas would be able to tell us a story that would help us go to bed without worrying about all the gruesome details of the day.

38

___

*"If I am in
Harmony with my family,
that's success."*
Ute Proverb

Aurora and Jane worked together, putting dinner on the table while John and Clay bathed in the bathtub behind the fireplace.

John said, "I hope never to see such a horrible thing again in my lifetime."

"I'm with you, Dad. I had no idea how awful it would be." Clay shuddered as he remembered the pieces of Lester Blunt either missing or lying around him while the vultures were having a feast.

John nodded. "I'm glad Thomas took Noah home with him. My guess is when the sheriff looked away about what he needed help with, Thomas picked up on the need for discretion."

"I'm glad he did. I hated what I saw. It's hard for me not to be glad

Lester Blunt is dead and gone, but damn! I never would have wished such an ending on anyone."

"I agree, son. Still, the cleaning up and taking the body back to town had to be done."

"I know, and a part of me is glad I helped."

"Why?"

"It isn't that I'm happy he's dead, for I'm not—but I am relieved that he is out of our lives. I might not have believed he was gone had I not seen him myself."

John sighed. "I can understand that, son."

"The worst part is that there have been many times I wished him dead and times I'd have been willing to kill him with my bare hands. Now I feel guilty as hell about those feelings."

"I understand. I've felt that way, too. However, feeling guilty about our feelings does not mean we are vile, hateful men. In point of fact, it proves we are men of good conscience. Otherwise, we'd be laughing and crowing at his demise."

Clay nodded and sighed, then blew out a long breath of relief. "Thanks, Dad. Your words help."

"Good. I'm glad it does. One of the things I've learned as a Chickasaw is that if we are in harmony with the earth, the people who love us, and not harm others, we can enjoy an honorable life."

"Well, I'm not Chickasaw, but I like how you think, Dad. I'll try to remember your words."

John smiled. "You are Chickasaw because you married my daughter and are raising your daughter as Chickasaw with Aurora. It's a circle of blessing and life."

Clay nodded. "I'm a lucky man."

"Yes, you are. Now dry off. I'm hungry."

"Me too!"

Both men laughed as they dried off and dressed.

Jane smiled, hearing their laughter. "They are getting more settled with all that has gone on this day. How are you, daughter?"

"Better. I think I was in shock, but I also am glad I was there when he died."

"Why?"

"I did not want anyone to do for me what I should do for myself. Conrad nearly forgot that."

"How do you know?"

"He said he should have invited me. It was only when he remembered the anxiety and grief was mine as much as his when he saw me following them. When he motioned for me to follow, I knew he was aware I needed to be a part of removing evil from my life—it couldn't be that I let him rescue me."

Jane hugged Aurora. "You and Conrad were brave and did exactly the right thing. Lester had choices and chose greed and evil instead."

"Yes. Right now, I'm ready to be with my loving family."

"Me too."

Aurora smiled as the men laughed behind the fireplace. "I'm glad to hear their laughter. It releases a burden around all that happened."

"So you are settled, daughter, that Lester Blunt has gone on to his next being?"

"Yes. He has many lessons to learn, but it is not for me to teach him. My life is to care for my daughter and husband, help other women birth their babies, and hopefully have a baby or two or three of my own body."

Jane laughed. "Be careful what you wish for, daughter. Hopes and dreams are powerful magic."

Aurora smiled. "As sure as the sun rises and sets, I believe in the magic of all around me."

Jane hugged her daughter, "Our men are ready for dinner."

"As am I."

EMMALINE TIED her horse to the fence post, took off her hat and perched it on the saddle horn, ran her fingers through her long, black hair, walked up the steps to the Grantham home, and raised her hand to knock on the door. Before she could knock, Joe opened the door and said, "I was watching for you."

"I'm glad you were."

"Momma Rose said to come on in. She's in the garden and will come in soon."

"Well, thank you very much. Where are Jolene and Adam?"

"They're helping Momma Rose. My job was to be the lookout.'

"You did a fine job, Joe. Shall we go to the garden to see if we can help?"

"Okay, but Momma Rose will make you work. She says we all have to work to make our lives full."

"She's smart, and I don't mind work."

Joe nodded and took Emma's hand. He led her through the house to a kitchen with a wood stove and sink with a pump handle and to a room where all sorts of boots, hats, sweaters, and coats were stored. She smiled and followed Joe out to the garden.

Rose looked up and smiled. "Come on over. We're nearly finished gathering the last of the pumpkins and squashes."

Emma nodded and looked across the garden. "You have a huge garden."

"I have to have a big garden to feed my children."

Jolene nodded and said, "Momma Rose calls us the hungry hoard."

"Do you know what that means?"

"Yep. We're a hungry bunch of children."

Emma laughed, and Rose blushed. "I keep trying to teach them a little, but there's always work. I'm better working in the garden and barns than with the teaching."

Emma smiled. "I can help you with the teaching. I'm useless in a garden, or so my mother says. I'm more likely to pull up the wrong thing or step on something important. She says it's because I have my head in the clouds."

Joe grinned. "That's what Momma Rose says about me, but sometimes there aren't any clouds around."

"My guess is they are waiting to sneak up on you."

"Really?"

"Well, I'm not certain you know, but it's a thought."

He nodded. "You're probably right. Momma Rose says you're the smartest friend she ever had."

Emma smiled and looked over at Rose. "Your Momma is a kind woman. I like reading and teaching and learning and sharing. I hate working in the garden."

Rose stood up, and Adam and Jolene each took a handle on the basket. Rose said, "Ya'll go on and set the basket in the mud room. Then you three hooligans go wash up. Dinner will be ready soon."

"I haven't been getting dirty. Do I have to?" Joe asked.

"Yes, even though you didn't get much dirt on you being the watchout, you still need to wash up. Go to the washroom, and Emma and I will have dinner on the table by the time you're finished."

The children entered the house with Joe holding the backdoor open for Jolene and Adam. Emma smiled and said, "They are great children."

"Yes, they are, and I love them like crazy, but they are a handful."

Emma took Rose's hand and said, "Come let me help you finish getting dinner on the table."

Rose looked down at their hands. "You're getting your hands dirty."

"I can wash them."

Rose squeezed her hand. "I've been nervous about you coming here this evening."

"Why?"

"Well, I used to watch you when you were teaching at Bloomfield, and I thought you were the most beautiful woman I'd ever seen."

"I'm glad and appreciate your words, but what made you feel nervous?"

"I was worried you were the usual sort of woman."

"You mean one who wants to marry a man and do his bidding for years and years?"

"Well, yes, sort of."

Emma smiled and kissed Rose's cheek. "I would never marry any man. If possible, I'd marry a woman—if I were to fall in love with her."

"Thank you for the kiss, Emma. We are of like minds."

"Good. Now, let's wash our hands and get dinner on the table."

"Good idea. The sooner we finish dinner, the sooner the children will be in bed, and we can have a deep talk."

Emma said, "Perfect."

Aurora kissed her mother and father goodnight and said, "Thanks, Dad, for all you did today to help Silas and Clay."

"You're welcome, but I did it for two reasons."

"Really?"

"Yes, it was the honorable thing to do to help a man who died today even though he wasn't an honorable or kind man. The second reason was that because he'd worked to harm you, I wanted to be sure he was dead and treated as well as possible. Then you are free of him, and I no longer have to worry about him."

Aurora kissed her father's cheek. "You are a wonderful father, and I'm glad you were here to help Clay and Silas with what must have been a terrible thing to do."

"It wasn't pleasant, but it had to be done."

"Good night, Daddy."

"Good night, Daughter." He kissed her cheek and went upstairs to join his wife in bed.

In their bedroom, Clay asked, "Are you all right with everything that happened today?"

"Yes, I am. First, sit with me, Clay. I have something to tell you."

He nodded and could tell by the tone of her voice that something had happened. He crossed his fingers, hoping it wasn't to do with her bleeding and that she was well.

He sat beside her on the bed, and she took his hand. She said, "I must tell you about Lester's death."

Clay bit his lip to say nothing but felt his wife's sorrow. He wanted to tell her everything would be all right, but he wasn't sure. He listened in awe as his wife told the story of Lester Blunt's death. He knew he could have never done what she and her friend Conrad had done.

At the end of the story, Aurora said, "Conrad and I sang Lester's death song. He had a choice even then to do the right thing, but it wasn't in him. I'm sorry he had to die, but there was nothing else for it."

He kissed her cheek and then asked, "Are you all right?"

"Not fully yet, but I will be. Momma helped with smudging Okchuli and me with sage. I don't harbor any grief, shame, or sorrow. I hope you understand I couldn't let Conrad do this alone."

"I do, darlin'. You are braver than I could have ever been."

She smiled softly and said, "Tomorrow, when the sun rises, I'll send a blessing to Lester that he finds an honorable way forward in his next plane of life."

"Good. Do you have any women who will be due soon?"

"Yes, two of them will need me any day now. I've talked with their husbands, and they understand my safety needs."

"Thank you for doing that, darlin'."

"There's one other thing I want to ask you."

"If I can say yes, of course I will. Anything."

She smiled. "This is important for me and my profession. I've found a young woman who wants to be a midwife."

"Is she Chickasaw?"

"Yes, and she is eager to learn. Her name is Evangeline Anna Baker, and she prefers to be called Eva."

"That's interesting."

Aurora looked at her husband and asked, "What's interesting?"

"Both you and Eva share the name Evangeline. For you, it is your middle name, but I think it is a name filled with goodness."

"Thanks, Clay. I don't think of my middle name very often."

He smiled and asked, "When do you start teaching Eva?"

"The Monday after Thanksgiving. I told her I wanted to wait until my parents returned home. She is seventeen years old and has been going to Bloomfield Academy but is ready to graduate. For now, she lives with her grandmother, Dorthea Baker, in Tishomingo."

"Where are her parents?"

"They are here for a few more days but are moving to Texas. Eva didn't want to go with them. She loves living here and wants to be a midwife here."

"What does her grandmother say?"

"She hasn't talked with Eva yet about her idea."

"What is her idea?"

"She wants to give her granddaughter one year to become a midwife. Dorthea will stay at her home in Tishomingo. After Eva's year of training, Dorthea will leave her house and land to Eva and join her son and his wife and their younger children in Galveston, Texas.

He nodded. "It sounds like a good plan, but is a year enough?"

"I don't know, but it will be long enough to get her started, at least. But it entirely depends on Eva's determination and what she already knows about how life comes to us all. Regardless, I'll be around to help her as needed, even when I think she is ready to be on her own. Eva will come here on Monday morning. I told her I wanted you to meet her before I would take her on."

"What does 'take her on' mean?"

"Well, most women who become midwives live with the woman who teaches her. It would greatly help me and her if she lived here with us until she is ready to be on her own."

"Then she would go back to her grandmother's home?"

"Yes. Her grandmother plans to deed her home and land to Eva. Of course, Eva also has her own allotment, which is next to her grandmother's land."

"How will you feel having another woman living with us?"

"Fine, I think. She could live here for a year, and then I'll follow up with her occasionally for a year or two once she is on her own.

She could learn much faster living here and could watch over Okchuli and the other children when I'm busy with Maggie and helping her around the farm.

"Have you talked with Maggie about all of this?"

"Yes, and she talked with Shirley and Mrs. Rittenhouse about her. Both women know the family and like her a lot. Mrs. Rittenhouse said Eva's parents wanted to move to Texas, where the climate is warmer. They have other families there, too, in the far south of Texas."

"What do you think about her from deep inside?"

Aurora smiled. "I introduced her to Momma as well. We both like her. We need more Chickasaw women who are midwives. Momma went and talked with her grandmother, too. They are all in agreement that Eva is a good and smart girl. Her grandmother says she works hard and is always kind and helpful."

Clay nodded. "It sounds like you all think she is a good person and willing to learn."

"I think so. She will be my first midwife to mentor. Plus, she can help around the house. Besides, I'm free of fear for Okchuli and me, and I want a new start for myself."

He grinned. "I agree. It sounds like a good plan. I also think you're eager to test your book."

Aurora smiled and nodded. "Yes, I am. Silas has planned to print a hundred copies of the book. He gave me two copies of the test printing of the book—one for me and one for my first mentorship."

"I'm happy to meet her on the Monday morning after Thanksgiving. After that, I'll head on into town to continue work on the cafe and library bookstore."

"Thank you, Clay."

He smiled, "You didn't have to ask, but I'm glad you did. My only concerns are for you and Okchuli. Everything else is the extras."

She kissed him and said, "Have you noticed that Okchuli is sleeping through the night every night."

"Yes, I have."

Aurora smiled, "If you're not too tired, I have a good idea."

He wrapped his arms around her and kissed her. He whispered, "What's your idea?"

"We could practice making babies."

He grinned. "I've heard practice makes perfect."

"That's what I heard too."

"Then we should listen to sound advice."

39

———

"The ones that
matter the most are the children.
They are the true Human Beings."
Lakota Proverb

Rose and Emma sat on the sofa before the fireplace, murmuring while the children slept upstairs. They spoke of their time at Bloomfield Academy and their efforts to fit in with others.

Emma said, "I finally decided to be me and not worry about what others think of me."

Rose said, "I noticed you wear men's pants under your dresses."

Emma smiled. "I notice you do the same. Do you hate wearing dresses?"

"Not really, but they aren't convenient when doing farm work."

"I'm sure you're right. I love to ride my horse everywhere I go. Having men's pants helps a lot, but I keep them hemmed up enough that they don't show much."

"Same here. I came up with a new idea about skirts and farming."

"Really?"

"Yep," Rose stood up, grinned, and untied her skirt and let it drop."

Emma laughed and clapped her hands. "What a great idea! It never occurred to me to separate the skirt from the top of the dress."

"I figured it out after years of wearing out my skirts. I make my tops long enough to tuck into the men's pants. I wear a belt through the pants' belt loops, then hem up the legs and tie on the skirt. It works great when working on the farm. I drop my skirt, hang it in the barn, and get busy working."

"Genius. I'll have to give that a try. Of course, my father will be incensed."

"He doesn't approve of your choice of mates?"

"Not at all. Although we've discussed it often, he is still incensed at the whole idea, mainly, I think, because he wants grandchildren."

"What about your mother," Rose asked.

"She doesn't love the idea but said if I found the woman of my heart, she'd take that woman into her heart, too."

Rose nodded. "I've just assumed there is no way to live with a woman I love. Of course, it's not like I've ever had a woman to love."

"It is difficult to do."

"Why should it be difficult or, better yet, something only men get to decide?"

Emma smiled, "Because our god is a man—at least, that's what I've been told."

Rose chuckled, then said, "You're probably right. I remember what my second mother told me, though. She said, 'When like spirits meet, they recognize each other, and gender has little to do with it all.' It was the first time I realized that gender was biological, but it had nothing to do with my heart—my spirit if you will. So, I've decided to let my spirit do the work my heart yearns for while I, physically and mentally, keep doing the work needed to keep my home and children."

Emma chuckled. "I love how you think. My mother told me something like that before I came out to visit you."

Rose tied on her skirt, sat back beside Emma, and tucked her arm through Emma's. "It seems too soon to tell how I feel emotionally about you, but I do like you. I like touching you, too."

"I agree. We've known each other for a few years—most of our lives, in fact—but only in the past several hours have we had any association of the possibility of something more for us."

Rose nodded. "Just to be clear, I don't believe in love at first sight."

"Nor do I. I'm not sure what sexual love is, but I do believe in learning how we feel about each other. We may be two women who are good friends and nothing more. However, it may be the beginning of something deeper."

"I agree. How about we spend time together whenever possible and see what happens as we go along?"

"Exactly what I want to do. For now, I need to get back home. Momma will worry if I'm out too late. Besides, tomorrow I have work to do getting the library and bookstore up and running."

"I don't want your mother to worry. Besides, I have to get up at dawn to get busy with my day's work."

Emma stood up and pulled Rose to stand with her. She wrapped her arms around Rose and said, "I need a kiss to see how I feel about you for now."

Rose smiled, reached up, touched Emma's cheek, and kissed her lightly.

Emma sighed. "Lovely. One more kiss, and I'll head home. I have lots of work to do tomorrow, as do you."

It was a few more than one kiss, but in a few moments, they both knew it was time to end the evening and think about all that had happened on this one lovely day. Emma got on her horse, and Rose waved goodbye.

When she closed the door, Rose said, "Now, that's what I want in a woman. Love, beauty, brains—she's the best thing this side of the Mississippi."

CONRAD SAT AT HIS CAMPFIRE, reading a new book—new for him at least—by his favorite author, Mark Twain, *Pudd'nhead Wilson*. Each page made him more glad than ever to be Chickasaw, for it seemed the African people had a more difficult life in this land of the free and home of the brave. He snorted and muttered, "As usual, the land is owned or stolen by the wealthy in their big homes, stepping on the heads of every other human being."

He'd spent much time thinking about Lester Blunt but felt no fear or guilt about the man's passing.

When Conrad was sleepy, he covered the fire with dirt, put his book in his saddle bag, and entered his canvas tent. It was small, and no floor was sewn into the tent, but it helped keep out the mosquitos and any rain that bothered to fall at night. He had a small tarp he used as a flooring to keep his blanket clean and block out the dampness of the forest floor.

He wrapped his warm blanket around his body and used another smaller blanket for his head as a pillow. He was quickly asleep, dreaming. He always welcomed his dreams, knowing that many times, they helped him understand what he should be doing. Sometimes, his dreams even showed him new paths, and generally, he knew before the telegram was sent that another family needed his services traveling to Indian Territory.

His sleep deepened, and then Lester came to him in his dream and said, "I know you didn't push me, but that old coyote nipped at my heels and startled me into falling to my death."

Conrad said, "Yes, that is what happened."

Lester asked, "Was there ever a treasure?"

"Yes, but you threw it away with your vile treatment of your wife and the other people around you. Treasure is often right before our faces and not in our pockets."

"Maybe. Sounds like silly talk to me."

"Well, while you try to figure it out, I will choose a different dream and rest easy."

"Okay, but I'm still unsure what to think."

"Think less, especially about money. It is the way I go, Lester. You'll be happier, and your life will be richer."

"Yeah, and look at you. Sleeping in a bit of a scrawny tent, lying on the ground, all alone in the wilderness with a rattlesnake wondering if you're worth killin'."

Conrad swallowed and carefully opened his eyes. He saw the snake crawling in under the edge of his tent. Conrad decided to wait and see what happened. He knew he couldn't move fast enough to avoid the snake's bite. So he waited. He closed his eyes and stilled his heart and mind. After several minutes, he opened his eyes to see the snake crawling out of his tent with his rattle as quiet and harmless as a sleeping baby.

Conrad looked up at the sky and whispered, "Thank you."

He closed his eyes and slept until the morning sun was beginning to rise. He woke when he heard Aurora singing a song of belonging and moving forward for Lester Blunt. When her song changed to one of gratitude to him, he smiled, knowing Aurora was doing well and his baby was in her rightful mother's home—Aurora's home—safe from men like Lester Blunt. His child was safe, loved, and blessed, and for all of that, he was grateful.

He stood up, folded his blankets and tent, and tied them behind his saddle. He walked a few steps away to relieve himself. As he did, he felt a searing pain in his heel. He jerked out his knife, dropped to his knees, cut off the head of the rattlesnake, and threw it away from where his camp had been. He groaned and shook his head as he sat by his cold fire and tried to think about what to do. Some folks thought cutting the area and sucking out the venom worked, but he knew better. That just made it worse.

He looked around and saw some herbs he remembered for rattlesnake bite. He pulled up the herbs, including the roots, started his fire again, filled his pan with water from his canteen, and, using his knife, cut up the roots—Prairie Rattlesnake Root. When the water was boiling, he filled his cup with the water, drank about half of it, and used the remainder to clean his wound.

He added more water to the pan and then started chewing the leaves. He was feeling a little less pain. He made a compress of the chewed leaves and charcoal dust from the fire's edge. He poured more hot herb-infused water over his wound and drank another cup full of the herbal water.

He pressed the compress on the wound and wrapped it with a wet leather strip. He limped over to his horse and got his empty extra water canteen. He went to the creek, filled both canteens with water, and boiled the water with more roots and leaves. He filled both canteens with the water he'd boiled. He pulled the boiled roots out, wrapped them in a pouch, dressed, and checked that everything was secure on his saddle.

He was beginning to be dizzy and worried he would faint or, worse yet, go to sleep. He wasn't sure if his dizziness was from the rattlesnake bite or the Prairie Rattlesnake Root water he'd been drinking.

It took several tries for him to get in the saddle, but he finally made it. With a piece of rope, he threaded the rope through his belt loops and tied it to the loops of his saddle, just in case he fainted. He told his horse, Soba, "On to the Mississippi girl. If I make it that far, I'll be fine."

The horse started walking faster than usual while Conrad sang his birth song. He'd drink a bit from his canteen every few fingers of the sun rising higher.

The rattlesnake was angry at having his head cut off. He told Conrad, "It wasn't my fault you were peeing on my favorite stump."

Conrad asked, "How was I to know?"

"If you had any sense, you'd know. How's your foot feeling, you silly human?"

"It's fine. I could dance all night on my foot."

"Right. Keep singing your song and sipping your water. Maybe you'll live. Maybe not. I don't much care since you already killed me."

And so the day went, with Conrad in and out of his mind. The snake whined about being dead. Lester bemoaned at his fate and at not having the treasure. On and on and on it went.

Now and again, Conrad would talk with people he loved who had gone on to their next existence. His mother repeatedly reminded him to keep singing his birth song and drinking the Rattlesnake Root tea he'd made.

His father said, "I'm proud of you son. Hang on. If you make it to the Big River, you'll be fine—sore but fine. Trust Soba and your Momma."

At times, he was ready to give up and die, but he sang his birth song and drank the Rattlesnake Root Tea every hour just as his mother urged him. He was sleepy and wanted to sleep but wasn't sure he'd wake up if he did. When he dozed too much or started snoring, the horse would trot—hard—pounding the trail and waking him. Once he was awake, Soba would stop the brutal trot and go faster and softer in her stride.

By midday, the rattlesnake and Lester Blunt had both stopped bothering him and whining about each other's demise, for which he was grateful.

His horse, Soba, stopped now and again to chew a little grass and drink from a stream or even a puddle, but she kept going east to the big river. Soba remembered where she and Conrad's people had been born for generations. She wanted to be by the big river if she had to die or Conrad had to die. She hoped they would both live, though. At one point, she thought, *maybe Huck Finn, Tom Sawyer, or Pudd'nhead Wilson would be there.*

A few miles later, she thought, *Mark will be there and help us if we're lucky.* She didn't know who Mark was, but Conrad thought he was an intelligent man and told great stories.

All Conrad could think of was living long enough to go back to Tishomingo, on the banks of Pennington Creek, to see Aurora holding his daughter in her arms with Clay standing by their side. He was relieved Clay took Okchuli as his daughter. He was a good father and a good man.

As the sun went down, the horse Soba and the man Conrad were losing hope. They had many miles yet to reach the Mississippi River —the Big River.

Soba was tired and worried she wouldn't reach the Big River.

Conrad was tired but hoped they would make it to the Big River.

At least Conrad's pain was less.

The big rocks at Devil's Den prayed for him. They wanted him back home in the shelter of their caves and crevices.

40

Early the next morning, long before sunrise, Aurora woke with a startle. She shook Clay and said, "I have to go outside, Clay. Conrad is in trouble."

He said, "Okay, darlin'. Give me a moment, and I'll come out with you."

Both got out of bed and quickly dressed. The sky was dark, and there was no moon. The stars seemed bigger and closer than usual. The Milky Way seemed to wrap itself around the couple. Clay started to light a lantern, but Aurora stopped him. "Conrad is near the Mississippi, and the night is dark. We must be in the dark."

He followed her outside, worried about snakes, but then remembered that most snakes don't bother to come out at night, especially in November when frost is on the ground. They stopped in the usual place where Aurora usually stood to greet the sun. As their eyes adjusted to the darkness, both Clay and Aurora began to be able to see a little better.

Clay stood quietly near his wife as she lifted her arms and began to sing her birth song. After a few minutes, she sang a different song and said, "It's your choice, Conrad. You are on the cusp."

Aurora and Clay turned when they heard Jane say, "Okchuli woke up crying."

"She's quiet now," Clay said.

Jane nodded, and Okchuli held out her arms and said, "Momma. Hold!"

Clay grinned and said, "That's a new word."

Aurora came to her mother and took Okchuli in her arms. She nodded to Clay and her mother, then quietly went back to her place of singing. Aurora began to sing Conrad's birth song again while Okchuli clapped her hands and said, "Wake! Wake! Wake!"

Clay was tempted to laugh at the pleasure of his daughter's speaking while Aurora sang a song he hadn't heard before. Jane reached out and took his hand. He looked at Jane, and she whispered, "Aurora and Okchuli are helping Conrad."

"Why? How?"

"I don't know, but be quiet!"

He nodded and listened to his wife singing and his daughter clapping her hands, repeatedly saying 'Wake!'.

CONRAD SWAYED, and Soba stomped her feet, splashing water on his legs. They were at the big river, and the horse walked into the water a little more. When Conrad felt the water on his legs, he opened his eyes, sighed, drank the last few drops of water in his canteen, and then began to sing his birth song.

When he heard Aurora singing with him, he smiled, and tears coursed down his face. He sang louder for a few minutes and then repeatedly heard Okchuli shouting, 'Wake!' He nodded. "I'm awake, daughter. Thank you for waking me."

He looked up at the stars and saw a snake, a coyote, and a big man. He waved to them and said, "Thank you for helping me understand."

He wasn't sure exactly what he understood but knew he would never take another man's or a snake's life unless necessary. The coyote howled a song of life and belonging.

ON THE BANKS of Pennington Creek, when a coyote began to howl over and over, Aurora said, "He's awake."

Okchuli laughed, clapped her hands and said, "Wake!"

Clay couldn't stop his tears when his daughter reached for him, said, "DaDa!" and hugged her father.

"Yes, girly, I'm your DaDa. Thank you for helping, Momma and Conrad."

She smacked her lips, and he said, "I have a feeling your Momma would love to feed you." He looked at his wife, who was beaming. He said, "I don't understand a damned thing that happened tonight, but I'm grateful."

Jane hugged his shoulders. "That's all that's needed, Clay. You're a good man, and I'm delighted you loved and married my daughter and love her daughter, too."

"I love them both so much it hurts sometimes."

"Exactly how it should be. Now, I'm going back to bed. I'm an old woman, and I'm tired."

Aurora smiled, "I'll let Okchuli nurse a bit and then return to my bed."

Clay said as they walked into the house, "I'll wait for you, darlin', and you can explain what happened here tonight."

"I will. It is every bit as much of a miracle as you imagine."

The mystery of miracles abounded and surrounded the family from the Mississippi River to Pennington Creek.

LATER THAT MORNING, Emma woke early, dressed in her oldest dress and the usual men's pants underneath her skirt. She gathered some rags and a bucket her mother used for cleaning. When she entered the kitchen, her mother asked, "Did you get a scrub brush?"

"No. I forgot."

"I laid one on the table for you."

Emma kissed her mother's cheek and said, "Thank you, Momma."

"You're welcome, daughter."

Her father walked into the kitchen, yawned, and said, "We need to talk, daughter."

She smiled, kissed her father's cheek, and said, "I'm happy to talk with you, Daddy. Let me help Momma set the breakfast on the table, and we'll talk."

He smiled, nodded, kissed her forehead, and sat at the table. He read the new *Weekly Beginnings* while the women finished cooking and setting breakfast. He smiled at his wife and daughter. "Thank you for blessing me with a good meal to start the day, Becca."

Emma's mother kissed the top of her husband's head and said, "It is always my pleasure, Harry."

He squeezed her hand and said, "I'll say grace, then we can eat and talk."

Once he said, "Amen," he reached for the platter of biscuits, took two, and put them on his plate. He handed the platter to his wife, who also took two biscuits. She smiled, gave the platter to Emma, and said, "Daughter, you're wearing tattered clothes today."

"Yes, Momma, I am. I plan to spend the day scrubbing and cleaning the library and bookstore. No point in ruining good clothes."

"Good idea."

Her father nodded and said, "Your mother and I would love to help today."

She smiled and nodded. Before she could say anything, her father said, "I love making you smile so bright, Emma."

"Thank you, Daddy."

He nodded and continued. "I'm proud of you, and I think being the librarian and selling books is a perfect occupation for you. I feel blessed because it will keep you here, close to us."

"I feel the same way," her mother said.

They were quiet momentarily as they buttered their biscuits, took bacon from the platter, and scrambled eggs. Finally, Emma said, "Now I understand why we're having a big breakfast. We'll all be working hard at the library building."

Her father nodded, "Yes, we will. I want to talk with you about Rose Grantham."

Emma stilled and was very quiet until she softly said, "I thought you would."

"Don't go cold on me, daughter. I know your spirit, but I can't say I'm delighted. A woman loving another woman rather than a man doesn't seem right." He shook his head and said, "I love you, but loving you doesn't change a thing for me. I don't think it's the right path you're choosing, but I love you too much to stand in your way."

She smiled. "If I could—if my spirit would let me, I would choose a different path, but I'm simply not a woman who wants a man in her bed. I want you to know I thank you, Daddy."

He held up a hand. "This isn't a blessing—yet. I'm asking you to take care. Some folks would rather beat you to death or stone you than let you share your heart and body with a woman. So please, take care, and hide as much as you can. I want to see you grow up to be an old, wrinkled woman with stringy and dingy gray hair."

Emma laughed. "Please don't paint such a picture, Daddy. But I promise I will be careful. Very careful. There are three little children to protect. It's not just Rose and me but also Joe, Jolene, and Adam."

"Thank you for understanding, Emma. I agree Rose is a good woman and has taken excellent care of her family and the farm."

"She has, and it is a lot of work, day in and day out."

"Well, for now, let's finish breakfast and get busy at your new place of work."

"Thank you, Daddy."

"You're welcome, Daughter."

CLAY RODE ABNER, his horse, into town with Noah riding Maggie's horse, Gypsy.

Noah asked, "Did you hear that coyote howling last night?"

"Yes, I did. He was loud."

"Yes, he was. I looked out my window but couldn't see him."

"Well, usually, they howl because they are calling a mate or another coyote. Sometimes, though, I think they howl because they can."

"He sounded happy to me."

"I thought so, too. Now, are you excited about today?"

"Yep. Momma said we wouldn't have any school until a week or so. She and Granny are working hard to make a special dinner for Thanksgiving."

Clay nodded and said, "I was surprised your Papa and Pops weren't coming with us this morning."

"Daddy said they'd be in soon. Pops wanted to see if they could round up a wild hog sow."

"Really?"

Noah nodded.

Clay said, "Well, I'd be surprised if they could get the hog into the pen without a fuss."

"Pops says he has a trick, and it's no big deal."

"Whew! He must be a man of magic if he can get a rooting sow into the pen with just your Papa and him."

Noah shrugged his shoulders. "He seemed pretty certain about it all."

"Well, we've got plenty of work to do today at the cafe."

"Where's Johnathan?"

"He said he'd come along a bit later." Clay shook his head. "You know what I think?"

"What?"

"Those three men are up to something."

"Like what?"

"A surprise, maybe."

Noah laughed. "I love surprises."

"Well, we'll see what happens with those three fellas later. For now, we're here and have work to do."

Noah pointed at the library building. "It looks like Miss Emma is already working."

"I'm sure she and Mrs. Rittenhouse are busy as bees."

They rode their horses around to the back of *Okchuli Press* and tied them up in the shed Silas had built for them.

Noah said. "That's how Momma, Granny, and Aurora are. They are either working or talking about working or sometimes both."

"I'll tell you a secret about women, Noah."

Noah grinned. He loved hearing adult secrets.

Clay patted his horse's rump and said, "Women make the world go round."

"By themselves?"

"Yep. Never think for a moment that men or children run things, son. It's women who run everything. Men are here just hanging around to help with the heavy lifting and reach things too high for the ladies to reach."

Noah nodded but had his doubts. Surely, there was more to being a man than lifting heavy things and reaching stuff that was too high.

Clay smiled as he opened the door to the cafe building, watching Noah, and said, "Of course, I'm not the sharpest axe in the shed, so you might want to ask someone else."

Lenora was already in the cafe working on cleaning the old stove. She looked up and said, "What should Noah ask about, Clay?"

"Go on, son, and ask Mrs. Blunt the question."

Noah nodded, then said, "It's just that Clay said women run the world, and men are just hanging around to help with the heavy lifting and reaching things that are too high for women to reach."

She smiled and said, "Noah, I believe Clay is smarter than he seems."

Clay laughed. "I told you so, Noah."

Noah shook his head but asked, "What do I get to hammer on first?"

"Follow me, lad, and I'll show you."

Noah followed Clay to the wall they were building, but now and again throughout the morning, he thought about how the world goes around. He wasn't sure if Mrs. Blunt and Clay were joshing him. Still, he felt his mother was the one who made everything happen in their lives—except for all the things Papa did.

Once Clay had Noah busy hammering in the stud bracings, he went to Lenora and quietly said, "I'm surprised to see you here, Lenora."

"Well, no matter what else happens today, I want to start working on my life."

"I understand, and I'm glad. Let me know if there's anything, anything at all, I can do to help you."

"Thank you, Clay. I may want to change a few things at the house, but not yet."

Clay looked over to see Noah pounding nails into boards. He stood closer to Lenora and said, "Silas, his dad, and Johnathan are working with the sheriff preparing a place for Lester's remains."

She nodded, looked up to be sure Noah was busy, and said, "That's the part of it all I didn't want to watch or have a part in doing. It felt too much like I was sending him away when he did that to himself—no matter how he died."

"I understand. I'll keep Noah busy, but let me know if there is anything I can do to help."

"Thank you, Clay. That's very generous of you, considering what my husband tried to do to your wife and home."

"Lenora, not one moment of your life should be taking up his guilt. All of that is on him."

She smiled. "Thanks for understanding. Will you and Aurora come when they have everything ready?"

"Yes. The women will come into town in a few hours. We'll all be there to support you. More importantly, we want to support you even after today."

"I appreciate your words. Now, if you'll get out of my way and get busy, I'll clean this stove and make it vermin-free."

Clay smiled and nodded. "Yes, ma'am."

41

Mrs. Rittenhouse was surprised to see both of Emma's parents carrying buckets, rags, and brushes. She smiled and said, "I see you've Tom Sawyered your parents into helping you."

Harold scratched his head and said, "I'm not sure what 'Tom Sawyered' is, but we're here to help."

Becca said, "It is obvious our daughter is better educated than her parents, but even I know what 'Tom Sawyered' means."

"Well, then, Becca, enlighten me so I don't stand here lookin' like an idiot."

She smiled and told him the story of Tom Sawyer and the fried chicken and getting his friends to paint the fence so he didn't have to.

He laughed and said, "Daughter, if you think I'm going to do all the work today while you eat fried chicken, you need to get your brain checked."

Emma laughed. "No way, Daddy. But I will enjoy your help and your suggestions."

"Well, if we were to move tables and shelves around where you want them, we'd have a better idea of what needs to be done regarding waxing, painting, and such."

"I agree. Mrs. Rittenhouse and I already did the sweeping and mopping yesterday."

Becca asked, "Why are all those rugs, chairs, and tables scattered around?"

"They are so we can set up quiet places for folks to sit and read or quietly talk about things."

Becca nodded. "Your father is right. But first, let's think about which areas might be suitable for quiet places. Then let's move the shelves, tables, and that marvelous desk where we think we want them. Finally, we can lay out the rugs, chairs, and tables."

Mrs. Rittenhouse said, "I have other work to do next door. Let me know if you need anything."

Harry asked, "Before you leave, do you know when Mr. Blunt's funeral will be?"

"This afternoon. Right now, some men are helping the sheriff dig his grave."

"It would be a kindness if you let us know when the time is near. I didn't care much for him, but he was still a part of our community, and I want to honor his wife."

"As do we all, Mr. Crawford. I'll let you know as soon as I know."

AURORA and her mother spent the morning cooking and cleaning while the men were in town digging Lester Blunt's grave. Aurora felt a little sad about it all, but only a little. She was glad everyone was pitching in to help Lenora officially send her husband to his next being.

She watched Okchuli play on the floor on a blanket. She said, "I love to see her playing with the wooden toys Daddy carved for her. I swear sometimes she talks to her doll, too."

Jane said, "You were like that too. I think babies know more than we can ever guess. She's not quite six months old and is already talking. She is going to grow up to be a spectacular woman."

"I think so too, Momma."

"How are you feeling today?"

"Much better. I hope Conrad is doing well. I dreamed a rattlesnake was involved, but I saw his spirit bright and alive."

"I felt his spirit, too. His horse has taken very good care of him."

"Momma, have you noticed how much like Conrad Okchuli is?"

"Yes, I have and agree about her ears too. I hope she grows up to be as in touch with the spirit world as he is."

"Me too, but it is sometimes a perilous pathway."

"Yes, but we all need those people in our lives."

Aurora nodded. "Watching her call to Conrad to wake was a true miracle."

"And we are all happy and blessed to have her in our lives."

As the day went on, Emma became more and more settled about her life. Her parents helping her was terrific. She felt closer to them than she had in several years. Her mother said, "You know, some posters, paintings, and photographs would be nice on the walls, especially of the life of our town around here."

"That's a great idea, Momma."

"Now, help me decide which rugs go where while your father finishes polishing the tall shelves."

Emma sighed and smiled as she looked around the space. "It does look like a library, Momma, doesn't it?"

"Yes, it does. I'd never have thought of having a library, but I'm eager for it now."

"Me too. Let's place the rugs and then stand back and see how we feel about it all."

The bell above the door tinkled, and Emma turned to see Rose with the children in tow behind her. She smiled and said, "Welcome to our library!"

Rose smiled and said, "It looks charming, Emma. I'd love to come here, sit and read, or check out books to take home. You and your parents have done a fine job."

Adam tugged on his sister's skirt and asked, "Momma Rose, is the library just for grownups, or can we use it, too?"

Emma smiled and said, "It will be for everyone. Would you like to meet my Momma and Daddy?"

Jolene said, "I want to!"

"Then follow me, children." She walked a few steps to stand by her mother and said, "This is my Momma. Her name is Rebecca, but everyone calls her Becca."

Jolene nodded and asked, "What do we call her?"

Emma was surprised at the question and turned to her mother. "I don't know."

Her mother shook her head and smiled. "Don't be silly, Emma. You children can call me Gramma Becca. I don't have any grandchildren, but I would love to have you think of me as a grandmother."

Jolene nodded. "That would be great. We don't have a Gramma or Granddaddy."

Rose smiled and said, "Thank you so much. The children will love having a Gramma."

Adam pointed to the back of the room and asked, "What about him?"

Harold turned around and said, "Well, since Gramma Becca has started with the naming, I suppose I can be Granddad. How does that sound?"

Adam grinned. "I like it."

Joe said, "Me too," then he ran over to stand by Harry and said, "Momma Rose is scared you won't like her."

"Really? Is she mean and ugly?"

"No! She is nice and pretty—for a girl, that is."

Harry laughed, "Then let's not borrow trouble."

"How do you borrow trouble?"

"You decide things will be terrible before you even know anything."

Joe nodded. "I'll try not to borrow trouble."

"Good, lad. Now, I need some help polishing these low shelves. Bending over hurts my back. Could you help me with that?"

"Sure. I know how to polish, too."

"What a relief for us all."

Emma laughed, Rose blushed, then turned to Becca and said, "Well, so far, so good. I was afraid about meeting you but decided it would be all right if you loved Emma."

Adam nodded. "Momma Rose said we had to behave, be nice, and not ask too many questions. Joe asks a lot of questions."

"Yep," Jolene said, "And now he's having to work."

Emma shook her head. "If you two would help polish the low shelves, we might be finished much quicker."

Jolene asked, "Can we call you Momma Emma?"

"Maybe soon, but not yet."

"Why not now?"

"We haven't decided."

"Who does the deciding?"

Rose interrupted the conversation, "Emma and I are the only ones who will decide, which will happen when we are ready. Now. You've done your fair share of talking and asking questions without polishing a single shelf."

Gramma Becca said, "Come on, Jolene, I'll help you. By the way, you should know I love your name."

Jolene smiled and said, "Me too!"

Adam shook his head. "I'll go help, and you two can talk about it all, but you should know we've already decided."

"Is that so?" Rose asked."

He nodded. "We want two mommas, and we like Emma a lot."

"Maybe, but not yet," Emma said. "We're just getting to know each other again and will decide when the time is right."

He shrugged. "Okay, but we decided already," then turned to help polish the shelves.

Rose shook her head and said, "I'm sorry. I did not mean to show up and push about us, but the children begged to come and see where your library would be. Frankly, I wanted to see you, too."

Emma took her hand and said, "It's fine. I love the children, too. The only thing is, I'm not someone who jumps in without thinking things through."

"I'm the one who simply goes along with whatever happens and then hopes I'm doing the right thing. It works out—mostly."

"Then, by all means, let's go slowly as long as possible and see how things might be for ourselves and together. We both deserve to ask for what we want and allow the other to choose something different if needed."

"Goodness gracious, that sounds wonderful. I've always just had to do what needed to be done. Here I am twenty-two years old and feel like a hundred and two."

Emma chuckled. "And here I am, twenty-five years old, and feel about five years old.

"Can we walk and talk about the possibilities and our desires while the children and your parents polish things?"

"Let me check with Momma and Daddy, and I'll be right back."

As the two women walked on the boardwalk, some folks were carefully watching, thinking that if they held hands, they would have to say something. Neither woman held the other's hand, but they simply talked.

Emma was so tempted to hold Rose's hand that she clasped her hands behind her back as they walked and talked.

Rose had trouble keeping her hands still, so she clasped them in front of her while holding her purse strings tightly.

Emma said, "Not touching you is difficult, Rose."

Rose agreed. "I know. I'm feeling the same way. But that's part of why I wanted to go for a walk in public. We need to learn how to be safe in public so we can live our lives how we wish in private."

"My heavens, but you are a smart woman."

"Thanks. I'm pretty much a tom-boy and have been all my life. I wish I could whack off all my hair like a man."

"I understand. I wish I could at least shorten my hair. I like having it brush my shoulders, but having it drag nearly to the floor is inconvenient sometimes."

"Why do you keep it so long?"

"It's what Momma has always said I should do."

"Why?"

"I'm not sure."

"Ask her, and then maybe you'll find a way to do exactly what you want."

Emma smiled and asked, "What about you?"

"I've been thinking about cutting off my hair and having a wig made of it. Then, I could wear my hair long in public but have it short at home and while working."

"Well, that sounds like a great idea. Why haven't you done it?"

"I worry that someone will see me with my hair short and say awful things."

"Like what?"

"That I'm trying to be a man or worse yet, call me awful names publicly."

Emma nodded. "Well, you're right about that. I've an idea."

"What?"

"Let me talk with Momma first, then I'll tell you."

"Good. We should go back to the library."

"Yes, we should. This was a great idea. Many folks have seen us walking and chatting but not holding hands or kissing, although that's exactly what I want to do."

"Me too. We need to go slowly and let things happen quietly, and then, fingers crossed," she crossed her fingers, "There will be no fuss about us being together."

WHEN THEY RETURNED to the library, Emma opened the door and grinned. "My goodness, Rose, you should have brought the children sooner. The library is lovely!"

Jolene approached Emma, tugged on her skirt, and said, "It was Gramma Becca's idea that we put the flowers on the tables in bowls."

"Well, it is charming."

Joe said, "Granddad said we should beat the rugs before we put them on the clean floor."

"How did that go?"

"It was great!" Adam said. We beat on the rugs with big sticks. It was lots of fun."

Emma looked up to see her father smiling, and he said, "The boys had a right old time, and Jolene picked every wildflower that hasn't died for the cold season behind the store. The children are handy to have around."

Emma went to her father and hugged him. She said, "Thank you, Daddy."

"Thank you, daughter. I needed these children in my life."

"Good. Rose and I will go slower than you and the children, but I know we'll get there."

He smiled and thought *I'm not sure what I was fussing about last night. Even old codgers can learn a bit about life and love.*

Before anyone could say anything more, Mrs. Rittenhouse said, "There will be a ceremony for Mr. Blunt about three o'clock this afternoon. Everyone is welcome to be there. We'll have a bit of shared reception afterward, here in the library, if it's okay with you, Emma."

"Certainly. The children have helped my parents. They worked together while Rose and I had a walk. Now they have everything here in ship-shape."

"I can see that. I'm happy for you all."

42

***

*"There would be
no rainbows if the eyes
had no tears."*
Native American Proverb

Most folks in Tishomingo did not like Lester Blunt, but almost everyone admired his wife, Lenora. She was a tall, elegant woman with black hair, dark brown eyes with touches of gold, and a soft, quiet voice. She was known far and wide for her cooking skills, but most folks felt sorry for her. Who would not feel sorry for her with the brutal Lester Blunt for her husband?

For most of her life, Lenora had followed the desires and wishes of first her father and, later, as an adult, her husband. Her mother stayed quiet and in the background while Lenora's father scolded and beat both her and her mother regularly. Lenora could escape for a few months when she went to boarding school at Bloomfield Academy. One night, when Lenora was at the Academy, her mother packed all her personal belongings while her father was down at the saloon, got on her horse, and left town. Lenora never had a chance to say goodbye to her mother, and her father did not attempt to find her either.

When Lenora's father said, "I've chosen Lester Blunt to be your husband," she didn't argue or think much about it. She didn't expect her life to be better married to Lester Blunt—and it wasn't.

Although several boys asked her out for dates or to go to community events, she'd never gone out with any boy. She always said, "I'll check with my father and let you know his answer." The answer was always 'no' until Lester Blunt entered their lives. Lenora had pleaded not to be married to a man fifteen years older than her, but her father beat her mercilessly until she yielded and married Lester Blunt.

So, at age fourteen, Lenora married Lester Blunt, who was thirty-one years old.

Her expectations were met. There was no loving life to be had, and her life was much the same as her mother's life. The one thing she made sure of was to drink the teas the midwife shared with her mother to keep her from bearing a child. Lenora worked hard to keep a clean and tidy home. She cooked only the foods Lester liked most.

Occasionally, Lester would try to be kind, but even then, it always ended with a slap or a punch. For Lenora, burying Lester behind the barn was for her benefit as much as Lester's. It was the only place he'd ever been kind to her. Now, at age twenty-four, the folks in Tishomingo hoped she'd find a man who could love her and be kind to her.

No one asked Lenora if she wanted to have any man in her life. She did want a man in her life and didn't need anyone in the community to help her find him. She planned to marry a kind, loving man and have children. She was determined she could be a good mother and protect any children she bore. She wanted to be a better mother than her mother had been. She had an idea of a man, but first, she must get through the funeral.

When the sheriff walked in before three that afternoon, he said,

"Lenora, whenever you're ready, we have things taken care of for Lester."

She smiled and said, "Thank you, Sam. You've been a good and kind friend to me."

"It's my pleasure, Lenora. Folks will be bringing a potluck dinner for after the funeral."

"Oh, no!"

"What's the matter, Lenora?"

"I haven't cleaned and tidied the house for company."

He chuckled. "Not to worry, Lenora. Folks will gather behind the barn to say farewell to Lester and then come to the space that will be the new library. Emma, her parents, Rose, and her children have got it all spit and polished and looking grand."

"I never would have thought the whole town would work to help me. I expected we'd toss some dirt over him and hope he stayed buried."

The Sheriff laughed. "Well, that's still my hope and expectation." He reached out, touched Lenora's hand, and said, "But don't for one second think anyone bears a grudge against you. Many of us want a better life for you."

She nodded and, brushing away a few tears, said, "I feel ashamed that I ever let him do the things he did, Sam."

"That's not on you, and besides, I think if you'd tried to stop him in any way at all, you would not have lived through the experience. Today is not just Lester's burial, Lenora. It is the whole town honoring you. We all know how cruel he has been to you and are glad it has ended."

"Thank you, Sam. Will you be back here at the library?"

"Yes. I plan to be your backup man for the rest of the day."

She smiled and blushed a little. "I will appreciate your help, Sam."

"Good. Now let me walk you back home. You can tidy yourself up a bit before the funeral. When you're ready, we'll all be behind the barn waiting for you."

She nodded and left the building where she would work

cooking for Silas Pennington's business in a few days. As she walked home with the Sheriff beside her, she felt some of the burdens of her life drop away. She was excited about her life for the first time she could remember. She felt a small thrill of happiness as they walked away from the building, the cafe where she would make the restaurant a high spot in town. She knew she was the cook for the endeavor, but it felt like her own business. She could hardly wait to start cooking—serving breakfast and lunch to the people of Tishomingo.

Sam looked down at Lenora and thought, *she is a beautiful woman, looking prettier with each step as she sheds the burden of Lester Blunt.*

Once Lenora had put on her dark blue dress and soft ivory shawl, she walked out the back door of her house. When she walked around the barn to the back, she was stunned to see so many people—maybe a hundred or more—standing and waiting for her to join them at her husband's grave. She smiled and nodded to the crowd as Josiah Hart-field, the Methodist Minister in her church. He reached out a hand to her to stand by him.

Once she was standing at the foot of her husband's grave, she looked down to see his rifle, his cigar box, his lighter, and three bottles of Tennesse whiskey. She smiled and nodded but wondered if maybe she should keep his rifle, but decided not to hold a weapon he'd used to try to harm people.

Reverend Hartfield asked, "Are you ready, Lenora."

She nodded but didn't say anything.

The minister opened his Bible and began to read: *To everything there is a season and a time to every purpose under the heaven...*

Lenora let the words from Ecclesiastes wash over her and begin to release the grief and horror of her marriage. Although she cried, it was primarily tears of relief—not joy but simple relief.

When the minister finished the Bible verse, he said,

"I am a man called by God to minister to this community.

Regarding Lester Blunt, I know some vile words and sometimes brutal actions have been said.

Still, I believe we all are children of God—even Lester Blunt, when he was at his worst and best, was and is a child of God. I implore you to pray for his soul and release any enmity you might have had against him. Holding such thoughts in your mind and heart does no pain to anyone but yourself.

Go home, read the Proverbs, the Twenty-third Psalm, and the passage I've read from Ecclesiastes. Let not your heart be troubled—that's from the book of John in the New Testament. Pray and release any mean thoughts in your soul. Peace, I leave with you this day in the place on Lenora and Lester's farm where Lester felt the most at peace and even sat with Lenora, from time to time, in peace, here at this spot.

I wish you the blessings of the day and request you all join us at the new library next door to *Okchuli Press*.

Amen."

Standing behind Lester Blunt's barn on a blustery November day, the people said, 'Amen.' A few folks had tears, but they were mainly for Lenora. As they left the gravesite, they walked or rode their horses, buggies, and wagons to the new library.

Johnathan, Thomas, Silas, and Clay filled the grave with the dirt they'd removed, leaving Lester Blunt buried behind his barn.

None of the men spoke as they walked to the library.

Nor did they shed tears.

As PEOPLE BEGAN to gather in the library, many brought books with them. Emma was overwhelmed with all the unexpected books. Rose said, "I'll help you sort them later. For now, let's accept the gift of words and be glad."

Lenora stood by the two women and said, "When folks asked me what they could do to help, I told them to bring books to donate to the library."

Emma hugged Lenora and said, "What a blessing you are! I've been wondering how best to get books, but you've taken care of it for me."

"Well, I felt there was nothing I needed. I'm not exactly happy Lester has died, but I do feel comfort in knowing I have my land and my house, and I'll be safe. For now, that will be enough."

Rose asked, "And after 'now'?"

"I don't know for sure. I am a woman who wants to be married, but I'm also a woman who never wants to have a man run rough-shod over me again."

Emma nodded. "I guess you'll find your best path forward as time goes on. Allow your heart, not your body, to guide you to the life you want to live."

"You're right, of course. I'm twenty-four years old, and I want babies."

"But you've been married for nearly ten years, Lenora."

"Yes, and with the help of some of Aurora's and Jane's teas, I haven't had a baby in my womb."

Emma smiled. "Good choice."

"Indeed. The only thing my mother ever told me before she left our house was never to become pregnant unless you're willing to put up with the man you live with."

"Why would she say that?"

"Because my father was a man exactly like Lester Blunt."

Rose sighed. "I'm so sorry. What about your mother?"

"The night after she talked with me about pregnancy was the last night I saw her. The next morning, I was sent back to Bloomfield Academy for the next term, like all the good Chickasaw girls were doing. She left the night after she talked with me about pregnancy. I don't know where she lives or whether she is alive."

"And your father?"

"I have no idea. Lester told me my father ran away rather than fight like a real man. I have no idea what that means, and when I tried to ask, Lester used his fists to keep me quiet."

Rose hugged her and said, "I'm so sorry. You can be our sister—Emma and me—and we'll help and look out for you."

"Thank you both. Now, I should thank all the people who have brought books and even those who did not."

She turned and walked away, and Emma said, "If we're going to be her sister, it is incumbent upon us to be sure she isn't settling with a man who simply wants her land and home."

"You're right about that."

The sheriff heard them and went to talk with them. "I don't think Lenora will jump off the deep end and have another brute like Lester in her life and bed."

Emma nodded. "Perhaps you're right for now, but my guess is there will be a lot of men who want to take advantage of her with their silvery words."

"Really?"

"Yes. Really. You seem like a good man, Sheriff, but you are woefully inadequate to protect Lenora if you think a man dressed in sheep's clothing won't tempt her."

He shook his head. "What can I do, then?"

Emma smiled. "I watched you walk with Lenora to the funeral, and I've watched you keep an eye on her throughout the rest of the day. Does she mean more to you than all the rest of us in town?"

He blushed, nodded, and sighed. "She means a lot to me. I tried to date her, but her father would have none of it. I'm a few years older than her, but I'm not wet behind the ears."

Emma laughed. "Are you sure?"

"Well, except about women. I don't understand the fairer part of humanity at all."

"Thus, you are a single man."

"Partly, but also, I wanted to help Lenora when the time came."

"And maybe she'd be willing to take your hand?"

He ran his finger around his collar and shook his head. "No. It's not like that. Any man would be honored and lucky to have her."

Rose touched his arm. "Are you worthy?"

"I'm working on it."

"Good, then, be sure it is you she thinks of, not the robbers in men's fancy clothing. There are a lot of men willing to marry a Chickasaw woman just because she has land."

"I take your meaning, ladies, and I appreciate it. I, too, am Chickasaw. I'll watch over her carefully."

Emma said, "And be the first one in line. Don't dawdle, Sheriff."

"Yes, ma'am."

He turned, walked to stand near Lenora, and watched as she spoke with everyone who wanted to be her friend. When people started drifting away toward their own homes, she turned and smiled at the Sheriff. "Samuel, would you please walk with me to my home? I'm drained and have lots of work tomorrow to prepare for my new cafe job. The sun will rise tomorrow, and I'll have work waiting for me."

"Yes, ma'am. I'd be delighted to walk you home."

"Please call me Nora. I've always wanted to be called Nora."

He smiled, "Then let's get you home, Nora. It would please me if you called me Sam."

"I will, Sam."

Rose and Emma smiled, and when the sheriff turned and doffed his hat at them, they laughed. Lenora grinned and waved at her two friends.

43

Hopi Proverb

As they walked, Sam pointed at the rainbow ahead of them and said, "I didn't know it rained."

Nora laughed. "It didn't rain here, but obviously, it rained somewhere between us and the sun."

Sam blushed and said, "Of course, you're right."

"Music to my ears," Nora said and chuckled.

He grinned and nodded. He didn't know what to say next.

Lenora said, "I've missed talking with a man willing to laugh and listen to my words."

"I like the sound of your voice, Nora."

"And I like the sound of yours, Sam."

They walked quietly, and then Sam said, "I know we just buried your husband today, Nora, but I want you to know I'm here for you and for anything you need."

"Well, since you started by reminding me that we buried my husband today, I think you have some ideas for yourself as well."

He nodded. "Is it too soon to say I want to spend time with you?"

"Not to my mind, but our social structure would say so."

"You're right, of course."

Nora touched his arm briefly, then pulled her hand away. "I need a few weeks or months to settle my heart and soul, Sam. After that, I'll be delighted to spend time with you."

"Thank you, Nora. Did you know I asked your father to let me go out with you?"

"No, I did not. When was that?"

"When you were fourteen and I was nineteen. A barn dance was coming up, and I thought I should ask him."

"You did the right and honorable thing."

"Maybe. Less than a month later, you were married to Lester Blunt. It was confusing to me."

"I'm sure it was, but I didn't have a choice in my marriage. I never loved Lester, though I tried hard to be a good wife. I never was able to meet his standards."

"What were his standards?"

"I still don't know, and now I'm thinking about it all, neither did he. He was a very solemn man sometimes—other times, he was a raging bull. I never knew which man would walk in the door."

"Maybe he had a brain or mind problem."

"Maybe, and I hope that was the case, but I'll never know."

"How do you feel about his death?"

"Honestly?"

"Of course, honestly! I never want to tell you a lie and hope you will never tell me a lie."

"I won't, Sam. I promise."

He smiled and nodded but said nothing more.

She said, "I'm relieved, excited, hurt, confused, but mostly, I'm ready to start my real life."

"I can see that."

"Do you think he was murdered?"

"No, I don't, despite there being good cause from many around us to do so. There were teeth marks on his heel. I think he was looking down from the edge of the boulder he was standing on, and something—perhaps a coyote or bobcat—came up behind him and bit his ankle."

"Wow. That must have scared him."

Sam shook his head. "I doubt it. My guess is it made him angry, and he was unbalanced and fell to his death. I found some bones of a rabbit near where he fell. The coyote waltzed in with his lunch and saw Lester as an interloper. Once Lester died, the coyote sat on the boulder and finished his lunch."

"Well, Lester never did know when to get out of folks's way."

Sam laughed. "I suppose you're right."

"Well, I'm glad he wasn't murdered. He was a terrible man and deserved getting killed, but I wouldn't want anyone else to carry a burden over him."

"I agree." He looked up and said, "Well, the rainbow is beginning to fade, and we're here at your house."

She nodded and walked up to the porch. She turned and said, "In a week or two, I'll invite you to dinner, Sam. How would that be?"

"That would be fine. Be sure you lock your doors and windows."

"Why?"

He shrugged and said, "I didn't know what else to say."

She laughed. "That's okay, Sam. I'll lock my doors and windows just for you."

He grinned and said, "I'm looking forward to spending more time with you, and I hear you're a passable cook."

She scowled and said, "Well, sheriff, we'll see."

He tipped his hat, grinned, and said, "Yes, ma'am." He leaned down and kissed her on the cheek."

She smiled and said, "Thank you, Sam."

"My pleasure entirely."

Aurora told Clay, "Before we return home, I want to see Lenora."

Her mother said, "Why don't Johnathan and I take Okchuli back home, and I start getting dinner ready? You can ride with Clay on his horse."

"That would be great, Momma. I want to chat with Lenora for a bit and be sure there's nothing I need to do for her."

"We'll see you back at your house," her father said. "Don't take too long, or I'll eat everything in sight."

Clay laughed, got on his horse, and reached out a hand to help Aurora ride behind him. Abner hadn't had two riding on him in a long time, but he loved Clay and Aurora and didn't mind a bit. They rode down the street toward Lenora's home.

Clay asked, "What do you want to talk with Lenora about?"

"Women's things."

"Ah. Enough said." He pointed ahead and said, "Look at that rainbow."

Aurora said, "Another blessing from the sun, and I hope it is a sign Lester will do better next time in his next life."

"My lord, if a rainbow can do all that, we should have them daily."

"Nope. If we had them all the time, we'd forget their blessing and the joy they bring us all."

"I suppose you're right. I see the sheriff standing on the porch talking with Lenora."

"Let's be sure not to ride too fast and interrupt them."

He slowed Abner to a slow walk, and just as the horse was getting bored, the sheriff bent and kissed Lenora on the cheek. Clay said, "Now, isn't that something."

"Yes, and I'm right to talk with her now."

Clay nodded. "Now I get it. You want her to take care not to be pregnant unless she is bound and determined to stick with a particular man."

"Exactly. If she chooses Sam, she'll have made a good choice."

"Sam?"

She laughed and shook her head. "That's the sheriff's given name, silly."

"Humph. I never thought of him having a name like us ordinary folks."

She laughed and said, "Oh, there's nothing ordinary about you, Clay."

"Thank you, darlin'. I think you're pretty special, too."

"Thanks, my love. Now the sheriff is leaving, so take me to Lenora. She and I will have a quick talk. You can wait on the porch or saddle. I won't be long."

LENORA OPENED THE DOOR, surprised to see Aurora, but then again, she came at precisely the right time.

She smiled and said, "Come in, Aurora. I was thinking about you a few minutes ago."

"Great minds do tend to think alike."

"Does Clay want to come in?"

"No. He gets a rash when we talk about women's things."

Lenora chuckled. "Poor fella. Must be rough married to a midwife."

"Oh, he's proud of me but doesn't want to know the details."

"Come, Aurora, and sit with me for a few minutes."

They sat at her kitchen table, and Lenora said, "I was thinking about things and wondered if I should quit drinking the tea you gave me to keep from having babies."

"Do you want to have babies?"

"Yes, I do."

Aurora smiled. "Then quit drinking the tea. More importantly, take care of yourself and watch your back."

"What do you mean?"

"You are a wealthy widow with a lot of land and holdings. Men are going to line up to marry you. Some of them will want to force you to marry them."

"How could they do that?"

"They could get someone to force you to say 'I do' when you want to scream 'I don't.' If you're unsure, keep drinking the tea. It won't hurt a thing for you to drink it. More importantly, keep your doors and windows locked all the time and maybe even ask the sheriff to walk with you to the cafe and back home."

"Why?"

"Well, for one thing, it would give the illusion—real or not—that you are a couple. That would stop many men from doing anything nefarious to you."

"That's a good idea."

"Yes, and it also might convey that you are under the sheriff's protection."

Lenora nodded. "Starting tomorrow, I'll ask Sam to walk me to and from the cafe."

Aurora smiled. "I know you just buried your husband today, but I also know the marriage has never been happy. You may be feeling a lot of grief but also be feeling a load of grief has been lifted from your shoulders."

Lenora nodded. "I feel no grief. I feel relief and feel there are much better possibilities than before."

Before she could say more, there was a knock on the door. Aurora said, "That's probably not Clay. He's sitting outside on his horse." She stood, walked across the room, and opened the door to find the sheriff standing before her. She smiled, turned to Lenora, and said, "I'll leave all the details up to you two, but be sure to take care, Lenora."

Lenora stood and smiled. "Thanks, Aurora. I appreciate your advice."

The sheriff nodded to Aurora, quickly stepped inside the house, and closed the door, just missing getting Aurora's skirt caught in the closing door. He walked over to Lenora and asked, "How many weeks has it been since you kissed me on the cheek, Nora?"

Lenora laughed, knowing what Sam knew. It had been only a few minutes—not weeks—since she had kissed him on the cheek. She was happy he'd returned quickly and said, "Come in, Sam, and sit with me on the sofa."

AURORA CHUCKLED as she went down the steps to Clay and Abner. He held a hand to help her settle behind him and the saddle. He grinned and said, "I can tell by the obvious joy on your face the sheriff showed up in the nick of time."

"Yes, he did."

"Love at first sight?"

"No, not even close to love at first sight. It's more like love at long last," Aurora said, laying her cheek against Clay's back. "Take me home, Clay, and let's keep our fingers crossed. I hope Momma and Daddy want to go to bed early."

"I'll pray it to be so," Clay said, urging Abner into a smooth canter to get them home quickly. Behind them, the rainbow was still there and doing what rainbows do—reminding everyone that despite their trials and tribulations, tears, and frustration, there was always another day and another way.

44

———————

*"If you see no
reason for giving thanks,
the fault lies in yourself."*
Maricopa Proverb

Noah woke early on Thanksgiving Day. He used the commode chair, emptied it in the bucket for waste, and went downstairs. No one else was awake, so he took the two big water buckets to the well. He knew his father and his friend Oscar Cassidy were making plans to have running water and even a bathroom in the house, and boy, was he ready for that!

He pumped water into both pails and carried them back to the house. The door opened before he was on the porch. His father stood there and said, "Son, I believe you must be excited."

Noah grinned. "Yes, Papa, I am. It's Thanksgiving Day, and Momma and Granny made pies and cakes yesterday. I'm already eager for dessert."

"You and me too, son. Thanks for bringing in the water. I'll go milk Patches if you and Sarah will gather the eggs."

"No need to wake her if she isn't awake. I don't mind getting the eggs."

"Will wonders never cease! Put the water by the fireplace, and let's head on out."

AT AURORA'S HOUSE, Clay and John were out in the barn milking the cow and gathering the eggs while Jane cooked breakfast and Aurora nursed Okchuli.

Aurora said, "I can't believe you are going home tomorrow. It's been a terrific visit."

"Yes, it has, and we'll miss you and your family."

"I'm pleased you and Daddy like Clay."

"It would take a hardhearted person not to like Clay. He is an amazing young man and a terrific husband and father."

"I think so, too. I can't imagine even a day without him in my life."

"That's how it's always been with John and me. True love makes for loving friends."

"Yes, it does. I can't imagine a day without Clay."

"It shows in everything you do for him and he for you. I'm very pleased with you, daughter."

"Thanks, Momma. I'm grateful for everything in my life."

"Even Lester Blunt?"

"Yes, even Lester Blunt. If he had not been so vile, I would not have met many people who stood by me and for me. If he had not been a part of the life of our town, there might be more bitterness and pain between the Chickasaw and the whites. Because of him, many of us banded together in ways we might not have done without his cruel way of life."

"I am proud of you, daughter, and grateful you understand that though life can be hard, it must be lived."

"Yes, exactly. I must live, and so must everyone else. Our lives depend on how we live and the choices we make."

Her mother smiled. "I hope Lenora will be okay and she has someone to be with on Thanksgiving."

"Oh, my best guess is the Sheriff will see to her needs."

"I wondered about that."

"Well, wonder no more."

SAM KNOCKED on Nora's door. She opened the door, and he handed her a bouquet of late wildflowers and sage. She smiled and said, "Come in, Sam. I've fixed us our first Thanksgiving Dinner."

"Sounds fine to me."

"Are you on duty today?"

"No, there are two deputies today and another for overnight. I can spend as much time with you today as you want."

"Good. I don't want to rush and worry about timing."

She led him into the living room and said, "Would you rather make love to me now or after dinner?"

"I can't do both?"

"Ah. Why don't we start now and see what happens after dinner."

"What are we having for dinner?"

"Rabbit stew with biscuits that we can eat any old time and a pumpkin pie."

"Sounds perfect."

She took his hand and said, "Leave your gun and your hat in here."

"What about my boots?"

"We'll see."

"Thank heavens."

"Maybe."

SHIRLEY JOINED THE MINISTER, his wife, and his family for Thanksgiving dinner. She brought fruit cake and whipped cream. She never liked to spend too much time at anyone's house but always accepted those who asked her first to join the family at special times like Easter, Christmas, and Thanksgiving.

In this way, she felt she was a part of many families in the town but did not have the burden of caring too much for everyone.

As soon as the dinner was over, she walked back to her home above the Dry Goods store, took off her shoes and stockings, and curled up in her favorite chair to read a new novel, *The Country of the Pointed Firs* by Sarah Orne Jewett. She was eager to learn of the rocky places on the east coast of this country. She'd been born in Texas and lived in Indian Territory for over twenty years. *It's easy to forget there are oceans when you live in the mountains and enjoy creeks and rivers,* she thought.

EMMA and her parents invited Rose and her siblings for Thanksgiving dinner. Joe, Jolene, and Adam were excited, as was Rose. The children chattered from their farm into town in their wagon.

Adam said, "I really like Emma's Momma and Daddy, but I especially like working with her Daddy. He calls me son and wants me to call him Granddad. Is that okay?"

"Sure it is. You can all call him Granddad and Emma's Momma Gramma."

"Yep. She said she wanted us to call her Gramma."

Jolene asked, "Why do they love us, Momma Rose?"

"Well, I'm not sure, but I'm happy they do."

"Because you love Emma?"

"In part, but also because I like having good people love us."

Joe nodded and said, "Because you love Momma Emma, right?"

Rose blushed and said, "I suppose that's right."

Adam shook his head. "I think if you're supposing you don't know. Don't you know?"

"Well, Adam, you are right. I do know."

Jolene nodded. "Yep, Momma Rose loves Momma Emma."

Rose laughed. "Love is a good thing."

Jolene said, "It's the best thing in the world except for pumpkin pie. Are we going to have pumpkin pie?"

"I don't know."

Adam said, "I like pecan pie better."

Jolene shook her head and muttered, "Boys."

Rose laughed, and as they arrived at Emma's parents' home, she decided.

Adam watched her and said, "Momma Emma is coming home with us, isn't she, Momma Rose."

"Would that be okay with you children?"

Adam grinned and looked at his brother and sister. They both nodded, but before he could answer, Joe said, "Of course she is."

Rose laughed and said, "Let's see what Momma Emma says about everything."

Jolene said, "She'll come. She loves us."

She did, and she does.

ADELLA RITTENHOUSE DID NOT GO to anyone's home for Thanksgiving. She also did not invite anyone to come to her home for Thanksgiving. Instead, she pulled out her new knitting basket and the new yarn she'd ordered from Ireland. She'd seen the Irish sweaters that were ivory in color, heavy and warm. The pattern she was knitting was a sweater that opened down the front and included many intricate designs of different cables and braids.

With her feet tucked under a blanket, she sat in her favorite chair, put her feet on the cushioned footrest, and started the project, casting on the loops for the first sweater ever she was making for herself. She smiled, glad to have the time and peace of sitting quietly and knitting. It was a gift she'd longed to give herself, and now, with her job secure, she could do so.

She was thankful.

A FEW DAYS after Thanksgiving Day, Conrad was preparing to lead the Barton family from the Mississippi River toward Broken Bow. He had been ill for a few days, but it worked out fine. The Bartons were a few days late in arriving at the crossing. His heel still hurt occasionally, but it was healed, and there was no residual bruising or swelling.

He had thought he would stay in Broken Bow for Thanksgiving, but he spent the day on the banks of the big river. Besides, it was never a celebration he was comfortable with. Once he took the Barton family to Broken Bow, he wanted to return to his home in Devil's Den. He needed to rest and sing his birth song in the place he loved the most. He was beginning to feel old and didn't understand why.

The snake knew. Even though Conrad would prefer many more years of life, the snake knew he would live fewer years than expected. Over the next several months, the poison would finally overtake Conrad. He would leave the Earth and the Devil's Den that he loved to begin a new life.

Several days after Thanksgiving, Conrad and his horse, Soba, felt great relief as they walked between the boulders to Conrad's home. He took his horse into his shelter, removed the saddle, brushed his back, and gave him fresh water and feed. When he had no more chores, Conrad smudged every nook and cranny with sage smoke and sat in front of his fireplace and drummed while singing his birth song.

As the burden of death eased his pain, Lester said, "So long, Conrad. I'm moving on. Seems I'm slated to be a better person this time around. We'll see."

The rattlesnake hissed and said, "No thanks to you. I'm moving on to being a buffalo. Such nasty-smelling creatures, but at least they are big and don't crawl on the ground."

Conrad smiled and wished them both a better life than they'd had before.

AT THIS MOMENT, everything is right in Tishomingo, Indian Territory.

THE END

"Be like the sun for grace and mercy.
Be like the night to cover others' faults.
Be like running water for generosity.
Be like death for rage and anger.
Be like the Earth for modesty.
Appear as you are.
Be as you appear."
Rumi

THANK YOU, DEAR READER

THANK YOU, DEAR READER

Thank you for reading our book. We hope you enjoyed reading or listening to our story as much as we enjoyed writing and recording it. If you enjoyed this book, please leave an honest review on Amazon or Goodreads. As independently published authors, the only way we become known to other readers is through your reviews and your sharing of our stories.

All of our books, whether written together or Glenda alone, are stories of women who keep their power close to themselves to create the best lives for themselves, their children, family, and friends.

Glenda and David have written seven novels in The Paradigm Books series. In this series, they wrote about women and their lives of love, belonging, and becoming—creating new paradigms for themselves and their families. The books are also available on Amazon and Audible.

1. *The Gloriana Paradigm*
2. *The Mother Paradigm*
3. *The Belle Paradigm*

4. *The Father Paradigm*
5. *The Cora Paradigm*
6. *The Dakota Paradigm*
7. *The Adoption Paradigm*

We have also written **The Shaman Chronicles** series. Although Glenda uses Core Shamanism in a lot of her books, in this series, not only do many of the characters practice Core Shamanism, but the mystic side of life becomes an important element. These books are also available on Amazon and Audible.

1. *Buffalo Dreams*
2. *Salmon Dreams*
3. *Bobcat Dreams*
4. *Sparrow Dreams*
5. *Crawdad Dreams*
6. *Elk Dreams*

The **Ouachita Mountain Tales** series is written by Glenda and focuses on women and children finding themselves and their place in the semi-rural southeastern Oklahoma area where Glenda grew up.

1. *The Mountain Beckons*
2. *Ring Around the Moon*
3. *The Water Flows*
4. *Sounds of the Night*
5. *Beaver Moon Rising*

Glenda and our granddaughter Marti have written *Nobody's Home*, a children's book about spending spring break at Grandma and Granddad's house during the COVID times.

The Redbud Stories, written by Glenda, are books close to Glenda's heart. The first book is mostly autobiographical, with many changes in the locals and people's names, although much of it is true. The other two books amalgamate some of the life in central Oklahoma while letting powerful women live their lives as they wish to.

1. *The Good and Holy Witch*
2. *The Keeper of All Things*
3. *The Creators of New Beginnings*

Glenda is pleased to inform you about the release of our newest collection, *The Minerva Mysteries*. These enchanting tales are overflowing with romance, sorcery, and courageous women who utilize their talents for the greater good. Glenda isn't sure if there will be more *Minerva Mysteries* but some folks have asked that there be more. We'll see.

1. *Minerva and The Runaway Train*
2. *Minerva and The Old Wood Stove*
3. *Minerva and The Upstairs Ghost*
4. *Minerva and The Rocking Chair*

The upcoming series, *Life on Pennington Creek,* will be available in late 2024 or early 2025. These are historical novels located in the town of Tishomingo, Indian Territory, during the last 4-5 years of the 1890s before Oklahoma was a state. The working titles so far are:

1. *Maggie's Home*
2. *Aurora Rising*
3. *Eva's Choice*

There will be at least two more, but probably 4 more books in the series.

Glenda has written another book, *Calista,* about one witch and a few other witches and even druids who live in Pink, Oklahoma. Pink is a real town. The characters are not! The book will come out in late 2024 or early 2025, depending on how the editing goes. Fingers crossed, there's a little magic involved.

All our books are available on Amazon as e-books, Kindle, or paperback books. They are also available as audible books on Audible and Amazon.

You can follow Glenda and David Clemens on Facebook, Amazon, or Goodreads.

AUTHOR'S NOTES

"Seek wisdom, not knowledge.
Knowledge is of the past,
Wisdom is of the future."
Lumbee Proverb

You know the old adage, *"History is written by the winners/victors."* Maybe, maybe not.

I came right up against that brick wall in trying to tell this fictionalized story as honestly as I could. No matter how many resources I read, none of them were the same—who did what, how, why, where, and when. UGH!!!

I looked up the old adage about winners on the internet and found it attributed to a lot of folks. It was rather like the history I was trying to tell while writing a book of fiction. I got a big laugh when I found this written by Matthew Phelan on **Slate**: *"Many attribute the adage to Winston Churchill, but it turns out he was just rewriting some losers."*

What a relief!

I'd read a few biographies of various people at the time of this story, a few histories of Tishomingo, Indian Territory, and even two different dissertations on the events told in my version of this story. I read newspaper reports (they always tell it exactly like it happened, right?), pamphlets, encyclopedias, etc., and they all tell *essentially* the same story. It was the details that didn't quite line up.

I became befuddled and anxious about getting it right, but getting it right seemed a monumental task. So, dear reader, I said my usual 'f-bomb' and went on my merry way, writing my version of the story. Besides, I wasn't writing a true story—although I wanted much of it to be true—I was writing a *fiction* story.

I'm a lover of Oklahoma and its history, even when I learn things that are painful. I spent much of my childhood in Southeast Oklahoma and had many loving times on Pennington Creek and the Blue River. When I was a child, Devil's Den was open to the public, and I was told many of the stories (true or otherwise) about the area.

When our son was in Boy Scouts, we spent many happy summers at the Boy Scout campground (known as Slippery Falls at that time). We played in the waters of Pennington Creek on the slippery boulders while we avoided rattlesnakes and mocassins. I especially avoided the tarantulas. No one ever avoided the ticks. But what is a spectacular natural garden without a bit of danger?

Here is a list of resources I used in telling the story. Some are background, and some are to get the times and details correct.

LINKS used for research: (in no particular order)

Building:

https://onlinebooks.library.upenn.edu/webbin/serial?id=builder

Pronunciation of Ishto Atumpa

(https://www.achickasawdictionary.com/search?q=giant).   The story is one the author created, not one that is in any list of stories of the Chickasaw Natives.

Reagan, Oklahoma (Johnston County)

https://en.wikipedia.org/wiki/Reagan,_Oklahoma

https://www.google.com/maps/place/Reagan,+OK+73460/@34.3489815,-96.7216715,15z/data=!3m1!4b1!4m6!3m5!1s0x87b34ae99dd18541:0x36a35ee03421e1f!8m2!3d34.348982!4d-96.7216715!16s%2Fm%2F04bh_dz

Indian Territory

https://www.okhistory.org/publications/enc/entry?entryname=INDIAN%20TERRITORY

https://www.okhistory.org/publications/enc/entry?entryname=SETTLEMENT%20PATTERN

https://www.okhistory.org/publications/enc/entry.php?entry=LA014#:~:text=By%20setting%20the%20stage%20for,Union%2C%20Oklahoma%2C%20in%201907

Devil's Den

https://en.wikipedia.org/wiki/Devil's_Den

Tishomingo

https://www.okhistory.org/publications/enc/entry?entry=TI008#:~:text=Prior%20to%20the%20founding%20of,Fort%20Washita%20to%20Fort%20Arbuckle

Trail of Tears

https://ualrexhibits.org/tribalwriters/artifacts/Family-Stories-Trail-of-Tears.html

Cities/Towns in Oklahoma

https://www.onlyinyourstate.com/oklahoma/oldest-towns-ok/?utm_source=pinterest&utm_medium=social

https://www.onlyinyourstate.com/oklahoma/small-town-tishomingo-ok/

https://www.hmdb.org/m.asp?m=184270

Pennington Creek Marker

https://s3.amazonaws.com/gs-waymarking-images/59270176-7be7-4cfb-ae74-258dc02e9c1e.jpg

Good Springs Marker

https://gateway.okhistory.org/ark:/67531/metadc962711/

Pennington Creek and Tishomingo Map 1892

https://www.loc.gov/resource/g4021e.ct000224/?r=0.487,0.511,0.
106,0.053,0

PENNINGTON CREEK: Alonzo Pennington (hanged 05.01.1846 in Kentucky after being arrested at what is now known to be Pennington Creek just north of Tishomingo, Oklahoma)

https://www.madillrecord.net/news/pennington-creek-important-location-chickasaw-nation

https://www.oklahomahistory.net/ttphotos8a/LonzPennington.pdf

Belle Starr

https://en.wikipedia.org/wiki/Belle_Starr

American Civil War

https://en.wikipedia.org/wiki/American_Civil_War

https://www.frontieramericanillustratednews.com/post/money-in-the-old-west-coins-of-america-s-dramatic-1840s-1870s

Jesus Loves The Little Children

https://en.wikipedia.org/wiki/George_Frederick_Root#:~:text=North%20Reading%2C%20Massachusetts.-,Legacy,the%20later%20God%20Save%20Ireland

The first Methodist Church began in 1843 in Tishomingo, Indian Territory, and later in Oklahoma. By 1844, there had begun to be buildings and a seminary.

https://www.facebook.com/tishfumc/

Poets

https://en.wikipedia.org/wiki/Category:18th-century_American_poets

Bedding

https://www.saatva.com/blog/history-of-mattresses/

https://www.thespruce.com/the-history-of-the-bed-4062296

Window Screens

https://en.wikipedia.org/wiki/Window_screen#:~:text=In%201861%20Gilbert%2C%20Bennett%20and,product%20became%20an%20immediate%20success

Mushrooms

https://www.wildfooduk.com/articles/how-to-tell-the-difference-between-poisonous-and-edible-mushrooms/

Columbia, South Carolina

https://en.wikipedia.org/wiki/Columbia,_South_Carolina

Chickasaw Tribal History

https://www.chickasaw.net/our-nation/history.aspx

Cherokee Freedmen named Pennington

https://en.wikipedia.org/wiki/Cherokee_freedmen_controversy

https://www.okhistory.org/research/dawesresults.php?cardnum=1034&tribe=Cherokee&type=Freedmen

Chickasaw Dictionary with vocalization of words

https://www.achickasawdictionary.com

Chickasaw life

https://www.bigorrin.org/chickasaw_kids.htm#:~:text=Chickasaw%20mothers%2C%20like%20many%20Native,war%20to%20protect%20their%20families

Chickasaw names

https://www.behindthename.com/submit/names/usage/chickasaw

Vernacular language

https://www.alphadictionary.com/slang/?term=&beginEra=1880&endEra=1890&clean=true&

Birthing

https://thereader.mitpress.mit.edu/birthing-furniture-an-illustrated-history/

Herbs and Midwife

https://www.holisticbirthingservices.com/midwife-blog/tag/Herbs

https://www.holisticbirthingservices.com/

https://www.wishgardenherbs.com/blogs/wishgarden/midwifery-roots-and-folk-herbalism

https://www.paullettgolden.com/post/midwifery-herbs

https://warwick.ac.uk/fac/arts/history/students/retrospectives/issues/8.pdf

Uterine and Cervical scarring

https://www.whria.com.au/for-patients/fertility/ashermans-syndrome/#:~:text=If%20the%20scarring%20involves%20the,this%20is%20not%20as%20common

https://boards.straightdope.com/t/a-morbid-question-about-gang-rape/583865/6

Birth Control and Women's Issues:

https://www.civilwarmed.org/birth-control/

https://www.healthline.com/health/birth-control/history-of-birth-control

https://www.tempdrop.com/blogs/blog/a-brief-history-of-basal-body-thermometers-fam

https://en.wikipedia.org/wiki/Julius_Schmid_(manufacturer) (he made condoms first with sausage casings and later rubber. He founded the Schimd contraceptive company with the products Fourex, Ramses, and Sheik. During the World Wars, he was the official supplier of condoms for the US Military.

https://www.womenhistoryblog.com/2014/06/19th-century-midwives.html#:~:text=In%20addition%20to%20assisting%20in,no%20painkillers%2C%20except%20for%20alcohol

Travel Time in Wagon in the late 1800's

https://www.fhwa.dot.gov/infrastructure/back0307.cfm#:~:text=The%20covered%20wagon%20made%208,longer%20to%20reach%20their%20destination

It is 1,032.7 miles from Columbia, SC, to Tishomingo, Oklahoma, so at a pace of 8-20 miles per day, it would take about 2-3 months to complete the journey.

Prouty Press and printing

https://www.printmuseum.org/1890-prouty-press#:~:text=And%20at%20the%20modest%20price,favorite%20of%20many%20country%20printers

https://www.okhistory.org/publications/enc/entry?entryname=PRINTING%20AND%20PUBLISHING%20INDUSTRY

Dugouts

https://www.awhc.org/dugout/

https://www.okhistory.org/publications/enc/entry?entry=DU003

https://www.motherearthnews.com/homesteading-and-livestock/frontier-homes-dugout-zmaz70sozgoe/

Railroads:

https://en.wikipedia.org/wiki/List_of_Oklahoma_railroads#Passenger_carriers

Miscellaneous:

https://en.wikipedia.org/wiki/William_H._Murray

https://en.wikipedia.org/wiki/Reading_law

In 1898, Murray moved to <u>Tishomingo.</u>

Murray's legal knowledge and colorful personality brought him to the attention of Douglas H. Johnston, the Governor of the Chickasaw Nation, who appointed him as legal advisor.

Although not American Indian, he was appointed by Johnston as the Chickasaw delegate to the 1905 Convention for the proposed State of Sequoyah. Later, he was elected as a delegate to the 1906 constitutional convention for the proposed state of Oklahoma. Oklahoma became the 50th state when it was admitted in 1907 to the United States.

https://www.okhistory.org/publications/enc/entry.php?entry=CH033

In April 1866, the Chickasaw and Choctaw were forced to sign a treaty renewing their compact with the U.S. government. They agreed to abolish slavery, recognize the rights of Freedmen, and provide railroad rights-of-way through their country.